FOOLSCAP

By Michael Malone

FICTION

Painting the Roses Red
The Delectable Mountains
Dingley Falls
Uncivil Seasons
Handling Sin
Time's Witness

NONFICTION

Psychetypes
Heroes of Eros

FOOLSCAP

A NOVEL BY
MICHAEL MALONE

LITTLE, BROWN AND COMPANY
BOSTON   TORONTO   LONDON

First Edition

The characters and events in this book are fictitious.
Any similarity to real persons, living or dead,
is coincidental and not intended by the author.

Library of Congress Cataloging-in-Publication Data

Malone, Michael.
   Foolscap : a novel / by Michael Malone. — 1st ed.
      p.   cm.
   ISBN 0-316-54527-9
   I. Title
PS3563.A43244F66   1991
813'.54—dc20   91-2957

10 9 8 7 6 5 4 3 2 1

MV-NY

*Published simultaneously in Canada
by Little, Brown & Company (Canada) Limited*

Printed in the United States of America

For
Tad and Jerri Meyer

and
in memory of
O. B. Hardison, Jr.

But men must know that in this theatre of man's life
it is reserved only for God and angels to be lookers on.

Francis Bacon, *Advancement of Learning*, xx, 8

Contents

FOOLSCAP

{Prologue}

IN THE West End of London, at eight o'clock on a cold starry evening, the red velvet curtain trembled and lifted a few inches off the floor of the great stage, letting out a shimmer of soft amber light. Expectation rustled through the handsomely dressed audience. Tonight was the world premiere of a play called *Foolscap*, the theatrical talk of the town, for months now a cynosure of critical controversy, academic squabbles, even lawsuits.

From his gilded box seat near the gold proscenium arch, a young American drama professor named Theo Ryan leaned forward, his hand pressing the rolled playbill against the starched white pleats of his shirt front. On the small brocaded chair beside him sat Dame Winifred Throckmorton, the retired Oxford don who had discovered *Foolscap*. And in the chairs in front sat the elegant Earl and Countess of Newbolt, smiling vaguely down at the crowd that gazed with careful nonchalance up at them. The earl was one of the owners of the play they were all about to see. Theo Ryan had been invited along as an interested friend.

"Scared, kid?" he heard a voice ask. "Me, I could never sit down at my premieres. Darted around like an old bobcat loose in the lobby till they ran me off."

Theo recognized the soft, slurred southern voice of the great American playwright Joshua "Ford" Rexford. The two of them had had years of such stage-talk conversations together.

Ford's voice said, "It's a hit, Theo. I could always tell."

"Oh, Ford," Theo thought. "No, you couldn't."

"You'll see. You can breathe it. Come on, Theo, this is why I brought you all the way over here. For this. Take a sniff of triumph."

All around him, murmuring hushed as hundreds of lights in the jeweled chandeliers dimmed. Theo turned sideways in the little chair, rested his arms on the gilt railing, looked down at the stage, and as the great velvet drapery of the curtain rushed upward, he breathed deeply in.

Theodore Ryan had never before watched a play's premiere from a gilded box seat, or, for that matter, from any seat in the audience of a theatre. Oh, he'd seen many shows open, and many shows close, hundreds and hundreds of shows from his earliest childhood on, but he'd seen them all from a backstage vantage point; his view of the drama had always been that peripheral view from the wings. For both his parents had worked all their lives in show business.

His mother, Lorraine Page, had performed in five Broadway musicals, in nine national tours, and in eighty-four stock companies. Theo's favorite childhood year had been 1959, when she had stayed home in New York to appear live on television once a week as the Luster Shampoo Girl. His father had traveled the entire country by bus more than a dozen times, singing his two gold record hits, "Prom Queen" and "Do the Duck." Benny Ryan had been a minor teenage idol, and in 1957 had made it all the way to number 3 on the rock and roll charts with "Do the Duck," which had started a short-lived dance craze. Lorraine had given birth to Theo in a small town between Nashville (where she was starring in *South Pacific*) and Atlanta (where Benny was scheduled to open for Elvis Presley at the fairgrounds).

Theo Ryan's early life had felt to him like one disorienting blur of grimy backstage corridors, interchangeable hotel rooms, and tacky restaurant lounges. He had never celebrated his birthday in the same place two years running, had never owned a bicycle, and had never lived in a house—until the house he'd bought for himself. He had bought this home near the university in the mountains of North Carolina where he'd taken his first teaching job, and where he had hoped to remain, on the same campus, in the same small town of Rome, for as long as half a century without ever being compelled to move so much as the wobbly metal lamp on the scratched and ink-stained desk in his office.

And so young Professor Ryan, although a scholar of the English Renaissance, had never even visited England until brought there by an odd set of circumstances that had led him to this theatre in the London West End, to this gilt and velvet box belonging to the Earl and Countess of Newbolt, to this seat beside Dame Winifred Throckmorton, who, like him, caught her breath as the curtain rose on *Foolscap*.

Lights blazed down on the set's dazzling metallic complexity, and the audience began to applaud. Theo heard Ford Rexford say, "You did it, kid."

Theo whispered aloud. "You're as responsible for this as I am."

"Rubbish," Dame Winifred whispered back, rapping Theo's shoulder with her thin, bent fingers. "I bear no responsibility at all. Your '*Destiny*,' Theo. . . . And, of course, Walter Raleigh's."

"Shhh!" hissed an indignant lady in the box next to theirs, with a pointed nod at the stage, where the play was beginning. With a smile of apology, Theo turned towards the lights, his heart rising inside him. Breathless, he held his cupped hands to his lips—just as he had done long ago when a small boy, when he had first stood backstage in the dim bustling wings of a theatre, somewhere on the road in America, and watched a heavy, frayed, patched, gilded curtain fall at some summer-stock play's end, watched it slowly close between the bowing forms of his parents Lorraine Page and Benny Ryan onstage, and the sharp echoing sound of strangers applauding out there in the dark.

I

{Scene: Rome, and the Neighborhood}

CHAPTER

1

{Whispers}

CHERBURTYKIN [*softly says*]:
Ta-ra-ra boom-de-ay, sit on the curb all day. . . .
It doesn't matter! It doesn't matter.
OLGA:
If only we knew, if only we knew.

[*The End*]

ON AN APRIL AFTERNOON, Theo Ryan sat impatiently in Ludd Lounge, thinking of endings. Exit lines. Curtain speeches. And as he thought, he was doodling. Swagged, tasseled, gilt-bordered, grand proscenium curtains, act drop, asbestos, teasers. He added wing drapes; in theatrical parlance—tormenters. Why tormenters? A pun? Polysemy signifying, of course, other signifiers—or so would have claimed his famous colleague Jane Nash-Gantz, the psychoanalytically inclined deconstructionist, had she bothered to attend these faculty meetings, which, of course, she rarely did. He tied bows to the tormenters, and centerstage added a stick figure, with a noose around its neck. It was still five minutes till four.

He had drawn the curtains in a homeopathic hope of bringing to an exit line the homily on "saving the canon" now being droned at them by Dr. Norman Bridges, earnest and unwilling chairman of the English Department until his successor could be elected. Bridges had just passed the half-hour mark, by no means a record at these gatherings in the Dina Sue Ludd Lounge.

Theo had stopped himself from drawing faces. They'd twisted into grimacing psychotics with hair like corkscrews and lidless eyes that spiraled into wider and wider circles of blind black madness. Oedipal, no doubt. Nearby, his worst enemy, medievalist

Marcus Thorney, leaned surreptitiously to peek at the page of scribbles, contempt flickering over his angular saturnine face. Theo crooked his arm around the legal pad, and turned his back. It had to be acknowledged that his doodlings these days tended towards the turbulent. Interesting (as his therapist annoyingly pointed out), that there should be such spasms of violence in so placid a person as Theo Ryan at least claimed to be. He added a trapdoor to his sketch.

Going into the meeting, Dr. Bridges had whispered in the doorway that he'd "like a word about something, Theo. Coffee afterwards?" Ryan had a good idea about what. The chairman would say again that Dean Tupper was still looking for a dynamic young man to run the university's new theatre center, and that he, Dr. Bridges (he occasionally referred to himself in the third person as Dr. Bridges), thought Theo Ryan should be that man.

Then Theo would say again, "Not me. I'm not a director, not a playwright; I don't know lights, sets, any of it."

And Bridges would flutter his hands. "So? You know the theatre!"

And he would say, "Thanks anyhow, Norman, but the truth is, I like my theatre on the page, not the stage."

Bridges would sigh. "Theo, Theo, how can someone with your background feel that way?"

And he would say, "That's why."

Actually, Theo had fudged the truth even in this hypothetical conversation; since adolescence he had been a closet playwright, and he'd written at least one play that he'd thought good enough to keep; one full, three-act play. The others, he'd destroyed the night he read *The Cherry Orchard*. This single saved work, completed in a summer workshop, was still in his bottom desk drawer. But not a soul knew about his creation, except for one person—a famous director named Scottie Smith—and Theo was sorry he'd ever allowed that monstrous individual to get his hands on it. The memory even now sent his pencil gouging through the eyehole of a sketched mask of tragedy. Marcus Thorney's brow arced into a suspicious position, and superciliously stayed there. Thorney, who wanted to be the new department chairman, suspected his colleagues of plotting against him, which several of them were.

"I don't disagree with you younger people," Chairman Bridges hemmed and hawed to his assembled faculty. "Perhaps we do need changes in our literary canon."

"We do!" someone shouted.

"And perhaps we do need a superstar of some sort here."

"We don't!" someone shouted.

"I'm only," Bridges sighed, "pointing out that my generation of scholars lived in a smaller, slower, and no doubt a less dazzling world. But perhaps I don't disagree with our older colleagues when they claim ours was somehow a . . . deeper world."

EDGAR:
We that are young,
Shall never see so much, nor live so long.

FINIS, thought Theo.

Nowhere near *finis*, Bridges rambled on, comparing the academic past and future—to, in the parlance, a dead house. Theo and his colleagues at least sat bored in comfort: for the lounge they sat in was the centerpiece of their newly renovated Ludd Hall, one of the finest buildings on the campus of Cavendish University, the "fastest growing college in the South." The hall's donor, Mrs. Ludd—to judge from her glazy eyes in the big oval oil painting above the silk-striped couch—was as dazed by Dr. Bridges's monologue as everyone else clustered at one end of her vast neoclassical faculty salon.

Ripping the sheet from his legal pad, Theo stretched a long arm down the conference table and flicked the ball of yellow paper. It bounced into the trash off the arm of the rotund young black woman next to him, his friend Jorvelle Wakefield, African-Americanist, who was startled out of a comatose trance. She mugged a theatrical sneer at him and muttered, "Honkie."

Stuffing the cuff of his flannel shirt in his mouth, he dampened the cloth with a yawn. Black fuzz stuck to his tongue, and he wiped the sleeve on his corduroy pants. At least he wasn't asleep, like Romantic Poetry and Victorian Novels, who always sat amiably slumped together in the shadows of the mustard-colored Empire couch against the wall, where they catnapped until nudged to leave. The lazy April sun hazing through the western windows, coupled with the unhurried hum of the chairman, was enough to lull into a snooze faculty far younger than those two grizzled venerables, who were now shoulder to shoulder in the middle of the couch, their foreheads nearly touching, like shy old lovers. Even the foot-jiggling and finger-thrumming of Jonas Marsh, the hyperkenetic Restoration specialist, had slowed to a languid tremor; coffee was not sloshing, pencils were not rolling off the cherrywood conference table as they usually did in Marsh's vicinity.

Theo was one of the most junior of the senior professors here in the lounge—three of whom had voted with Marcus Thorney against him when he'd come up for tenure last fall. He knew exactly who those three were, because Steve Weiner (Southern Fiction) had rushed straight to his house the minute the voting was over, and blabbed the results. Steve had yelled the score right from the car, his bushy black beard descending with the lowered window glass. He'd bellowed, "You got tenure! Know what they used to give you with tenure here? Your own personal plot in the Cavendish cemetery! I'm not kidding, tenure *is* forever."

Steve Weiner was Theo's oldest friend at Cavendish. He was a Jew from Brooklyn, whose fatal weakness for southern fiction and department politics had now held him hostage eleven years in the boondocks of the North Carolina hills. When Steve had heard about the arrival for a job interview of a theatre scholar who had lived at least some of his life in Manhattan, and whose mother, at least, was Jewish, he'd driven to the airport and hugged Theo Schneider Ryan right there at the baggage-claim carousel.

That was seven years ago. Their friendship had flourished; now they were pointed out on campus tours as Doctors Mutt and Jeff: Steve, short and wiry, explosively gesticulating in that barrage of caustic aggressiveness with which he'd at first asked people in Rome for directions. (As a result of which, he'd rarely received any answers from locals, who couldn't understand his fast Yankee patois anyhow.) Theo, with his long limbs and his long hands and feet, mildly nodding as he loped along beside his friend. The two were a Cavendish landmark. They'd seen each other through Steve's divorce and through the recent breakup of Theo's three-year affair with a woman in Art History. They'd settled in. They even rooted for the football team.

Far from explosive this afternoon, Steve Weiner sat upright and motionless in a Windsor chair, his eyes fixed. He appeared to be either enchanted or dead. Theo lifted two fingers at him in salutation, but there was no response. Noticing them, Marcus Thorney lowered thin eyebrows over baleful eyes. Theo and Jorvelle Wakefield were supporting their friend Steve Weiner in the upcoming election for the new chairman. Three supporters of Marcus Thorney glared at them. One of the ancients gargled in his sleep.

Portly Dr. Bridges was passing out another of his lengthy packets of material for discussion. "And so I think we all think it's time," he bobbed, his plump pink features a grin of feverish collegiality above his round collar and paisley tie, "that we here in the English Department at Cavendish need to step forward, to leap forward, I should say, with both our feet, into the eighties."

As the year was now 1989, no one could dispute that, indeed, if ever, the time to move into the eighties was now. Jorvelle let her elbow jerk off the table in a parody of falling asleep.

Dr. Bridges was pointing to the oval painting, with a respectful bow. "Thanks to the wonderful generosity of Mrs. Ludd . . ." No one bothered to look at her. "The window of opportunity is ours. What happened to History can, and must, and will, happen to us." Everyone in Ludd Hall was painfully aware of what had happened to History, and of the cankerous jealousy felt by Dr. Bridges as a result.

Six short years ago, a Georgia insecticide king, Class of '57, dying of emphysema, had donated thirty-five million dollars in order to bring renowned historians to Cavendish University so that they might, in the words of the bequest, "teach the great lessons of America's past to the leaders of the world's future." By lavish offers of fat salaries, little or no teaching, luxurious subsidized travel junkets, and office suites designed by I. M. Pei, the lucky History Department had promptly hired a handful of celebrity scholars from around the Ivies. As a result they were soon ranked in the top ten nationwide in three separate polls prominently framed in their gleaming new lobby. Four falls back, they'd soared into the top *five* by luring Herbert Crawford, superstar Marxist, from Oxford (from *Oxford!*, as Bridges moaned in his nightmares), by agreeing to build the renowned cultural materialist a lap pool in his basement. The pool was now in a lakefront chalet the school had helped the Britisher purchase by picking up the tab for the interest on his mortgage payments. They'd also agreed to fly his wife over from England one weekend a month for conjugal visits (though so far no one had seen her). Dr. Crawford—Herbie to his students—wore black leather pants and jackets, with a T-shirt, to all college functions; he taught only one course a term, the hugely popular "Modern Capitalism: Origins to Collapse," during which he interpreted the great lessons of the American past in ways the dead insecticide king probably had not anticipated.

When the rating polls had first appeared, the provost of the university, Dean Buddy Tupper, Jr., had outraged English further by not only giving History a dozen new fellowships with which to hire graduate students to grade all their professors' papers and exams for them, but by handing over to History, during the Pei construction, the entire fourth floor of the English Department building itself. While at the time this floor had been unused except as a place to store mildewed zoology exhibits—fish fossils, stuffed otters, pig fetuses in formaldehyde—still, English was incensed by the injustice of such rank favoritism.

Weak with indignation and envy, Dr. Bridges, till then a timorous man, had forced himself to crawl on his knees (his wife's phrase) to Dina Sue Ludd, granddaughter of the college founder, recent widow of a canned-goods mogul, and passionate believer in the study of Literature, her own major way back when. In the most successfully seductive moment of his fifty-five years (his wife, Tara, had seduced *him*, while he was preoccupied writing his dissertation), Norman Bridges persuaded Mrs. Ludd to give the English Department forty million dollars, in installments to be doled out by her cousin Buddy Tupper, so that English could hire academic stars to outshine in the polls those of History. Tupper told them they had two years to make appointments to three Ludd Chairs, as the richly endowed posts were to be called, and that they were to "make them good, and visible too." Mrs. Ludd specified that two of the chairs should be, as she was herself, female, and that the third might be, if they chose, "a creative sort."

English had gotten off to an excellent start. Flush from his conquest of Mrs. Ludd, Bridges flew north that first Christmas to the Modern Language Association's annual convention at a pitch of invincibility so intense it made him (according to his wife) almost sexy, and went looking for visible women. (At the time, there were no senior women in the Cavendish department, and had been none since the death of Miss Mabel Chiddick, M.A., chair from 1938 to 1957, *Beowulf* to Milton, and the retirement of her long-time companion, Dr. Elsie Spence, Ph.D., *Rape of the Lock* to Sandburg.)

Chairman Bridges's extraordinary coup, at that crowded holiday convention, was to lure a consensus out of his senior faculty (inebriated into a rare fellowship by three days of nonstop drinking at open bars hosted by all the other English departments in the country). Miraculously, this hitherto utterly divisive group voted to let him make two Ludd Chair offers. And astonishingly Bridges got those offers accepted, out from under the noses of Harvard and Yale, by two senior women. (These women were senior in status only, not in years; a fact which rankled some of the elder males back home at Cavendish—as poor Bridges was later to discover.) One of these women was Jane Nash-Gantz (author of five collections of her own essays, and editor of seven collections of essays by her friends, winner of the N.B.C.C. criticism prize for *The M/other Self: Discourses of Gender de/Construction*). She was only thirty-nine. The other was Jorvelle Wakefield (top draft-pick out of her graduate school, with twenty-seven job interviews and twenty job offers; author of *Black on Black: African-American Literary Theory since Watts,* and subject of a Bill Moyers program). She had reportedly just turned thirty. Somehow Norman Bridges, who could rarely talk his wife into anything, had talked both these women into moving to Rome, North Carolina, and teaching at Cavendish. How he did it was anybody's guess—and most of the guesses were in the six figures, and bitter.

He'd also hired Jane Nash-Gantz's husband, Victor Gantz, an amiable, hardworking Anglo-Saxonist, who'd written a number of books, but wasn't famous, and therefore couldn't be a Ludd Chair himself. But everyone liked Vic, for he taught lots of classes, served on lots of committees, and—from loneliness (his wife was in high demand on the international lecture circuit)—attended lots of parties, where he came in handy as an extra male.

Still, these great visible-women coups had occurred more than two years ago. Since then, while the short list of distinguished candidates for the final Ludd Chair grew as long and convoluted as a metaphysical conceit, no consensus could be cajoled out of the rancorous crew with whom poor Dr. Bridges was obliged to row his academic ship of state. Everyone submitted plenty of Ludd-worthy names, names of scholars or "creative sorts" they considered distinguished (including their own, and those of old friends), but everybody blackballed as totally *un*distinguished any names submitted by anyone else. Theo himself proposed bringing back from retirement, and over from England, Dame Winifred Throckmorton, the great Elizabethan drama specialist, angrily denying his colleagues' claims that she was long dead, notoriously senile, too obvious, and too obscure. He got nowhere.

Friday after Friday, semester after semester, allegations, innuendos, and reckless libel flew around the Dina Sue Ludd Lounge like bats in a burning barn: A Chaucerian was vetoed by the up-to-date set as "hopelessly concrete," a popular culture theorist was pooh-poohed by the old establishment as "a moronic boob tuber" after publicly stating that MTV was the cutting edge of postmodernist narrative and that John Lennon was better than John Donne. An eighteenth-century critic was dismissed as a compulsive and clumsy plagiarist, and a novelist fell by the wayside after the public posting of an old yellowed newspaper clipping in which he urged the nuclear bombing of Hanoi.

Anonymous memos, with exclamation points in red magic marker, appeared in department mailboxes claiming that a renowned Melville man was trying to hush up six charges of sexual harassment, and that a poet was a kleptomaniac. On her way home from the Asheville airport, Jane Nash-Gantz vetoed, via the cellular phone in her Mercedes, a foreign playwright who'd just been exposed at a conference in Budapest as a Nazi collaborator. John Hood, the department's gentle Miltonist, left the room in tears on being informed by Marcus Thorney that his Renaissance candidate didn't have a brain in her head, had lied about her salary, and was spreading herpes along the Northeast Corridor.

Tempers flared. Only two months ago, Marcus Thorney had threatened to resign if his own candidate wasn't offered the Ludd post. Steve Weiner had snapped, "So *go!*" and the two men had actually surged out of their chairs, with nostrils wide, until Jorvelle Wakefield had broken the tension by laughing despite noisy efforts to hold her breath. At that meeting the department had formally split between factions of Weinereans and Thorneyites, but it was a loose and jagged division. Temporary coalitions formed only to break up other temporary coalitions, then turned on each other. At least the excitable Jonas Marsh was consistent: He voted "No" on everyone except Dame Winifred Throckmorton, including (as Thorney nastily reminded him) one scholar he himself had nominated the year before! Dr. Bridges was eating five or six Almond Joys a day from nervous tension, and could no longer get into his tuxedo for trustee banquets. He told his wife, Tara, that he had stopped believing in democracy—a horrible thing for a Walt Whitman scholar to say.

Besides, as Theo pointed out to Steve, temperamentally Norman Bridges was incapable of anything *but* democracy. Whatever the greatest number wanted at any given meeting (even if that number was only three on one side, two on another, and four against both), Bridges was constitutionally convinced that that majority had possession of the greatest good. He could not swim against the tide to save his life, and so in this whirlpool of random riptides, he was constantly drowning. For most of his three terms as chair, he'd been trying to resign, on the British precedent that he'd clearly failed to receive a vote of confidence. But if he'd thought he'd suffered migraines from trying to bring the department to agree on hiring an outsider, then what happened to his nervous system when he started asking them to choose *one of themselves* to replace him was, in his wife's phrase, something you wouldn't want sleeping in the same bed with you. She certainly didn't, and ordered a set of twin maplewood four-posters.

The provost had finally demanded that Bridges's colleagues elect a new chairman by the end of April, or he'd appoint one himself.

That election was scheduled for next week. Meanwhile, until his successor arrived to relieve him, Dr. Bridges (believing that leadership had its duties as well as its—presumed—privileges), took a Valium every Thursday, and carried on.

"I tell you frankly, gentlemen—" Dr. Bridges caught sight of Theo pointing ostentatiously at Jorvelle Wakefield, the sole woman in the room (for Jane Nash-Gantz was away, as usual, lecturing in Europe). Dr. Bridges fussily puckered his lips, as if to say, "I knew!" But then he only made matters worse (as his wife often remarked), by adding, "Gentlemen, *and* our one lovely lady, Jorvelle . . ."

Jorvelle crossed her eyes flamboyantly at Theo. Dr. Bridges didn't see her; he was dropping two thick packets onto the laps of the napping Romantic Poetry and Victorian Novels, small elderly Southerners tenured before the days of publish-or-perish, and entirely unpublished (indeed for all anyone knew for certain, entirely unread), dubbed "Dee and Dum" by Theo after the nasty beanied schoolboys in *Alice in Wonderland.* They twitched with little exasperated jerks when the packets hit them, but immediately settled back down to their slumbers.

Dr. Bridges tugged at his argyle sweater vest. "We *have* to come to a decision by next week. Here's our final ranked list of candidates—"

"Who ranked it?" growled Jonas Marsh, who always said aloud what everyone else was thinking—one of the warning signs of what everyone else called insanity.

Bridges ignored this violation of Robert's Rules of Order. "—With a little more material I've put together—" He ignored a sound suspiciously like a groan. "—about each person. We have to stop, well, this, friendly fire . . ." He waited for a laugh, but didn't get it. ". . . and come together on this thing." He sighed. "And make, I repeat, *make* an acceptable and advantageous appointment before the term is over. Or—" And for emphasis he took off his glasses. "*Or*, and this, my friends, is the news." Bridges started to pull at his hair, remembering only at the last second that it wasn't his hair, but a toupee. "If we don't, Dean

Tupper has called me in, and told me flatly that he is going to take that third Ludd Chair, and give it . . ." The chairman paused, sucked in his stomach and snarled, "To the French Department!"

A pause. Followed by a loud slap from the end of the table. "Let the whoreson Tupper give it to the bloody Frogs then!"

Everyone looked at Jonas Marsh. The Restoration man had blown again. He did so as regularly as a geyser. First, his foot-jiggling sped up until his handsewn slip-on was kicking the underside of the table; then his hands began to squeeze both lapels of his custom-made jacket, then they started rubbing in a frenzy of zigzags across his handsome face as if it were crawling with flies.

"Here we go again," sneered Marcus Thorney, sotto voce to his current minion (Rice, Early American), and everyone went back to whatever they'd been doing for the past hour—chewing erasers, grading quizzes, counting venetian blind slats, doodling curtains.

"Now, Jonas, you don't mean that." Bridges gave Marsh a placating smile. The chairman seemed determined to go on believing his colleague was joking, as opposed to confronting the fact that Marsh seemed to be under the impression that he lived in seventeenth-century London, where men of letters were blunt, rather than in modern North Carolina, where they were considerably less so.

"Outrageous!" Marsh snapped. "Tupper? That cretinous syphilitic backwater swamp-bred FUNDI?"

"Now, Jonas."

Marsh stood, his wide-cuffed Jermyn Street trousers falling in exquisite lines. "Dean Buddy Tupper, JUNIOR, threatens us? That poodle-fornicator?!"

John Hood, the gentle Miltonist, gasped.

Steve Weiner gawked at Theo, and asked aloud, "Dean Tupper is a poodle-fornicator? I didn't know that."

"Yes." Marsh turned to him in a gleeful quiver. "Yes, yes, yes. *What else* do you call a whoreson panderer who spends his life trying to fleece old women out of their assets while their mongrels hump his shinbones."

"I don't know," Steve admitted.

Marcus Thorney tapped his packet of folders with an angry forefinger. "Why is *my* candidate ranked *fourth*, may I ask?"

Steve Weiner snorted loudly. "Marcus, he's a moron—"

"Now, Steve," said Bridges.

Thorney rose. "How *dare* you?"

Jonas Marsh interrupted. "His last book is dull, derivative drivel."

"Now, Jonas," said Bridges.

"Marsh, you ought to be locked up!" Thorney shouted.

"Oh, dear, oh dear," whispered Hood, the gentle Miltonist.

"Frankly," Jorvelle Wakefield said, "I agree with Jonas."

"Marcus, I'm telling yah," said Steve Weiner, "this guy said in public, on a S.A.M.L.A. *panel,* that the only black literature ever written worth reading was by Alexander Dumas! The only black literature worth reading!"

"What does Dumas have to do with it?" wondered an Americanist.

A languid stir from the couch, and a yawning drawl from old Dee. "Mulatto. Mixed blood. Known fact. Dumas *père* had Negro blood in him."

"Oh, who doesn't!" Steve snarled.

The lounge erupted. Theo heard his stomach rumble, but knew there was little chance anyone else would.

Bridges tried beating on the table with his copy of *Leaves of Grass,* gave up and waited. When the shouts subsided, he coughed, held out his wrist to display his watchface, and sighed. "Next week we also need to vote on whether or not to drop the Spenser course from the undergraduate major requirements."

"Right! No one needs to read *The Faerie Queene* in the nineteen nineties!" shouted one of the younger professors.

"Oh reason not the need," sadly whispered the gentle Miltonist.

"Drop the bloody Romantics. Throw Shelley out!" Marsh yelled.

Bridges looked desperately around the beautiful room.

Theo took the hint, and raised his arm. "I move we adjourn."

From the mustard couch came another rustle, then from both

the venerables a thin sharp synchronized rasp perfectly audible, "Ah second."

{*Curtain*}, thought Theo.

Norman Bridges had hurried away to answer an emergency call from the provost. Out in the corridor waiting for him, Theo leaned against the wall, noting who walked out with whom, who clustered, who got snubbed. He himself got snubbed by Dum and Dee and by Thorney, but that was nothing new. The ancients disliked him only because they couldn't cope with the way Cavendish had been invaded by more and more "Yankees." But the lean medievalist and Theo disliked each other personally. In Theo's view, Thorney had only two kinds of relationships: He attached himself to power, like a bird hitchhiking on the back of a rhino, or he played rhino to smaller birds. And Theo had been unwilling to play fowl for him. Rice, Thorney's newest hitchhiker, had his beak deep in the man's ego now, sucking away by making nasty cracks about the jet-setting Jane Nash-Gantz as they hurried down the hall past old Dum and Dee, who were toddling off, looking refreshed.

Contemporary Poetry walked out, hoping, despite the last-minute notice, that Vic Gantz could come to dinner. As always, Vic could. Modern British Novels walked out and brushed past Jonas Marsh, who was emerging blind from the lounge, talking to himself, though Hood the Miltonist kindly walked beside him so it wouldn't look that way.

JONAS: "Unconscionable! Excrescence!"

HOOD: "Yessss. Umm. Hmmm."

When Theo's best friends Jorvelle Wakefield and Steve Weiner jostled together through the lounge doors, Critical Theory from the junior faculty raced out of his office after them, again trying to wheedle information from Jorvelle about her salary, as he'd been doing since the university's youngest full professor had first arrived there in a red turbo Saab convertible.

CRITICAL THEORY (obsequious): "We're all just curious, Jorvelle, I mean, the junior faculty. We share our salaries, I mean the information, we share the information—"

THEO: "Oh, make him suffer, Jorvelle. Tell him."

JORVELLE (grinding her teeth cheerfully around an unlit cigarette): "I'll tell you this. If I was a white man, I'd be ashamed to take all that money."

CRITICAL THEORY (nervous): "She's joking."

STEVE (straightening the younger man's bow-tie): "Look, Jim, lobby for me for chairman, and I'll make Jorvelle let you ride in her new helicopter, deal? Did she tell you they gave her a helicopter?"

CRITICAL THEORY: "Is that *true*?"

THEO: "Is it because you theorists think language is meaningless that you'll believe anything?"

Critical Theory thought this over, biting at his fingernails, then wandered away to the library, where foreign exchange students and the untenured faculty carried on till late hours the life of the mind.

Though Jorvelle was fleshy and Steve was thin, they were the same height, had the same close-cropped black curly hair, and wore the same clothes—baggy shirts in natural fibers, earth-colored, pleated baggy trousers with thin belts, and shoes like bedroom slippers. Theo, on the other hand, was no clotheshorse, although he was by far the best-looking of the three. In fact, a group of female graduate students had often commented together on Professor Ryan's close resemblance to the young Gary Cooper; but then Cooper hadn't been much of a clotheshorse either. At home Theo wore jeans and sweatshirts; his teaching wardrobe consisted of three corduroy suits—Old, Not So Old, and Pretty New—though Jonas Marsh had told him that one corduroy suit was one too damnable many. Steve had often offered to drive him to a "great discount mall" only fifty miles away, but Theo wasn't interested.

His black flannel shirt rolled to the elbows, hands in the pockets of Not So Old black trousers, he now leaned against the wall, listening as his friends went on with their increasingly flirtatious bickering. It had been two years since Steve's wife had left him to work full-time for the George Bush campaign with a corporate banker from Charlotte, whom she'd afterwards married. Lately, thought Theo, Steve was acting besotted with the new Ludd Chair.

JORVELLE: [lighting up]: "Steve, if you lose to Marcus Thorney, I'm gonna take the Yale offer."

STEVE: [lighting up too]: "You're gonna leave a place that's giving you eighty-five thousand a year to deconstruct *The Color Purple*?"

JORVELLE: "I don't do deconstruction, boy. I do demolition. Didn't you read that in *People* magazine? I blow up canons. Meanwhile, I love for William Faulkner to *hear* what you're doing to *The Sound and the Fury*."

They puffed away at each other companionably, smiling through the stinky clouds. Then Jorvelle gave Theo a hug. "So long, DWEMs, I've got a radio interview." (DWEMs were the Dead-White-European-Males who'd once been running the world and telling everybody in it what books to read.)

"Hey, who's dead? I'm still a Weem," Theo protested.

"Today's Weem, tomorrow's Dweem," Jorvelle cheerfully predicted. She waved, on the run, broad hips swaying.

Steve couldn't let her go. "I'm a Dweemboat," he shouted, and chased after her down the hall, not even pausing at the men's room door to chat up the emerging Contemporary Poetry, a vote allegedly leaning his way.

It must be spring, thought the unattached Theo Ryan with envy.

MOTHER COURAGE:
Get out of bed and look alive.
{Exit}

CHAPTER
2

{A Cry Within}

There has been much throwing about of brains.

Hamlet

IN 1924 a Piedmont tobacco czar named Ubal Cavendish had built himself an isolated Christian college in which to pen his worthless sons. He'd built it far from home, in the western part of North Carolina, built it of Georgian brick and Gothic stone in a sylvan setting in a fundamentalist county, huddled by a lake, surrounded by wooded hillocks, and guarded by an impoverished faculty of fanatical evangelicals convinced that the game of football was God's favorite pastime. In the beginning, the student body was male, rural, local, and as sophisticated as a bootlegger's still hidden behind a patch of jimsonweed. Back then, students were required to pray, forbidden to dance, and encouraged to smoke. Now they were warned against smoking, but praying and dancing were optional. Back then, the school was as poor as the state. Now it was rich; so were most of the students, and the faculty was looking to catch up. Football was still sacred.

Football was sacred despite the scandals of '64, in which the alumni Goalpost Club had been exposed for buying the head coach a beach house and the star quarterback a Corvette; or the shock of '75, in which the defensive line had been arrested for betting on games with professional bookies; or the upheaval of '82, in which three faculty members had turned state's evidence and confessed to handing out passing grades to scholarship players in courses that presupposed an ability to (a) do long division, (b) identify rocks, (c) read newspapers in Spanish—none of which skills the players appeared, under the most generous interpretation, to possess in the slightest. It didn't matter. In '87, the Cavendish Cougars had been ranked sixth in the nation. In '88, they'd won the Peach Bowl for the fifth time since the Buddy Tupper days. They'd beaten their great rival across the hills, Waldo College, forty-nine times in sixty-four years. The college stadium seated fifty thousand happy alumni. There were never any empty seats. This was still the South. Football was sacred.

Over the years the college had become a university, called Cavendish after its founder; the town that grew up around it was called Rome after the Empire. Across from the building that housed the English Department, now renamed Ludd in honor of the daughter of one of those original worthless Cavendish sons, was the Forum, an outdoor café set amidst fake broken-off Roman columns. There, Theo's bedraggled chairman, Norman Bridges, was treating his protégé to coffee and himself to two cinnamon buns. The Forum bordered Vance Walk, a cobbled path that wound on a pretty diagonal across the pastoral campus. The scene was idyllic, every tree patiently and expensively raised to form a grove of academe. The town of Rome, such as it was, was there to serve the school; it never imposed except to deliver mail and pizzas. The campus offered Nature at its monied best, Architecture at its most serene; upon the green landscape, well-fed youthful bodies lay lusciously about the grass nearly naked, sharing knowledge, like a vision of the Golden Age.

Theo glanced with pleasure at the yellow stone of the huge library glowing mellow in the afternoon sun. Ivy twined round the casement windows of rose-bricked Ludd Hall. An Ionic frieze of tobacco sheaves and Indian maidens graced Calvin Coolidge, the administration building, named by the tobacco czar for that pro-business president who'd helped him make his fortune in the twenties by staying out of his way. Daffodils and tulips patterned the lawn leading to the stately new Palladian temple of History, designed by I. M. Pei and paid for by the Georgia insecticide king. The chime of bells (or at least a recording of the chime of bells) pealed sweetly from the white spire of the college chapel. And in the center of the quad, bushy red rhododendron flamed at the base of the statue of Reverend Amos Latchett, the college's first president, as if he were a martyr being burned at the stake for his devotion to a higher and purer education.

"I do love this place," Dr. Bridges reminded himself as he morosely licked cinnamon sugar from his fingers. "So, Theo! What do you hear from your mother?"

"She and Dad are doing *The Pajama Game*—I think it's *Pajama Game*—somewhere, Connecticut, I guess." On a napkin Theo started doodling the original set for the American playwright Ford Rexford's *Desert Slow Dance*, which he was teaching Monday in "Classics of the Stage: Sophocles to Rexford," his spring term perennial. Ford Rexford was in a way a friend of his, and they were, in fact, supposed to have dinner together tomorrow evening.

"Lorraine Page!" Bridges sighed. "My goodness. I can't get over my saving that *Bells Are Ringing* playbill."

Theo nodded and scratched at his tawny mustache. They'd gone through this—how many times?

Decades ago, Norman Bridges had seen his first Broadway musical on one of the nights when Theo's mother had happened to go on in it as the understudy for Judy Holliday. Bridges, enthralled, hadn't even known Lorraine Page *wasn't* Judy Holliday, until he'd asked for her autograph at the stage door. The chairman now shook his head fondly, and wandered back into the past. Waiting for him to return, Theo stared as six beautiful short-skirted young women lined up across the quad; suddenly they leapt in unison off the ground, each forming the shape of a Saint Andrew's cross.

"Well, Theo. I've got some exciting news about the Ludd Chair. . . ."

Theo had known Bridges would be drawn back to "shop talk" like a moth to an electric zapper. Still watching the young women, he brushed a bee from his coffee. "Norman, you know—"

The cheerleaders screamed; an enormous sweat-suited young man charged into their midst, and galloped away with a blonde slung over his shoulder like a Sabine captive.

"My gosh! Wasn't that Cathy Bannister, one of our honors majors?" asked Bridges, squinting through his glasses.

"Yes. That's Joe Botzchick making off with her."

"The quarterback?"

"Half." Theo was staring at a dark-haired girl in shorts, lying in a spring fever in the grass nearby, her knees bent, her arms outflung, fingers feeling through the green blades. He rubbed his eyes. "You already know my opinion. If no one will agree with me about offering Dame Winifred—"

"I'm afraid no one will. Except Jonas."

"Then I say we should give John Hood his Renaissance candidate—"

"Yes, but what about this herpes rumor?"

Theo laughed. "Do we have to sleep with her to hire her? Besides, you don't even know it's true."

"She doesn't have much visibility. At least, as a scholar."

"Oh, the star theory!" Theo made a disgusted face.

"The consensus is we need a star. And that brings me to—"

Theo interrupted. "Make Mortimer and Lovell retire. . . . (These were the real names of the ancient Dee and Dum.) Replace them with Hood's candidate. Hire some famous female novelist. We need more women."

"More women?"

"Yes."

Theo needed *one*, at least. He had a feeling today, almost tingling, a stirring he hadn't felt since the departure of the art historian. But maybe the feeling was only April in the mountains. A jumble of songs of the sort his father and mother were continually belting out in his childhood jingled through his head, as they'd had a strange habit of doing this spring. April in dada, chestnuts in dada. . . . Why, it's almost like being in— He pushed away lyrics about hearing music when there's no one there, and drank his coffee.

Dr. Bridges looked at the young man with the paternal affection a chunky little spaniel might feel for an adopted baby Saint Bernard. He thought of Theo Ryan, whom he'd hired and had nudged through finishing his first book (on clowns in Shakespeare), as his academic son and heir. His successor, his success. "Theo, Theo. Why can't the rest of the department be as reasonable as you! I've got a building full of Napoleons and no army. Did I tell you my internist thinks I'm developing an ulcer?"

"You mentioned it." Theo stretched his long legs out into the walkway. "When I think of Napoleon, I think of ending up on Elba."

"That's your one problem. You're not ambitious, Theo." The chairman wagged his pudgy finger.

"Not virtue?" Across the quad, approaching the Coolidge steps, Theo saw a small group of students, dressed in black and carrying a big red banner. They appeared to be staging a grisly pantomime with some sort of human effigy. He thought he recognized his best graduate student, Jenny Harte, among them. It looked as if she was waving at him; she was very pretty. Theo reminded himself that he was Jenny's faculty adviser; she was as morally off-limits as a cloistered nun. She was very pretty.

Bridges was gulping down a large pill taken from the prescription bottle he kept in his vest pocket. "The way academia is today, Theo, only the *very* ambitious make it to the top. And the top is all there is now. Even for those who aren't in it. In my time, you could live a happy, productive life in the middle. Now the middle is simply not the top. You could be the top, if you'd only try."

"Norman, you sound like a Cole Porter song. Besides, a minute ago you were wishing everyone else could be *like* me."

"Theoretically." The chairman smothered a soft belch behind his hand. "Let Dr. Bridges be frank with a friend," he murmured. "All right?"

Theo nodded unhappily. The frankness of friendship had, since they'd met, flowed only in one direction. All right over the years for Dr. Bridges to tell him that if he didn't "chat up" old Mortimer and Lovell at his visiting lecture, and "talk some football" to Dean Tupper at his first interview, he wouldn't get the job; that if he didn't finish his "clown book" and have it accepted by a "major press," he wouldn't get tenure; that if he didn't stir himself and get married soon, he wouldn't have children. And that if he didn't capitalize on the success of the clown book and on his "fantastic chance" to write the official biography of Ford Rexford, America's greatest living playwright, he would not only not get promoted to "full," he would sink from the Limbo of the Middle into an abyss of anonymity on the Bottom. All that was friendly frankness.

Whereas it was Theo's strong impression that it would *not* be all right for him to remind Norman Bridges that he himself had been working on the same book for eighteen years. That if he didn't stop overeating, he would go from looking like Porky Pig, who was at least cute, to resembling the latter-day Orson Welles, who was a mess. That if he didn't gag most of his faculty, the lucky History Department (an oligarchy of catholic conformity) would never stop smirking out their I. M. Pei windows at the anarchy of radical protestants squabbling in Ludd Hall.

Not for Theo to point out that Bridges himself was married, and had children. That his wife, Tara, a Virginia belle who was sorry she'd ever left Charlottesville, lost no public opportunity for sarcasm at his expense, and four years back, after too much punch, had thrown a mousse paté in his face at the department Christmas party. That his Visigoth of a teenaged son had trashed downtown Rome one Saturday night in his pickup truck and, skipping bail, had vanished in a trail of exorbitant Visa charges. That his daughter (who made her father look slim) had declined to attend Cavendish, or any other college, or to move out of the house, where (at thirty-two) she still lived, passing her days watching the soaps and sullenly stuffing college fund-drive envelopes for $5.50 an hour. No, frankness was not called for on Theo's part.

"How's the Rexford book coming?" Norman asked.

"Coming," said Theo.

"You're due for promotion in the fall, you know?"

He knew.

"It's going to be a big book, Theo."

It certainly was.

"How is Mr. Rexford?" asked the chairman shyly. "Feeling better?"

"Much."

"Did he really fall off his balcony, or was he, well, drinking again?"

"Both."

"Ah, ha."

Although not a vulgar man, Norman Bridges was a star-gazer. His attraction to Theo Ryan, as Theo knew, had followed close on his spotting two comets that had trailed the tall young man into Rome. First of all, there were Theo's parents, Benny and Lorraine. While by no means ever the greatest celebrities, and by now (to their chagrin) entirely unknown to the general public, the two had enjoyed their glittering moments up there in the same sky with brighter stars. Everybody in America who'd watched *Luster Playhouse* on Friday nights in 1959 had watched Lorraine Page lather up her strawberry-blonde curls at 8:14 P.M. and comb them out at 8:27. Norman Bridges had been one of those millions of Americans. Plus, back in 1957, while an undergraduate at the University of Kentucky, he had attempted (along with everyone else in the country under twenty) to "Do the Duck" with Benny Ryan, although he had never mastered the back-slide.

Even more important among Theo's assets was the playwright Ford Rexford. For Theo was not merely Rexford's official biographer, he was likely to be his literary executor—with final say on the resting place of all the Rexford papers—papers that Harvard, UCLA, and Carnegie Mellon had already tried in vain to persuade the writer to leave to them. It was thrilling to Bridges that the best-known publisher in New York had flown down to Rome (well, to Asheville, and then rented a car) to meet with Theo and Rexford. Theo S. Ryan might not yet dazzle, himself—although those who loved him, and Bridges did, believed there was, well, sparkle in him—but life had already dusted him with the glitter of others; he might not be a star, but he certainly hung out with them.

Theo knew this: that behind the chairman's incessant promotion of his candidacy for the directorship of Cavendish's new Spitz Center was the hope of getting Rexford's papers. In fact, Theo was waiting for Bridges to say something more about that Spitz job right now. Seated in the sunset at the Forum, watching the bronze head of Reverend Latchett blaze with indignation at the disrespectful young protestors on Coolidge steps, Theo was absolutely certain he knew what was coming. The chairman was leading straight to that "word" he'd said earlier he wanted to have with his protégé. He would once again begin pleading with Theo to agree to run the Spitz Center.

In this assumption, Theo was absolutely and horrendously wrong.

The plump chairman wiped his glasses with his napkin. (A mistake, as the napkin was covered with sticky sugar.) He said, "Damn." Then he cleared his throat nervously. "Theo. I'll make the announcement tomorrow, but I wanted you to hear it personally. You know that Dr. Bridges has always been your strongest supporter."

Theo smiled patiently.

"But, well, I've had to face the fact—and there was no way to convince Buddy Tupper you were exactly eager, when you weren't . . ."

Theo stopped doodling, and stared at Bridges, who looked as if he were having gas pains, which was possible. "Is this about the Spitz Center?"

The plump man patted his heart, or intestines. "Well, yes. Remember that multimedia thing they offered Herbie Crawford's wife? I have to hand it to Buddy on this one. He's pulled off quite a coup."

"She's coming?"

"No, thank God. We would have never heard the end of History's hideous gloating." Bridges swiveled to shake his pudgy fist at the I. M. Pei building. "No, but Buddy put a multimedia package together, with Mr. Spitz, you know, the theatre donor, and the upshot is we're going to get something really major here. Theatre, film studies, television studio, an annual festival! Bigger than—"

"Sounds fantastic, Norman, but I keep telling you, it's just not my—"

Bridges rushed ahead, hands dancing. "To run it, Spitz wanted, and Buddy and Mrs. Ludd wanted, somebody, well, a *star.* Now, the amazing thing is—"

Theo began to suspect. ". . . A star?"

"The amazing thing is, they put out some feelers, made the approach. . . . And, I've got to hand it to them, they think they've got him!"

". . . Him?" It's a sad fact of human nature that we don't care to be rejected even by that which we are quite prepared to reject. Theo's first sensation was a spasm of hurt, a jab of envy. But all that might have been recovered from by bedtime, all that was nothing, compared to the jolt that shook him at the two words he now heard like a hiss from the suddenly serpentine tongue of his old advocate.

The words were "Scottie Smith."

Theo's coffee splashed. "Excuse me? Scottie Smith? The Broadway director?" Maybe he'd misheard; maybe Norman, whose face had turned into that of a leering python, had lost control of his lips.

But no, there was no mistake. The cheerful fiend hissed on, repeating a name that had curdled Theo's stomach for four years. "Yes! Yes! Scottie Smith. He's in the magazines all the time. I think he's only like thirty-two or so, about your age, but famous. He does all those high-concept interpretations? *Othello* as a minstrel show, and *Lady Windemere's Fan* at Attica prison."

"I know who he is. Dean Tupper wants to offer him a job here?"

"And tentatively he's said *yes*. Can you believe it? That was the phone call I had to take just now! I wasn't at liberty to mention it before; it seemed so unlikely he'd agree. But he said he'd love it!" Bridges's round pink face metamorphosed into that of a bloated pig, as he talked on and on. "Says he can turn Cavendish into a combination Spoleto and Cannes. Scottie Smith! And he'll have an appointment in English. He'll be the third Ludd Chair. An incredible feather in our cap!"

Theo sputtered. "But we didn't vote for him."

Bridges brushed this airily aside. "Oh, the department will be thrilled. Besides, otherwise, the French get the chair. Still, I need you, Theo, as, you know, our other theatre person, to make sure everybody understands what a remarkable catch Smith will be. Isn't it remarkable?"

Theo made a sound somewhat similar to speech.

"What?"

He tried again, gave up, and shook his head.

Bridges leaned across the table. "Of course, we'll make sure Smith won't step on your toes, Theo. I mean, you'll be doing your theatre lecture courses like always. You can work it all out. He'll do a playwriting workshop or something. Creative-type thing. Type of thing that doesn't interest you. . . ."

"Scottie Smith said he'd come to Cavendish?"

"Tentatively. Of course, there're salary questions. Fall after next . . . Theo? I hope this hasn't upset you."

Theo said, "No, of course not," but it didn't come out right.

Bridges took on a defensive, truculent tone. "You *said* you weren't interested in the Spitz . . ."

Theo jerked himself back into focus. He stammered that he was fine, surprised, that's all. He'd have to think about Smith. Yes, a star was needed if what they wanted was a performing arts center. But Smith? Yes, to become the Southern Yale Rep would be a coup for Cavendish. But Smith?

"Why do you keep saying 'but Smith'? Do you know something about Scottie Smith? I realize you know the theatre, Theo."

"Let me think," said the drama professor. And he pleaded an evening engagement with Ford Rexford.

Bridges fawned at the name. "You'll tell Rexford about Smith, I hope?"

"I certainly will."

Relieved by these assurances, Bridges walked the younger man to his bicycle, patting his arm from time to time along the way. The bike was chained in front of Ludd Hall. Among the clutter of fluttering posters stapled to the kiosk there was one announcing auditions tonight for the Cavendish Faculty Drama Club's spring musical. *Guys and Dolls.* Theo winced at the sign. As a child he must have sat through a half-dozen productions of *Guys and Dolls.* Dr. Bridges winced too, because his wife always played a role in these productions, leaving him during the weeks of apparently nonstop rehearsals to eat his way through an international series of microwave gourmet dinners.

Before pedaling off, Theo agreed to pass on to Ford Rexford an invitation to join the Bridgeses for dinner on any date that suited him. Then the chairman waddled away to search for his station wagon, which—despite its distinctive VIRGINIA IS FOR LOVERS bumper sticker glued there by his wife—he always had trouble locating.

As Theo biked furiously back home, he reminded himself that, after all, Norman Bridges was innocent, that Norman had no way of knowing that some years ago Theo Ryan had spent his summer in a playwrighting workshop in the Berkshires, where for five unresting weeks he'd rendered his heart and cleaved his soul into the form of a three-act play about Walter Raleigh which he'd called *Foolscap*. Norman had never seen the frayed manuscript in Theo's bottom desk drawer, had never deciphered the short red scrawl of the workshop's celebrity teacher that bled across the final page.

> Nice moments, but not ready for prime time.
> Americans shouldn't try this sort of thing anyhow.
>   Best of luck, Scottie Smith

How many times had Theo heard the words shriek from the page? He heard them now in the weak screech of his bike chain as his legs, deadened weights, heavily pushed at the pedals. He heard them in the grating chitter of birds in ugly trees and in the whine of car tires on the pale street as he climbed the long steep hill towards home.

> There is a far-off sound as if out of the sky, the sound of a snapped string, dying away, sad. A stillness falls, and there is only the thud of an axe on a tree, far away in the cherry orchard.

> thought Theo,

> *{the Curtain slowly descends}*

CHAPTER

3

{Flourish}

What is our life? a play of passion.

Sir Walter Raleigh

WHEN HAMLET met the Ghost, the kingly spectre said, "Mark me." And the Prince of Denmark said, "I will."

When Theo Ryan met Joshua "Ford" Rexford, the great playwright said, "You're damn big for a Jew."

And Theo replied, "Well, to tell you the truth, I thought *you'd* be a whole lot bigger."

Rexford grinned at him. He said, "I am."

"I know," nodded Theo.

"How's that?"

"I teach your plays."

"That's a damn funny thing to do to plays—teach 'em."

The two men met because Cavendish University was near the once fashionable mountain resort of Tilting Rock, North Carolina. And in Tilting Rock was the hunting lodge to which America's most famous living playwright had suddenly retired for a rest. A lanky, liquor-gutted man, with bowed-out legs, gray hair, and droopy-lidded, very blue eyes, Ford Rexford appeared, at first sight, to need a rest. He barely resembled at all the young tousled Texan playwright in jeans who'd squinted out from a 1949 cover of *Life*—as gorgeous as a cowboy movie star. Theo had for years kept a framed copy of that *Life* cover on the wall of his study;

and there was no denying he was disappointed by his first sight in the flesh of the four-time Tony, three-time Pulitzer Prize winner.

It was Theo's parents who had arranged his meeting with Rexford. The Ryans, native New Yorkers—convinced that their son would wither from loneliness down in the southern wilds—were always culling their vast Rolodex for anyone who might know somebody crazy enough to move anywhere near Rome, North Carolina. They had never "played those hills"—was there even anything besides that outdoor pageant about Daniel Boone down there *to* play?—and they imagined their only child living on the set for *Tobacco Road*.

For years, the Ryans had known a man named Bernard Bittermann, whose father had done character parts on the Borscht circuit. As it happened, Bittermann was Ford Rexford's business manager. So when the Ryans mentioned that Theo was now a drama professor living only thirty miles from his client's retreat, Bittermann gave them the great man's phone number. Knowing they couldn't trust Theo to "follow up" on this opportunity (they were always telling him to call on strangers, and he never did it), they phoned the playwright themselves, describing Theo lavishly as a passionate worshipper of every word of Rexford's work. To their delight, Rexford had said he was already an admirer of their son's book on Shakespeare's clowns, and he'd immediately invited the young professor over to Tilting Rock for a dinner of bootleg alcohol, turnip greens in fatback, squirrel stew, and peach pie.

That first evening, Theo (unused to 200-proof grain alcohol) did things that caused him at five in the morning to leap out of his bed hyperventilating. They were the very things that started Ford Rexford thinking about the young scholar as his authorized biographer. First of all, Theo, drunk before he knew it, recited a soliloquy from Marlowe's *Tamburlaine*, then put on a Fred Astaire record and tap-danced (which he hadn't done since last on stage with his parents—in a stock company production of *George M!*). At midnight, Rexford drove him to a bar named Cherokee's, where Theo was cheered for his rendition of "Blue Bayou." At 2:00 A.M., they went waterskiing out on a lake where the playwright broke his arm. It was the kind of evening that was known to appeal to Ford Rexford.

Over the next year, their relationship (despite Theo's subsequent sobriety) deepened. Rexford consoled him about the loss of the art historian, or at least suggested she was no real loss. Eventually the playwright began writing a new play about a young drama teacher. Eventually Theo began writing the playwright's life, and two years after their first meeting, he had finished four hundred pages of this "official critical biography." Even so he had only reached the year 1944, when his subject was still a nineteen-year-old grunt in World War II, filching scotch from his C.O.'s footlocker in Palermo, with few thoughts about writing so much as a one-act. In fact, according to the playwright's lurid recollections, recorded by Theo on five dozen tape cassettes, in his youth Ford Rexford hadn't shown the slightest intimation that he'd ever think about a thing in his life except (as the great man had phrased it for Theo the day they met): "Hooch, cooze, and rhythm 'n blues."

No denying, Theo had been disappointed by that original meeting, by what he'd seen, and by what he'd heard burbling out of the mouth of the nation's Chekhov. It had been difficult to connect this scatological sot who indiscriminately slurred gentiles, Jews, women, men, children, and animals, with the author of sixteen wise, large-hearted three-act plays, and dozens of wonderful one-act plays, glorifying them all. At that first meeting, Rexford had looked spent and shrunk, too battered a vessel to hold ordinary good sense, much less any wise-hearted insights. Two years later, he didn't look much better. Still, he was only sixty-six, and while, in his phrase, he'd "packed a shitload of boogying" into those three score and six, and indeed did seem as decayed as a compost heap these days, he had, he said, no intention of really retiring. He fully expected to make a comeback, and "wipe his worn-out backside on Broadway" once again.

"Retire" was merely Rexford's euphemism for run away. He'd run away to the mountains from his producers, who wanted their large advance back; from his psychiatrist, who wanted to have him committed to a sanatorium, after collecting from him seventeen thousand dollars for more than three years of triweekly sessions (half of which the playwright had failed to attend). He'd run away from the police, who wanted to question him about shooting his fourth (now ex) wife; and from his fourth ex-wife, a mediocre actress with remarkable physical assets, who wanted to "sue the redneck S.O.B." for shooting at her.

Rexford's hunting lodge near Tilting Rock was one of the many retreats his frazzled business manager, Bernard Bittermann, had bought him over the years as a tax dodge (some of which he then had been forced to sell fast, because of yet another of the writer's sudden cash-flow emergencies—like that bad roulette run in Reno in '63, or that palimony suit in '79). Sometimes Bittermann would sit up nights in the kitchen of his brownstone in Brooklyn Heights, and add on his machine the millions of dollars squandered by "the ignoramus" (as he called the man the MacArthur Foundation called "the finest genius of the American theatre"). The, yes, *millions* squandered in forty years of indiscriminate profligacy—all gone, including the generous grant from the Mac- Arthur Foundation. Sometimes, staring at those figures would make the Republican C.P.A. toy theoretically with the notion of justifiable embezzlement.

In the sixties alone, Rexford had earned $12,543,768.22. After all, as Bittermann explained with leaden sarcasm to his wife, when you have four hits running on Broadway simultaneously, at six percent of the box-office gross, you earn over fifty thousand a week from one city alone; when you then sell all four of those plays to theatres in every city in the world civilized enough to have a theatre, and to book publishers in every country in the world literate enough to have publishers, *and* to Hollywood, well, you need a lot of lodges for tax dodges.

"Bernie! You made a rhyme!" gaily said Bittermann's wife, but the C.P.A. scowled at her. He preferred numbers to words. And as far as he could tell, Rexford had no head for numbers, or much else in the "real world." The writer had even had to call in the middle of the night to ask where exactly this particular hunting lodge of his was located. At the same time he'd warned Bittermann—under hazard of his returning to New York to "saw your cojones off with a hoof-file"—not to tell another soul where he'd gone, including his mother-fucked, head-diddling bull-pizzle of a shrink, and the fart-bloated, slab-brained cops.

"Including your wife?" asked the C.P.A.

"That central sieve of the city's sewers!" said Rexford, and slammed down the phone. Or dropped it.

Packing garbage bags with manuscripts and Wild Turkey, the playwright had then driven nonstop to North Carolina in a rental car, a new deluxe Lincoln Continental, which he'd neglected to turn in for so long that the business manager was obliged to buy it outright for him (the rental agency didn't want it back anyhow, considering what it looked and smelled like by then); Bittermann also had had to pay off speeding tickets impressively collected from six separate states within a seven-hour span.

Ford Rexford's first sight of the natural landmark for which the town of Tilting Rock was named, as it suddenly loomed out above the highway when he rounded a curve, scared him into thinking he had the D.T.'s again. (That's when the Lincoln had suffered the most severe body damage.) The discovery that he had moved to a "dry county," an expression he wasn't familiar with, was even more terrifying. All one could buy in public in Tilting was beer and wine; and Rexford drank beer and wine only when he was on the wagon. He almost turned around and drove straight back to Manhattan.

Instead, the writer had passed the evening at Cherokee's, a local roadside dive where he'd been introduced to the first of the three solaces which soon proved so pleasant he'd settled into a bucolic contentment that had now lasted for two years. It was the longest he'd ever stayed anywhere since he'd run away from home at fourteen, after seducing a married choir singer in the Pentecostal church where his father was the minister.

That first solace was a beautiful and strong-willed twenty-five-year-old woman named Rhodora Potts, lead singer with a honky-tonk combo playing at Cherokee's called the Dead Indians. The second was Rhodora's brother, T. W. Potts, who manufactured excellent whisky in his cow shed. The third solace was Theo Ryan.

Between them, Theo and the Potts siblings carried the jaded writer back to the simple days of his childhood in rural Texas. With their help, he moved into his yellow pine lodge in the hollow of a pretty little mountain he appeared to own, and which he renamed Rhodora in Miss Potts's honor. There he slept under patchwork quilts, rolled his Bull Durham, clogged at the V.F.W. Post until he broke his ankle, raised his own chickens until they ran off, and sat up nights on the porch watching owls eat mice. T. W. Potts took him hunting for deer and bear, and kept him (after the initial binge had subsided) down to a half pint a day. Theo took him to his writing desk. Rhodora took him, he said, to paradise and back.

Best of all, from Rexford's business manager's point of view, he wasn't spending any money; there was not much to spend it on in Tilting Rock. Back in Manhattan, Bittermann and three lawyers were able to buy off the psychiatrist, and stall the producers by claiming Rexford was locked up in a santorium working night and day on his best play ever. They were able to get the assault charges dropped, and to settle out of court with their client's ex-wife number four, by pointing out that she'd stabbed Rexford with a letter opener before he'd shot her (which was true) and by threatening to tell the police about her cocaine habit. They'd also agreed to a generous alimony settlement, including all foreign royalties on *Desert Slow Dance,* and the penthouse. On the phone to Tilting Rock, Bittermann had offered the writer the choice between the penthouse and letting Mrs. Rexford have the lead in the upcoming London production of *Her Pride of Place.* Rexford said he'd rather lose the house. He added, "But if I ever write a one-woman show for a douchebag cocksucker, tell her she can come try out for the part, using a rusted muffler off an old Chevy truck."

Unlike Theo, the business manager no longer paid much attention to his famous client's foulmouthed badinage; once it had offended him; now it just sounded like Rexfordese, the way other clients sounded Japanese or Bostonian. So all he said on the phone then was, "Well, you better think of writing *something,* Ford. And soon. I'm doing my best, but you don't—"

"Don't shit a shitkicker, Bernie. Been socking my dough away in Switzerland all these years, is that it? Been off snorting cocaine, off muff-diving for poontang?"

The manager, who had spent a good part of all those years trying his best to keep Ford Rexford out of bankruptcy and/or jail, took a deep breath, and let the air boil out the sides of his mouth. "At your current rate, and without any sudden additional expenses, you'll last six months—"

"*Whoa!* A goddamn minute ago, Paramount wanted to buy *Bunches of Roses.*"

"True." Bernie Bittermann, a man of discipline, went on adding numbers as he talked. "But, Ford, you don't own *Bunches of Roses.* Your first wife owns *Bunches of Roses.* Your sister Ruth owns *Maiden Name.* Your third wife owns *The Valley of the Shadow.* Your agent owns *Preacher's Boy.* Your son Pawnee owns *The Long Way Home,* or did until he sold it. As I keep endeavoring to make clear, you own very few rights to very few of your plays. You have bribed with, made gifts of, bartered away, or sold off almost everything you've ever written. Can you understand that?"

". . . Well, fuck."

Yet, while the manager took this stern stance with his client, he privately felt rather encouraged by the end of the second "mountain year." There was no income, true, but there was considerably less outgo. And if Ford would only stay put, maybe he'd even finish writing something new. "America's National Treasure" (according to the Pulitzer committee) presumably hadn't written a word for a solid year after (as far as Theo could reconstruct the sequence from Ford's narration) the following had happened within a six-day period: He'd found his fourth wife embracing her personal trainer and was knocked cold when he attacked this large, physically fit individual; his new play, *Out of Bounds,* opened, was panned by the *Times,* and closed; in Sardi's his younger son, Pawnee, publicly renounced him forever (his older son, Josh, Jr., had done the same twenty years earlier); his fourth wife found him in the Jacuzzi with the show's leading lady and tried to electrocute them both; she then changed the locks on their penthouse, and boasted through the chain that, the night before, she'd tossed his computer containing his only copies of *A Waste of Spirit* (his play in progress) off the balcony into the traffic on Central Park West, twenty floors below; she then stabbed him when he shot the lock off the penthouse door in order to see if she'd really thrown out his computer (she had); he shot at his fourth wife; his lawyer kept him waiting in jail overnight; his psychiatrist tried to have him committed; and a parking garage gave his Ferrari to somebody else.

As, in a more peaceful mood, cuddled on the porch swing with Rhodora Potts, Rexford had summed it up for her and Theo, it had been "Lord, boys and girls, just one of those real bad weeks."

But by the end of mountain-year-2, Bernie Bittermann had begun to hope that down there in that dry county, far from temptation, Ford Rexford could make a full moral, physical, artistic (and consequently, a full financial) comeback. For the physical regeneration, Bittermann counted on Rhodora Potts. For the artistic recovery, he counted on Theo Ryan.

Now, despite what Theo's parents had said, it wasn't true that he knew every word of Rexford's work by heart, or that he "worshipped" the work. And he certainly didn't worship the man— even before he'd met him. But it was true that Theo believed in his bones that Joshua "Ford" Rexford's plays were as good, at times, as plays ever got. What became clear after he met the man was that Rexford didn't know when those times were. Or at least he behaved as if he didn't. He behaved as if he couldn't *read*, much less write.

A scholar trained in current critical theories, Theo knew that any objectives of that human creature, the writer, were entirely beside the point; that the *text's* intentions were irrelevant and the *author* was absolutely a goner—as dead to the modern world as God—with no more authority over creation than a rose has over its scent. Still, deep in Theo's bones tradition pulled; he hankered for meaning and purpose. He was troubled by Plato's notion of the artist-as-divine-moron; he was annoyed by that recent play in which Mozart came across as a lewd, giggling, imbecilic conduit for the divine harmonies of the universe. Was it really plausible that Shakespeare could have been as dumb as Shaw thought him? Was it conceivable that Michelangelo didn't have a clue as to what the David was going to end up looking like? Could anyone ever seriously believe that Jane Austen might be stupid?

But Ford Rexford, the man who'd written with such understanding and admiration about the Mexican family in *The Valley of the Shadow*, how could he possibly tell those sophomoric racial jokes? How could the man who'd written *Preacher's Boy*—a play

that made fathers and sons all over the world weep to reconcile—
have so irrevocably abandoned his own father and so alienated his
own sons? How could the man who'd written *Desert Slow Dance*,
that wonderful love song to women, have failed so miserably in
four marriages? Surely, Rexford was joking when he claimed that
Bunches of Roses was "just about having some fun while the get-
tin's good," and that he couldn't recall what *The Long Way Home*
was about. It was almost enough to reconcile Theo to the worst
excesses of modern criticism. Better that the poet have nothing to
say about the poem, better that the plays be snatched by the critical
midwife at the moment of delivery, than that fecund fools like
Ford Rexford be allowed to bring them up.

That's what Theo Ryan had thought when he'd first met the
man whose biography he now appeared to know better than the
subject himself. And that's what he still thought two years later,
when, already in a bad mood on this sunny afternoon, late April
in the Carolina mountains, he rode his bicycle wobbling up the
gravel drive to his small house near the campus of Cavendish University.

For first he saw the battered, mud-splattered gold Lincoln by
(or rather, on) his lawn, then he spotted Ford Rexford urinating
off the side of his porch, just missing his careful beds of new
blooming tulips and daffodils.

CHAPTER

4

{Aside}

If it must all come out, why let 'em know it; tis but the way of the world.

Congreve, The Way of the World

LATE THAT SAME AFTERNOON, Dean Buddy Tupper, Jr. stood in his luxurious suite of offices atop the Coolidge Building, from which, like Patton, he studied the field of battle below. He could see trouble coming like a swarm of Rommel's tanks. Let it come, he growled. Tupper ran this university under the official title of provost. He continued to call himself "Dean Tupper" only because he liked a brisk title, rather like "Coach," stuck in front of his name, and "Provost Tupper" didn't, in his phrase, cut it. He was a bull-necked, big-thighed man who still had the flattop he'd worn when he'd played offensive line the year he'd slammed, bucked, and shoved Cavendish all the way to the Peach Bowl; when they'd named him Buddy the Bone-Cruncher Tupper. The smell of blood didn't scare Tupper at all. He loved it.

Down below on campus, Herbert Crawford, star professor of History, and Maude Fletcher, acting Cavendish chaplain, were still stationed behind a microphone at the doors of Bleecker Dining Hall, where they'd been shouting at the cafeteria workers to unite because they had nothing to lose but their Tupper-forged chains. Above the doors flapped a big red banner that read, BOYCOTT BLEECKER. Crawford had been trying to stir things up from the inside for weeks. Now this. While at first the workers had clearly been put off by the British professor's black leather outfit and his Ortega sunglasses; while many obviously hadn't been able to follow his Cockney-accented call to arms; and while most had little idea what it meant to be a labor-intensive mode of capitalistic production; still, every one of them had quickly grasped the idea that an eight-percent raise for eight-percent fewer hours was something to think about. They didn't need Herbie Crawford and the damn (temporary, thank God) chaplain, Maude Fletcher, out there distributing fliers urging them to strike for incredible wages in order to realize they were "slaving for slave pay." Buddy Tupper had known it himself when he'd negotiated their contracts.

Worse, today Crawford and Co. had collected a squadron of followers among the young faculty and students, all of them dressed in black and wearing those damn red 8% buttons, who were out there with him now in the picket line, calling on the undergraduates to boycott the dining hall. Tupper could hear their ridiculous chant from his window right this minute.

> Don't eat Tupper's supper!
> Don't eat Tupper's supper!
> Boycott Bleecker! Boycott Bleeker!

The provost butted his shoulder hard against the plate glass. Crawford, who only last month had announced that starting next year he'd be alternating his popular "Modern Capitalism: Origins to Collapse" with a new course, "Modern Communism: Origins to Collapse," had pulled a fast one. The Commie bastard really was a Commie, despite the History Department's fervent assurances that Professor Crawford's ideology was all in his head, and would stay there. Why, they'd claimed that Crawford hung around the cafeteria workers only to take notes on their dialects, for an article on the ethnosemiotics of migrated blacks in rural Appalachia; they'd even shown him the article, and if it was in English, you couldn't prove it by Buddy Tupper, who held a Ph.D. himself (Cavendish, '48, Social Sciences). Somebody ought to write an article on Commie Crawford's negotiations for shameless salary supplements in nontaxable grants, noninterest mortgage loans, and incentive perks like lap pools unreported to the I.R.S. — in the haggling over which he'd displayed an entrepre-

neurial ruthlessness J. P. Morgan would have envied. Tupper had
heard that Crawford had been pestering those cafeteria workers
since they'd opened for breakfast. What was the man doing up at
six-thirty anyhow?—after he'd refused to teach a single morning
class. "Like Caruso, before noon, mate, I don't even spit," he'd
told Tupper, laughing. And why didn't he get his teeth fixed, now
that he was in America! God knows, he could afford to have every
crooked one of them capped in pearl.

At 5:00 P.M. on this April afternoon, Herbie Crawford was
not Tupper's only problem. Tupper's "major prob" was—as
always—Claudia Pratt, the woman the trustees had put in over
his objections as dean of the college, when, after twenty years at
that post, he'd been promoted. This bleeding-heart, yellow-bellied
woman, with no savvy about the real way of the world, had already been in here this morning jabbering junk about providing
sympathetic arenas for discussion with the cafeteria workers. He'd
had to pretend to take a call from the governor to get rid of her.
(His secretary knew to buzz him with long-distance calls whenever
Dean Pratt got going good.)

It was no slouch job running a university. Like all days, today
had been long and hard. His secretary had left at noon, just because she had a temperature of 102°. Her temporary replacement
didn't appear to know longhand, much less shorthand. The provost had had a phone call (collect from London) with the stage
director Scottie Smith, who'd talked like a high-strung six-year-
old, and who was asking for a salary that Vince Lombardi would
have choked on. (Maybe they should have gone with Theo Ryan
after all.) He'd had a telegram from Cavendish's most famous law
professor, off for some reason to Rio, demanding a raise that
Tupper had initially assumed was a Western Union typing error.

He'd received a memo from the chairman of Romance Languages, advising him that in the heat of a tenure review, a senior
member of the Spanish Department had "regrettably rather seriously bitten through" the forefinger of a senior member of the
Italian Department. Tupper's immediate phone call to demand
why such news should be reported by (slow) campus post, rather
than the expensive system of computer-screen E Mail with which
they'd been provided, elicited the update that Dr. Montemaggio's

finger had required twenty-two stiches, and that he was screaming about suing the university.

"Tell him to sue Dr. Torres!" the provost shouted. "What have we got to do with it?" He was told that Dr. Torres was still in the hospital with a burst blood vessel in his eye, and he too was considering bringing suit.

"Fire them both!" growled Tupper.

The chairman gasped. "Buddy, for heaven's sake, they're *tenured.*"

Damn tenure!, Tupper thought, and stopped himself from blurting out a witticism about the place of wops on the evolutionary scale—which would have doubtless left him vulnerable to another suit for racial discrimination from the chair of Romance Languages, whose name, he recalled just in time, was Sebastiani.

If there was one thing Tupper hated, it was the system called tenure. Thank God that so-called reverend, Maude Fletcher, didn't have it yet. Tenure was a choke hold whereby the faculty who grabbed it were never to be shaken loose unless so senile they couldn't locate their classrooms, or so depraved they debauched dogs in public. Short of those sins, the whole university had itself turned into one big sanctuary harboring the merely mad, the simply slothful, and the routinely immoral, ignorant, inept, obtuse, and inebriated. What C.E.O. of any other multimillion-dollar industry was so ridiculously hamstrung, so blocked from his goals, so unable to fire at will?!

And if there was one thing Tupper hated more than tenured mediocrities, it was tenured celebrities like Crawford, it was that stable of pampered prize-winners forced upon him by academia's stampede to go Hollywood—and not even the good old Hollywood, where as head of the studio he could have signed, traded, and indentured his stars in the imperious fashion of Louis B. Mayer; no, here he was in the new Hollywood, where the lunatics were running the asylum, where he had to put up with craziness like an economics professor who flew off to the White House every other week, and actually had his own public relations man. Craziness like departments calling themselves "Cultural Studies" and teaching comic books. Or calling themselves "Native American Studies" and hiring boozed-out half-breeds from Boone (and what a laugh those old geezers were having on Cavendish) to hop up and down howling (so they claimed) authentic Algonquin into tape recorders. Or calling themselves "Women's Studies" and getting two hundred kids to enroll for something listed in the catalogue as "The Power of Gender" or "The Gender of Power"—he couldn't remember which. Craziness like Herbie Crawford.

Tupper's meditations were interrupted by a late phone call from Norman Bridges saying Federal Express had just picked up a package from Jorvelle Wakefield addressed to Yale, which could very well mean Yale was making her an offer, so maybe Cavendish should be ready with a quick counteroffer. That wimp Norman Bridges would agree to a punt on second down if enough of the huddle asked him to! "Forget it!" Tupper barked. "Nobody with a new Saab is gonna park it in downtown New Haven."

His mood burned hotter as the provost read the next item on his desk, a ten-page letter from the mother of a senior coed, one Cathy Bannister, in which Mrs. Bannister wondered why she and her overworked husband paid $19,674.50 a year, as well as contributed heavily to the Alumni Fund Drive, so that their daughter could (a) write a honors thesis under the supervision of Jane Nash-Gantz entitled "Clitoral Imagery in Contemporary Lesbian Poetry," (b) telephone her mother and tell her that on the basis of recent insights gleaned from her famous psychology professor, she felt fairly certain that her father had been sexually abused, (c) announce to her entire family after church on Easter Sunday (having attended those services in a black leather jacket) that Modern Capitalism had collapsed, that so had Christianity, and she herself had turned into a Neo-Marxist. This was not the Cavendish the correspondent and her husband had attended twenty-five years ago, not "by a long shot," and therefore the Bannisters were "compelled to wonder."

Tupper telephoned immediately to Dr. Nash-Gantz, and was told by her secretary (she had her own secretary!) that Jane (her secretary called her Jane!) had flown that morning (why didn't she stay home with her husband where she belonged?) to be a keynote speaker at an international women's conference in Warsaw. Warsaw? By God, Nash-Gantz was a Commie too! And to hell with this new notion that not even the Communists were Commies anymore. Tupper glanced quickly around his palatial office suite as if to plan the barricades behind which he could dig in to pepper these overpaid proletariats. He probably had more of them here on the Cavendish campus than were left in all of Eastern Europe!

Tupper's roving glance caught sight of the stooped lean silhouette of his ostensible boss, President Irwin Kaney (Brigadier General, U.S. Army, Retired), a man of eighty who looked like a withered bald eagle, and behaved (in Tupper's phrase) like a doddering dodo.

Now, many years back, Tupper himself had been a fervent advocate of Irwin Kaney's appointment as Cavendish's president: A bomber pilot hero of World War II, in his mid-sixties a field commander in Vietnam, General Kaney would be sure to have— or so Tupper had thought—the kind of no-nonsense military mentality this school could use. As it happened, the military mentality was there all right, but the search committee should have probed a little deeper into the no-nonsense. For the years had, in Tupper's subsequent appraisal, dimmed out of the Old Man what had most likely been very low wattage to begin with.

The general now walked past the big desk, on his way to Tupper's private bathroom again; unable to recall that this was no longer his office, nor his toilet. The provost bellowed, "IRWIN!" at him. But in vain; the Old Man was deaf and doubtless legally blind as well. The bathroom door slammed shut. By the time Kaney came back out again, Tupper was in a worse mood, having finished an interview in the *Chronicle of Higher Education* with English professor Jonas Marsh in which that (tenured) maniac denounced the university for everything from its South African stocks to its undergraduates' IQs. "When will Cavendish stop admitting these shallow blonde streams of idiotic southern belles, these dumb sons of rich rednecks?" ran one boxed quote. "When will our cowardly faculty stop bestowing A's on the mediocre and B's on the mentally defective? Why, today, a C is cause for a faculty conference, and a D grounds for a legal suit!"

The bathroom door flew open. No toilet flush—as usual. President Kaney, immaculately dressed except that his pinstriped vest was on inside-out, nodded pleasantly, but without a glimmer of recognition, at Dean Tupper. "Irwin, your bathroom is down the hall, in your office! Irwin! *General Kaney!*"

The general wheeled, saluted smartly, marched to the plate-glass window under the impression that it was an exit, and stopped. He stared down at the students picketing Bleecker Dining Hall. "Officer," he said to his provost in his soft Mississippi slur, "that village down there is crawling with V.C. Radio fire base for some air support." He shook his head sadly and ambled away.

Dean Claudia Pratt's secretary came back in smirking with the bad news that his own temporary couldn't figure out the telephone, that his cousin Dina Sue Ludd was on line five wanting to know if it could possibly be true, as rumor had reached her—and as she had just chewed Norman Bridges out for babbling nonsense about academic freedom to excuse it—that one of her Ludd Chairs (Nantz-Gap, or whatever her name was) had used a Ludd Hall lecture room to accuse Emily Dickinson of unnatural desires? Was that why she was giving the English Department forty million dollars? And Norman Bridges was back on line three, calling from home, begging to be allowed to retire early. And a Channel 10 News van had just pulled up in front of Bleecker Hall; a woman with a TV camera was hopping out. And a (black) fast-food magnate with *four* children enrolled in Cavendish was waiting on line six to learn if indeed the richest university in the South paid its (mostly black) cafeteria workers slave wages. And a committee of undergraduates who wanted the land Cavendish sat on returned to the Cherokee Indians from whom it had been stolen by Andrew Jackson was outside waiting to see him.

"Let them wait." Dean Tupper grimaced. It took a tough man to run a university these days. But he was a tough man. He clutched at the bronze football displayed on his desk, and took the call from Dina Sue Ludd.

CHAPTER

5

{A Bell Rings}

The poets' persons and doings are but pictures what should be, and not stories what have been.

Sidney, Apology for Poetry

"SON, GET ME A PREACHER!" shouted the playwright, zipping up his jeans, and pulling a half pint from the green suede vest he wore over an aquamarine T-shirt with the logo of his flopped play, *Out of Bounds,* on it.

"Jesus, not on my porch, Ford! Not on my flowers!"

Rexford took the last swig from the little bottle, shook it, flung it up in the air, and mercifully caught it in the Chicago Cubs cap he wore. "I'm old, cowboy, but I can aim," he protested.

Theo looked around. "I've got neighbors!" Neighbors who had in fact already complained about the playwright.

"Theo! Say hello, dammit!" Ford replied.

It was somewhat peevishly that Theo shook hands with the man who, in Norman Bridges's prediction, could give him "a national reputation." "Hello. How's your collarbone?"

"Perfect." The playwright had recently broken it, falling off his balcony.

"I expected you tomorrow," Theo uselessly added. "Does Rhodora know you drove over here?"

A sheepish chuckle. "The Dead Indians took her to Gatlinburg to play some hillbilly roadhouse gig tonight. That woman's too good for those dumb ugawugs."

In other words, no, Rhodora didn't know where Ford was. And his sky-blue eyes had that red-streaked, muddied look of having traveled beyond the two-drink limit. Now he stared with pleased awe at his hands, then wriggled the fingers. "Isn't it something, Theo, how everything on the vast majority of us works to start with and goes on working?" He pointed about his body. "Eyes see, ears hear, lungs go in, out, in, out; heart goes lub dub, lub dub. Look at you—ten movable fingers, ten movable toes. Look at me—absolutely more or less the same . . . I think." He took off one boot and sock.

Theo jerked his bike up onto the porch. "Yes, Ford. Go inside, will you? The provost's secretary's over there staring out her window at you."

A mistake. Rexford swung out from the porch rail and squeezed his crotch at her. Quickly unlocking his front door, Theo nudged the older man through it ahead of him. "Go!"

The old mill house of whitewashed stone in which Theo Ryan lived was only a few blocks from the university, yet open to hills in the back where a wide creek reached to rising woods beyond. Across the street, however, he faced a drab fifties split-level and two ersatz Victorians. Even as he kicked open the door, he glimpsed Buddy Tupper's malevolent secretary, who lived in the green pseudo–Carpenter Gothic, staring down at them from her upstairs window like Judith Anderson in *Rebecca*. "Inside!" Theo hissed.

Only saints stay heroes to their biographers. Any awe felt by the young professor for Rexford had long ago been driven off, dragging deference after it. In fact, Theo was often pushed by the playwright's behavior into emphatic, even overt orders. He had noticed other people taking the same exasperated peremptory tone with the man (Rhodora, for example, sounding like a sour schoolmarm when she forbade her lover to drive his own car). Theo often wondered if Rexford didn't encourage this treatment by others, thereby freeing his mind from the time-consuming chore of running his own life.

Rexford stomped into his boot as he hopped through the small, neat rooms back to the kitchen. He opened the refrigerator and stuck his head in. "What's the matter with you?" he yelled.

Theo set down his briefcase where he always did, on his bleached pine floor beside his desk, and examined his white-walled and sunny house; everything arranged just so in the open-beamed rooms. He squared a stack of books on the oak chest. Good. Everything in its place. (Once the playwright had broken in, and roasted extremely greasy sausages in his fireplace.)

"Tortellini and prosciutto salad," shouted Rexford. "It's hand-written on the package, with circles dotting the *i*'s, I swear! Plus some Hanoi-type goo, yogurt on a stick, and endive! I want food! Food!"

Refusing to be hurried, plumping a back pillow on the green rocker, straightening an old signed photograph of Ginger Rogers on the wall, pushing in a chair as he passed the dining room, Theo walked to the doorway of the kitchen. It was narrow enough for him to touch both walls with his arms outstretched, and he did that now, as if to reassure himself of the room's stability. "What are you looking for, Ford? A possum leg? Bobcat liver?"

"I'm looking for something a man has to do some work to chew," Rexford growled as he handed Theo a beer. He took a can for himself, swilled down two aspirins with it. "Rhodora's so right. Stay off the hard stuff."

"Then why don't you listen to her?"

The playwright shrugged; unwrapping a chicken breast, he washed away the sesame sauce under the faucet, and tore off a chunk with his teeth as he headed back to the living room.

"So, how are you, son of Do-the-Duck Ryan?" The playwright executed that song's buttocks-quivering backslide, with which Theo was all too familiar, and then plopped down in the old up-holstered reading chair next to the open hearth. "How's life?"

"Weary, stale, flat, and unprofitable," said Theo.

"Yeah, you are lookin' pretty sickled o'er with the pale cast. I've got to get you out of this damn college awhile."

"Ford, you just don't like academics."

"Are you kidding? Without academics, I'll be dead as a doornail in another hundred years."

Theo sank into the rocker across from him. "I've had a bad day."

"Well, get over it! Assume an antic disposition, and it will soon be yours. What are you wearing all black for? You're young, it's spring, follow your dick." Rexford waved his arm out stiffly, like a diviner's rod. "It's gonna fall off if you don't use it soon."

"Ford, I've been in a faculty meeting for two hours. I've got thirty term papers on tragedy to grade."

While chewing, Rexford grinned. "That's your life? You're right; that's flat. Well, how's *my* life then?"

Theo stretched out his legs to the rug fringe. "You're about to leave Sicily, and invade Italy."

"Have I killed those two Krauts that trapped me in the barn?"

"Two Krauts?" Theo rubbed the cool beer can on his temples. "You said it was an Italian deserter who trapped you in that barn. You said he made you hand over all your rations. You were in there with that Australian nurse from the medics' unit, re-member?"

"Eleanor . . . Christ, she had gorgeous feet. An excellent thing in a woman. Big, but perfect." Rexford nostalgically stuck out his own boots, sucked at the chicken bone, then pointed at Theo's dirty tennis shoes. "My God, talk about big feet!"

Theo looked at his stretched-out legs. Their length continued to surprise him. He had grown into his own big-boned frame so quietly and so late in his adolescence that he kept forgetting that he was, in fact, distinctly large. He pulled his feet under the chair. "Eleanor? I don't recall your mentioning any Eleanor before. This nurse's name was Agatha."

"Was it?"

One of the reasons the Official Life of Rexford was taking so long to write was that the poor biographer never knew which version of any episode to include in it, or indeed, which to believe. Over the years Theo had variously decided that Ford Rexford was forgetful to the point of senility, a perverse practical joker, or a creature with so porous a membrane between fact and fiction that he simply didn't know the difference between what had happened and what could or should have. He indiscriminately mixed charac-ters in his plays with people from his past whom he'd turned into characters in his plays. He never told a story the same way twice. Outside confirmation was not only necessary, it was usually a shock. When Theo had met Ford's first wife, he'd been staggered by her . . . ordinariness.

The publisher of the biography—the renowned Adolphus Mahan of Mahan and Son—was—well, perhaps "frantic" was too strong a word for so well-groomed a man—was eager to have the manuscript in hand, so that the presses could roll when demand was highest; that is, the minute Ford Rexford dropped dead, an event Mahan saw as imminent (even desirable, he admitted without remorse), given Rexford's rowdy habits, both physical and social. The publisher's impatience was forgivable, considering that the book had been originally signed up ten years earlier as an *autobi*ography to be written by the playwright, who had conned Mahan into a sizable advance for it, confessed six years later that he hadn't written a word; and then had conned Mahan and Theo both into having Theo write the book instead as a biography. "All you would have gotten from me was a bunch of bullshit anyhow," he'd predicted with annoying candor.

But Theo had come to wonder if it wouldn't be easier to, as it were, sort through the debris of The Life *after* the hurricane had passed, rather than while the gale blew and the gates, windows, and signposts were still flying around in air, memories and fabrications slammed in splinters together. After Ford Rexford returned to his Maker, then in the quiet of the archives, then perhaps Theo Ryan could better reconstruct the playwright's story.

As for that "Maker," that melodramatist God, that reckless, unruly creator of improbable characters like Ford Rexford, God obviously had no respect for the unities, not the slightest regard for Aristotle's *peripeteia* or for Freytag's pyramidal structure, could care less about the orderly progression of rising action, complication, crisis, reversal, and resolution. God didn't write well-made plays. Now in the mess of life, Theo was obliged to ask, "What do you want a preacher for?"

"Rhodora," said Ford, and threw the chicken bones into a wastebasket across the room. "I want to marry her."

Theo felt a surprising weight sink through him. "You want to marry Rhodora?"

"Sure do. But she won't have me. Lived with me three years—"

"You've only been here two."

"—and won't marry me." Ford popped up, wiped his hands on his jeans, and started pawing through a built-in bookshelf of drama journals, play collections, and volumes of theatre history.

"She won't?" Actually, Theo wasn't all that surprised to hear it. Plenty of young women might be found who would marry a world-famous millionaire (at least, in his will, worth millions), who was forty years their senior, and on his last legs. Rhodora Potts wasn't one of them.

Theo was very fond of Rhodora. He thought of his fondness as friendship; at least he tried to, but he had several times dreamed of sleeping with her. He knew she was fond of him too, as well as considering him "a good influence" on Rexford. With her smoky voice, long straight black hair, lithe figure and astonishing sexual self-possession, Rhodora Potts was extremely attractive. She was also bright, and a talented singer. She had an aggressive nihilism about most of the modern world that appealed to Theo because it never stopped her from acting on things; whereas his own melancholia could erode his will until he vacillated over even the choice of toothpaste. But Rhodora never hesitated; she was gritty and blunt—like a rural Barbara Stanwyck, if such a paradox were possible.

No, it wouldn't be Ford's age that would hold her back from marriage; besides, though by his own admission now "beat to gook," in his youth the man had looked like a movie star, and must still have some kind of physical appeal. Even if only a tenth of his lurid recollections were true, women had been all over him all of his life. Theo had often been embarrassed by the way Rhodora slid a hand inside Ford's shirt, or slunk down in her chair to reach out her leg and rub her bare foot against his thigh as the writer sat narrating tall tales about his life into the tape recorder.

"Did she say why she won't?" Theo asked. His own mind crowded with answers, too impolitic to pose: Your drunken binges? Four previous wives? Shabby health? Foul mouth? Rotten temper? Lousy driving? "Did Rhodora give any reason?"

"Yeah." Ford flipped through two thin paperbacks, both recent plays, and threw first one, then the other on the floor. "Those plays are bullshit. Don't waste the space." He pulled out a third volume, kissed it, and put it back. It was, Theo noticed, a rather obscure drama by Gerhart Hauptmann, which might mean that Ford had read it, and might not.

"And?" Theo prodded.

Ford punched the wall. "I'm down on God."

Theo was surprised. "What in the world does that mean?"

"Rhodora says, 'Ford, if you won't go to a shrink, why don't you go talk to a *preacher*? Then find a church that's willing to put up with you long enough for us to say 'I do,' and then maybe I'll marry your dumb ass.' "

"Rhodora's a Christian? But she's so . . . cynical."

"Her and God both. . . . So, Theo—" Ford turned and slapped the younger man on the shoulder. "I want you to find me a fuckin' preacher in these calvinistical mountains who's not going to send me to hell, ask me for cash, or shove my hand down in a bucket of rattlesnakes and expect me to blabber at him in Babylonian. Let's go."

" 'Let's go'?" Rexford's request was even more surprising than the revelation that Christianity was apparently exempt from Rhodora Potts's sardonic worldview. Why, whole doctoral theses had been written on Ford Rexford's hatred of organized religion. Theo's own colleague, the Freudian deconstructionist Jane Nash-Gantz, had a piece in her fifth collection of essays, *The Father Devoured,* entitled "Phallocentric Feud: Castration Anxiety in Rexford's *Preacher's Boy.*"

Theo combed at his rust-gold mustache with his fingers, a nervous habit. "Ford? You want religious counseling?"

Suddenly, the playwright threw out his arms, and moaned, "Oh gentle Proteus, Love's a mighty Lord." (While always at pains to parade himself before the public as an illiterate redneck rube, Rexford sometimes slipped up and exposed an extraordinary familiarity with the literary classics he derided as the Oldies but Moldies.) "But I don't need God. That *woman* is my salvation. I *am* born again. I can write again, I can fuck again, I can shit again! Saved, and not a decade too soon!" He dropped like a plumb line to his knees, hands waving. "Praise her!"

A throb pulsed in Theo's heart, and looking away from Rexford, he turned to the photo on his wall of Ginger Rogers, immortal in black and white, smiling, leaping free of the tug of gravity. He'd loved Ginger Rogers. And Margot Fonteyn and Moira Shearer, and other airborne dreams. But love on the ground was what Theo wanted now. And here he was in his dull, safe life— with ecstasy, marriage, blood, bliss, all untasted. And here on his knees in the earth was this greedy old glutton Ford Rexford, this unslakable great gulper of life, starting in on wife number five!

Theo looked back at the playwright still swaying as he knelt, arms wriggling. Here was Ford Rexford unbroken, bucking off the past, kicking the world into chaos, then starting in again, and again, and again, racing gleefully around the course of time, when the man's scrawny legs should have broken and his fatty heart burst *decades* ago from misuse; while Theo felt that he himself was still, at thirty-five, trapped in the starting gate.

As Theo's therapist Dr. Joan Ko often noted, he had a problem with these seizures of low self-esteem. In such moods, he fell into depressions over inadequacies both real and imagined, hating the procrastinating way he would let possibilities—pleasures, rigor in his work, honesty in his relations—just slide, slide out of his life. In such moods, he dismissed himself whole-cloth as a stupid, envious, and cowardly second-rater, finding intolerable the very sound of his voice in classrooms, hating even the shape of his ears—whereas he had won the Cavendish Distinguished Teaching Prize only last spring, and he had perfectly attractive ears; indeed, as Dr. Ko tried to point out, was a perfectly (in fact unusually) attractive, intelligent, appealing young man. "I notice you didn't say I wasn't a coward," Theo, in such moods, would mutter. "And an observant man," smiled the therapist.

All right, maybe he judged his flaws a bit too harshly, but good God, wasn't that better than the blind self-acceptance of the Ford Rexfords of the world (not, thank heaven, that there were any others like him)? Why, thought Theo, if he had Rexford's warts of character and blemishes of behavior, he'd hang himself!

"Sorry. I don't know any preachers," Theo tersely said.

Ford returned to the bookshelf by the desk, yanking things out, just stuffing them back helter-skelter. "Maybe Rhodora would go for a rabbi."

Theo said that he knew little of either the Jewish or the Christian faith, for he had been raised by his parents in the church of The-Show-Must-Go-On. "Synagogue was out for Mom because of Saturday-night curtains, and mass was out for Dad because he was getting ready for the matinee."

The playwright ran his spotted hand down a row of books. "Well, fuck. I haven't been in a church since my S.O.B. papa kicked my ass down the steps of Bowie's First Pentecostal, and broke my goddamn collarbone."

"He didn't kick you down the steps; he knocked you into a choir stall and fractured your jaw." Theo glanced at his watch. "And you married your second wife in a very fancy church on Park Avenue."

"Whatever."

The room was quiet. Then, on this Thursday in April, spring busy in the earth, sunlight glowing on the hills, a small, seemingly insignificant statement was made that was to change the rest of Theo Ryan's life. Ford Rexford made it. As he threw a slender hardcover onto the floor, he sneered, "Scottie Smith! *A Theory of Theatricality*! That stupid little schmuck thinks he knows the theatre. He wanted to direct something of mine, showed me a scale model of his 'concept,' and I vomited on it."

Theo's heart tightened. "You know Scottie Smith?"

"He doesn't know fuck about shit." The playwright kicked *A Theory of Theatricality* with his boot.

Theo, who moments earlier had been wondering why Rexford didn't commit suicide in self-disgust, now bounced out of his chair, lifted the smaller man, and hugged him. He said, "I hate Scottie Smith."

Rexford socked at him. "I'm glad to hear it."

"The Pit 'n Grill, okay?" Theo ran from the room, calling back. "It's redneck, just your style."

When Theo returned with a briefcase under his arm, the playwright stood and groaned. "You'll have to pay. I'm busted flat." He flicked his cigarette into the open hearth, from which Theo quickly removed it, stubbing it out on the chimney brick.

"Ford," said Theo as they left the house. "How can a man who's made the kind of money you have, who's made *millions* of dollars, be broke?"

Rexford shrugged. "Beats me. But don't say that when you write my 'Life.' Make up something with a little more intentionality, all right?"

"Intentionality is irrelevant." The critic smiled.

"You're telling me?" agreed the playwright.

CHAPTER
6

{*Music Is Heard*}

The play's the thing.

Hamlet

FORD REXFORD raised his voice over the twanging jukebox of the Pit 'n Grill, and tapped his chest with his fork. "Morris, one of my producers, fixed up a meeting so this schlemiel kid Smith could show *me his* stuff. That pretentious trendie-bender Amanda Mahan, Morris's partner, had gone hog-wild for Smith. So this kid had a fancy little model all rigged to demonstrate how he was gonna set *Her Pride of Place* in a giant red womb!"

"A womb?" Theo paused with the sparerib nearly in his mouth.

"Yeah. Whole stage was gonna be this *womb* with thirty-foot fallopian tubes waving all over the place and ovaries dangling and sperm zipping in and out on a back scrim." His arm raised high, Rexford squirted erratic swirls of catsup down on his french fries.

Theo thought over this description of Scottie Smith's plans for *Her Pride of Place,* one of his favorite Rexford plays. "He didn't want it set in Miss Rachel Green's funeral parlor?"

"Nope. All those bereaved folks, *and* the corpses both, were supposed to stand around shooting the breeze in old Rachel's womb. Swear I did, Theo; I puked right on it."

Theo frowned. Earth mother giving birth to life through death? Capitalism as the root of infertility? "On the model?" he said.

Rexford grinned shrugging. "Probably shouldn't have mixed all those margaritas with the gumbo at lunch." His tan wrinkled throat lifted as he swallowed beer. "Imagine? I told Scottie Smith, what I did was *sweet*, compared to what an unmarried lady like Rachel wouldda done, she'd known some little putz was planning to invite all of Broadway in to gawk at her womb. Then, you'll love this, Theo, this brass-balled brat hands me a copy of my own script where he'd inked in his 'editing suggestions'! Looked like his coked-out nose had bled all over it. 'Cut this.' 'Move that.' The booze threw my timing off or I'd have clocked him, instead of poor old Morris who was just trying to calm me down. Amanda was livid. That's what she said, 'Ford, I'm livid.' I told her she'd be black-and-blue if she ever let Smith *near* one of my shows. I don't know why Adolphus Mahan married that bitch. He already had plenty of money." Rexford ordered another pitcher of beer.

Quickly, before he could change his mind, Theo reached for the briefcase. It sat beside him in the dark booth, where wood was gouged with the initialed generations of collegiate love affairs. His heart was thudding. "Ford? Ever seen a production that Scottie Smith's actually done?"

"Two. Two's enough from that California cutie."

"California? I thought he was British!"

"Bullshit. He got that accent off *Masterpiece Theatre*. He's not British. He's not even Southern. He's from a San Fernando Valley shopping mall. He's from a vacuum, a vapor—"

"Well, a lot of critics think he's the best director in America."

"A lot of critics," mumbled the writer, stuffing the last of a chiliburger past his lips, "thought *Moby-Dick* sucked. The best director in America is a fat young broad running a theatre in the Village. Barbara Sanchez's her name. She did a *Desert Slow Dance* that made *me* cry!"

Theo unbuckled his briefcase and took out a smudged manuscript, with a rust spot under the big paper clip, and FOOLSCAP typed across the cover. He had removed it from the bottom of his locked desk drawer just before they'd left the house.

"Ford?"

"Yeah?"

"I want to ask you a favor."

"You can't fuck Rhodora. I know how much you want to."

Theo blushed. "Isn't that, after all, her decision, not yours?" Had she ever thought of it? he wondered.

"Oh, I expect it's crossed Rhodora's lustful mind," said the playwright, as if his ear were so good he could hear unspoken dialogue. "But she says fidelity's the best bet for a peaceful home life. So give it up." He licked his fingers. "What's the favor? Want a loan?"

"You said you were broke." Indeed, Theo wouldn't be surprised if he had more cash than the wealthy playwright—who had borrowed fifty dollars from him last November and had not yet repaid it. "No, I'd like to ask you if you'd read something of mine."

How often over the last two years had Theo thought of doing this, but held back—because, while he was at times forced to doubt that Rexford knew what his own plays *meant*, the writer undoubtedly knew that they *worked;* he knew what would play, and what wouldn't, and would say so.

"I wrote a play. A while ago." His long arms outstretched as if he carried a flaming plate, Theo held up the manuscript of *Foolscap*.

Rexford crooked his chin in his palm. Smoke curled around his liver-spotted hand. "Yeah, I figured when I read *Shakespeare's Clowns.*"

"Figured?"

"It was in you. But one lousy play, and you're thirty-three?"

"Well, no, I wrote some others, but I threw them away, they weren't any good. But this one. . . . I wrote it in a workshop. With Scottie Smith. He didn't like it."

"So?"

Scottie Smith, the *bête noir* of Theo's nightmares, just a wisp of breath blown to nothingness with a "So?"!

"So, I—"

"Quit?" Rexford wedged his back into the corner of the booth, scratched his ankle under his boot, and reached for the dog-eared typescript. "This one any good?" Theo shrugged, but didn't answer. "Come on, professor, you tell *me.* If you don't know, I'm gonna get me a new literary biographer. The thing any good? Your book's damn good. Alive, feeling, gorgeous. I'm surprised it didn't ruin your career. But a play's—"

"It's good." Theo blushed, but he nodded.

"Oh, Lord," the playwright said. "I hate reading other folks' stuff. If it's bad, it bores me. If it's good, I get jealous. But I'll make you a deal. Grab the check, find me a preacher, and I'll read your play."

Energy swelled back in Theo, he who'd been of late so hesitant, so slow of pace. "I'll take you right now to Cavendish Chapel. Norman Bridges mentioned something about a new chaplain there who's—I think he said—up-and-coming, or up-to-date, something like that." He watched with some trepidation as Rexford stuffed the manuscript into the big pocket of his suede vest. "Ford . . . Maybe I should Xerox it first. That's my only copy."

"I don't lose plays, kid." Rexford's knees creaked as he slid from the booth. "And I won't bullshit you," he growled. "Bullshit's scary." He threw Theo the car keys. "You drive. Rhodora's on the rampage about me driving without a license."

In response to their inquiry at the college chapel, an elderly sexton snarled at them, "She's over there at that auditorium."

"The college chaplain is a woman?" Theo was surprised. "Reverend M. E. Fletcher?"

"Name's Maude. A woman priest!" mourned the grim old sexton. To his added disgust, the Reverend Fletcher was right now over at Cavendish's new Spitz Center, trying out for a part in the Faculty Drama Club's production of *Guys and Dolls*. "A woman priest. Tap dancing!" he sighed.

Ford Rexford circled his biographer's shoulder. "Theo, she sounds like the preacher for me."

In the enormous Spitz Center, auditions were in progress, and no one participating in them looked remotely clerical. Now, standing in the back of the tiered semicircle of luxuriously cushioned seats, Theo felt the old rush that always shot through him whenever he stepped inside a theatre. "It's excitement," said his therapist. "Fear and loathing," Theo growled.

He stood there listening to a tall slender dark-haired woman in a black blouse singing on stage. She was singing, "Ask me how do I feel . . . well, if I were a bell, I'd go ding dong ding dong ding."

Theo whispered, "Who's that?"

Rexford grabbed him. "My God, I can't believe it!"

Theo shook off the arm. "Try not to forget you're in love with Rhodora."

Rexford pulled down the younger man's head and kissed him. "I'm in love every minute I'm alive. What are you? Father Time?"

"Come on, stop!" said Theo, jerking away to look back at the stage.

"One of these days, let's fucking hope, you're going to be in love too, babe," the playwright predicted, proving himself indeed, as Ryan had once written of him, "the poet of the heart." For Theo felt right now like falling in love that very minute.

But the desire that had brightened Ford Rexford's battered face when he first saw the stage was desire not for anyone on it, but for the Spitz Center itself. "I can't believe this!" He whistled. "Look at that raked thrust! Look at those sight lines!" He took in the gigantic space, the acoustical wall panels, the high hydraulic flies, and it was love at first sight. The old pro felt as a great jockey might feel to see Secretariat used to trot toddlers around in circles at a church fair. "Jesus God, Theo!" he spluttered. "Joe Papp would kill for this! You son of a bitch! You didn't tell me about this! Where'd they get it?"

"Some rich alumnus donated it." Theo explained, as he walked Rexford down the plush carpeted aisle. "And just wait'll you hear who they're planning to turn it over to. Scottie Smith, that's who. They're planning to hire him as artistic director."

"Scottie Smith! Bullshit! Well, stop 'em, for Christ sake!"

"How am I supposed to do that?"

"Who cares? Do it! They want an artistic director? Hell, I'll get 'em Barbara Sanchez. She's sick of getting mugged up there in SoHo anyhow."

"You'll help?" And as Theo asked this, a plan began to slide like mist out of a dark burrow of his mind.

II

{Scene: A Playhouse}

CHAPTER

7

{Here a Dance}

For what's a play without a woman in it?
Kyd, The Spanish Tragedy

THE ARNOLD AND INEZ SPITZ CENTER, Cavendish University's new theatre complex, was the gift of a Mr. Doug Spitz, which is why gilded S's were embroidered into the wing curtains. Immediately after graduation, this young man, making practical use of his economics major, had sold sufficient junk bonds to buy two fast-food chains and a Hollywood movie studio; in gratitude, he'd built his alma mater a theatre; in filial devotion, he'd named it after his dead parents, Arnold and Inez Spitz of Kansas City. Mom and Dad had loved nothing better, he'd told Dean Tupper, than going to shows, especially musicals, particularly in dinner theatres serving good buffets. Mrs. Spitz had walked down the aisle at her wedding to "People Will Say We're in Love" from *Oklahoma,* and at the Spitzes' silver anniversary, "It's Almost Like Being in Love" from *Brigadoon* had been their first dance. "Climb Ev'ry Mountain" was sung at their funeral, after a weekend of Broadway shows ended in a tragic plane crash. Young Spitz and his tax lawyers had wanted the best for his parents' cenotaph, and he'd certainly gotten it, as the profane exclamations of Ford Rexford (wandering backstage now) would seem to attest.

All that Cavendish had to agree to do, as beneficiary of this munificent gift, was to put on two of the senior Spitzes' favorite musicals every year; other than that, they could do whatever they liked with the place. Since there was (as yet) no official drama school, what Cavendish did was use the Spitz Center for official university functions like the monthly brawl known as the Faculty Senate, for band concerts, and for highly attended classes like Herbie Crawford's "Modern Capitalism: Origins to Collapse" (he did a lot of what he called "visuals," among them film clips of *Potemkin* and music videos of the Rolling Stones, and needed the projection booth). The rest of the time the Spitz Center was rented out to anyone who wanted it.

But given the location—"Let's face it," said Doug Spitz, "*not* L.A."—and with the town of Rome being on the small side, few clubs and civic groups had need of a thousand-seater for their modest get-togethers. The Friends of the Rome Library had felt fairly lost when only fourteen members showed up for a discussion of Iris Murdoch. The Rotarians never came back, and neither did the Medieval Woodwind Ensemble. Billy Graham, of course, had packed them in, and due to a Jaycees' boycott, the national touring company of *La Cage aux Folles* did very well. But such sure-fire draws were rare in the hills, and often the great modern spaces of the Spitz Center sat dark and empty.

As for the college's commitment to the memory of the tune-loving Arnold and Inez, Dean Buddy Tupper, Jr. managed that nicely. (He managed all the university's business, for its elderly president was a figurehead, pure and simple—indeed, "pure and simple" characterized General Kaney precisely.) Dean Tupper arranged for a coup of professors to take over the Cavendish Faculty Drama Club who would vote to put on a musical comedy in Spitz every January and every May. At first, the rank-and-file of C.F.D.C. grumbled at this typical administrative intrusion on academic freedom—since 1928 they'd devoted themselves to headier stuff, like Maeterlinck and Gorky performed in the basement auditorium of the old science building—but they soon yielded to coercion and greed. Beginning with *Annie*, then *Brigadoon*, on Doug Spitz's long list of his parents' favorite shows, the Drama Club was charging fifteen dollars a seat by the time they got to *Fiddler on the Roof*. Affluence seduced them; frankly, even free, *The Lower Depths* had been sparsely attended. By now, only diehards continued to plead for Pirandello, and to refer to their leader, Dr. Thayer Iddesleigh, as "Tupper's puppet."

As acting head of the Spitz and director of these shows, adjunct professor of music Dr. Iddesleigh, the Cavendish marching band conductor, was king, but no Hal Prince. Although he'd taken to dressing in black like the Bob Fosse character in *All That Jazz*, and to yelling at his casts like Warner Baxter in *42nd Street*, and while he was exactly the same size as Mickey Rooney in *Babes in Arms*—these surface resemblances to the Greats had gained him only muffled mockery from some of his disrespectful players, who felt that Iddesleigh's approach was too heavily influenced by his background in football stadiums. For example, he'd had the dancers in *A Chorus Line* form a giant "C" that marched sideways offstage at the finale, with the four Iddesleigh children trotting in their midst under a huge sequined top hat. For the number "You Gotta Have Heart," the shirt backs of the baseball players in *Damn Yankees* were seen to spell out "H.E.A.R.T." in neon, when one by one they turned cartwheels at the footlights. And two winters back, to the annoyance of Tara Bridges who'd played the part, Evita's followers waved green pompoms in her face the whole time she was singing "Don't Cry for Me, Argentina." Now, they were doing *Guys and Dolls*, and Theo Ryan was certain that Iddy (Thayer Iddesleigh's *nom de théâtre*), was planning extensive precision drills for the Salvation Army's first big entrance.

Iddy also upset textual purists by his Protean attitude about making whatever changes in his scripts he needed to meet the limits of his casts: the old became young, men became women, the wealthy lost their servants, and cities lost their streets. If speeches could not be said well, he cut them; if songs were nicely sung, he repeated them. "Use what you've got" was his motto, to which he often added, "And if you've got nothing, make it up."

Theo had never been a part of C.F.D.C. While unwilling to take on the burden of direction himself, and refusing (despite the pleas of Tara Bridges, who'd heard him sing) even to participate in the club's productions, the young drama professor was human enough to assume that *were* he to do it, he would do it much better. After all (as Dr. Bridges kept reminding him), Theo did know the theatre. He knew it inside out. But not even Bridges was aware of the lessons in everything from tap-dancing to juggling, taught by his parents and their friends, that had been practiced on Theo since infancy; that as a result of thousands of hours spent trapped in rehearsals, or squirming on stage whenever an extra baby/child/teenager was needed, Theo Ryan had memorized the scores, the dialogue, and even a little of the choreography for most of the canonical American musicals—including *Guys and Dolls.*

For his part, Iddesleigh (drugged on the smell of greasepaint) had come to believe he *was* Bob Fosse (and who in Rome could say him nay?); consequently, he disliked Theo Ryan. He thought it grossly unfair that while he, Iddy, was out there on stage shrieking himself hoarse year after year, Norman Bridges was up in Coolidge Building begging the provost, Dean Tupper, to let Theo Ryan take over the directorship of the Spitz Center. At least that's what Iddy had heard from Tupper's secretary; although when he'd confronted the provost with his fear that he was "being used like a finger in a dike," Tupper had blandly denied the rumors. But Iddy remained eaten with envy. He continued to suspect that the monstrous Theo Ryan was only holding out for more money before swooping in, and dropping the curtain on him.

The band leader constantly told his wife that running the Spitz shows was a thankless pain in the you-know-what: the stage crews persecuted him and the casts had no more notion of the absolute authority accorded directors by *real* performers (documented in the thousands of show-biz books and movies Iddesleigh had studied) than wild savages know about traffic lights. When his wife suggested that if he felt so misused, he should resign, he bellowed at her that she was against him too. Dr. Iddesleigh didn't want to resign; he wanted the roar of the crowd, wanted it *indoors,* and for longer than a half-time intermission. He had nightmares that Theo Ryan would displace him before he made it down the alphabetical list he was methodically following to the *M*'s and so to that great showpiece from *The Music Man,* "Seventy-six Trombones"—for which he planned to close drill on stage the entire one-hundred-and-ten-man Cavendish marching band.

Theo knew how Iddesleigh felt about him. And he'd thought,

when walking into the theatre tonight: Poor Iddy, wasting his time being jealous of me. He hasn't heard yet that a star named Scottie Smith is set to crash like a meteor onto that big stage of the Spitz Center, smashing to dusty oblivion the glitter and glory of the Iddesleigh Years. Unless Theo himself could stop Smith. And even if he could, how well would Iddy get along with a "short fat broad" from SoHo named Barbara Sanchez?

On stage, the dark-haired woman was dancing. Her pleated skirt swirled tight around her legs, then swirled floating back open as she finished her tryout with a double shuffle wing kick combination. A jolt rushed round the lining of Theo's brain like nicotine, and made the whole theatre change shape and color. And then a hideous whistle blew, the one Iddy wore on a chain about his neck.

"Thank you, Reverend Fletcher."

Reverend Fletcher! This woman was the Cavendish chaplain?

"Next!"

Next? How could there be any next! Theo wanted to squeeze his hands around the black turtlenecked throat of that inert little clod, Thayer Iddesleigh, and so cut off his heartless "Next!" Instead he loped down the aisle towards the orchestra pit, to introduce himself to Maude Fletcher when she left the stage. But she stopped beside the piano, holding her tap shoes by their ribboned laces, and from there watched the audition of some cipher in female form, whom he remotely recalled as an assistant professor in the Music Department, someone he'd dated once and considered quite pretty. Pretty? Compared to Maude Fletcher, she was a smudge, a smear, a blur, a shadow of an eclipse.

As soon as the professor finished her tryout, and stuffed her sheet music in her bag, a man and a woman lugged a fifteen-foot tube of huge gray papier-mâché sewer pipe onto the middle of the stage and dropped it. Thayer Iddesleigh shouted at them, "This isn't the time! Get that out of here!" The man crossed his arms, offended. He said, "We worked hard on this, okay?" The woman said, "If you don't like it, make the rest yourself!" They stomped off, leaving the pipe on the stage. Then a big fellow in a sweat suit (with a huge bandage on his finger)—a man Theo thought he

recognized (from Romance Languages, maybe?)—lumbered over
to the piano, and sang in a slight Italian accent, "Sit Down, You're
Rocking the Boat," as if he'd kill you if you didn't.

After him, Tara Bridges, the English Department chairman's
extremely thin wife, strode forward in tights and high heels, carrying a long opalescent scarf. With a cough, she fluffed out her
gray pageboy. Then she stood with her feet spread wide, put her
hands on her hips, and bizarrely trilled in piercing soprano, with
Virginian accent, "Ahhhhhhh, sweet mystery of life, at last I've
found you."

Pounding out the tune funereally on the Center's new spinet was
Dr. Bridges's own secretary, Effie Fruchaff, a minuscule leathery
widow probably—despite her red bobbed hair—far past the mandatory retirement age. (No one in Ludd Hall had dared to suggest
that she leave; they were all terrified of her.) Slouched down to
reach the pedals, Mrs. Fruchaff looked as if she'd modeled her
piano-playing style on Hoagy Carmichael—even to the cigarette
hanging precariously from her lips. Tara Bridges called on her for
a quicker tempo by lashing out with her scarf. "Ahhhh, at-last-I-
know-the-meaning-of it all!"

A tense hand clapped Theo's shoulder, and Steve Weiner squatted, stylish but woebegone, beside him. "Well, *I* believe Tara
Bridges knows the meaning of it all. But does Norman know she
knows, isn't that the question? . . . What are you doing here,
Theo?"

"Hi. Do you know the new chaplain?"

"Who?"

"Her!" Theo pointed. "Maude Fletcher."

"Nah. That her?" Steve shrugged. "What do you want a chaplain for anyhow? Spiritual crisis?"

"Ford wants her."

"Ford wants any woman he can get."

"Shut up, Steve."

Theo's friend looked at him puzzled. "Sorry. I guess we
shouldn't speak ill of the Official Life until you get it published."

Mrs. Cloverton, Financial Aid, staggered in from the wings,
immense piles of gaudy burlesque outfits on each arm. "Iddy,

couldn't we use these outfits left over from *Funny Girl?*" she called, spitting at the ostrich feather tickling her face.

"Not now! Karen, please! *Next!*"

"Well, you tell me where I'm supposed to find six mink coats then!" She tossed the costumes on top of the sewer pipe, and left.

Steve nudged Theo. "Did you see Jorvelle's audition, for this part called Miss Adelaide? I helped her with her Brooklyn accent."

"*Next!*"

"Jorvelle's here?"

Yes, there on the stage steps lounged the youngest Ludd Chair professor, lushly straining the seams of her leotard top, a bandanna circling her Afro. With her were Vic Gantz and Theo's graduate student, Jenny Harte. Sitting beside them, staring slack-jawed at Tara Bridges, was Robey Something from Philosophy, in open shirt with the sleeves tightly rolled, and a thin belt around his waist, like Gene Kelly.

"I should be off schmoozing votes," snarled Steve.

"Why aren't you?"

"Robey's after Jorvelle."

"Robey's gay," Theo reminded him.

"Who says?"

"He does."

"Yeah, but what if he isn't really? He'll be with her night and day."

Theo looked around. Maude Fletcher was now sitting in the front row of the orchestra, searching in her purse. "So you admit it," he said to Steve.

"Admit what? Robey's just wrong for her, that's all."

"Particularly if he's right that he's gay." It must be spring, thought Theo. "Admit you're falling for Jorvelle, that's what."

Steve nodded, flushed. "So? Okay, maybe I don't have your looks, but I'm *alive*, Ryan. I'm not schlepping through my life lately like it was a dull book I didn't particularly want to read."

Theo stared hard at his friend. He stared at the stage he'd avoided for seven years. Then in an irresistible surge, he felt himself lifted to his long legs. He vaulted right over Steve, who fell backwards with a grunt.

"Hey! Watch it! Where you going, Theo? Come on, I was kidding."

"You were *right*."

"Quiet!" called Iddesleigh. "*Next! Anybody else?*"

Theo was trotting backwards as he called to Steve. "Ford's here to see the preacher."

"Ford's getting married? Again?"

"*Quiet!*" Thayer Iddesleigh spun about, and nearly swallowed the whistle he'd raised to his lips, when he saw Theo Ryan all in black striding down the theatre aisle, waving long arms at him, just like in his nightmares. Of course, since they'd never been more than nodding acquaintances, the director couldn't, without appearing hasty, simply throw this usurper out of his kingdom, unless he had a reason. So he said, "Yes?"

"Hi, Iddy. I want to audition." Maude Fletcher was smiling at him. He added, "For Sky Masterson?"

Tara Bridges squealed. "Theo, that's wonderful!"

Iddy spat out his whistle. After three years, the man waltzes in here, and asks for the lead?! "These are closed auditions. C.F.D.C. members only." He hugged himself hard. Ryan was standing in the *pit,* and they were almost eye-to-eye.

"I'm a C.F.D.C. member."

Iddy grinned, teeth gnashed tightly. "No, you're not."

But Theo was. His dues were fully paid every year—as Tara Bridges, Treasurer (who'd browbeat him into paying them, even if he wouldn't join in), pointed out. He could have kissed her on her glossy plum-colored lips.

Tara Bridges fluttered towards him. "I knew you couldn't resist, honey." She told the crowd, "His daddy's the one who made 'Prom Queen' and 'Do the Duck,' y'all remember? And his mama was Lorraine Page."

Great, thought Iddy. It really wasn't fair.

Theo grabbed an audition form from the stage manager and started scribbling on it fast. Meanwhile, Mrs. Bridges, an incorrigible flirt, took the small band director aside and swiped at him with her shimmery scarf. "Oh, Iddy, now you let him try out," she cooed, and twirled the two little pink angora balls hanging from the scooped neck of her sweater.

"All right, all right!" Iddesleigh swatted the scarf out of his face.

So up on the stage Benny and Lorraine's son bounded, up, up, up, until Thayer Iddesleigh was staring at the pen in the pocket of his black shirt. The young man beamed down at him. "Thanks," he said.

"What'll it be, kid?" Mrs. Fruchaff—cigarette bobbing, eyelashes twitching from the constant stream of smoke—swung around on the piano stool.

Theo clutched at memories. His dad with a summer stock company in—was it the Catskills or the Poconos?—a bright blue tie, black shirt, white suit, with a wad of play money in one fist, dice in the other. But what was the plot, what were the words? He cleared his throat. "Luck Be a Lady Tonight."

"You got it." Mrs. Fruchaff swung back, flipped through a tattered music book. "Take it," she growled.

Theo took it. And when his throat opened, the song burst through the dark mood that had constricted him, and out soared all the energy of youth on an April night. The tall dark-haired young woman paused in the aisle, turned, her head tilted, her hand inside the collar of her black blouse massaging her neck as she listened.

When the audition finished, Iddesleigh shrieked, "Next!"

"I can tap," Theo panted, brushing sweat from his eyes. " 'Singin' in the Rain,' Effie!" And he gave them, unasked, a combination step Donald O'Connor himself had taught him when he was ten.

Jorvelle Wakefield whistled, and Jenny Harte jumped up, shouting. Mrs. Bridges hugged him, smelling of Shalimar and gin. Maude Fletcher clapped, then turned away with a smile, walking up the carpeted aisle towards the rear doors.

Steve Weiner was still staring with amazement, even hurt, at his friend Theo Ryan; he felt as if he'd just lectured a cripple to go out and buy some crutches, when the man had suddenly hopped up and turned a back flip on him. Theo Ryan, who for months had slumped against walls at parties, staring at his shoes, had just leapt and slid and spun and flung himself down on his knees, wildly shaking imaginary dice; Theo Ryan had just belted out enormous high long musical notes, Theo Ryan had just done a dance step that looked like something Steve had seen in an M.G.M. musical!

"Thank you," Thayer Iddesleigh smiled with his teeth clamped. "*Who's next!*"

CHAPTER

8

{They Speak Together}

As an imperfect actor on the stage,
Who with his fear is put besides his part

Shakespeare, Sonnett XXIII

THEO had already bounded towards the lobby when Ford Rexford walked onto the Spitz stage and said, "Fuck 'next.' Give the big guy the goddamn part."

Dr. Iddesleigh stared at Rexford, ambling over in muddy jeans, as the president of the United States might look at a wino who'd somehow strolled into the Oval Office and growled, "Fuck Congress. Give me a billion dollars."

"Who do you think you are! Get off this stage," the little director spluttered. "You can't use that kind of language in my theatre!"

But other people had recognized the Great Man—either from *Life* or *Time*, or books or Broadway, or from the *National Enquirer*, or from Cherokee's bar in Tilting Rock. One of them whispered something to Iddy, who then looked as the president might if told by an aide that the disheveled derelict he'd just had thrown out of the White House was Albert Einstein. For while the band leader didn't know the face, he certainly knew the name. He'd even seen the movies made of five of Ford Rexford's plays. He'd even been told by his source in Coolidge Building that Norman Bridges had claimed the cursed Theo Ryan might be able to persuade Rexford to premiere a play at the Spitz Center, so that precisely "that kind of language" would be used there. It was just

Iddy's you-know-what luck that he'd stuffed his small loafered foot in his mouth, and would never hear the end of it.

But Rexford was holding up his arms in friendly surrender. "Whoa, guy. Your decision. Director's the boss." He laughed, and then everyone else laughed too. "Great space you've got here," the playwright added, and he affably agreed to sign autographs for the gushing group of stagestruck amateurs who'd swarmed shyly around him.

Meanwhile, out in the lobby, Theo Ryan would have liked his first words to Maude Fletcher, when he caught her at the doors, to have been more memorable than "Stop! Just a minute!"

And exhilarated as he was by his performance, ready to fall instantly in love, he would have liked her first words to him to have been something memorable too, like:

> Good pilgrim, you do wrong your hand too much,
> Which mannerly devotion shows in this.
> For saints have hands that pilgrims' hands do touch.

But in fact, alarmed by his urgency, she said only, "What's the matter!" Then she smiled. "Oh, hi! You were great in there."

Theo stared at her, still panting from his dance.

"You'll get the part," she said. "I blew my last note. Was it noticeable?"

He shook his head.

She stood waiting, brushed the short, lustrous black hair behind her ear. Her eyes were dark green like forest in the hills behind his home. She kept smiling, a puzzled smile. He stared at a large red button on her blouse that for some reason said "8%!" Finally he blurted out. "A friend of mine needs to talk to a minister. Ford Rexford."

Her eyes widened. "I *thought* that's who that was. Wants to talk to me?"

But at that instant, Ford himself burst into the lobby, swooping down on them with warm easy words. "Theo, you were damn good! You too, darlin'. Maude, right? Maude, can I talk to you in private just a second? Theo, wait right here. You know, Reverend Fletcher, my daddy was a preacher, but he was a S.O.B. and ugly besides. Now *you* . . . ." And he led her out the wide glass doors into the night.

Theo waited right there.

He was still waiting when Jenny Harte came looking for him. Theo had seen this young woman nearly every day for three years; she had been his best graduate student, was writing her dissertation with him, and was the teaching assistant for his large drama survey course. Still, he'd had no idea she was involved in these musicals. Twenty-six, blonde, Jenny wore dancer's shorts and tap shoes. Theo reminded himself that she owed him two chapters on her dissertation. She was very pretty.

She smiled up at him. "There you are! Hi! I just wanted to—" She slapped his hands together in hers, then hers flew away. "You were *fantastic!* Really! Did you sing professionally? I bet you did. Wait'll the class sees you in this!"

"Oh, hi, Jenny. Thanks." He ran his hand through his wavy hair, a gesture that increased his marked (and much remarked on) resemblance to the young Gary Cooper. "I just did it, you know, on the spur of the moment."

"You're kidding! Well, you're really good!"

"That's nice of you. . . ." He noticed over the pocket of her black blouse one of the red buttons that said "8%!" "What's that button for? They're all over the place."

"Bleecker. We want an eight-percent raise for the Bleecker cafeteria workers. Take one."

Theo absentmindedly pinned it to his shirt. "Did you try out too?" he asked, staring past her towards the doors.

"Sure. I'm usually in these shows. I'm not all that good, but I love it. I played Dorothy at camp, and after that I wanted to be Judy Garland." She hunched her shoulders wryly.

Theo, who'd met Judy Garland backstage once when he was six, said, "Happier, I hope." Then he stepped around her to push open one of the glass doors. He saw Rexford already coming back up the steps alone. "Where'd Reverend Fletcher go?" Theo asked him, holding the door.

Rexford waved at Jenny. "Home, I guess. Said she lived next to the chapel. Got in a sports car with a guy wearing a leather jacket. Hey, she agreed to do this counseling bit with me. Praise

Jesus!" shouted the playwright. "Goddamn, if women like her had preached the word in Bowie, Texas, I'd still be washed in the blood of the Lamb. . . ." He spun in a circle, and threw open his arms. "Theo, babe, you did good! It was just bubbling away down there in your blood, and whoosh, out it came!"

Theo muttered, "Guy in a leather jacket?"

But Rexford turned to Jenny, pressed her hand in both of his. "Jenny Harte, you are the heart of this beautiful country. I look at you, I see midwestern wheat and big white clouds, blue sky on gold hills."

She laughed cheerfully. "Ford, you can lay it on."

"I sure can," he agreed, and invited her to come have a beer with everybody at the Bomb Shelter. Theo was surprised that she appeared to know Rexford fairly well; but her dissertation was about the endings of modern plays, including Ford Rexford's, and no doubt she'd interviewed him. Not that you had to know the man well to call him by his first name. Thousands of people did.

The Bomb Shelter was Rome's (in Steve Weiner's phrase) "art-fart hangout," as opposed to its "upscale New South" and "down-home white trash" hangouts. It was lined with vinyl booths and crammed with fifties' memorabilia—from nude mannequins wearing "I Like Ike" buttons as pasties to posters of Ronald Reagan advertising Arrow shirts. Cajoling the deejay there into playing only solid fifties gold, Ford Rexford led onto the dance floor a Stroll line of all the drama club members he'd invited along. They did old dances that Jenny Harte had never heard of. The Hully-Gully, the Hokie-Pokie, the Shag. Jorvelle Wakefield then tried to get Theo to teach them all how to Do the Duck, but by then he had burned out the surge that had carried him through his audition. Suddenly exhausted, he begged off, saying he felt like taking a walk alone.

After Theo left, the group drank more pitchers of beer, and when the Bomb Shelter evicted them, they bunny-hopped out into the silent streets of Rome, where at 2:00 A.M., Steve Weiner and Jorvelle Wakefield were given a warning by the police for creating a public disturbance. They'd been cheering on Ford Rexford, who, after swilling a pint of bourbon hidden in his glove compartment, had drag-raced his grimy gold Lincoln down Main Street, smacked it into a telephone pole, and socked the policeman who'd helped him out of the car.

At 2:00 A.M., Thayer Iddesleigh was also in trouble. In bed beside his wife (as she tried to sleep with the covers over her head), he asked her one too many times if she thought it would offend people in Rome to have a black woman pretend to be in love with a white man, and vice versa, even if Jorvelle Wakefield had a comedy role and, according to his source, Bill Robey was a homosexual anyhow.

"Thayer, please! I honestly just don't give a shit," snapped Mrs. Iddesleigh, burrowing under her pillow.

Iddy sprang out of the canopied bed in his *Chorus Line* nightshirt. "Doris, I won't listen to you talk like that!" Maybe a famous playwright could speak to him obscenely, but not his own wife!

"Then leave," was the mutinous muffled response.

So, back at the kitchen table (alone and lonely, as all leaders must ultimately be), the director sat studying his *Guys and Dolls* cast list. Montemaggio for Big Julie, easy. Jenny Harte could dance in the Hot Box Club and march in the Salvation Army, both; she was the hardest worker he had. Iddy put an arrow here, scratched a hopeful there, and finally, feeling proud of himself, drew interlocking circles around the names Jorvelle Wakefield and Bill Robey. If the Jaycees boycotted them, they'd sell out the house! Then he had a glass of warm milk. Then he stared at the words *Theo Ryan*. And the words *Maude Fletcher*.

It should be said, to the credit of Dr. Iddesleigh, that in struggling towards a decision, he was not swayed by the fame of Ford Rexford (if anything, that man's dirty-mouthed recommendation of "the big guy" was further ammunition—if any were needed—in his animosity towards Ryan), nor by the flirtatious friendship of Tara Bridges (a friendship probably about to come to an end, once she learned that she was playing a Hot Box Club hoofer—when she'd always played a lead—and that she'd lost her part to someone much younger, a black woman hired by her own husband, and paid—according to Iddy's source—as much as her husband was). No, Dr. Iddesleigh was swayed only by his addiction to that intoxicant, the Stage. He wanted to do the best *Guys and*

Dolls he possibly could. When he played his tape of the original Broadway cast, he wanted *that*. He wanted the show to go on, right.

Maude Fletcher. He tapped her audition sheet. New member, Religion Department, acting chaplain while the real one was on leave. Some tap and jazz. Divinity school—lead in *Godspell*. It wasn't much. Nice voice though. Nice face. But too tall. Good gimmick, though, to have the college chaplain play a Salvation Army goodie-two-shoes. But with Joel Elliott (Sociology), penciled in as Sky Masterson, much too tall.

Theo Ryan: college, grad school leads. Come on, what was this supposed to mean? "Small parts, professional stock, national tours, off-Broadway, etc.," and then over two dozen shows scrawled out in odd abbreviations—*Okla., Call Madam, Sound Music, H. Dolly, S. Pacific, P.J. Game*. Sure! Where, when? The creature was an academic. He'd spent his life in college (Yale!); he'd been here at Cavendish seven years. What had he done, crawled onto those professional stages in his diapers? "Voice, tap, little piano, guitar, juggling"! Come on! "Some ventriloquism, fencing and card tricks"? What a preposterous liar the creature was. And yet, he was handsome, that had to be admitted. And he could certainly carry a tune; in fact, he had a definite take on that song already; you'd have to say, he gave it his all tonight. And you could *hear* him—more than was always true with Joel Elliott. He could dance; despite the ridiculous size of his feet. "Six-three; one-ninety-two." God, he was big. Even barefoot, Maude Fletcher would tower over Joel Elliott. Why did people have to be so tall?

And wouldn't there be a sweet kind of noblesse oblige in casting his rival? In *directing* his rival? Telling his rival, do this, do that, no good, again, again. "Director's the boss." The great Ford Rexford himself had said it, and surely Ryan must take that man's word as Gospel. Iddy sipped his milk, tapped his pencil.

As Theo's fate was being decided in the country kitchen of that raised ranch a mile away from campus, and while the reveling thespians downtown were dancing out of the Bomb Shelter and into the arms of the Rome police, the tall tawny-haired drama professor was standing on the sidewalk beside Wilton Chapel, looking at a light high up in the rounded bay window of a white-framed Victorian house that stood bristling back at him with pointed peaks and latticed turrets. He leaned against its crooked iron gate, and waited.

But the Reverend Maude Fletcher failed to open her window—if indeed that was her window where the light still burned. Unlike Juliet, she declined to appear and call down to him her thoughts about Echo's cave and birds on silken threads, or her ideas about parting being any kind of sorrow at all. Theo waited until he heard the clock bells of the chapel chime two deep, sonorous peals. Then he started home, so preoccupied with his thoughts that, while he heard a motor's roar, and even hurried across the street at the sound, he failed to notice that the car thundering past him towards the chapel was a black Mazda sportscar. He certainly didn't see the man and the woman inside it, nor realize that the car was slowing to a stop in front of the crooked iron gate, that the Cavendish chaplain Maude Fletcher was getting out, leaning over to give Herbert Crawford, Professor of History, one last long kiss.

On Vance Walk, Theo stopped and listened to the night. It was so quiet he felt as if he could hear the petals of white cherry blossoms floating down in moonlight onto the glinting stone path. Then he jogged on through the streets of Rome—where Steve Weiner, staggering down Main Street, said to Jorvelle Wakefield, whose shoulders he was holding on to, "That looked like Theo wandering across the intersection up there!"

An hour later, Dr. Thayer Iddesleigh finally made his decision. Bob Fosse, Gower Champion, Hal Prince would have been proud of him. *He* was proud of him. Maude Fletcher for Sergeant Sarah Brown. Joel Elliott for Nicely-Nicely. And Theo Ryan, whom he hated the sight of, for the leading role of Sky Masterson. He'd make the phone calls tomorrow morning, before he changed his mind. Iddy put down his pencil, and tiptoed upstairs. He checked the bunkbeds of his sleeping sons, and the twin beds of his sleeping daughters, and then he rejoined his wife, removing the pillow from her rumpled hair.

At dawn Rhodora Potts returned from Gatlinburg and listened to

Ford's phone message to come get him out of jail. She called Theo, and then she drove to Rome in her brother T.W.'s truck, still wearing her fringed sequined cowgirl skirt from her gig with the Dead Indians. As Theo was phoning Bernie Bittermann for the bail, Rhodora slapped the playwright through the bars of his cell. She then left him there, with instructions to grow up before he died, predictions that he didn't have long to do it in, and vows not to marry him even if he did. He asked her why, with his best lopsided grin.

"You're an asshole, that's why," said Rhodora. She flung her long ebony hair back off her shoulder, gave her lover a well-known gesture with one long scarlet-nailed finger, told the sheriff, "Throw the goddamn book at him," grabbed Theo's arm, and left.

As they stood beside the truck, the sky indigo blue against the mountains, Theo leaned over to kiss Rhodora goodnight. He meant to kiss her cheek, but somehow his lips were against hers, and somehow she was kissing him back. They kissed a long time. Then they both pulled away, alarmed.

"Goddammit," said Rhodora, angrily shaking back her hair. "I've got enough problems without adding this on. Let's just forget about this right now. All right?"

"All right," Theo said, but his body wasn't forgetting at all.

CHAPTER

9

{Enter Disguised}

Hamlet: You played once i' th' university, you say?
Polonius: That I did, my lord.

ON A CRISP MAY MORNING, two weeks after Theo Ryan had
accepted his new role as a leading man, he was on his way to see
Dean Buddy Tupper, Jr. Despite a grueling rehearsal last night,
and little sleep after that, he swung his briefcase as he strode along
Vance Walk; he tapped, kicked, paused, corrected his footwork,
strode on.

Here came the ancient English professors, Dum and Dee,
both—despite the season—in tartan plaid hunting caps with the
flaps lowered, scurrying towards him, out for their early-morning
constitutional; Dum in the lead, Dee hobbling after him, shouting,
"Slow down, gawddammit, Fred! Slow down!"

"Morning, Dr. Lovell. Morning, Dr. Mortimer," called Theo
cheerfully.

"Humf!" said Dum, his nostrils flared.

"Mawnin', young man, lovely mawnin'," said Dee.

Dum stopped to pinch his old friend's arm spitefully. "What
are you being so nice to *him* for?!"

"Stop that, Fred! Who?"

"That was that Theo Ryan!"

"No, it wasn't!" Dee pushed disgustedly past his old friend into
the lead, and they hurried on.

Theo smiled benevolently after them, twirled the briefcase by its handle, hopped back, tapped forward, strode on.

He wasn't really surprised that old Mortimer failed to recognize him. For one thing, he wasn't wearing corduroys; he had on the new white pleated trousers and the new white linen sports jacket he'd just bought, and the new leather loafers with which he'd replaced his scruffed sneakers. That high roller Sky Masterson was such a flamboyant dresser that after his first costume fitting, Theo had begun to feel a little drab even in his Pretty New corduroys, and had secretly traveled to Asheville to make these purchases. Despite his horror at the obvious rise in the cost of clothes since he'd last been forced to buy any, he'd proved a large lump of malleable clay in the fluttering hands of an artistic sales clerk who'd worked on him for hours before finally sighing, "There now! Look in the mirror."

For another thing, Theo had been ordered by Iddesleigh to shave off his mustache and to wear contact lenses instead of his black-rimmed glasses. "Director's the boss," Iddy had smugly quoted Ford Rexford at him. So far the new performer had declined Iddy's advice that he carry a pair of dice in his pocket in order to "feel his way into the characterization," but Sky Masterson, on his own, was feeling his way into Theo Ryan.

His friends Jorvelle and Steve of course had noticed that he walked faster, hummed when he walked, and smiled at everyone he saw, sometimes to their alarm. They told him so enthusiastically what a great improvement it all was, from—in their blithely heartless phrase—"Theo the Moper," that he was quite hurt. Jorvelle commented frequently on his improved appearance. "Now you can see 'em, you got the thickest eyelashes I ever saw on a white man," she said on one evening out. And "Honkie, you are one good-lookin' hunk" she said on another. "Don't overdo it," said Steve. But apart from them, his delighted therapist Dr. Ko, and now old Mortimer, no one else had said anything about the difference in Theo the Singing, Dancing Guy of *Guys and Dolls*, and the apparently drab shadow of a self who'd bumbled by in the past months. Maude Fletcher certainly hadn't made any observations about his eyelashes.

Not that he still had seen Maude Fletcher anywhere but on the stage of the Spitz Center during rehearsals; every night as Sergeant Sarah Brown, she acted as if she were falling in love with him; every night as Maude Fletcher, she pleasantly declined all invitations to coffee, or anything else, as soon as the rehearsals ended. There was, Theo noticed, a black Mazda that occasionally waited outside the theatre, and there was a shadowy man in black leather driving it, but so far Theo had no idea who the man was. To him, Maude Fletcher was always pleasant, friendly, and in a hurry.

Perhaps in her theological sessions with Ford Rexford, she was saving the playwright's soul, but if so neither had confided in Theo. Rexford hadn't mentioned her when he called to give Theo the "Poop" about Scottie Smith, or when he'd called to admit that he hadn't gotten around yet to reading *Foolscap*. (No surprise there.) That Rexford was back in Rhodora's good graces after signing up with a chaplain, Theo had learned from Rhodora herself when they'd met a few days ago at the deli in the Super Winn-Dixie (the only place in the county that sold pastrami). He'd been avoiding her since the unexpected kiss outside the police station, and when they met he was both relieved and disappointed that she acted as if it hadn't happened.

"Ford," she said, holding her long black hair off the back of her neck to cool it, "Ford jist miaght be gittin' his shit together, 'stead of tryin' to kill his dumb self," leaving her to make the travel arrangements for shipping his "used-up carcass on home to that dump, Bowie, Texas," where apparently in a maudlin moment he'd begged her, and she'd promised, to bury him. "Nobody," said Rhodora, "can be that mad at God without a whole lot of faith. The asshole's just got God mixed up with his daddy." (This was precisely, if more bluntly phrased, the gist of the Nash-Gantz essay "Phallocentric Feud.")

Theo continued to find Rhodora's own faith in the power of religion peculiar, given her contempt for the rest of civilization, but she was apparently determined to marry in a church in June, or not at all. Asked why, she said frankly, "When Ford says, 'I do,' I want him paying attention; I want him scared shitless of a lie. And I don't know anabody mean enough to scare that snake, but me and Almighty God. You know he's scared of me, don't you, Theo?"

"I wouldn't be at all surprised." He held up his hands in surrender.

She laughed. "You look real handsome today. You got pretty eyes. Those dumbass glasses didn't do a thing for you. And that mustache looked like something off a dead fox."

"Gee, thanks, Rhodora."

"Well, I said you look good now. I'm an honest woman, Theo Ryan. You know where you stand. That's what scares that fucker Ford; he's so used to evahbody lickin' his butt."

She added, when they bumped into each other again at organic vegetables, "Your preacher friend better not try haulin' Ford's ashes, you tell her that, hear? I'll rip her goddamn head off, and beat him to death with it."

"I hardly think Maude's likely to do that!" Theo snapped, glaring at Rhodora through mist sprayed so thickly down on the lettuce that they might have been chatting in a rain forest.

"You're real sweet, sugar," was Miss Potts's cryptic reply, as she dumped a bunch of kale into her cart and rattled off, in tight shorts and an electric-blue tank top.

"Ford loves you," he yelled after her.

"I guess," Rhodora called over her bare shoulder.

Theo stared at those shoulders until she disappeared around a corner. He stuffed his hands in his pockets, and squeezed his nails into his palms. As he stood there, a thin woman in a pink pantsuit abruptly thrust a tomato in his face. "Look here!" she exclaimed. "Somebody ate a little teeny bite out of half a dozen of these tomatoes, and then put them back with the teeth holes facing down. Burns me to bits. Doesn't it you?"

"It certainly does," Theo agreed, only recognizing Tara Bridges when she shook her hands in front of his eyes and shouted, "Theo! Where are you?" (Very much as his mother had so often done in the past.) "I swear, you're as bad as Norman. Now listen. Are you doing anything to stop Marcus from taking over the department like he's always wanted to?"

Theo pulled himself into focus. "I'm telling everybody Steve would be a better chairman. All Marcus wants is the title and the props, not the job."

"I'm mad at Steve. He encouraged that Jorvelle to push her way into C.F.D.C. and hog one of the leads."

Ever since Tara Bridges had lost the part of Miss Adelaide, she'd been referring to the youngest Ludd Chair as "that Jorvelle." "Oh, Tara, she didn't," said Theo. "That's the whole fun of amateur theatre to me, that people *don't* push and hog."

Mrs. Bridges's laugh was caustic. "Honey, you and my husband are nothing but little babies in the woods." With that contemptuous appraisal, she waved goodbye, swerving her cart deftly around him; it was filled with dozens of gourmet microwave meals. Theo walked on, annoyed by all these accusations of naïveté, angered by Rhodora's lack of faith in Rexford, whom presumably she intended to marry in a month.

Rexford's manager, Bernie Bittermann, had gotten in the habit of calling Theo from New York for updates on his client. By now a devoted believer in Miss Potts, Bittermann had defended her skepticism in their talk that evening. The C.P.A. was himself suspicious of "the born-again phase," particularly after hearing that Reverend Fletcher was an unmarried female; but if Rhodora wanted to hope religion might help, let her. In Bittermann's own opinion, surely any deities still in the business had given up on Rexford's promises to reform long before now. The financial manager certainly had. His hopes, he confided to Theo, were more modest: That Rexford wouldn't lose interest in Rhodora Potts before he finished his long overdue play, or before his producers sued him for their advance on it. "I don't know," he sighed over the phone from his Brooklyn brownstone, "what that young woman is holding over Ford, but if my wife plans to remodel our upstairs bath, she better pray Miss Potts doesn't let go of it."

What Rhodora held over Ford Rexford was, Theo told him, that primordial source, according to songs, of the circumrotation of the earth. That love makes the world go round, Theo had always been fully willing to believe. And now he could see planets turning all about him at the Spitz—among them, Steve Weiner and Jorvelle Wakefield, Bill Robey and Joel Elliott. And he too, glowing bright, was ready to cross stars with Maude Fletcher, if only the universe would whirl her into his orbit.

Thinking in this vein about love, Theo paused in midcampus on his way to his appointment with Dean Tupper, and rubbed for luck the foot of the statue of the prudish Amos Latchett.

"Hi, Dr. Ryan!!" a female voice called enthusiastically. Theo waved at a young woman sprinting towards him across the green. It was Cathy Bannister, the honors senior in his "Classics of the Stage" class; behind her walked Jenny Harte; they appeared to be friends despite their chasm of academic rank. Both wore black T-shirts dotted with red "8%" buttons. Reaching him, Cathy thrust a flier in his pocket, and slid a red rosebud into the lapel of his jacket. Jenny pointed at his upper lip where his mustache had been, then gave him an okay sign. They were both quite beautiful, he noticed, luscious as the rosebuds they carried; they both seemed so happy to see him, too; no doubt about it.

Cathy said, "I've got my *Streetcar* costume all set, Dr. Ryan. The whole class just loves it, you know, doing real scenes in class instead of, you know, just that boring read-and-take-notes stuff."

"I told you they would," Jenny said.

"Except Joe." Cathy frowned. "Joe thinks acting's weird. He hates me to do anything weird. He's just a big ole horrible macho pig."

"Joe Botzchick's her fiancé," Jenny explained. "And he's an ox, really, not a pig."

"Aw, he's a sweetie," Cathy protested happily.

Theo glanced at his flier. "BOYCOTT BLEECKER!" ran the headline. The reasons why were listed below, as were plans for an upcoming rally in front of Coolidge Building. "Is this the Herbert Crawford in the History Department who's behind this?" he asked.

"Herbie!" Cathy did a mock swoon. "If I didn't love Joe, I could go for Herbie in a major way! Herbie's great. Right, Jenny?" Giggling, she knocked herself playfully into her friend's side.

Theo spoke firmly. "Cathy, Dr. Crawford is married."

"Oh, he's separated from her." She shrugged. "I mean legally."

How did undergraduates know these things? "Well, still . . ." He checked his watch. "Look, I've got to run," he told them.

"Bye, Dr. Ryan!" Cathy caroled, twisted him around, and patted her hands across his back.

Jenny Harte turned once, to wave at him, and to call, "Goodbye, Sky!"

Off they breezed like the wind, blonde hair sprayed out behind them. Beautiful.

CHAPTER
10

{Aloft}

They have tied me to a stake, I cannot fly,
But bearlike I must fight the course.

Macbeth

ATOP THE COOLIDGE BUILDING Dean Buddy Tupper, Jr. stood at his post by the huge window watching his enemies below.

Down on the campus, Professor Herbert Crawford and Reverend Maude Fletcher stood where they'd been stationed for weeks, right in front of the doors of Bleecker Dining Hall. Above the doors still flew the big red banner that read "BOYCOTT BLEECKER." The black-dressed, red-buttoned crowd of radicals with them had swelled in number. Tupper watched his secretary, whom he'd sent to reconnoiter, milling about on the steps, taking down the names of faculty picketers. Suddenly Crawford spotted her, and shouted in the poor woman's face:

> Don't eat Tupper's supper!
> Don't eat Tupper's supper!
> Boycott Bleecker! Boycott Bleecker!

Watching his secretary flee back down the steps and scurry off, the provost slammed the plate glass with his fist, then returned to his desk and other problems. The Physics Department needed an extra $670,000 for "lab equipment." What were they building over there, hydrogen bombs? Plus, he'd just gotten rid of a nutcase from the Classics Department who claimed he'd been denied tenure because he was a vegetarian. Plus, Dean Claudia Pratt had been in here about more tuition rebates for graduate students, and had taken the opportunity to predict "the Bleecker thing isn't going away."

And now he had an upcoming appointment with Theo Ryan, who was probably going to whine about why he'd been passed over for the position Scottie Smith was trying to dick them around about. It was always something.

As the provost rose to shake hands with the big ruddy young man, he found himself favorably surprised by Theo Ryan's appearance. He hadn't remembered him as quite so well-groomed a figure. Maybe he should add him to the list of faculty eligible for display purposes at dinner parties to which potential donors were lured.

It was always Tupper's habit to squeeze as much information out of supplicants as he could before they started squeezing him for whatever it was they wanted. (And he didn't fool himself: no one ever came to see him without wanting something—including his wife.) So he forestalled Ryan by growling immediately, "John Hood's just backed out of running your London Year Abroad program in the fall. Says his mother's got cancer." (Tupper looked skeptical, either about the fact, or its relevancy.) "Can you think of anybody else might be good?"

Theo pulled in his long legs, his knees nearly chest high; the visitor's chair was elegant but rather small—a strategy of Tupper's to diminish whoever sat there. "Well, sir, Dean Tupper, yes. I'd recommend Jonas Marsh. I've talked to him about the London program often—he's applied a number of times—and he has very sensible ideas."

Amazing: If this young man had gotten anything resembling sense out of Jonas Marsh at all, perhaps he was administrative material. Tupper tapped the ring against the bronze football on his mammoth desk. "Marcus Thorney suggests this guy Rice."

Theo said nothing.

"Fact, Norm and I were set to give the program to Thorney himself. But now he's up for chairman. Whadda you think?"

"I'm a supporter of Steve Weiner's."

"Hmmm."

"He'd make a great chairman."

"You don't think Thorney would?"

Theo stopped himself from resting his chin on his knees. "Dr. Thorney and I are not particularly congenial."

"Um hum." That was for sure; Tupper had read the scathing letter Marcus Thorney had written opposing Ryan's tenure promotion. He raked his hand down his flattop. "What's he got against you?"

Getting ready to say "I don't know," Theo changed his mind. "You'll have to ask him that; my theories are necessarily prejudicial. But I do think Dr. Thorney'd be an excellent choice . . . for London."

The young fellow was politic, and witty too, mused the provost. Maybe this time there was something *to* all of Norman's gushing. Tupper found himself feeling warmly about this good-looking kid; he was big, even taller than the Bone-Cruncher himself, and it was comfortable being with other big people, instead of your run-of-the-mill wimpy academic runts. He rubbed the football, and grumbled, "Jonas Marsh, hunh? Kind of a nutcase, isn't he? Between you and me?"

"Jonas cares passionately about things. He's intemperate, but I don't think he's crazy."

Stood up for his friends too, even the ones that were bonkers. Tupper rapped his class ring on the desk edge. "You played college ball, Ryan; Yale man, right? You were big enough, that's for damn sure."

"Yes, sir. But I was out the last two years with a knee injury." Frankly, the end of his football career had not exactly broken Theo's heart, but he certainly wasn't about to say so. "Had to be operated on." That was true; in the fall of his junior year, he'd been knocked down by stampeding fans at a Mets game his father had taken him to.

"Too bad," Tupper mumbled, and slapped the football. "Okay. I figure you're coming in here to bitch about wanting to run the Spitz Center. Norman Bridges pushed hard for you on that."

Theo nodded. "I'm very grateful for Norman's support, but as I've told him, I'm not qualified to turn the Spitz into what it could be."

Modest, too. "So what do you think of this Scottie Smith guy?" Theo said, "I think he's famous."

Dean Tupper scratched an eyebrow with the ring, then he looked at Theo, then he grinned. "Yeah, he's famous."

"Dean Tupper. That's why I'm here." Theo opened his briefcase, took out a sheaf of papers. "I oppose Smith's appointment strongly. Oh, he's slick maybe, but at base he's only an opportunist."

"Opportunist?" (Ryan didn't even know the half of it, unless he'd listened in on Smith's phone call demanding one hundred and fifty thousand dollars a year!) "But you guys in English are the ones bitching about reputation, reputation. And they say Smith's a name." Tupper picked up a national magazine with Scottie Smith's face on the cover; the youthful American director, his head shaved, and wearing satin knee pants and a gold brocaded vest, was seated cross-legged on an outmoded electric chair in Attica prison.

Theo shook the magazine indignantly. "Well, look at this! That's my point. He's just a fad. Fads fade. I know the theatre, Dean Tupper, and I know that's true."

Tupper frowned suspiciously. "But Norm said you'd be all for this. He says the rest of the English Department is happy as dogs in a butcher shop."

Theo handed the provost the first page of his papers. "I've put together some background on Scottie Smith."

"Listen, I already know he's a fag. We can't hold sexual preference against him." Tupper twisted his face into a smile. "Hell, half my goddamn faculty's queer already, from what I hear."

"Sexual preference isn't what I'm talking about." Theo pointed at the paper.

As he read, Tupper's slab of a face turned the color of raw steak. "Crap Above! Is this all *true?* Three times in the Betty Ford Center, and *still* hooked on alcohol and cocaine? What kind of willpower is that!"

Theo nodded, handing the provost the second sheet of paper. "This information comes from professional theatre people who have worked with and know Smith."

"Boy prostitutes? Arrested in a private S-and-M club for doing *what!* . . . Well, now, wait a minute, this bit here, not being really British, that's not a negative. We've got too damn many foreigners on this campus as it is."

Theo placed the third piece of paper on Tupper's desk.

Tendons twitching, the provost spluttered, "Went into this theatre's endowment? Spent their *endowment!* His last producer filed Chapter Eleven! In God's blue heaven what is the matter with Norman? Telling me to hire the filthiest pervert that ever lived!"

"Norman of course didn't know. It's just that I have a lot of contacts in the business. Smith has been very discreet really."

"Discreet! He's been in *jail!*"

"Only the once."

"Why didn't you tell Norman!"

"Norman was so eager, and the department is in such a fractious—"

"That's for damn sure!"

"I came to you first, Dean Tupper. If you've committed to Scottie Smith already, then—"

Tupper beat at the grinning face on the magazine cover. "Committed! Forget committed! Why I wouldn't let that creep drink stale water from my dead dog's bowl. Listen, Ryan, I'm glad somebody's playing defense here!"

It was now time for Theo to set before the provost his alternate proposal, neatly typed on triple-spaced pages, and signed by eight friends of his in the English Department. It suggested that a committee be formed to study the need to establish, independent of English, an undergraduate program in theatre studies at Cavendish, based in the Spitz Center. It suggested that in the meantime, (1) Thayer Iddesleigh be retained as the programs coordinator of the Center, (2) in the following year an N.Y.U. adjunct professor named Barbara Sanchez, who'd directed two dozen off-Broadway shows, be hired as artistic director of the Spitz Theatre, (3) her salary be paid by the Spitz Endowment, leaving free the third Ludd Chair, (4) the third Ludd Chair be bestowed on Norman Bridges, who after his long services to Ludd Hall certainly deserved the recognition, and the raise.

The provost looked up and stared at Theo, who stared back. "Well, well," Tupper growled. "Well, well. Interesting ideas."

"Thank you," said Theo. "Let me also say that if you bring in this Barbara Sanchez, who comes very highly recommended, I can guarantee you a deal that will put the Spitz on the map from its opening night."

Tupper pulled contemplatively on his ear. "Shoot."

"A world premiere by the biggest name in the American theatre."

"Which is?"

"Joshua 'Ford' Rexford."

Tupper was not a man who followed the arts, but even those who've never followed baseball recognize the name of Babe Ruth. He leaned back in his leather chair. "Can we afford Rexford?"

Theo smiled. "He's not interested in money."

"That'd be a change." The provost picked up the bronze football and slapped it from hand to hand. "Why would he do it?"

"Ford?" Theo didn't miss the twitch of the provost's eye at this easy use of the first name. "He told me he would. Barbara Sanchez was his suggestion."

Tupper looked at the magazine cover of Scottie Smith. "It's a thought. Let me think about it." He stood, and rapped his ring twice on the desk top.

"Thank you very much, Dean Tupper." Theo stood.

At this moment Lady Luck, to whom Theo had sung in his audition, rescued him from a sudden spin down to the bottom of fortune's wheel. Just as he was about to exit, and so expose his back to Tupper, Luck sent President Kaney in, unannounced, through the door. "As you were," Kaney announced pleasantly.

Theo had never personally met the Old Man, though he recognized him, and of course had heard the rumors. He started to hold out his hand, but the general paraded straight over to the desk, and so blocked from Tupper's view the sight of young Dr. Ryan suddenly catching a horrified glimpse of the back of his jacket, reflected in the mirror above a table crowded with gleaming football trophies. He was horrified because taped across the shoulders of his new linen sports coat was a wide sticker that read "DON'T EAT TUPPER'S SUPPER." So much for Cathy Bannister's simply patting his back out of high-spirited affection!

Could he now back all the way out of the opulent room without knocking into a lamp? Perhaps he could, since President Kaney had Tupper's full attention; for some reason he was sternly telling the provost, to whom he was not related, "Your mother was a virgin when we married, and I expect the same behavior from you, young man."

Backstepping, Theo reached frantically behind him to rip off the sticker. He had half of it balled in his fist, when Kaney abruptly snatched the bronze football out of Tupper's hand and hurled it at the plate-glass window, which being very thick, didn't shatter.

"Manly sports are very well in their place," Kaney announced in his southern slur, "but this is not the place, and this is not the time." Then he wheeled on Theo, who by now was pulling off the last bit of tape, and shook a thin finger at him. "Stop scratching." He wheeled on the provost. "This soldier here is thoroughly infested with lice. Or worse." He marched over, inches from Theo's face. "Pull yourself together, son. Remember the Spartan boy who let a fox chew up his little stomach and never broke rank."

Theo stuffed the sticky wad in his pocket. "Yes, sir, General Kaney, sir," he replied. And then he saluted.

Quick on his feet too, thought Tupper. And it was truer than he knew.

Out in the reception room, Theo astonished the provost's secretary, who'd just returned from spying on the protesters. She was Theo's churlish next-door neighbor, the one who'd called the police on him twice, once when Ford Rexford had blown out his speakers playing Ethel Merman hits, and once when his drama students had built him in the front yard a surprise snowman meant to represent the God of Classical Comedy—a fat Greek fellow wearing a chaplet of grapes, bright socks strapped with leather, and a gargantuan erection.

Theo astonished her by leaning over her desk and handing her, with his Sky Masterson smile, the red rose.

CHAPTER

11

{Enter a Messenger with a Letter}

The players cannot keep counsel. They'll tell all.

Hamlet

THEO SAW, massed on the desk in the anteroom to the chairman's office at Ludd Hall, an enormous heaped pile of envelopes, manuscripts, and folders veiled in smoke, as if stacked there for a bonfire and already smoldering. Behind this hump, the top of a red bobbed head suddenly moved. "Hi ya," mumbled Mrs. Fruchaff, cigarette dangling from the corner of her lip. Her thick-lensed glasses enlarged her eyes like those of a fish staring out of an aquarium.

"Hi, Effie. Norman in?"

She ran a yellowed finger across her throat. "Our 'benefactress' Dina Sue Ludd chewed him out this morning, and now Norman thinks he's passing a stone. He ran off to the doctor's."

"A kidney stone? That's supposed to be the worst pain in the world! Did you call Tara?"

"It's just nerves. Norman's cracking up." Tears streamed from the tiny old woman's magnified eyes, but from smoke, not sympathy. "That bleeding heart can't take the pace." She pawed through papers. "Here's your check. You oughta ask for a raise. And here's a letter from some woman in England; tell her it was twenty-seven cents postage due."

A jolt went through Theo as he read the sturdy up-tilted penstrokes of the return address.

Winifred Throckmorton
Lark Cottage, Barnet-on-Urswick
Devonshire, England

A letter from Dame Winifred, the Elizabethan drama scholar, retired from Oxford, and in Theo's opinion shamefully disregarded
by most of a newer, forgetful generation of critics. Dame Winifred's many books had inspired his first one, and he kept all ten
of hers, carefully taped and patched, on a special shelf above his
desk. Recently he'd published in a journal a long essay about her
contribution to the field of Renaissance studies, but he'd never
thought she'd respond so quickly, if at all. The sight of her name
on the thin blue page thrilled him.

It was a short note, rather oddly capitalized, thanking Mr. Ryan
for his "Generous words" about her, telling him that she'd
read with interest his own "brilliant" book on Shakespearean
clowns—"written with Marvellous Style and Power"—and noting that she had "a few Quibbles" about the argument. Should he
be interested, she'd be glad to write them to him. Or, if he were
ever near Devonshire (perhaps to "Visit Ralegh's manor at Sherborne?"), she hoped he'd "feel Free to pay a Call." She added that
she was "on" to something "most Exciting," for which she had as
yet only "tiny Bits" of evidence. "My God," Theo said. "Isn't
that wonderful! 'On to something.' She never quits."

"Brit girl friend?" asked the old secretary.

"She's a very old woman." He smiled.

"So what? Am I dead?" Mrs. Fruchaff pointed her extra-length
cigarette at him. "Now that you're showing a little life again,
Theo, little juice, take my advice. Stop mooning over Maude
Fletcher—"

"What do you mean, mooning over Maude Fletcher?"

"Get somebody who'll give you the time of day. Well, don't
put on that look. Who told you it wasn't going to work out with
that woman in Art History? Me."

"It worked for three years."

She shrugged. "Jenny Harte had a crush on you last spring."

"Effie, come on! Jenny's my student!"

"Student schmudent. She's twenty-six, you're so fixated on

women's ages. Okay, there's plenty others. With those eyes, that voice, piece of beefcake like you could get just about any woman you wanted."

"I don't want any woman. I want the right woman."

"So, pick one. You'd be surprised at the amount of sex up for grabs in this building. And you're not getting any."

The tough-minded Mrs. Fruchaff had no compunctions about nosing into the privacy of all who labored in what for nearly half a century she'd called "my sweatshop." As she said, she'd seen them come and go. The philologist who'd run off with a male graduate, leaving the department's first chair, Miss Mabel Chiddick, to tell his wife. The Americanist who had broken down and sobbed when Dr. Elsie Spence told him he'd been denied tenure, until they'd finally had to make him breathe into a paper bag. The Swift man who'd shot the windows out of the dean's office when he hadn't been promoted. The Romanticist who'd sold his novel to Scribner's and quit the same day. The Victorian man who'd married the Tudor woman, and she'd had to leave and go teach in a community college because of nepotism rules, rules now abandoned in favor of hiring all the celebrity couples available on the market. Times changed. Effie Fruchaff had been there when professors taught for a dollar a year, because gentlemen didn't need salaries. She'd been there when graduate schools were crammed with draft dodgers, and Ph.D.s were lucky to find jobs selling Avon door-to-door. She'd lived to see English teachers earning six figures a year and driving Mercedes sedans with cellular phones. Triumphs, failures, friendships, bitter venom, she'd seen it all.

To Mrs. Fruchaff, Norman Bridges was a child, and Theo Ryan a baby. She'd known Dee and Dum when they were pipsqueaks in baggy golf knickers, both with blond slicked-back hair and crazy about Greta Garbo, Ezra Pound, and the rumba: It was hard for Theo to imagine those two old men swaying their small behinds to the rattle of maracas, but Mrs. Fruchaff claimed to have danced with each of them the day Prohibition was repealed. Now she jabbed her cigarette in Theo's direction. "There was a guy here in the fifties—a poet—he got two students *pregnant* in one year. This was before they ever heard of sexual harassment—"

"Or birth control either apparently."

"Well, let me tell you, it caused some stink."

Dismissing this gossip with a tolerant headshake, Theo asked, "Where's Jonas?" as he carefully folded the blue note.

"The Madman's down the hall teaching. Can't you hear him? Most everybody else has gone home, or they're over at Bleecker stirring up the masses."

"Boycott Bleecker."

"I've been boycotting Bleecker for fifty years, and beats me if they've cleaned the coffeepot once in that entire time. Listen, sweet-pie, turn in your ballot for chairman. Poll closes tomorrow at three." The secretary's ash dropped off her cigarette as she disappeared under a hillock of manila envelopes.

"I'll do it now." Theo took a page from her memo pad, wrote down a name, folded the paper. Mrs. Fruchaff reemerged with a miniature bottle of Kahlua; in the past she had collected a huge assortment of them from airplane trips taken by faculty members on boondoggles. After a chug, she sucked on her teeth as she opened his ballot. "Steve Weiner," she said, unsurprised. "The Bronx bomber'll have to pull it out hard in the stretch. So far all he's got's your vote, Hood's, Marsh's, Jorvelle's, and what little of the chicken-livered junior faculty not busy sucking up to the old farts. Marcus Thorney's in the lead, plus he voted for himself. Vic Gantz voted for his wife, who's not even on the ballot. Touching."

No sense in making rhetorical remarks about weren't the votes supposed to be confidential. He said, "Jane wouldn't be a bad chair, if she were ever around."

"Big if. Jane's what Dina Sue's been on a rampage about. She's heard N.-G.'s been up to something smutty with Emily Dickinson's labia." Mrs. Fruchaff snorted. "One thing's sure; N.-G. hasn't stuck around long enough to do anything smutty with Vic. Unless they do it in her Mercedes on the way to the airport."

Clearing away a manuscript with "Unmitigated Rubbish!!!" scrawled on its cover, Theo sat on the desk edge. "Give Jane a chance. I like her."

Another derisive snort. "You're 'bout as discriminating as a whore with the rent due. But you're sweet." She slapped hard at his hip bone.

No point in taking offense; so he just gave her the finger non-chalantly, and she cackled. He said, "You're the second person who's called me 'sweet' and made it sound like an insult. And I don't like everybody. I don't like Marcus Thorney."

Stabbing out her cigarette on something (an ashtray, one hoped) under a mound of papers, she muttered, "Then you'll be sick to hear he won the Ludd Book Award this morning."

He did feel sick. "You're kidding! For that Chaucer thing?"

She chuckled. "Tell it to Ludd. The Grease-Man's been playing her like a big bass fiddle. And don't think Dina Sue's not casting her vote for chairman too, and believe me, some votes are more equal than others."

Theo hopped off the desk. "I'm going. You're depressing me. Hey, what about this Jorvelle-getting-a-Yale-offer rumor?"

The old secretary scattered folders. A miniature bottle of Cherry Herring rolled off the desk. "Eighty-two thou." Useless to ask her how she knew. "But five-to-one she says no. Her mom lives in Greensboro. Plus, she and Weiner got something going. A Jew dating a black woman and he's running for chairman down here in Jesse Helms country? The kid's got chutzpah. All I did was marry a Jew, a white one, fifty-two years ago and he's been dead, God rest him, thirty-one of those, and my family's still not speaking to me."

Theo handed her back the little bottle. "See yah. And pick up the tempo on my first number tonight." He snapped his fingers at her in a rhythm, walking backwards as he left to find Jonas Marsh.

In the hall, Jane Nash-Gantz herself—tall, svelte, with striking spiked hair—was hurrying along with a leather suitbag over her shoulder. Her plump secretary raced along beside her taking notes.

"Jane, hi!" called Theo. "I hear Dina Sue's breathing fire!"

"Hi, gorgeous." She stopped, grabbed him, hugged him, and rolled her shrewd, slightly crossed eyes to the ceiling. "Theo, may the Great Goddess inflict that sex-crazed cow Ludd with the mange. She's driving me nuts. I'm talking about poetry, and she thinks I'm talking about pussy!"

Her secretary tugged at her boss's glamorous baggy silk jacket. "Jane, you'll miss your flight."

Jane rubbed her lipstick briskly from Theo's cheek. "Hi, bye. Tell Steve he's got my vote. Kiss Vic for me if you see him. Off to Barcelona."

"Lecturing?"

"God, yes, if I can get the damn thing written on the plane. 'The Anorexic Text: Minimalism as Sexual Politics.' What do you think?"

"In Barcelona?"

"Oh, *huge* conference. 'Reproductions of Oppression' and of course vice versa."

"Jane . . ." Her secretary tugged at her again.

Jane waved. "You know what success is, Theo? Success is exhaustion."

The two women clattered in their heels down the marble stairs.

At nearly three, the few classes in session on the fourth floor were just emptying. Students tiptoed thoughtfully out of the room where old Dr. Mortimer snoozed at his desk, his chin resting on his plaid bow-tie, his volume of Romantic poetry open to Wordsworth's "Intimations of Immortality" ode.

Only one teacher was still going strong. In front of the blackboard, on which was hugely chalked, "FOR GOD'S SAKE, THINK!," Jonas Marsh, in Liberty of London braces, a striped shirt, and a fuchsia tie, looked to be dancing the carioca. Through the propped-open door, Theo watched as students squirmed in their seats.

"Dolts! Dullards!" Marsh bellowed. "Have you no ears! Have you no souls, you lethargic progeny of Philistines? This is Herrick! This is poetry! How can you listen to that poem and not want to rip off every shred of your thoroughly undistinguished clothing!"

Giggles, one hoot, a shouted "Go for it, Kevin!" as a young man in the front row made a pretense of pulling off his polo shirt.

Marsh raced over, squatted, grabbed the wide-eyed boy's desk top and shook it back and forth. "You want a woman, Kevin! You want her to go to bed with you before you're old, a decayed rotting putrification. You want to get her in the mood. How, you somnambulistic blockhead? With rock 'n' roll?" Marsh leapt up, flung himself into gyrations, shouting:

I want some sex!
Who'll be next?
How 'bout you?
Yeah, you'll do!

Now general applause and a few Rebel yells.

"Isn't that it?! You play her your troglodyte notion of a sexy song! Well, Robert Herrick writes *sexy songs!*"

A young woman came half out of her seat, angry. "What's sexy about having your virginity treated like a fort somebody's charging at with a battering ram? Or a flower, and here come the scissors, snip, snap? I'll take Donne over Herrick any day."

"Good for you, Laura!" Marsh shouted at her.

Cathy Bannister raised her hand. "Dr. Marsh. Do you think Herrick might be a repressed homosexual?"

General guffaws from the males.

Facing the blackboard, Marsh knocked his head into his fist, once, twice, a third time. "I despair. Leave me. Go, go. 'Go gather ye rosebuds while ye may. Old Time is still a'flying.' " He spun around on them. "Does that ring a BELL, you imbecilic LUMPEN?"

Some sheepish, some chortling, they left him.

In Jonas Marsh's office (which resembled the reading room of a cramped but posh Victorian club—red leather wing chair, rolling library ladder, brass cuspidor, and elephant foot hassock), Theo sipped a glass of port while Jonas, after scrubbing his hands and face with Handi-Wipes, unwrapped for him a morocco-bound first edition of MacPherson's 1760 *Fragments of Ancient Poetry Collected in the Highlands of Scotland;* sent on approval, he said, by his antiquarian bookseller. The Restoration specialist was an insatiable collector of rare books, holographs, and manuscripts, and apparently something of an expert on them. Theo and Steve had often speculated on where he got the money to pay for such rarities, as well as for his antique furnishings, and his handsewn outfits. Jonas was always cavalierly dropping exorbitant figures into the conversation about the cost of that breakfront ($7,000) and this bottle of Bordeaux ($290), and if the figures were only half true, he'd still easily run through his entire annual salary in a month's time. They'd decided it must be family money, until Mrs. Fruchaff told them Jonas's father had worked till he died behind a ticket counter at the Minneapolis airport. But even Mrs. Fruchaff couldn't explain his income. "Drug pusher?" she suggested.

Theo had come to show Jonas Marsh his letter from Dame Winifred, and to tell him he should keep pressuring Norman Bridges about letting him run the London program. "If John can't go, and you want to, why not?"

"Why not? Because my influence in this department is precisely NIL. I do not stoop to conquer. And bent-over is the preferred position."

"Dammit, why should Thorney get everything his way? You hear about the Ludd Book Prize yet?"

"What about it?"

"Marcus won it."

Marsh started a rapid shoe-kicking against his Marlborough desk. "Bugger him! And that's a curse, Ryan, not a suggestion. Thorney a medievalist! Rubbish! I showed him a manuscript page, thirteenth-century French. Couldn't read it. Could not read it! Translation of Boethius. Didn't know it from a bloody broadside ballad. That whoreson quack future CHAIRMAN calls himself a Chaucerian!" Marsh's hands were getting away from him, swatting at his leonine head. "Charlatan!"

"But you don't think Steve's going to lose?"

The slender blades of Marsh's shoulders spasmed. "Of course Steve's going to lose! Just because he's published four good books, teaches the biggest classes in the department, and serves on ten university committees, you think he deserves to win? Why even Norman will vote for Thorney. The old boys will all stumble into a circle like smug, sluggish musk-oxen, their flabby buttocks to the winds of change! Lose? Yes, yes, YES!"

"Well, I guess I keep hoping . . . Anyhow," Theo added quickly to plug the flood of words. "I've been meaning to thank you again for supporting me on Dame Winifred, even if it didn't—"

Marsh clawed at his tie. "Dame Winifred Throckmorton is a great scholar. A *real* scholar. That woman discovered and identified a Kyd play, a Marlowe fragment, and three Raleigh essays! If she'd done nothing else in her life but that and belch in public, she'd more deserve a bloody Ludd chair in this backwater hovel of intellectual pygmies than the rest of our miserable faculty put together and invigorated by electric prods! The cretinous swine!"

"Well, yes, I suppose."

"You *suppose!*"

To distract him, Theo opened a leather portfolio lying on the desk. "Jonas! This is a David Garrick letter!"

"Don't touch it!" Marsh clapped his hands together as if at a child.

"Sorry. . . ." Hands behind his back, Theo read the splotchy lines of faded ink. "Actors never change, do they? Garrick bitches just like my parents. . . . Well, listen, if you do get to England in the fall, maybe I'll come over and we could go see some plays together. Maybe we could even go visit Dame Winifred."

Marsh was wrapping the MacPherson volume in cloth. "I'll be in London all summer," he remarked blandly. "I'm there every summer. And every Christmas."

"You are?"

"Why on earth would I stay here?"

"You know, Jonas, here I am teaching Shakespeare and I've never been to London. Isn't that stupid?"

"Very."

"Every summer?" Theo was struck by how little he knew about Jonas Marsh. His high-strung colleague had never been to his house; although invited to the half-dozen cocktail parties Theo had hosted over the years, he'd always sent his regrets on rich creamy note cards with his name engraved on top. Nor had Theo, or anyone Theo knew, ever been in Marsh's own home, which was apparently in Asheville, twenty miles away from Rome. Presumably he lived there alone. Steve said the old department joke was that Marsh had been slipping out of a mental institution daily for decades, showing up at Cavendish to teach, then returning at night to his padded cell.

"How much is that worth?" Theo pointed at the leather-bound *Fragments of Ancient Poetry,* which Jonas was then locking in a desk drawer. When the bibliophile named a sum in the thousands, Theo expressed surprise. "But it's an eighteenth-century forgery!"

"Ah!" Marsh nodded cheerfully. "But a very famous forgery."

He slid the desk key under an ornate oriental figurine that looked suspiciously like solid jade. "An extraordinary forgery is naturally more valuable than an ordinary original. Of course, just imagine what it would be worth if there really had been a Scots Gaelic epic by a bard named Ossian?" The man's dark eyes glittered. "Or imagine if *A Man for All Seasons* had been *Shakespeare's* lost play about Sir Thomas More, instead of just some twentieth-century costume drama!" Marsh placed a long slender foot on the rung of his library ladder and flicked a speck from the burnished leather of the wing-tipped shoe. "I wonder," he smiled, "if it ever occurred to Robert Bolt to write *A Man for All Seasons* that way instead? I mean, as if it were contemporary with its period. . . . Interesting."

Theo considered inviting Marsh home to dinner with him tonight, of talking more about such things, but after watching the elegantly dressed man race his ladder in a frenzy back and forth in front of the bookshelves, charity failed him. Probably Marsh would have declined anyhow. Still it seemed to him that the Restoration specialist looked lonely as he left him there in the otherwise deserted Ludd Hall, crouched atop his mahogany ladder, brushing dust from his beautiful books with his ivory white handkerchief.

CHAPTER

12

{A Trumpet Sounds}

SNEER:
The devil!—did he mean all that by shaking his head?

PUFF:
Every word of it. If he shook his head as I taught him.

Sheridan, The Critic

BOTH LONELY AND WITHOUT PRIVACY, the only child of chaotic
parents, Theo had begun at age three to carry around with him
talismans of domestic stability, and the first thing he did when
deposited in a new hotel suite or an unfamiliar dressing room was
to unsnap his heavy brown suitcase, and place in order on bureau
or shelf, his iconic home—a ratty Winnie-the-Pooh bear, an old
Madame Alexander doll that looked to him like his mother, a
cardboard figure of his father doing the duck dance, a blue plastic
telephone. Every place he traveled, this ritual of routine was his
first, invariable habit. As he grew older, the objects changed, but
not the impulse to impose continuity on change. Never a collector
in Jonas Marsh's league or of his inclination, Theo's icons remained few and profoundly personal. Now, of course, that he had
lived alone in the same house for years, disorder never disturbed
his careful arrangement of his treasures. Or almost never.

But when he returned home this afternoon, he found Ford
Rexford in his bed, asleep, covered with sheets of paper, wearing
muddy sneakers. The framed Popova sketch of a Chekhov set for
Moscow's Meyerhold Theatre had obviously been carelessly used
as a lap desk, and was now on the floor. The drawing had been
his grandfather's. Cigarette butts floated in a coffee mug that sat

on top of his (rare, 78 rpm) Helen Morgan record album. Helen Morgan's voice on the old recordings—high, plaintive, sure as a bird's—Theo had loved as he'd loved Ginger Rogers's brisk, earnest dancing, as he'd loved Simone Signoret's world-weary eyes, and the line of Vivien Leigh's neck. He owned all these actresses' signed photographs, and kept them not as collectibles but like romantic tokens, intimations of the beloved to come. Now his photograph of Jeanne Moreau lay on the floor.

"*Ford!*" Theo snatched up the objects more in horror than rage, and placed them on his dresser. "*Ford!* Wake up."

The grizzled playwright bolted to his elbows, and blinked in confusion. Then he reached up, pulled Theo onto the bed, and rolled him back and forth in a warm, sinewy, scratchy embrace, strongly smelling of tobacco, bourbon, wood chips, and roses. There were in fact, Theo saw, crushed red rose petals and pencil shavings all over his white down comforter.

Rexford growled in his ear. "Where you been! You son of a bitch!"

"What's wrong?"

"You sneaky bastard! This thing is *good*, it's damn good!"

Bewildered and frankly terrified, Theo fought his way free of the hugging arms and legs, and scrambled off the bed. It was then that he realized that the papers strewn all over the place were the pages of his play, *Foolscap*. His heart knocked wildly at his chest. "My play?"

"Yeah, your play. I'm not going to shit you. I didn't expect it." Rexford sat up, legs crossed, and rubbed his gray hair. "I mean I knew you could *write*, but I wasn't sure you could *write write*. Well, babe, you can!"

"My play *is* good?"

"When I saw the thing was set in the Jesus Christ sixteen hundreds, and you got Sir Walter Raleigh a Jesus Christ old man in the Tower the night before he gets the ax, and he's in there making up new endings to the play of his life, well, fuck. . . . I said, 'Don't even read this, Ford. It's gonna hurt.' But Theo, I've been at it for two days now, and it *works*, by God. It *plays!!*"

Theo's knees buckled, and he sat on the edge of the bed. "It does?"

"Almost." Rexford crawled around, gathering pages; they were scribbled all over with penciled marks. "Go get me a drink. Legal pad, and got a corkboard?"

"What? Do what?" Theo began spinning on the floor, picking up the rest of the paper, his hands shaking.

"We need a big table." Ford was already on his way out of the room, Theo so close behind that he stepped on his heel. "First thing," said the older man, "start here on page three. This opening's shit. You don't need it. Somebody should have told Will Shakespeare it sucked every time he did it too. Next scene"—he turned and smacked his lips—"Perfect, beautiful, don't touch it."

"Don't touch it."

"No, wait, cut the last line. Last two lines. Redo this whole speech, let's get some iambs working for us now and then, undercurrent. Da dúm da dúm da dúm, break, 'the wrecks of time.' "

"More iambic there."

"Now, big things. What you need—save Elizabeth, don't bring her on so fast. Hold her back, build it. She's gotta strut in on that cloak right next to the trip up the Amazon."

"In the dream sequence, Orinoco next to Elizabeth."

"Her and the treasure hunt. Back and forth, bing, bong, bing, bong. The old stud's two great golden maidenheads. God, I love this guy! I envy this guy!" Rexford threw the pages on the dining room table. He gestured as if he were spinning a rope overhead, hurling it, climbing it hand over hand. "Now, listen, you throw the hook into the next scene, you pull through it; you don't push, you *pull.* You're headed someplace, right? You're not just cruising around hoping you'll bump into the fucking road." He tore off pieces of paper and starting writing numbers on them, I, 1; I, 2; I, 3. "You're not just whacking off in the dark. Okay, wait a minute, where's the little bit with his drowned brother Gilbert—"

Four hours later, Ford Rexford had gone through—lightning fast—a pound of salami, five beers, and Theo's play. The young man had touched nothing, but he felt drunk. Rexford, with all his tales of Texas brawls and Broadway smut, had never talked to him like this before. In four hours, Theo learned more about writing plays than he'd known after thirteen years of studying and teaching them, and the awful weeks with Scottie Smith were no more than a speck of dirt that in his eye had caused terrible pain, but once washed out was too small even to be found. The truth of what the old playwright said stunned him. "Right," he whispered again and again, staring at the corkboard tacked with dozens of scraps of paper.

"Do you see?" Rexford kept asking.

"Right. I see."

Not that he saw through Rexford's metaphorical microscope, which remained largely scatological ("Clear out this steaming pile of shit") or sexual ("Kid, you gotta *come* right here. You got about twenty minutes till curtain. You can't go on rubbing it with a fuckin' feather. Get it *in*. You get in there, that woman's gonna take you to Paradise. Pump, pump, pump, *come!*"). Indeed, Theo was sure that Jane Nash-Gantz, having written so vigorously on Rexford's castration anxieties, would love to bring her tools of Freudian deconstruction to bear on his image of art as vaginal penetration. But what Theo saw, through Rexford's lens, was *Foolscap* coming to sharp quick life.

For three days they worked together in this way on *Foolscap*, with Theo rushing home from classes with beer and chiliburgers to find Rexford at the computer in his dirty clothes, impatiently typing up the finished scenes from the morning session. For three days, he appeared in no hurry to go back to Tilting Rock: Rhodora, he said, was away with the Dead Indians in Nashville playing a week's gig, and talking to record producers. He appeared not to want to work on his own play, about which he would say only that it was "stuck." (If there was in fact a new play at all—no one had ever seen it.) Each night after Theo returned from *Guys and Dolls* rehearsals, Rexford would give him notes for revisions, and then leave—for where he didn't say, but Theo would hear him stumbling in through the front door at dawn, yelling "Back to work! Rise and shine, Ryan. Let's do it!" He appeared to be intensely determined that they should "do it" until it was done. Theo had never worked with such concentration before in his life.

"Okay," growled Rexford on the third evening. "Give me a new ending line." He tore off half the last page.

"Me?" Theo rubbed at his reddened eyes.

"Is Marlowe in the kitchen?"

"Last line?"

"What? Am I asking you to blow me? Give me the line."

Theo gave him a line.

"No."

". . . So the book can be closed—"

"Rhythm's off. You don't want da da dúm, da da dúm. We ain't waltzing here, we're getting our fuckin' heads chopped off." The playwright beat the table with his palm. "*Dúm* da. *Dúm* da. *Dúm, Dúm. Dúm,* pause, *Dúm.* Funeral beat, see. Give me the line."

". . . Shut tight the book. Now . . . night . . . calls."

"Better."

Theo stared into the fireplace, tried again.

"Almost."

Theo walked to the kitchen and came back with a line.

"Okay, that's it! Write that down. Let me kiss you, you big Jew S.O.B." And Rexford grabbed his head, pulled it down, and nuzzled in the tawny hair. "That's it. That's a play."

Theo struggled to speak, then blurted out, "Ford . . ."

"You're right. You can't thank me." Scooping up the pages as they came from the printer, Rexford stacked together the script, slipped it into a manila folder, and stuffed it into his old leather jacket on the chair back. He began to talk about his intentions to express *Foolscap* to this agent and to call these producers, and he jabbered on about how Theo should plan to be in New York all next year, because while New York was a rank fetid cesspool where only sharks and trashfish survived, New York was Alpha and Omega, Parnassus, and Sinai. It was the Great White Way to theatrical glory. There was no other true Mecca, even for those who died there of neglect. To live elsewhere, even richly, was not fully to live.

". . . New York," the young man mumbled. "I don't know . . ."

Since childhood, Theo Ryan had responded only after, in his quick impatient mother's words, "mulling and mulling and *more* mulling!" He'd lived in a dream world, his mother had said (an odd criticism from one who made her living playing make-believe), and she had frequently rapped her fist in front of his forehead, calling, "Anybody home at Pooh Bear's house?" So

Theo was still trying to assimilate the changes in his play, while Ford was tearing through his future, like someone throwing clothes into a suitcase.

Slowly the younger man repeated, "I don't know. I can't just take off. I mean I have to earn a living. And I've promised Adolphus Mahan the draft of your biography—"

"Oh fuck me!" Rexford flung a beer can in the vicinity of a wastebasket. "Stop writing my life, and go live your own." The playwright pulled off his lumpy sweater, revealing white hairs above a sleeveless T-shirt.

"Don't finish the biography, Ford?" Theo tightened his large hands on the chair back.

"Let 'em wait till I'm dead. Let Nash-Gantz finish it. She'll have a field day when she finds out I was cornholed by my drill sergeant."

"Is that true?"

"Who knows?" Rexford threw open his bare stringy arms. "And, babe, who cares?"

The telephone shrieked at them. Theo looked around, realized it was black night outside; looked at his watch, and burst out, "Oh my God." He ran to the kitchen, fumbling for the receiver in the dark.

"Theo!" It was Jorvelle Wakefield. "Where are you? It's eight-fifteen. Iddy's hopping!"

"I'm coming! Oh my God! I'm sorry!"

Theo Ryan had been raised by his parents to believe in a number of inviolate truths—among them the Bill of Rights, the Democratic Party, the primacy of blood relations, and, grafted deep, deep in the bone, the Law of the Theatre: You never miss a performance, even should you break your leg while leaving your mother's deathbed. And even in a subway strike in a blizzard during a nuclear attack, You Are Never Late to Rehearsals. And only three rehearsals away from Opening Night too!

"You Are Never Late to Rehearsals. You Are Never Late to Rehearsals," throbbed like a great gong in Theo's head as he skidded back into the dining room, grabbing his sheet music off his stereo as he passed it. "Ford, I gotta go! I'm an hour late to rehearsal! Lock up!"

"I'll drive you!" Rexford snatched up his jacket, groped for his car keys. "You forgot a *rehearsal?*"

Two minutes later they were bouncing over the speed bumps on Campus Drive, glimpsing, as they flew by, a noisy swarm of students waving torches and placards on the green in front of Coolidge Building. "I thought the big rally was tomorrow," Theo said.

"Let 'em torch it. It's scary when the young don't want to torch the old. The world fills up with crap. Like me." Rexford pounded his chest. "Where's somebody to do to me what I did to O'Neill and Williams?"

"You're as far from old as it gets, Ford."

"That's not far enough. . . ." Rexford sighed.

"Did you see Maude this afternoon?" Theo asked him.

Ford squeezed his hairy shoulders up to his ears. "I can hack just so much of that sweet Jesus baloney, even from a radical activist."

"Well, don't you figure as long as you show up at the church, Rhodora'll take the rest on faith?"

"Rhodora deserves better," Rexford snapped, as if she were to blame for it. "Rhodora's something else, kid. She scares the shit out of me."

"That's what she says."

"Yeah? She's fucking real, Theo. . . ." Ford ran his hands up and down the steering wheel. "You know, I've gotten rich and famous off acting up, wild and moody, hard to handle. America demands that kind of adolescent assholery from its serious artists, and ambitious boy that I was, not to mention authentically out of control, I gave it to them. But it never much appealed to Rhodora. With her, bullshit's got no room to glide. . . . Hell, I don't know. . . ."

Theo glanced nervously at the way Ford was swerving the steering wheel (and therefore the car) from side to side. "You don't know what?"

"A lot." Ford shook his head. "Listen, babe. Let's worry about *you.* I want you to find yourself somebody to love."

Theo looked over at him curiously. "I'm trying to. I can't seem to get anywhere with Maude."

"Because Maude's not the one. You need a spitfire; big passive-aggressive guy like you needs a ball-buster." Rexford shook the young man's long sturdy thigh, then slapped it. "We both know who the one is, right?"

"What do you mean?"

Rexford leaned over and squeezed hard on Theo's leg. All he said was, "You wrote a good play." The battered Lincoln skidded onto the curb at the Spitz Center, and Theo ran around the front of the car. "Go on," the playwright said, sliding out the door.

"See you later," Theo yelled over his shoulder.

"Knock 'em dead, kid. I love yah."

Theo turned halfway up the steps and waved the rolled baton of sheet music down at Ford Rexford. Spotlighted by the street lamp, the playwright looked white and frail as he leaned against the gold car, shivering in his rumpled sleeveless T-shirt. Then he slipped back into the front seat, and reached over to the glove compartment for the hidden pint of amber whiskey, which he held out the window in a brief twinkling salute.

Theo was always sorry he hadn't said anything then about his belief that Ford was better than O'Neill and better than Williams, and that without writing another word remained the greatest playwright in America. He was sorry that he hadn't at least called out one more "Thank you" for *Foolscap*, even though Ford Rexford was to disappoint him so painfully, certainly was never to make phone calls or to express manuscripts; was to do far worse than that, was in many ways to betray him.

Still, a part of Theo was always sorry, remembering that the great playwright's last words to him had been I love you. Da dúm da.

CHAPTER

13

{Thunder and Lightning}

He that outlives this day and comes safe home,
Will stand a'tip-toe when this day is named.

Henry V

SO SINCERE was young Ryan's apology, so earnest and obedient had been his behavior throughout the weeks of rehearsal, that Thayer Iddesleigh was disposed to forgo the blistering sarcasm he'd sketched out to inflict on his leading man for his tardiness, particularly as the director hadn't yet reached a scene with Sky Masterson in it tonight.

Iddy had started strong at seven, but, as was his fate, he'd been slowed down. Slowed down by Harry the Horse's need to explain why he'd had to bring his hyperactive seven-year-old, Nash Gantz, along, and why he'd have to bring him every night from now on. By Costume's need to say why she wouldn't be treated anymore like an insect to be stepped on by the stage manager. By Sets' refusal to rebuild the Havana nightclub front so that it wasn't shorter than the people who were sitting outside it. By Mrs. Fruchaff's burning a hole through "A Bushel and a Peck."

But, thought Iddy, knocking back a slug of codeine-laced cough syrup, things were actually going pretty well; compared, that is, to when the two leads had refused to speak to each other, or to him, during the last week of *Damn Yankees*, or when the cow had died onstage at the dress rehearsal for *Fiddler*. No, thought Iddy, things could be much worse. He had Thursday and Friday, and

even Saturday until the curtain went up, left to rehearse in, with
full orchestra. And Saturday was sold out. As the lovers, Fletcher
and Ryan weren't bad at all. His lighting designer had quit a few
minutes ago, but he always did about this time, and he always
returned. Jenny Harte had failed to appear for rehearsal tonight,
when she was always so reliable, but she was only a chorus member, and there were too many of them anyhow. If Bill Robey
could stop worrying about the "psychological subtext" behind his
postponing for fourteen years his marriage to Miss Adelaide, he'd
be (while no Sinatra) a respectable Nathan Detroit. Nobody would
be looking at Robey anyhow, because (as Iddesleigh with great
self-satisfaction told his wife every night), the real show-stealer
was going to be Jorvelle Wakefield. "She's a natural! She can sing,
she can dance, she's got incredible comic timing—"

From under the pillow, Doris Iddesleigh had mumbled, "I don't
think black people like to be told they're naturals anymore,
Thayer. Please turn that video off and go to sleep. If I have to
listen to Frank Sinatra sing 'Sue Me' one more time, that's just
what I'm going to do to you in a divorce court."

"Very funny, Doris, very funny."

On stage now Iddy was watching the Hot Box girls' number,
"Take Back Your Mink." (Still without minks, the girls were
flinging in each other's faces a colorful flurry of raincoats, parkas,
and leather bomber jackets.) The director was trying to handle
Tara Bridges's sulky efforts to upstage Jorvelle (whom she hadn't
forgiven for getting to play Miss Adelaide), when the first sirens
wailed by the Spitz Center.

Of course, any world there may be outside the walls of a theatre,
is not a world of interest to those inside it. Mrs. Fruchaff
kept playing. Iddy kept darting in and out of the line of women,
shouting, "Pick it up. Right left right kick. Move your you-
know-whats!" There was a rumbling of thunder, very faint in the
soundproofed space. Ten minutes later, a second, louder, longer
set of sirens flew wailing past. More heads turned, turned back.
The show went on.

From their seats in the orchestra, where they were conferring
about some new business they planned to add to her drunk scene,

Maude Fletcher leaned over to whisper to Theo, the white silk of her blouse brushing his arm. "Is that a fire?"

Theo listened. "I noticed a bunch of students massed around Coolidge when I drove by. Some of them did have torches. Maybe they set fire to the place."

"Are you serious!" Maude Fletcher leapt to her feet, and ran up the aisle. "Something's happened at Bleecker!" she shouted back at him. "Tell Iddy I had to go!"

"Maude! Wait! You can't leave rehearsal!" Was this what Ford had meant by her "radical activism"?

"*Quiet!*" the director shouted from the stage. Then, "Where does *she* think she's going?!"

"She'll be right back," Theo promised.

But she wasn't. And it wasn't a fire. The Bleecker boycotters, learning this evening that Dean Tupper had not only denied them the right to hold their rally tomorrow, but that he'd summarily fired ten of the cafeteria workers, had just stormed Coolidge Building, where the provost was apparently holed up in his offices. Steve Weiner burst into the Spitz Center to tell the cast the news. Drenched, he ran up onto the stage, and over to Jorvelle by the piano. Mrs. Fruchaff's hands lifted stoically from the keys.

"They're arresting students over at Coolidge!" he said. "They were burning Tupper in effigy, and he called the cops on them! A fight's broken out!"

Everyone stopped where they were—in midkick, midstitch, midstaple. They looked at each other, and at Thayer Iddesleigh, who stared aghast at Steve Weiner (he recognized the short bearded man as the intruder who hung around Jorvelle Wakefield, who'd had the effrontery to claim to be her "voice coach"). Iddy hugged his black *Cabaret* sweatshirt, and turned red in the face. Not from fury against the fascistic Dean Tupper, either. From rage that an outsider had disrupted his rehearsal for something less momentous than news that the Spitz Center was at that instant an inferno of raging conflagration.

The shock paralyzed him a minute too long. Before he could move, his entire cast and crew, even his stage manager, even his four children, bolted. "Stop! Come back here!" he screamed to no avail. They scrambled off the stage, raced up the aisles, and poured out the exits. In seconds the whole huge beautiful space was empty and silent.

Silent, except for the mournful plink of notes on the piano as Mrs. Fruchaff slowly one-fingered "Take Back Your Mink." The old secretary had seen them come and go, young protesters and irascible police; she'd heard the shouts and the sirens through fifty years of grievance. Over Sacco and Vanzetti, Guernica, the Rosenbergs, Birmingham, Nixon, Soweto. Over everything from nuclear waste to curfews on campus. "They'll be back, Iddy," she called to the forlorn little man slumped in his black Bob Fosse pants on the edge of his director's stool.

He nodded morosely. Hadn't he just told himself things could get worse? He shouldn't forget it. He should remember the opening night of *Annie*, when the singing orphans had lost control of F.D.R.'s wheelchair, and plunged him into the orchestra pit.

On the campus green, pelting rain and stabs of lightning shooting all over the sky had driven off most of the festive students who'd come to support the fired Bleecker workers less out of political fervor than a desire to be caught up in mass hysteria, whatever its nature. And the arrival of two squad cars and the Rome police van with helmeted, armed men jumping out of it had proved enough to scare off the sincere but timid. Still others had been persuaded to slip away by reports that the administration was taking names. That still left about sixty students, twenty cafeteria workers, and a dozen faculty members to taunt Dean Buddy Tupper, Jr. as he stood on the Coolidge steps, rain pouring off his flattop, and glared down at them. The arrival of the police had caused a swell of obscene chants and boos, a rattling of placards, and a confused stampede, during which two deputies had gotten whacked with soggy torches. They'd retaliated by conking whatever they could reach with their swat sticks; unfortunately, in the confusion, one stick connected with the head of a female undergraduate, and knocked her unconscious. An ambulance was rushed to the scene to take her away. The police were now hauling the ringleaders up into the van by their hands and feet—all of them had dropped limply into the mud, just the way Professor Herbert Crawford was shouting at them to do.

The ringleaders were Crawford, a Bleecker salad chef, three dishwashers, and the two students who had used their torches to ignite a kerosene-soaked, eight-foot cloth dummy with a gray flattop and TUPPER painted across its fat stomach. Hung from the limb of a giant oak near the steps, the effigy smoldered in the rain now, but the storm had arrived too late to stop it from blazing into a charred rag of disrespect.

But Buddy Tupper was not about to be intimidated, as he'd explained emphatically through his megaphone two hours ago. He'd told them then to disperse, and no hard feelings. He'd told them then there was a university rule on the books against assemblage of more than twenty-five students after dark without written permission from the provost's office (his secretary had found this rule at 6:49). He'd told them that if they attached that effigy to a university tree and lit it, they'd be subject to arrest as well as disciplinary action. He'd warned them. They didn't know the Bone-Cruncher if they'd banked on his backing off. He hadn't backed off when unions had tried to infiltrate the campus; he hadn't backed off against Georgia Tech in much worse weather than this, with Cavendish down thirteen points in the fourth quarter, and two of his fingers broken.

While the camera of Channel 10 whirred, the provost stood, feet apart (like the opening of *Patton,* his favorite film next to *Knute Rockne, All American*), and stuck out his chin. He could see an indistinct huddle of half-dressed spectators watching him from the shelter of the nearby Forum café awning—among whom he thought he spotted Tara Bridges in pink tights. Well, they'd see a *Man* against a mob! He hadn't been happier since '73, when he'd routed the hippies who'd stormed Coolidge over the bombing of Cambodia.

Sure, he was a little surprised; this was '89, these weren't unwashed long-hairs, these were Reagan's children, future commodities traders and corporate execs. But last fall, they'd staged that El Salvador demonstration, and then they'd tried to clutter the campus with that South African shantytown, and now here they were up to this malarky. That idiot Herbert Crawford must have brainwashed them with his MTV and his Commie films and his old sixties footage of hippies wild in the streets. Listen to the Limey now, squealing, "Thah 'ole world's whatchin', yah bleedin' bloody bastards!" You wish! Well, let's see how 'Erbie likes a night in a Yank holding cell, instead of a swim in his lap pool.

But Tupper didn't see his major prob as Crawford (now being whisked away in the van with his comrades). Nor did he give a thought to Gen. Irwin Kaney, who, somehow escaping from the middle-aged daughter responsible for putting him to bed each night, had trotted across the lawn from the President's House, and pushed his way into the crowd. It had taken only minutes for Tupper's secretary to capture the Mississippian general, and relieve him of the umbrella with which he'd been poking at the protesters, as he ordered them with yipped Rebel yells to "Close up those lines! Remember why you're here, boys! You're here to liberate the people of South Vietnam from Northern Aggression! Go git 'em!"

As ever Tupper's major prob was Dean Claudia Pratt. The small woman of fifty, now in a yellow slicker, kept grabbing at his trench coat sleeve and hissing at him that he was out of his mind, and that she was taking the whole affair to the trustees. Let her. The best defensive was forever a good offense. Yanking his arm free, Tupper raised the megaphone, spit out the water, and bellowed at the crowd, "Listen to me! Those people just taken off, *including* those students, will all be charged with criminal offenses. Anyone who does not immediately clear this area will be arrested too. Any student who disobeys these instructions will also be expelled from this university. You have one minute to disperse!"

Dean Pratt shook his arm. "Buddy, you're going too far!"

As if they'd heard her and agreed, the crowd yelled back, "FIRE TUPPER! FIRE TUPPER! FIRE TUPPER!"

This wave of hate slapped at the provost's thrust-out chest without budging him. He showed the crowd his watch. "The clock is running!" Thunder crackled in echo, and a bolt of lightning lit up the bronze statue of Amos Latchett. Half the students and all the untenured faculty broke rank, dispirited by the storm and the departure of their leader, and began to shuffle aimlessly from cluster to cluster.

Then, out of the crowd ran a tall young dark-haired woman in black slacks and a short-sleeved white blouse. She flew up the steps, right beside Tupper, cupped her hands around her mouth, and shouted, "STRIKE! STRIKE! NOW!"

An instant of silence. And then the cafeteria workers started shouting it back at Reverend Maude Fletcher, "STRIKE! STRIKE! STRIKE! STRIKE!"

And then the students joined in, stamping their feet, jabbing their placards in air. "STRIKE! STRIKE! STRIKE! STRIKE!"

Maude Fletcher shouted, "THE CHAPEL! GO TO THE CHAPEL!" She rushed down the steps, and ran, waving her arm, back into the night. The whole crowd stirred, turned, and fled away—either after her, or back home—while the four remaining Rome policemen, frankly relieved, watched them go, and Channel 10 followed the action.

"Was that that goddamn Fletcher woman?" bellowed Tupper at the dean, flabbergasted.

"I hope you're satisfied," Dean Claudia Pratt snapped at him. "Yes, that was Reverend Fletcher. Our chaplain."

"Not for long," Tupper growled. "That's not what I call a minister of God. Not at Cavendish University!"

"Buddy, remember Tyler Gym!"

This was a below-the-belt reference to that damn Affirmative Action fracas when those damn lesbo feminist gym teachers had got the feds to cut off funding for the new phys-ed plant because the men had forty showers and they only had two.

Tupper swelled over the small dean. "Yeah, Claudia, well, don't talk to me about academic freedom. You're the one who tried to muzzle Burke Spooner!" (This counterblow was a reference to the fracas Pratt had stirred up over Professor Spooner's lecturing to Anthro 210 about the genetic inferiority of the Negro race.)

Dean Pratt wiped rain from her face in wild exasperation. "I am not talking about academic freedom, Buddy! I am talking about *all hell breaking loose here!* One of our students was just taken to the hospital! I don't know where in the world you think you are, but we are not behind the Iron Curtain in the nineteen fifties!"

"And never will be," vowed the provost. "If I have to arrest every man, woman, and child on this campus. You call this hell? This kind of gunfight doesn't scare me one iota."

Dean Pratt, a sensible woman, calmed herself and retied her

plastic rain hat. "I'm glad to hear it," she predicted. "Because we're about to get bombed good and heavy. See you in the bunker in the morning."

Here Claudia Pratt showed the foresight that was to make her president of Cavendish University when, three years after these events, General Kaney suddenly passed away—very suddenly, for possibly under the impression that he was back in a B-52 freeing South Korea from Northern Aggression, he drove his golf cart over the hill at Hillcrest Country Club and into the Rome reservoir below.

As Dean Pratt foresaw, on Thursday morning the Cavendish administration suffered saturation bombing. The girl who'd been struck on the head was in intensive care with a serious concussion. The whole story was on the morning news. The whole campus went on strike.

CHAPTER

14

{Storm Still}

O, I am fortune's fool.

Romeo and Juliet

THE BLEECKER STRIKE (organized that night in Wilton Chapel) spread like fire across the mountains of the campus. All university activities came to a halt. Cooks stopped cooking, teachers stopped teaching, students stopped doing much of anything except camping out with pizzas and Sony Walkmans on the green in front of Coolidge; yelling "OINK! OINK!" or "SIEG HEIL!" at the provost every time he stomped past them. On Thursday, his office resembled the U.S. Embassy in Saigon on that afternoon in '75 when the light at the end of the tunnel finally went out. From the crack he opened in his door, Tupper couldn't even see his secretary through the mayhem of students, parents of students, professors, clergymen, civic leaders, and television crew all crabbing at her to let them in. Most of these people thought, like Dean Claudia Pratt, that Buddy Tupper had gone too far.

Well, he didn't think so. Except for that girl who'd gotten herself knocked on the head (and that was a shame), he didn't think he'd gone far enough. Naturally, the ringleaders had got out of jail by dawn. Due to a gutless judge, they were let off with miserable minor charges for inciting riots and singeing that magnificent oak tree branch, and Herbert Crawford would have no trouble hiring a fancy defense lawyer (considering the fortune Cavendish was paying him!) to get those piddling charges thrown out. Tupper couldn't even fire Crawford due to his damn tenure.

But he had fired the salad chef and dishwashers (on top of the ten workers he'd already dismissed), and he had expelled the two students, and he had sworn publicly to expel every student and to fire every (untenured) teacher and every cafeteria worker who wasn't back on the job by 9:00 A.M. on Friday—which gave them a whole day to come to their senses. Fair warning. And that Maude Fletcher (whose three-year contract, thank God for small favors, ran out in June)—that harpy was out of here!

As for everyone's boo-hooing about the poor cafeteria workers, and about how shocking it was to hear how little those workers earned—well, they'd been earning that little for a long time, during which none of these sob sisters had ever given them a minute's thought. As for the sniveling parents, let them tell their brats to attend the classes they were paying nineteen thousand a year for, and then they wouldn't be expelled. As for the administrators whining about bad publicity, and the History Department whining about guest speakers refusing to cross picket lines to appear at their conference, and even as for the football coach moaning because his best halfback, Joe Botzchick, had been arrested and expelled; let them all bite the same bullet Tupper was staunchly grinding between his teeth. Nothing was going to push the Bone-Cruncher back from his position on the line of scrimmage. Losing yardage was not the way to stay number one.

Remember Waldo College, that once worthy rival of Cavendish on the other side of the mountains? Waldo had gotten soft, voted unions in, put students on the board of trustees, dropped the core curriculum *and* grades, let women try out for baseball; in general rushed off like lemmings over the cliff of kneejerk liberal politics into a sea of sentimental slop, and where had it led them? They'd been *bought by the Japanese,* that's where! Japan owned Waldo College, fifty miles away! And Claudia Pratt thought he'd gone too far! What did she want, what had happened at Stanford? The whole student body out screaming, "Hey hey ho ho! Western Culture's got to go," with Jesse Jackson leading the chorus? If Western Culture went, who the hell would pay people like her and Herbie Crawford big fat salaries to sit around griping about Western Culture?

Red lights were flashing on the provost's phone like flak over Hamburg. That little jerk Thayer Iddesleigh had been calling every hour. And Norman Bridges was back on line three. Tupper barked at his secretary to tell those two fairies either to take the goddamn heat or get out of the goddamn kitchen. She decided to paraphrase this message, explaining that Dean Tupper was still in a meeting and unable to come to the phone.

Thayer Iddesleigh was a wreck. Even his wife (who'd been buffeted by so many years of Iddy's theatrical tempests that she could sleep upon the raft of their bed through his most torrential gales), even she was worried about him. He sat with all the lights out in his den, in the director's chair with his name on it, sat there limply, dialing the phone in his lap, hour after hour, without a word. She couldn't goad him into a groan, much less a shriek. They'd canceled his play. His own cast and crew and orchestra had done it to him. They'd met this morning behind his back, under the instigation of that female Judas, that Benedict Arnold to the Theatre, that witch Maude Fletcher, his *leading lady* (ha, ha, that would teach him to give outsiders a chance); and they had voted to "honor the strike" by refusing to perform on campus.

The Spitz Center was dark. But not as dark as Iddy's soul, from which all light had been snuffed, leaving him in black despair. And irony of ironies, who was the one person to stand up for the play's-the-thing, for the Honor of the Glorious Tradition that the Show Must Go On? Theo Ryan, that's who. Ha ha. Fat lot of good it had done Ryan, of course, trying to convince those *amateurs* of their Duty to the Stage. Never again. Never again. He'd resign from C.F.D.C. as soon as that you-know-what Tupper answered his phone.

Norman Bridges was a wreck. He'd passed the morning unable to decide whether to honor the strike by canceling Thursday's regular senior faculty meeting (as seven members of the department insisted), or to disavow the strike by holding the meeting anyhow (as eight members demanded). Finally Bridges put memos in everyone's mailbox urging each to follow his or her individual conscience and attend or not attend a meeting that would be held, but not held in Ludd Lounge; it would be moved to the Bridgeses' living room, off campus.

This agonized attempt at compromise by the chairman was scorned by the few Luddites who bothered to check their mailboxes that afternoon. Jonas Marsh fired off a two-page fulmination, jammed it in Bridges's mailbox, and went back to the library. Jorvelle Wakefield and Steve Weiner returned to the picket line outside Bleecker. Marcus Thorney and four of his followers joined the snoozing old Mortimer and Lovell in Ludd Lounge, and waited there fuming for half an hour for an official announcement of the results of the vote for the new chairman. Finally, they gave up and left to get ready to drive to Mrs. Ludd's estate in Asheville for the black-tie dinner party in honor of Thorney's winning the Ludd Book Prize.

Promptly at four, John Hood showed up at the Bridges home with a bottle of sherry, and found Norman in the living room trying to talk his daughter into turning off her soap opera so he could introduce her to Vic Gantz. It was a meeting that only they and Theo Ryan attended, and at which Theo spent most of the time arguing with Tara and Vic in the kitchen about whether or not they should put on *Guys and Dolls*.

"We don't appear to have a quorum," sighed Bridges, alternatively clutching his stomach and his head. "I guess we should cancel the meeting. What do you think, John?"

"Dear me. I suppose we should," said the gentle Miltonist.

Bridges had only two solaces: One was that he didn't have to announce that Dean Tupper appeared to have suddenly developed reservations about offering that last Ludd Chair to Scottie Smith, and might be secretly planning to give it to the French Department as he'd threatened to do. The other consolation was that he wouldn't have to tell three men who disliked Marcus Thorney that it looked as if Marcus Thorney was going to be their new chairman. Well, at least, he sighed, after this interminable term was over, they wouldn't have Dr. Bridges to kick around anymore. Maybe now Tupper would let him take early retirement. Maybe

Tara and he could leave their daughter the house here, and move to Florida, and he could write that Whitman book, and Tara could . . . Norman Bridges pulled himself together, and offered his guests some chocolate eclairs.

Theo Ryan was a wreck. Working on his play with Ford Rexford would have been by itself enough stimulation to last him a month. Then add the rehearsals. Add seeing Maude Fletcher rush up the Coolidge steps and start the strike. Add the all-night meeting in the chapel, the sign-painting, the telephoning. Then elation plummeting to gloom in the morning.

He was leaving the chapel with Steve and Jorvelle to go get breakfast when the black Mazda sports car pulled up. It was Herbert Crawford, in black leather, who bounced out of the driver's seat. "Steve-o!" he yelled, and they all turned. "Where's Maude?" he called. But the tall, dark-haired woman was already rushing down the steps towards him. And—as Effie Fruchaff had predicted only yesterday—she didn't give Theo the time of day when she flew past, and flung herself into the arms of the revolutionary leader, who embraced her with obvious familiarity. "Maudie, girl, you did it! A bloody strike!" They spun each other in circles of delight, then sped away together in the Mazda.

"I tried to tell you," Steve said.

"No, you didn't," Theo snapped. "Tell me what?"

"The Marxist and the minister," Jorvelle said. "Maybe it's just political," she added with an attempt at a comforting smile.

"Maybe it's the lap pool," Steve shrugged.

"I never liked her for you anyhow," Jorvelle said.

"You sound like an oddsmaker at the track," Steve told her. Theo strode off, ignoring them.

At noon when the brief *Guys and Dolls* meeting took place, Theo's mind felt curiously cool and clear. And although he lost the argument not to cancel the play, he had at least stood up and argued, cheeks hot, heart thumping, even in the face of attacks on his politics, his character, and his intelligence. Even when Jorvelle herself had shouted at him, and Maude Fletcher had cut him off in midsentence to call for a vote. Relentlessly he'd offered analogies, compromises, counterproposals. One of his ideas had been to put on the play for the *benefit* of the fired cafeteria workers. But some of the cast thought this too weak a statement of solidarity; others thought it too strong. In the end, the consensus of the group was to do what everybody else was doing. Shut down. Still, Theo told himself, he'd spoken out, although surprised to find his the voice of the opposition.

On Thursday night Theo suffered still more blows. Until then, he hadn't been back to his house since he'd run out of it with Ford Rexford, late to his Wednesday rehearsal. When he finally did return home, he found the place the mess he'd left it. Ford had never come back. Worse, there'd obviously been a long power failure during the lightning storm the night before; the clocks were hours late, the refrigerator was smelly. Worse, Ford had clearly not bothered to shut off the computer before they'd rushed off; the hard drive had crashed, taking with it into oblivion the revised version of Theo's play. Ford didn't appear to have made any back-up copies, or at least Theo couldn't find any. And, as it proved, worst of all, there was a note stuck in his screen door. It said:

Call me. Rhodora.

She answered on the first ring, and didn't waste words. "Where is he?" she said. "And don't lie to me."

"Ford?"

"I got home from Nashville last night, no note, no Ford. And I haven't seen or heard squat since." Rhodora's voice sounded more angry than frightened.

"Ford?" Theo pulled over a kitchen chair and sat down.

"Shit, Theo! Yes, *Ford!*"

Theo was very tired, and not really worried. Rexford was, after all, notoriously erratic. "I don't know, Rhodora. he dropped me off at rehearsal last night about eight. I thought he was coming back here. He's been here helping me with my play." Moving the phone to his other hand, he opened his refrigerator and began sniffing its contents. "Have you called—"

Her voice sharpened. "Yes, dammit! Highway patrol, hospitals, Cherokee's, T.W.'s. What's been wrong with your damn machine all night!"

"I'm sorry. The power was off, and I was gone. We've been in the middle of a strike on campus. You try Bernie Bittermann?"

"Yes. He said to try the morgue. No such luck. You sure you're not coverin' for Ford? Don't put me through this."

"Rhodora, Jesus." Theo turned to the sink and splashed water on his face. "I don't know! He could be anywhere." He glanced out at the dining room table where the corkboard still lay, pinned with scraps of paper. "He's not dead, you'd have heard!"

"He's gonna wish he was." Rhodora hung up.

Pulling off his grubby shirt, Theo went to clear his head in the shower. Afterwards, he called the local bars; nothing. Was it possible that Rexford had joined the riot? It was just the sort of thing he'd do. But the playwright hadn't been arrested, and he hadn't come with the crowd to the chapel. Theo gritted his teeth, and called Maude at the chapel office; she said Rexford had skipped their last session, and had spent the one before that alternatively fighting about the existence of God and reciting Hank Williams songs. "Try the local bars," she suggested.

While his pasta boiled, he called Bernie Bittermann, who said, "What else is new?"

At his counter eating the spaghetti, Theo called the Rome police and described the gold Lincoln. Nothing. After two more talks with Rhodora, he even called Ford's son Pawnee in Taos, who said sarcastically, "Ford who?" and added, "I don't want him buried next to my mother if he *is* dead."

Steve Weiner and Vic Gantz were no help; neither of them had seen the playwright since he'd been with them that night at the Bomb Shelter.

Who else had been with them that night at the Bomb Shelter?

Jenny Harte. She seemed to know Ford. Where was she? She'd missed the rehearsal Wednesday, hadn't she? And the meeting about whether to strike, she'd missed that too, hadn't she? When Theo got no answer at her apartment, he started phoning anyone he could think of who might know her, troubled to realize he knew so little about Jenny's life, when he was after all supposed to be her "adviser." His stomach had begun souring. Finally he reached Cathy Bannister. Cathy was too worried about her fiancé Joe Botzchick (who'd been not only arrested, but expelled—

which meant the end of his football scholarship, his pro career, and all their plans) to get upset about Jenny Harte. She didn't even know her all that well. But she was pretty sure she had seen Jenny yesterday . . . at the Bomb Shelter . . . early on, in the afternoon.

With somebody?

Yes, she thought so. "Mr. Rexford was with her."

Color sank out of Theo's face. "Ford Rexford?"

"Remember, Dr. Ryan, you had him talk to our class last year?" She thought a bit, then added, "Somebody else, seems like, said Jenny'd gone out with him a couple of times lately." Cathy tried to be helpful. "Is it important for you to get in touch with her? You could try her folks in Charlotte."

By morning, Jenny Harte's parents also wanted to know where she was. But no one appeared to be able to tell them.

As fate, always promiscuous and wasteful, would have it—on Friday Theo's opposition to the play's cancellation became moot. Dean Pratt had her way. In emergency session that morning, members of the board of trustees of Cavendish University (as many of them as could get there) met first alone, then with the top-level administrators, then, by courtesy, with President Kaney, who from time to time advised then strenuously to "Fall back and take cover!"

They did just that. They sat the administration down with a group of cafeteria workers, a group of faculty members (chaired by Herbert Crawford and Maude Fletcher), and a group of students. They interviewed privately the police chief and the football coach and Dean Pratt. And then they called in Buddy Tupper, and in his phrase, the whole bunch went offsides, grabbed him by the short hairs, and busted his chops. Although long after Tupper had retired with his trophies to Pineshurst, he would deny that he'd ever surrendered, he did something that could be paraphrased as that. His other option was to resign, and he wouldn't give them the satisfaction. At three-thirty, the white flag flew from the suite atop Coolidge Building.

The fired Bleecker workers were reinstated. The salaries of all cafeteria workers were raised by six-and-a-half percent. (Tupper's only comfort was that it was still not enough to live on.) Classes resumed. (At least the goldbricking faculty would have to show up to teach them.) Lines formed at Bleecker Dining Hall. (At least the students would have to eat the junk served there.) The expulsion of the two students was reduced to a week's suspension, and Buddy Tupper signed a personal letter of regret to the parents of the girl in the hospital with the concussion. The strike was over.

But at least some of the administrators and some of the faculty (including Marcus Thorney) had sent the provost messages that they'd been wholeheartedly on his side. And the same Rome clergyman who'd called Maude Fletcher "a modern Joan of Arc," took it back when he heard she was reputed to be having an affair with Herbert Crawford, a British Marxist separated from his wife. These were the small comforts that kept Tupper company in his lonely bunker, as he looked down Friday afternoon at shirtless boys and barefoot girls climbing all over the statue of poor Amos Latchett, who had a sombrero on his head and a beer bottle in his hand.

And so Friday evening, Doris Iddesleigh had the odd experience of feeling delight when her husband emerged from their bedroom in his black Bob Fosse T-shirt, when he lowered his whistle around his neck and marched once more into the breach of Show Biz. His cast, crew, and orchestra returned; all was, if not forgiven, forgotten in the mayhem as rehearsals at the Spitz Center frantically resumed where they'd left off in the middle of "Take Back Your Mink," and went on all night long.

Yet, sadly, Theo Ryan could not enjoy his inadvertent victory over the those who'd cried cancel. Too much else had happened. He could not retrieve his play from the computer, he could not stop wishing Herbie Crawford would drop dead, he could not find Ford Rexford, or Jenny Harte. Of course, Ford might have flown to Key West to go fishing or to Las Vegas to lose his shirt. Jenny Harte might gone to the Library of Congress to work on her dissertation. Herbie Crawford might in fact drop dead. But Theo didn't really believe in any of these possibilities. On Saturday night, the show went on without Jenny, as by that miracle of communal will, the show always does go on, and Theo Ryan, the trouper his parents had trained him to be, went on with it, playing the role of the lucky Sky Masterson.

Everyone said *Guys and Dolls* was a triumph; even Iddy admitted that nothing really too noticeable had gone wrong. True, John Montemaggio had a fever of 101° from the infection in the twenty-two stiches on his finger, but it gave his portrayal of Big Julie a nasty heated quality that fit the part. True, little Nash Gantz had refused to be parted from his father, Harry the Horse, and had clung to him onstage through the whole show, but apparently everyone thought it a nice modern touch to make one of the gamblers a single parent. True, the Havana nightclub had toppled over during the fight scene, but in an expressionistic way that might have looked planned. As expected, Nathan Detroit had forgotten the words to "Sue Me," but no one had much noticed, for as Iddy had predicted, the audience went so wild for Miss Adelaide they gave her a standing ovation.

But if Jorvelle Wakefield stole the show, Theo Ryan had never performed so well before in his life. He was performing in the most absolute sense, of acting what he did not feel, was sure he would never feel again, even if the *Rome Gazette* had described his performance as "the magnetic and charming birth of a new Spitz star." By Saturday night he did not feel like singing and dancing and falling in love. He felt like crawling in a hole.

By Saturday afternoon Jenny Harte's parents knew where their daughter was. And they telephoned Theo Ryan, who had to tell Rhodora Potts, who accused him, unjustly, of having known all along. After all, he was the girl's faculty adviser; not that Jenny Harte was a girl (in fact, she was a year older than Rhodora); and not that she'd come to him for advice, or to anyone else apparently. Jenny had already made her decision when she phoned her parents from London and told them she'd flown to England with a man, but that they shouldn't worry about her. She planned to work there on her dissertation (on endings—suitably enough).

She told her parents she thought this man and she might go to Cornwall on the southwest coast of England, which—as she had always loved the Arthurian legends—she had always dreamed of seeing.

So Ford Rexford had flown her there. He had a way of making people's dreams come true.

III

{*Scene: An Island*}

CHAPTER

15

{Enter Time, a Chorus}

Time travels in divers paces with divers persons.

As You Like It

MAY WAS IN THE MOUNTAINS, profligate with beauty. On the Cavendish campus, rose vines climbed the walls; students collected like tulips on the green, their faces lifted to the sun. Classes had ended; exams were brief distractions; young bodies were restive for summer.

But all was suddenly Russian winter in the eyes of Theo Ryan. In every direction the sky darkened, with no dawns in sight. In the fall Marcus Thorney would be chairman. Dean Tupper had made the announcement "with pleasure." Tupper's pleasure was no doubt sincere, since Thorney had stood by him (at least in his heart) during the Bleecker strike; since certain things (both political and personal) had since been heard about Steve Weiner and Jorvelle Wakefield; since Thorney was Mrs. Ludd's choice; and since (which was helpful) Thorney was apparently also the will of the department—by a two-vote majority.

It was ironic to Theo that the only blue speck in his sky was that Tupper had dumped Scottie Smith before finding out that (1) Theo had also been one of those all-nighters at Wilton Chapel, and (2) that Theo had spoken too soon when he'd claimed he could guarantee Ford Rexford's premiering a play at the Spitz Center. Imagine telling the provost that Ford Rexford would commit himself to anything an hour from now, much less a year. Stupid. As stupid as (yes, Effie Fruchaff was right) not seeing that Maude Fletcher and Crawford were obviously the talk of the campus. Where were his eyes? He was too dumb to have deserved tenure. Except what was tenure but the misery of being stuck at Cavendish until he was lowered into his reserved gravesite? Stuck at Cavendish forever, and alone. Or so he said to Steve and Jorvelle as the three sat morosely in a dark booth of the Bomb Shelter, pouring beer after beer on their wounds.

"I should have never come back to North Carolina," Jorvelle sighed.

"I should never have trusted Ford. Or Jenny. Or Maude," Theo sighed.

Jorvelle shook her head in a wobble. "Oh, come on! Maude was involved with Herbie before you ever met her."

"Why do you have to argue about everything?" Theo snapped.

"I'm sorry, Thee."

"I'm sorry, Jor."

They drank more beer.

"At least you got contact lenses out of that show," Jorvelle said after a while. "Even if you are back to those old corduroys."

"Oh, leave me alone."

"I'm sorry."

"I'm sorry."

"We should have never let ourselves start thinking I could win," Steve sighed. "Call Yale back, Jor. Take the offer."

"You take the Columbia offer," she sighed. Both knew they wouldn't do it. She would go to Amsterdam on her Guggenheim to study slave trade records for her book *Decolonizing the Canon*. Steve would go to Bread Loaf to teach Southern fiction out of the heat. In September they'd both come back to Cavendish. They knew that.

Theo, who had no offers not to take, didn't know exactly what to do. And yet he found he had not dropped into a slump at the bottom of the slough of despond, despite his old habit. Through the next few weeks, rage against Ford Rexford pinched him everywhere in sharp hot bites, and kept him in constant motion. To think of his wonderful revision of *Foolscap* was a gnawing ache. For, on top of everything else, Rexford had unforgivably taken off with the one copy of the revised play that he had printed. Had tossed it somewhere in the rat's nest of that miserable gold Lincoln, and then no doubt tossed away the Lincoln too. Just the way he had tossed away Rhodora Potts.

As for Rhodora, Theo told himself she had had no right to blame him for Ford's leaving her. But it was no use. Blame buzzed in his head while he was grading papers until he had to reread the same scribbled bluebook half a dozen times. He blamed himself not only for Rhodora's abandonment but for Jenny Harte's seduction. The loss of his play and (as he saw it) the inevitable ruin of his graduate student fused in his thoughts until the manuscript and the young woman became one grand theft by the man whose Official Life *ought* to be published, as a warning to anyone else foolish enough to trust a faithless irresponsible bastard like Joshua Ford Rexford. Theo tortured himself with how he might have stopped Ford if only he hadn't invited him to lecture to his class, hadn't taken him to the Spitz Center; if only he had never recommended Jenny Harte for graduate school, never advised her to work on the endings of plays.

If only he had made Rhodora listen carefully to those tapes of Rexford's past—those haphazard chronicles of a hit-and-run life, crowded with accidents, littered with waste; she would have known it had to end this way. Ford had been bolting from commitment for half a century. Theo could have quoted to her Rexford's own dictum on playcraft: "The end must be in the beginning. Look for it there." He always said: See how life imitates art.

So obsessive on the subject was Theo that even Dr. Ko (who was paid to listen) said she was tired of hearing about it, and that he talked as if Jenny Harte were a helpless child snatched from her nursery while the watchdog (that is, Theo) failed to keep awake. "Plus, he didn't leave you," the therapist added in her infuriatingly sensible voice. "Rhodora's the one who got left."

"He took my play!"

"He took the revisions. Can't you redo them from your draft?"

"He ruined my computer! And he tore the draft in a thousand pieces!"

"Well, before Ford pushed you, hadn't it been sitting in a drawer for years?"

"Thanks a lot, Dr. Ko! I've been coming here for years and where has that gotten me?!"

"For one thing, you know how upset you are."

"You think I'm upset, you should see Rhodora."

"You keep talking about Rhodora. How do you feel about her?"

"I feel *awful.*"

Rhodora was not taking things sitting still. When Theo had asked her if there were anything he could do for her, she said, "Kill him." Then she said, "No. Find him, so I can kill him myself."

As soon as she'd learned for certain that Rexford had left her, she had left his house. She had stuffed her two enormous vinyl suitcases with her clothes, picked up her blue guitar, her tapes and records, and all her bright potted flowers, and moved out of the beautiful yellow pine chalet high above Tilting Rock.

Theo was there that Sunday to help her pack. He heard her when she called Bernie Bittermann and told him, "I'm going, I'm not takin' a thang I didn't come with, I want that understood for a fact. And if y'all want all this shit just left sitting here, and this ton of dead meat Ford shot cleaned outta this 'frigerator 'fore it rots, you're gonna have to hire somebody to come do somethin' with it. 'Cause I'm not." Then, in her brother's truck, she had driven without a backward glance down the mountain named in her honor; she hadn't so much as closed the windows, or locked the door.

Bittermann's sympathetic assurance to Rhodora that Ford didn't deserve her met with, as he told Theo, a curse so chilling it belonged in a Rexford play—and indeed would probably appear in one if Rhodora had ever expressed the same sentiment to the man directly, and if the man ever wrote another play. Bittermann knew enough of the moods of, as he called them, "Ford victims" not to bother begging Rhodora please to reconsider. And as for her younger brother, T.W. had said succinctly that if he ever got near that house again it would be to throw kerosene at it and torch the place, and the same was true if he ever got near Ford Rexford.

So it was Theo whom Bittermann persuaded to close the lodge, and arrange to hire a local housekeeper. Theo agreed after Bittermann told him he'd had a letter from Rexford with instructions to make over by deed to Rhodora the chalet (and the mountain). All Ford wanted from it was the army trunk with his manuscripts in it, and the personal effects on his desk. Rhodora was also assigned, as of now, all the royalties from his play *Her Pride of Place,* and all future royalties from the play he'd started writing while living with her. The business manager asked Theo if he would find Miss Potts and tell her that the documents of ownership, signed and legalized, had been sent to her, c/o Rexford's local bank.

"All right," said Theo, "But Ford's a complete asshole if he thinks he can justify what he did with goddamn presents!"

Bittermann sighed into the phone. "Young man, this is no news to anyone, including Ford."

"Where is he, dammit! If he's calling you and writing you, I bet you know where he is, Bernie, and you're just not telling me!"

The business manager did not take offense at this shouted accusation; it was the rustle of doves compared to many decades of other voices raised in his ear about his famous client. His phone, his ear, were only conduits between the lightning and the man the lightning would have struck if it had only been able to find him. Mildly, Bittermann continued, "He's in England. The letter was sent by Josef Middendorf, his London agent."

"Christ Almighty, I know who Buzzy Middendorf is, Bernie. I've wasted the last two years of my life finding out about Ford Rexford's."

"Then maybe *you* can find out where he called from. I can't, as I am only a C.P.A. and not the FBI."

"How do you think Jenny Harte's parents feel!"

"Theo, I've haven't an inkling in the world. But, let's give the devil his due, he doesn't appear to have *shanghaied* Miss Harte, who is after all considerably beyond her majority."

"I want my play back!"

"So you've explained, and when he runs out of money and calls again, I'll see if he knows where it might be."

"You do that!"

Bittermann, unruffled, asked the young professor to pass along his warm wishes to Miss Potts, of whom he was as fond as he'd been of the third Mrs. Rexford, his favorite of the four certified wives. "I did let myself hope," he sighed, "that she'd make it till he finished the play."

Rhodora, barefoot, wearing no makeup, her tight jeans and halter as black as the hair that fell in two straight pigtails down to her lap, sat playing her guitar on the stoop of her brother's little split-level when Theo drove up the dirt driveway. Her response to the, as it were, separation settlement was to throw her coffee mug at the mailbox. A hot line of stain sprayed across Theo's shirt sleeve. "Oh, shit, I'm sorry," she said. "But that bastard didn't have the sleazebag guts to tell me to my face he was runnin' like a rabbit. Not even a gawddamn note. And now he's sending me *deeds!?* Sending me *contracts!* Come on in, dammit, Theo. Deeds! Care of his agent care of his manager care of his fuckin' bank? That bastard."

She didn't want the chalet or the mountain, and she didn't want any royalties on *Her Pride of Place,* or any new play that Ford might finish either. "He don't know finishing anyhow," she said, her eyes bitter. "He just knows quittin'. You want some coffee? In a cup this time? And, hey, sugar, I'm sorry I missed your show."

"Don't worry about it."

"You know I'd of come if I hadn't had to be at Cherokee's both nights. Lord, I didn't know what the hell I was singing half the time anyhow. I'd totally lost my mind that whole weekend long. How'd *Guys and Dolls* go?"

"They say, fine. I was pretty crazy myself. But I guess 'the show goes on' okay even when we're nuts, right?" He rubbed her shoulder. "Sell the chalet then, Rhodora. Or rent it out, and get yourself a new place. You don't plan to stay here at T.W.'s? You could use the money, couldn't you?"

"Lissen! I had a job singing at Cherokee's when I met that asshole, and I still got a job." They went inside and she handed him a mug of coffee. "I even got a goddamn Nashville record company that wants me to do some of my songs for them."

"You do? That's great."

"Yeah, everything's great."

"Which songs?"

She shrugged. "I don't know. The mood I'm in now I can think of a heap of sad, mean ones." She leaned across the white tin kitchen table where they were sitting, and grabbed away her coffee mug so fast he was afraid she might be going to throw this one at him too, but instead she took it to the cheap new two-burner stove and poured herself another cup. "What'd he pick *Pride of Place* to give me for anyhow?" she snarled. "Some old dried-up spinster running a funeral parlor! Whatta you bet, he's imagining me *dead,* so he can cry about it and stop feeling guilty, that's what I bet!"

"You used to say you loved that play."

Her eyes were hot, frowning against the tears. "Yeah. I used to say I loved the asshole that wrote it too." She reached over and pressed her hand like a slap stopped before it reached his cheek. Two blue beaded bracelets slid up her bare arm. "I did, too. I loved him. Didn't you?"

Theo nodded, his chest tight. "Bastard."

"Right." She scrubbed at the table top with a napkin. "Couple of jerks, that's us. We both got fucked. And while we're sitting here crying in the woods, he's off buying evahbody drinks at some gawd-damn English pub, evahbody shouting, 'We love you, Ford.' "

He shook his head. "Poor Jenny Harte."

Rhodora threw the napkin at the sink. "Poor Jenny Harte, my ass! Why don't you take my wedding dress and send it to poor Jenny Harte, and she can wear it to Buckingham Palace!"

"Oh, Rhodora. I know." He took her hand and held it against his face.

Theo left her seated again on the front door stoop, her blue-painted guitar cradled in her lap, her long red fingernails plucking from its steel strings a hard grieving sound.

"If I could stick a sharp clean knife in my head and cut every-thing that's him out of it, I would," she called to Theo as he walked away. "But isn't that the sad part, how the mind just goes on? Come see me. Don't be a stranger." She leaned down over the guitar.

"That's a nice tune," he turned and said. "Take care, Rhodora."

✻   ✻   ✻

The day after the spring term officially ended at Cavendish, Theo drove back over to Tilting Rock, up the high winding road bordered with bright foxglove that led to the top of "Rhodora's Mountain." The big vaulted living room of the chalet smelled of wood and ash still in the fireplace. Shriveled petals of yellow lilies lay curled at the foot of their vases, and a dead bee floated in the whiskey glass beside the photograph of Rhodora singing at Cherokee's bar. Collecting the bills and papers cluttered on the giant oak door Ford used for a desk, Theo threw them on top of all the scripts packed in the dented black army footlocker near the man's writing chair. It was a sprung-cushion, drink-stained, cigarette-scarred armchair. Its name was Chester, as the desk was called Sharon, the car Abe, and the birch tree outside the study window, Lavinia. Rexford named all the objects in his life, treated them like people; and, it seemed, thought Theo, as if the reverse were also true.

On the desk under a biography of Sir Walter Raleigh checked out of the Tilting Rock library, Theo found carelessly piled eighty or so pages of typed paper. Three-fourths of an unfinished play. The play's title was *Principles of Aesthetic Distance*. It seemed to have a woman like Rhodora in it. It seemed to be about a love affair between her and a young professor who taught drama theory. This man loved plays passionately, but lived without love or passion.

"Bastard," said Theo Ryan.

He sat down in the chair with the pages resting on his knees. After an hour, the last page dropped from his hand, and his eyes closed. What he had read was as good as anything Ford Rexford had ever written, and that he was right about that, the young professor who loved plays knew absolutely, beyond the possibility of denial.

". . . Bastard," he said quietly again.

Then he stretched up out of the chair, wiped his face against his sleeve, and picked up the telephone on the desk beside Rhodora's picture. He called Bernie Bittermann in New York. First he discussed methods of shipping the footlocker to Rexford's agent in London.

"Did you look for a manuscript?" the C.P.A. asked eagerly.

"Ford told Buzzy Middendorf he'd finished his play, but he didn't have a copy with him. Said he'd had to leave for England on the spur of the moment—"

"Goddamn right!"

"—and he'd left the manuscript in Tilting Rock. Was that a complete fabrication? IS there a new play, Theo? Believe me, a lot of people need to know. Morris and Amanda are out of their minds."

Theo looked at the photograph of Rhodora, then out the wide window that opened onto hills, pine green, ridging the sky. As his head turned, a blackbird winged past as if it had flown out of Rhodora's hair and soared into the dark hushed woodland of her mountain.

"Yes, there's a new play, Bernie."

Bittermann's relief came whistling through the phone all the way down the coast of America. "Great! For God's sake, make a copy and send it to me."

"No," Theo said.

"No? What do you mean 'no'?"

"You tell Ford," Theo said, "that *I* have his play. And that I'm coming over there to get mine."

" 'Coming over there?' Coming where? You don't know where he is."

"England."

"Theo, you're sounding crazy. Why do you think we have postal systems? Just send me the play. Did you read it?"

"Yes."

"And?"

"It's wonderful." Why mention that it wasn't finished?

"Send it! And I swear to you, Theo, I swear, I'll do what I can to locate yours. Maybe Ford didn't even take it with him."

"Then I'll ask him where he left it." Theo rolled the manuscript against his side, and slapped it against the desk. "That's the deal, Bernie."

Bittermann groaned in disgust. "You're going to fly to England, you're going to wander around who knows where, looking for Ford who could be, I swear to you, *anywhere,* just so you can maybe take a God forbid swing at him, and maybe kill him before we can get his play on so Morris and Amanda don't sue the idiot's estate for what he owes them? For that, you're flying to England? You're as big a lunatic as he is."

Theo put the picture of Rhodora in his pocket. He said, "No, I'm not. But I am damn big for a Jew."

Bittermann spluttered, "What are you talking like that to me for?"

"I'm quoting your client, Bernie. That's the first thing he ever said to me. 'You're damn big for a Jew.' Well, when I put my big fist in his redneck face, he's going to find out how right he was."

"Fists, racial slurs. You sound like Ford." A long sigh, heavy with years of Rexford, blew gently through the receiver. "In the end, they always do. They turn violent. They start calling him 'redneck,' " said Bittermann. "God knows, that's the least of the man's sins. . . . Okay. So call me if you find him. And give him a little clonk on the head from me. Just don't knock anything loose. Looser . . . You need a loan for the plane?"

A week later, Rhodora Potts sublet Theo's house for the summer. The day she moved in, he left for New York, surprised to hear himself telling people that he was flying home.

CHAPTER
16

{A Banquet Is Prepared}

The course of true love never did run smooth.

A Midsummer Night's Dream

INDIFFERENT TO JUNE, as to so many other things, Manhattan was cold and rainy. All the taxis had gone on strike, which made little difference to those in need of them; the cabs would only be bouncing derisively in and out of potholes, splashing desperate waving customers with filthy water. Manhattanites, considering rain an imposition, were crankier than usual. Annoyed purveyors of stolen watches and sunglasses shut up their portable shops and scurried home. Sidewalk three-card monte sharps threw their soggy aces away in disgust. Under awnings, beggars and bankers cursed the weather and each other while the city shook off wetness like a giant put-upon cat and went scrambling about its business. Only Theo Ryan was whistling as he stepped out of the lobby of his childhood home, spryly dodged a green mountain of plastic garbage bags, and apologized to the woman whose three foul-tempered poodles had just tangled their leashes around his legs.

Theo's parents lived in an old-fashionably large apartment in the Upper West Side, where they were periodically mugged and vandalized, and out of which he could not persuade them to move. They were native New Yorkers, for whom being robbed from time to time was one of the acceptable costs of life in the world's greatest city. Besides, the Ryans were theatre people, and for theatre people, the rest of the United States was simply a three-thousand-mile stretch of sticks.

This evening the Ryans were hosting a welcome home party for their only child. He didn't want a party. "Oh, sure you do, Pooh Bear," his father, Benny Ryan, promised in the sweet throaty voice that had changed no more with the years than his Black Irish good-looking face, though both had slightly thickened. "We'll have a B.A.L.L." (hugging him, dancing him in a circle). And that was the way it had always been.

Darting from room to room like a swarm of hornets, Theo's mother, Lorraine Page, small, slender, and as strawberry blonde as she'd been decades ago on *Luster Playhouse,* didn't know why she was bothering, when they were no help, parties were no fun, most of the guests owed *them,* and she was still so mad at Theo, why hadn't he just flown straight to England without deigning to drop by for two lousy days, *two* lousy days, which wasn't even, thank you very much, worth it, even if he'd given them decent notice, which he hadn't—not that he ever told them anything about his life, not even a goddamn starring role in a play!—and then taking off for ridiculous London, after that stupid playwright jerk, so why was she killing herself for him to have this party, in the, naturally, *rain,* when he obviously didn't give a, frankly, shit, about it, and she wasn't—move that table against the wall, no, over *there,* what was the matter with them!—wasn't, frankly, sure he *was* welcome home. And that was the way it had always been, too.

The party was for Theo, but the guests would be his parents' age—which was also the way it had always been—with the two constant exceptions of "the youngsters": his dull cousin Dan, a forty-year-old data processor who still lived at home with his mother; and Bette, the interior-decorator daughter of the man who'd written both of Benny Ryan's biggest hit songs, "Prom Queen" and "Do the Duck." Benny had been telling Theo and Bette to get married since they'd been toddlers. They'd never liked each other.

Other than the youngsters and Steve Weiner (with whom Theo was angry anyhow, for having blabbed to the Ryans that their son had starred in *Guys and Dolls* without informing them about it), all the other guests were from fifty to seventy, and all of them were in show business, or living on pensions, or doing something else "temporarily" (even if "temporarily" had lasted ten years), until another break came along. Another "Prom Queen," another *Luster Playhouse*. His mother's cousin Buster McBride (Ike Schneider) would be there, a ventriloquist who had appeared twice on the Ed Sullivan show. And Catherine Cassell, who'd played a long-suffering mother on a soap opera for eighteen years, until she'd been run over by a drunk driver. And Sweets Pudney, half a century ago a tiny child movie actor whose gap-toothed black face had grinned its way through a hundred M.G.M. movies, plus one scene of *Gone With the Wind*. And Benny's brother Arthur, a professional contestant on fixed game shows who'd gone to jail. And twenty or thirty more old friends whose presence through his childhood had made home feel much the same as hotels, a bustle of people "in the business." Anyone not in the business, as his parents had often told him, was a "civilian," to be (unless in an audience) pitied and borrowed from. Anyone who was in the business was "family," to be loved, but not loaned money to. The Ryans had invited family to this party.

It was Theo's party only in the sense that he was the main dish, like the great spiral of slivered turkey flanked by pyramided breads; like the capers around the immense length of smoked salmon; the shaved almonds atop the towering mocha cake. In the sense that on the marble breakfront in the hall, *Shakespeare's Clowns: Improvisation and Textuality* by Theodore S. Ryan was propped up for display, centered between his bronzed childhood tap shoes and his Ph.D. diploma from Yale. In the sense that, thanks to that idiot Steve Weiner, his parents would undoubtedly be running, right there in the living room, the damn videotape of *Guys and Dolls*, which guests would wander over to watch whenever someone yelled, "Quick! Theo's back on!"

At which point, his mother, whisking by so fast with the heaped platter of fat pink shrimp that her jangle of earrings shook, would call out, "I could care!"

And his father would sing over his broad shoulder, "Oh, Rainie, now, come look! Pooh's singing! That's my boy!"

And all of it would be the way it had always been.

Theo Ryan made these predictions about his parents (whom he loved, he reminded himself), as he swayed in the steamy crush of the downtown subway, poked by random elbows and umbrellas, on his way to the Russian Tea Room, to meet with his publisher; at least his former publisher, as soon as Mr. Mahan learned that the Official Life of Ford Rexford had, as far as its biographer was concerned, come to an End. As much as Theo dreaded this meeting, its necessity had provoked his whistling. For it had gotten him out of the apartment, where his father was following his mother from one big, junk-crammed room to the next, driving her crazy by trying to cajole her into a good mood, as his father had been trying to do for forty years, until he inevitably ended up, baffled and hurt, "back on the shit list, for *some* reason, and I wish you'd ask your mother why, because I've had it! I'm never opening my mouth to that lady again!" His father inevitably unable to sustain such vows of eternal silence for more than an hour—being constitutionally incapable of solitude—soon slamming in and out of the long hall of high-ceilinged rooms until he found her again and was bellowing at her, "We can't go on like this! Let's get a divorce." She inevitably shouting in reply, "Call the lawyer, you stupid son of a bitch!" And the two then going busily back to their favorite pastime, which was fighting with each other about their complete incompatibility.

Not that they were wrong to think so, mused Theo, stepping over smelly heaps of rags left by panhandlers on the subway steps. Lorraine Page (born Rosie Schneider) was quick, anxious, and negative. Benny Ryan (born Benedict O'Ryan) was slow, complacent, and sanguine. They were thoroughly incompatible. And utterly inseparable. They couldn't leave each other alone. Theo had never had a long-distance phone call from them—or indeed an answering-machine message (and he'd received one or the other at least twice a month for fifteen years)—that didn't end up with the two, on different lines, contradicting whatever the other said until they'd spiraled into some satisfying argument, often on the subject of their marriage, and why it should never have taken place—with Theo forgotten, sighing into the receiver; his periodic interjections ("Mom," "Dad") ignored.

Down Sixth Avenue he walked, or was shoved along with the

crowd by the blustering wind, everyone shuddering and snarling as packages were knocked into gutters, buses pulled heartlessly away from those racing towards them, and umbrellas blew inside out, flying around intersections like black tumbleweeds. His father had given him maddeningly detailed instructions on how to make his way to the Russian Tea Room; his mother had shouted contradictions from the "library," where she'd set up the office of her new "Help for Hire" service—finding out-of-work actors temporary jobs as servants at yuppie parties. "I know, I know! I know how to get there!" Theo spluttered, pulling away from his father's efforts to button his raincoat.

"Don't take the local. Get off at Fifty-ninth!" screamed his mother.

No wonder, thought Theo as he glanced into the lobby of Carnegie Hall, no wonder he'd fled into libraries and the quietness of books. He had always been exhausted by his parents' endless energy for emotional chaos, for what when he was a child his father would explain (finding the small Theo hidden in the bathroom, hands over his ears) was "just the human side of life, Old Bear. Why I love your mother more than the world and all its gold. She's my queen. I don't know exactly what's set her off this time, but let's just lie low till it blows over. Hey, I know, why don't you go ask your mother if she wants to go to the movies with us, Pooh? Give her a hug, see what the matter is. Don't tell her I asked you."

His mother would corner him at the breakfast table, ignoring the schoolbook he held up against her like a shield. "Theo, I married a moron. A self-centered, self-indulgent, thick-headed moron. And go ahead and say it; that makes me a moron too. Please tell Benedict O'Ryan, the next time he signs a *dumb* contract like that without discussing it with me, he should just stay in L.A., just stay there!"

From his earliest memory, Theo had served as messenger between his parents, racing back and forth with challenges, negotiating settlements. He was their confidant, their marriage counselor. And he realized, though they loved him with (provoking) intensity, he was not nearly as important to either as they were to each other. He learned that while they'd been onstage together in dozens of shows (sometimes singing entire duets glowering with rage), their favorite roles took place on the grand stage of their marriage, and that was basically a two-character play, with Theo in a very minor part.

During his boyhood, his allegiances shifted back and forth, but finally he settled himself on the pivot of the balance, at each end of which his parents furiously seesawed, as if determined to bounce each other off. It was transparent to the boy that Benny Ryan adored his wife, admired her beauty and her talent, bragged to everyone about her "steel-trap mind" and her "will of iron." It was equally transparent that these same metallic qualities nonplussed, terrified, and exasperated him. As a child, Theo thought that Rainie, his father's nickname for his mother, derived, not from her stage name Lorraine, but from the sobbing temper that blew like a rainstorm through their lives.

That Lorraine loved her husband was not as clear until Theo grew older, and could take less literally her claims that she'd like to blow the stupid S.O.B. away with a machine gun. "He drives me mad," she would confide to her son as he sat on the floor beside her vanity table, watching in fear and pleasure as she yanked the comb so savagely through the red curls that it broke and she flung it at the mirror. "Listen!" (And Theo would obediently listen to his father's voice like warm syrup being played loudly on a record in another room.) "In there moping. And how long was I in Chicago? Ten days! Who's the one who just announced he's playing two weeks in Las Vegas and he's leaving *tomorrow!?*"

"Mom, I think maybe Dad's crying."

"Oh, he cries when a fucking flag goes by. He *loves* to cry. I *hate* it," and she would burst furiously into tears, glaring at her face in the mirror as if she hated herself too; studying herself cry.

As Theo grew older, he came to see what was so maddening about his father. He came to see what was so impossible about his mother. That their marriage never should have taken place seemed a logical conclusion—one that in his adolescence, he'd occasionally encouraged them to act on. "Will you two please just get a divorce and shut up about it!" Now he knew that divorce was no more likely than harmony. Some chemical amalgam of strength and weakness, permanently unstable, met in them and bonded.

They were as addicted as drunks to what they claimed was ruining their lives, though their lives—after forty inseparable years— showed every sign of vitality. They were always up to some- thing—from signing on as singing waiters at McMullin's Tavern around the corner to backpacking in the Badlands, driven into life by her whirring metabolism and his stamina for new experience. Their phone rang incessantly; they'd both run for it every time, calling hopefully, "It's for me!" As he grew older, Theo came to (almost) envy them. And he loved them. They just drove him crazy.

After two days back home, the impersonal hostility of the streets of Manhattan was a relief.

CHAPTER

17

{Enter a Gentleman}

To see and to be seen, in heaps they run;
Some to undo, and some to be undone.

Dryden

"THEO? Adolphus Mahan, Theo. Sorry you had to come out in this miserable rain. Wonderful to see you. And rather more . . . sartorially resplendent than when we last met."

Theo smiled. "Thank you. You're looking as distinguished as ever, Mr. Mahan."

"Adolphus, for heaven's sake. Here, let's get rid of this foul-weather gear, shall we? Over here. Frances, hello!"

"Dapper" was the word Ford Rexford had always used for Adolphus Mahan, but "distinguished" was better; "dapper" implied an acquired skill, a forced effort, and Mahan gave the impression that he'd been born in his three-piece suit and small dotted bow tie, born wearing round horn-rimmed glasses, with his gray hair perfectly trimmed over his small perfect ears. Born running the publishing firm of Mahan and Son (as indeed he had been, for his father was Son before him). Born knowing everyone at the Russian Tea Room, for in addition to his own power in the American arts, he was married to a woman descended from a family of illustrious theatrical producers—she herself in fact, in partnership with Morris Schwinn, had produced five of Ford Rexford's Broadway successes.

"Ah, Mr. Mahan, such weather," said the cloakroom lady.

"Mr. Mahan, what chaos, your booth," said the maître d'. "Adolphus, still on for tonight?" said a man all in beige. "Dolly! Call me!" said a glittery-eyed woman leaning out from her table to squeeze his arm as they passed. "Mr. Mahan, blinis and champagne?" said the waiter.

"I seem to eat here a lot," confessed the publisher with the polite pretense of anonymity with which he'd come forward in the entranceway to introduce himself to Theo Ryan.

Theo grinned. "I don't blame you. I used to love to come here with my parents. It always sounded so loud and happy." Yes, how much louder here, he thought, than in the Cavendish Faculty Club back in Rome, where one went on special occasions, in one's best suit, and quietly complained to a few of one's colleagues about all the rest of one's colleagues, or sat stiffly serving anecdotes to visiting speakers when signaled to do so by Norman Bridges. "I mean, the sound of success," said Theo to Mr. Mahan, "is noisy in a very pleasant chinkling kind of way."

"Quite true." His host smiled. "I never thought of that."

Yes, in the Russian Tea Room there was a humming hubbub of rich noises—the tinkle of crystal, the clatter of silver on china, outbursts of laughter, and eager overlapping gossip among a hundred people who were all enjoying good fortune at hand and all sanguine of more good fortune to come. Here were dozens of men and women in the arts who were as well known in Rome, Italy, as in Rome, North Carolina. And all the celebrity academics who expounded on the arts to one another, all those academic stars whom Theo could at times not help but envy, here in the Russian Tea Room it was unlikely that anyone had ever heard of the most famous of them. "So?" Theo could hear Ford Rexford saying. "And a lot of genius African woodcarvers and great Burmese dancers never heard of the Russian Tea Room. So what does that tell you? Do it 'cause you love it. Or fuck it."

"Champagne?" asked Mahan.

"Please. That's Katharine Hepburn!"

"I believe it is." Mahan offered a cigarette from a slender case, smiling as if with envy when Theo said he no longer smoked. "Yes, you can always tell the movie stars in here, because they're wearing T-shirts with baggy trousers. Agents and publishers look like bankers." He pointed at his suit. "Film producers look like teenagers, and often are."

"Mr. Mahan—"

"Excuse me. Charles, wonderful to see you! Amanda sends love to Beryl." Settling back against the plump red leather booth, Mahan lowered the glasses on his straight slender nose. "Now, Theo, until coffee, we'll do what was once called civilized conversation, but is now known as schmoozing. And then I'll begin to badger you about The Book, how's that?"

That was fine.

"How is academe? I gather you've been bought by the Japanese."

"No, not Cavendish. You're thinking of Waldo College. They're our rival across the mountain."

"Yes, of course. The Japanese have bought most of my rivals too. Much more sensible approach to conquest than Pearl Harbor. I remember once lunching in Tokyo with— Ah, Harrison, how *are* you?"

Adolphus Mahan told charming stories, knew that he did so, and spared his companion the burden of reciprocating without making him feel either dull or slighted. Throughout the meal, these stories were interrupted by a stream of visitors to their booth. While Mahan was preoccupied with them, Theo ate his crepes and eavesdropped on the other guests as they floated about to neighboring tables. (The show-business equivalent of Publish or Perish was clearly Be Seen or Vanish.) Two novelists apparently had been married to the same woman (judging from their remarks at her expense). An actor Theo recognized kept drifting off in the direction of the men's room for long stays. At the table next to their booth a beautiful young woman with wild blonde hair periodically checked her reflection in a mirrored compact as if afraid she might have disappeared. She smiled at him.

Nearby a playwright complained to his agent that after twenty-four rewrites and seventy-nine backers' auditions, he appeared to be no closer to a Broadway stage than he'd been when he'd won first prize at the Louisville Festival six years ago. The playwright waved at a black comedienne in jeans, wearing sneakers with little puppets of Ronald and Nancy Reagan on the toes, who was wandering around, growling "Gimme a quarter," just as she did in her famous television routine. Everyone laughed. It was much funnier than being told "Gimme a quarter" by the black panhandlers standing outside the Russian Tea Room.

Theo listened to an austere young woman try to sell a treatment of a story (which was in fact the plot, scene for scene, of *Crime and Punishment*) to one of the teenaged movie producers, a thin man in a voluminous pink shirt with black piping. The producer did not appear to know the story, and thought it had possibilities. Both of them drank water and nibbled at endive. Theo told Mahan Ford's description of Hollywoodeans as "small-town shop girls and bellboys crowned at a Kansas sockhop, whose idea of spending money is still a fucking *car!* 'Least when I was out there," he had said, "you could get a lot of good booze and beef. Now they've given those up for salmon pizza and buddy basketball."

"You imitate him well." The publisher smiled.

"I ought to by now," snarled Theo.

He even was table-hopped himself, when a short bosomy tan woman suddenly squeezed into the booth beside him and rasped hoarsely, "My God! Aren't you Benny and Lorraine's boy? You don't remember me." (It was true; he didn't.) "Joanie Berlin! I produced *O Mistress Mine.* What a turkey, my GOD, but your mother was heaven. Look at YOU! Shawn, right?"

"Theo."

"Close enough, for a ditzy broad with Alzheimer's, har har! You were the prettiest little boy anybody ever saw. We told Lorraine, 'Commercials. He could make a fortune in commercials.' But she wanted you to have a normal life. My GOD, Leo, and here you are a grown man. Kiss your mother. Bye!"

When their coffee arrived, Mahan stirred in a sugar lump with the small silver spoon. "—And so Beckett said to me, 'No, I don't much care for Tennessee Williams. But I was a very great fancier of *Esther* Williams. *Dangerous When Wet* is my particular favorite. Was she Tennessee's sister?' "

Theo, laughing, "Is that true?"

"Ah, 'Is it true?' The biographer's question."

And so finally the breach of The Book was opened. Theo charged into it by announcing bluntly, "I should tell you first,

Mr. Mahan, that Ford Rexford deserted his fiancée in Tilting Rock in the most callous way, and ran off to England with my graduate student."

"Ah yes, Miss Harte. Wonderful wide blue eyes." Mahan's own blue eyes searched for something and found it. " 'Jenny kissed me when we met/Jumping from the chair she sat in . . . Say I'm growing old, but add/Jenny kissed me.' Leigh Hunt, wasn't it? 'Your' graduate student? I congratulate you. She certainly appeared to know more about Ford's oeuvre than he did. Charming about the photos in my office."

Doubtless it shouldn't have been a surprise to hear that Ford Rexford had "dropped by" with Jenny Harte in tow, nor that while there he had "ruthlessly manipulated an excessive advance" from the publisher for a new play "rather oddly" entitled *Principles of Aesthetic Distance.*

Theo bit down on his upper lip. "And did he *show* you this play?"

"Heavens, no. Said his London agent had the only copy. Well, you know Ford. . . . Don't care for the cheesecake?"

Theo put down the fork with which he was stabbing his dessert. "He said Josef Middendorf had the only copy?"

Nodding, Mahan popped a strawberry past his small perfect teeth. "Typical Ford. Of course, my wife and Morris Schwinn are going mad. As you know, they're supposed to be producing this whatever-it-is. Buzzy has been behaving oddly too. Playing cat-and-mouse, pretending not to be there when Amanda calls."

"Did Middendorf happen to say where in England Ford was?"

"Claimed to have no idea. Amanda thinks Buzzy may be up to something shifty. Theatre people! Myself, I'm only a reader. *Aesthetic Distance*—whatever in heaven's name does that title mean?—will make an even dozen of Ford's plays we've published individually, plus the collected volumes. A great source of pride to the house." Mahan sipped delicately at his coffee. "But the best news is, Ford says he's delighted with your biography! And that you're really very close to finishing. I know you plan a big push this summer, and that should do it, hmm?" He tapped the large creamy napkin against his mouth, then chose another cigarette from the thin case. "Ford says—"

Theo's coffee cup clattered from rage as he replaced it in the saucer. "Mr. Mahan—"

"Adolphus."

"Ford Rexford is a liar. An immoral, irresponsible, manipulative, perverse, and excuse me, but really a *shitty* liar."

Mahan smiled. "Ah, but we knew that before you began your research. Is that then the general theme you intend to follow in the book?"

"He's a bastard."

Mahan smiled again. "Now, that is news. I'd always understood him to say that his parents were veritable Babbitts of conformity. Suzanne! How wonderful to see you. Yes, *much* too long."

Between Mahan's witticisms and his popularity with the Tea Room's clientele, quite a bit of time elapsed before Theo could make clear that, far from finished, the Official Life consisted of a crate of index cards, a carton of tapes, and four hundred and fifty pages of draft, all of which covered only the years 1923 to 1949 (when Ford's first play opened off-Broadway), and was probably riddled with lies anyhow. That the Official Subject had vanished. That the Official Biographer, believing as he did that scholarship must be without bias, and feeling as he did that he could happily murder Ford Rexford with his bare hands, had come to the conclusion, with apologies, that he could not, and would not, go on with the book.

"Don't be silly, Theo," said Mahan. "More coffee?"

Theo charged ahead: That he felt terrible for any inconvenience his (irrevocable) decision would cause Mahan and Son, but that he was willing to turn over the draft and all his (considerable) research to the publishers in recompense for the first half of the advance they'd given him, which he frankly could not hope to repay in any lump sum, as he'd used it as part of the down payment on his house. But in fairness, there were the four hundred plus pages, and it shouldn't be hard to find another writer to put it all together—

"Really," said Mahan, still smiling, though somewhat less agreeably. "Suppose I hired you to build me a house. Suppose you unloaded heaps of lumber in my yard and drove away calling, 'Just put it all together.' Hmmm? Would you expect to be paid even partially for that? Now what really seems to be the problem?

You're distressed by Ford's character? But if biographers wrote only about decent people, who would read their books? Extremity, that's what we want to hear about—the extravagantly promiscuous, the colossally ruthless, the excessive. Marilyn Monroe. Ernest Hemingway. It's exorbitant good fortune and catastrophic bad luck that make a life worth reading. Do you think a monogamous J.F.K. declining into a sedate old age would sell even ten thousand copies? Why, remainder tables are filled with Jimmy Carter's fidelity to Rosalind. Carter was never a man destined to be shot at."

"You anticipate Ford's being gunned down?"

"He's certainly the type, wouldn't you say? A dark star. Murder, suicide, overdose. The fascinating type . . . Don't change the subject, Theo."

"Did I?"

"We agree the book's already overdue?"

Wretched with guilt, Theo struggled with explanations, stumbling over excuses. Inside, he heard Ford's voice—one of Ford's "lessons on the world," given on the porch of the pine chalet one soft summer night. "Kid, you fretting about being late? After that pissant advance of Mahan's? Why, they've thrown me dumb cocktail parties cost more than they gave you. Listen, when dealing with the Mahans and the Shuberts and probably the Buddy Tuppers too, never justify, you hear me?, never apologize. They see a throat, they bare their teeth. You make 'em beg, they lick your hand. So just look 'em in the eye and don't say a word. Just nod. See—Listen up, Rhodora; okay, don't. You could learn from me, sweet lady, and you and your Dead Indians could stop singing for beer nuts at Cherokee's. Yeah, likewise to you, babe.—Theo, here's the bulletin: the Mahans of the world think money's everything, but deep down they're scared maybe it's not. Maybe art's got more mojo than money. 'Specially if it doesn't seem to give a flying fuck about *their* money. Indifference makes 'em real nervous. 'Course, money *is* everything, at least everything the world's got to offer. And the world's all they live in, the poor dumb shitkickers."

Theo could hear Ford's voice, but he went on thrusting excuses at Adolphus Mahan, who parried them easily with sharp-edged smiles, and then proved the truth of Ford's lesson by blandly adding that he was sure Theo acknowledged his responsibility: by contract and by conscience, he had an obligation to turn in an acceptable book in September, or to return without delay the full sum of money he'd accepted for it. This was said to Theo, a poor academic!, when by Mahan's own admission he'd just handed over who knows how much money to Ford for a play he hadn't seen (and though Mahan didn't know this, might never see, nor his wife ever produce it). No, the lowly scholar was to be called to account, when the great playwright had never repaid a cent of the huge advance Mahan had given him eight years ago to write his own damn life!

Beside them a famous film goddess sneaked up and bit the back of a bald man's neck. The man swatted behind him in terror until he realized who'd assaulted him, then shrieked "YOU!" with overwrought delight.

Theo's hands clinched his knees. "Even if I felt I could honestly continue, I wouldn't be able to work on it this summer. Something's happened. I'm going to England tomorrow, and I don't know when I'll be back. You see, I've written a play—"

"*You've* written a play? Oh dear me." Mahan lowered his glasses to suggest amusement. "Under Ford's influence? Not exactly what we had in mind. Theo, you're much too sensible a man to write plays."

"Possibly so." From the heat of his ears, Theo suspected they were the color of the booth. "My point is, he took my only copy to England—"

"Check please, Karl. Thank you. Delicious, everything, yes."

"—And as a matter of fact, Ford lied to you, because *I* have the only copy of *his* play, *Principles of Aesthetic Distance*. I know it's the only copy, because Bittermann and Middendorf have both been having fits on the phone to me trying to get me to send it to Ford in England, so I'm—"

"*You* have Ford's play?" Mahan, whose interest had been visibly waning, now paused while uncapping his distinguished gold pen. "*You* have it?"

"Yes."

"Have you read it?"

Theo almost said, "What there is of it," but he stopped himself suddenly, thought a moment, and instead just nodded yes.

"Is it good?"

He thought of Ford. Another nod. "Very."

Mahan took off his glasses as if to get a different view of the young man across from him. "I'd very much like to see it."

A pause. "So would a lot of people, including I imagine Mrs. Mahan and Morris Schwinn. Including Ford."

A longer pause; Adolphus Mahan, as might be expected of so eminent an editor, read between the lines. Then he frowned. "Do I gather that you decline to return this manuscript?"

"That's right." Theo folded his hands on the table edge. "Not until I find Ford. This is between me and him."

Mahan put back his glasses, and looked for the first time *at* Theo Ryan. "Your relationship with Ford appears to have gotten rather intense."

Theo looked back at Mahan.

"Whatever your personal feelings, Theo, and I can certainly understand them, I can't believe you of all people would destroy a Rexford play. Possibly the *last* Rexford play." Mahan sighed—no doubt dreaming again of the sales that would follow the playwright's (violent) demise.

Theo said nothing.

Mahan fiddled thoughtfully with his pen. "Has Ford *stolen* this play of yours? How did he get it?"

"We were working on it together. My computer crashed, and he ran off with the only copy we'd printed."

Mahan considered. "Just a moment. Is this a play you two collaborated on? We're talking about *two* Rexford plays here?"

Theo looked the publisher in the eye and didn't say a word.

"Well, well, well." Mahan signed in a quick neat hand the charge slip held out to him. "And Ford took it to England."

"Yes, and I'm holding on to *Aesthetic Distance* until I get it back."

"Well, well, well."

Theo looked deliberately at his watch as he said, "I'm afraid I have to get going. Thank you very much for listening and for lunch, Mr. Mahan. Please think over what I said. How far is it to Random House from here, walking?"

Mahan told him as he slid his pen back into his dark, smooth jacket. "Business with Random House?"

Theo was in fact going to Random House to meet Steve Weiner, who was doing a book with them, but seeing the concern his question had evoked in Mahan, he simply nodded yes, and slid out of the booth.

While Mahan was collecting their raincoats from the cloakroom, the young woman with wild hair suddenly appeared at Theo's side and thrust an eight-by-ten glossy photo of herself into his hand. Her voice had a trained breathlessness. "I happened to overhear. You've written a play with Ford Rexford? Here. In case I'm right for anything. My agent's on the back." She showed him the name with a lethal-looking purple fingernail.

"I don't think—" began Theo.

But she'd floated quickly back into the hubbub of fame.

"So you're off to England." Mahan held out the coat politely. "I envy you. Let's say you'll call me when you return, shall we? This autumn. And don't worry about the book. In fact, I've had an idea. Send me the four hundred pages—"

"—I did send them to you. I mailed them from Rome before I left."

"Good, good. They're probably somewhere in the wilderness of my office. I'll read them with this new idea in mind." He smiled radiantly at Theo, his eyes twinkling behind the distinguished horn-rimmed spectacles. "A multivolume! How about that? A trilogy. Why not? Ford deserves a trilogy. Call the first one something like 'The Early Years.' No, that was Churchill. 'The Texas Years.' No. 'Preacher's Boy.' How's that? I like that."

"I just can't think about it right now." Theo shook his head.

"Of course you can't." The publisher nodded with sympathy. "Not now. Go get this play thing settled first. You and Ford will work it out, I feel sure. Of course, I certainly hope so." (A warm chuckle.) "Before Amanda has a nervous breakdown. Excuse me. Bill! No, just leaving. Well, all right, I can stay a few minutes. Bill, meet Theo Ryan, one of our prized authors. Doing the Rexford biography. Goodbye then, Theo. Call me from London. I'll read the manuscript right away. Wonderful to see you!"

In the Russian Tea Room, success glowed in the sheen of famous faces turning from side to side to see and be seen.

CHAPTER
18

{Enter Several Strange Shapes}

Let the world slide.

Beaumont and Fletcher

THEO, Steve Weiner, Bette the interior decorator, and Dan the dull data-processor cousin were in the kitchen taking a break from Theo's party. Like their cohorts nationwide, they were far less saturnalian than their parents' generation, and expressed some wonder at the display of frivolity and filthy habits now rampant in the living room at one in the morning. Steve was driving Theo at 4:00 A.M. to Newark Airport, where they were meeting Jorvelle, who had a stopover on her way from North Carolina to Holland. Later in the day, they'd drop Theo off at the inexpensive charter flight that would take him to Gatwick, England, via Iceland. His bags sat already packed, looking eager to go, on his bed.

As the youngsters lounged about, sedately munching appetizers, Theo's father burst through the kitchen door, letting in shouts, shrieks, and thumping piano music. "*Whole lot of shaking goin' on!*" sang Benny Ryan, lavishly sloshing gin into a glass pitcher. "Whatsa maddah, you bambini? Come out in the living room!" He shook the pitcher at them. "*Maybelline, why can't you be true?* Nobody can play the old tunes the way your dad can, Bette. Give Papa Bear a hug."

Bette, a severely sleek woman of thirty-six, suffered the embrace with unconvincing good humor.

"These boys are morons not to snap you up!" The elder Ryan turned her to face them. "Hey, Stevereeno, how 'bout this lady!" He swung her back. "Steve just had his book accepted by Random House."

"I know," said Bette, disentangling herself. "He told me."

"Serious stuff. Not my bag, but I love you, Steve." (Steve Weiner also endured a fierce hug from the ebullient Mr. Ryan.) "And my boy Theo's writing the Ford Rexford story for Mahan and Son. He and Mr. Mahan had lunch today at the Russian Tea Room."

"I know," said Bette.

"Get out there and dance, youngsters! *Try your luck, everybody, do the duck, hey, hey, do the duck.* Come on, Pooh Bear!" Ryan, black curly hair tipped with gray, chest swelling under the burgundy cashmere turtleneck, danced his son in a circle, then backstepped in a long slide down the hall towards the roar of the party.

"Amazing," said Steve. "How old is he?"

Theo shrugged. "Fourteen, fifteen maybe."

"Must have been weird to have a dad like that. 'What does your dad do?' 'He's a rock 'n' roll singer.' " Steve hoisted his small frame up onto the long oak refectory table in the center of the kitchen, ducking copper pots hung from the ceiling. "My dad sold cardboard containers."

Bette snapped a radish with her teeth. "I wish Benny would keep in mind that I'm a lesbian."

"I don't think anyone's told him," Theo explained.

"*I've* told him." She washed the radish down with mineral water.

Dan made one of his rare remarks, most of which sounded ironic but weren't. "I guess it hasn't sunk in." He went back to scooping troughs with a celery stalk through a mound of chicken liver pâté, his fat white hairy hand steering graceful curves around the coiled pimientos.

The kitchen door crashed open. Lorraine Page banged through it carrying a platter of dirty plates littered with shrimp tails and gnawed chicken bones. "Don't anyone make a move to help, Theo, thank you very much!" she said with an immensely bright smile, and jabbed the platter at him as he raced forward. "Dan, stop playing in that pâté. Your mother wants you. She can't find her antidepressants." Dan hurried away, pear-shaped in pale blue trousers, knocking his shoulder into the door frame as he left.

"God, he should take a handful of those pills himself!" Theo's mother shook her head, the strawberry curls throwing off glints of artificial gold. With a colorful batch of bracelets and earrings, she wore a black silk sleeveless pantsuit; at the ends of its flowing trousers red-painted toenails wriggled impatiently. "Theo, go rescue Inez Bernheim. Your stupid father's spinning her all over the furniture like a rag doll. They already broke a lamp. Not that it wasn't a piece of junk."

The door banged open again. A good-looking woman, whose ample breasts quivered dangerously at the edge of a stretchy red bodice, teetered a weaving course up the kitchen hall in absurdly high heels. "Where's my husband?" she asked, looking about the room.

Lorraine said pleasantly, "Why, Ziti, darling, I don't know. I haven't had him for years."

At this, the woman doubled over with gasps of laughter, exposing her breasts to the riveted stares of the two younger men. Helplessly she swiveled, still bent double, and hobbled laughing back down the hall.

Later, in came a short svelte man with thick spectacles, whom Theo called "Uncle Wally" although they weren't related; the man fished an ice cube out of his scotch glass. There was a big fly in the cube. "Lorraine, this is disgusting!" he said in a high exaggerated lisp.

"Oh, cut it out, Wally." She handed him back the cube.

"I'm gonna puke!" he shouted. Clutching his stomach, he gagged long and noisily, bent over, then pointed at the floor where lay a large viscous blob of pink vomit. "I told you!"

"Good God," said Steve Weiner.

Theo picked up the blob—it was rubber—and stuffed it in the pocket of the man's red tuxedo jacket. "Hi, Uncle Wally."

Two decks of cards suddenly appeared in the man's hands. He fanned and twirled them like a Spanish dancer. "Theo. Pick a card." He grinned.

Theo showed Steve the ace of spades, then returned it to the deck. "They're all aces of spades," he whispered.

"Says who?" Wally closed the fans, shot his hands up in the air, and instead of cards, red and blue paper flowers floated all over the kitchen.

Lorraine brushed them out of her hair. "Wally, get out of here. Go saw Ziti Klein in half."

Steve laughed nervously as Wally's hand (it was rubber) came off in his when he shook it goodbye.

"Stephen, if I cared what you thought of us, darling!" Lorraine wheeled on Bette who sat in the breakfast nook reading *Architectural Digest*. "Don't spare me!" she told her. "How much would it cost to throw out everything in this whole goddamn apartment, and start over?"

"Including Benny?" smiled the interior decorator.

Lorraine caroled a merry scale of laughter, at the end of which Benny himself reappeared at the end of the kitchen hall, calling out like the Philip Morris bellboy: "*Guys and Dolls*. Theo's back on! Videotape of *Guys and Dolls* again."

Lorraine said, "I could care!" and violently banged the top of a jar of caviar on the sink edge.

Theo's father sang, "Oh, Rainie, you've watched it twice already! Pooh, you've got my vibrato! Last call! *Guys and Dolls!*"

Later still, crashes, shouts, and song blared from the living room. Thudding shook through the floors. A man in a satin vest ran in and hauled on Bette, "We need you, okay?"

"Jesus," she sighed, and let him drag her out.

A big gray-haired black man, wearing jeans, pointed metal-tipped boots, and a pink Brooks Brothers shirt rolled to his biceps, squeezed past them into the kitchen. "They're wild out there," he said in a rumbling bass. "That big Chinese vase on the coffee table's gone for good, Lorraine." He made a hurling motion with a long sinewy brown arm.

"Goddammit."

Theo introduced Steve to the former child star Sweets Pudney.

"Good God." Steve shook hands eagerly. "I just saw you a week ago on the late show. Mr. Pudney, I've got a friend who teaches a cultural studies course with a lot of those M.G.M. movies of yours in it."

Lorraine laughed. "That's you, okay, Sweets, a cultural study."

Steve was earnest. "A course on 'Transgressions of Race and Gender.' "

"Well, I got those covered." Pudney grinned.

"You ought to come down to Cavendish someday and do a guest lecture for her."

Pudney smiled his old movie smile. "Lawsie, Mistuh Steve, you mighty flatterin' to ole Sweets. You tell your friend, for one thousand dollars, I'll reminisce about race and gender, and for two thousand, I'll spit watermelon seeds just like in the old days."

Unfazed, Steve grinned back. "Hey, for fifty bucks, I'll catch 'em in my teeth."

"Deal." They shook hands again.

Lorraine was flipping spoonfuls of caviar at one cracker after another. "Why isn't Andrew here? He said he was coming. Oh!" She paused, spoon raised. "Did he get that part! Is he in L.A.? Oh, the lucky shit!"

Pudney rubbed the same side of his head he'd always rubbed in the movies. "He's home pouting. We had a little snit-fit last night and he's not talking to me."

"Divorce the son of a bitch" was Lorraine's advice.

He rubbed her arm with old affection. "After thirty-odd years, makes you look kind of dumb you didn't do it sooner."

"You're telling me? The only reason I don't is I don't want to give him the satisfaction." They laughed together bitterly.

Pudney rearranged a row of crackers, then held out his hand, palm up, at Theo. "Theo, baby, when you either gonna get yourself a girl, or a guy?"

Theo slapped the large long hand. "I'm still looking for the right one, Uncle Sweets."

"Lookin' both ways?" The deep laugh rumbled off down the hall.

"Sweets Pudney!" mused Steve. "Maybe Jorvelle *could* get him down to talk at Cavendish."

"Cavendish, Cavendish. Shut up about Cavendish!" Lorraine

sprayed onion slivers on the caviar dabs. "Bad enough it had to steal my son."

"Right, Mom." Theo shook his head. "Six months, you didn't even know where I was. You thought I was in North Dakota."

"North Carolina, North Dakota—hicks in the sticks. Bad enough they pay you bupkis. Bad enough you had to meet Ford Rexford."

"You set it up!"

"He had to drive you crazy so you're chasing him all the way to ridiculous London. He quit Dr. Ko, did you know that, Steve?"

"Mom! She told me to!"

"You're so much healthier than I am? I've been in therapy twenty years, and I haven't even scratched the surface. If you're so healthy, why do you keep breaking up with your girlfriends? It breaks my heart. Look, tears."

"It's the onions," Theo said.

She wiped her eyes. "At least you got Mahan off your back till September. The anxiety attack you were having this morning, you acted like he was going to repossess your house."

"Who told you he's off my back?"

"Stephen, who else."

Steve shrugged off Theo's scowl. "See, Rosie, if it wasn't for Cavendish, we'd never have met." Steve was the only person Theo had ever known to call Lorraine Page by her given name.

"Don't!" she snapped. "Don't defend that place after what it's done to you. Your wife runs off to work for *George Bush*."

"We can't blame Cavendish for that."

"And Marcus Thorney's going to be chairman! The prick that tried to stop Theo's promotion." She darted towards Steve, leaving the pink imprint of her lips on his cheek. "What a frankly stupid thing, letting yourself get beaten out by that reptile. There's no justice."

Steve held up his arms, shrugging. "So, Rosie, who thought there was?" He winced. "Anyhow, it was a long shot."

"You deserve what happened," she said, her small ringed hands a flurry of motion as she dealt more crackers like a hand of solitaire across the tray. "You and Theo both. Moving down there with toothless hillbillies. When they start burning crosses on your lawn, maybe you'll take that job at Columbia like I told you two years ago. Is my table a chair? Off, off."

"At least down there I've got a lawn." Steve slid away to pick at a skeleton of smoked salmon.

"You wanna talk lawn?" She licked caviar from the spoon. "Look out my windows. Central Park. That's a lawn."

"Yeah, but mine's not full of junkies and muggers."

"No, it's full of redneck sheriffs wearing white sheets over their heads. Theo!" Lorraine grabbed him by the arm and shook it. "Go mix with your guests. They came to see *you*."

"Really?" Theo cupped his hand to his ear. "Sounds to me like they came to boogy-down with Dad."

Reverberant thuds rattled the copper pots on the ceiling. A drum set had been added to the piano.

"Go tell your idiot father that if Mrs. Schultz calls the cops again, it's on his head." She pushed her son towards the hall. "And if he's got his long Irish nose back in Ziti Klein's cleavage, he's a dead man."

Theo allowed himself to be nudged along. "You're trying to get rid of me so you can worm stuff out of Steve. I can't imagine what else you think there is. He's already blabbed my whole life to you."

"God, I hope not," she snapped. "I hope there's more to it than that!"

"Thanks, Mom." At the door, Theo gave Steve a significant glare. "Do not mention the clergy. Understand?"

Lorraine threw her hands to her temples. "Great. My beautiful son's become a goddamn priest. I want babies! I'll never have grandchildren."

"Rosie, you're such a fake." Steve laughed. "If anybody ever called you Grandma, you'd slit your throat."

The small woman put her hand to her throat and slowly felt it. Her eyes darkened, filling with tears. "Probably," she said with a nervous smile. "I suppose that's true."

"Oh, Mom," Theo called. "Steve's kidding."

Steve patted her bare slender shoulder. "God, I'm sorry, Rosie."

"It's onions," she said.

"Oh, Mom."

CHAPTER

19

{Exit Disguised and Muffled}

He shall with speed to England.

Hamlet

MOST of the Ryans' furniture had been toppled into corners. A gray-haired couple cuddled on an overturned couch. A rain-soaked portly man straddled precariously the ledge of an opened window, calling to pedestrians fifteen stories below—who couldn't possibly hear him—"Come up! Come up!" Bette's father in a half-crouch at the piano pounded out "Life is a cabaret" on the baby grand. At an ottoman beside him, Bette beat on a drum set—one abandoned decades ago by Theo—as if she hoped to demolish it. She was good, though clearly took little pleasure in her talent. Theo's cousin Dan stood in a corner sucking clam dip off potato chips. Despite (or because of) their relatively advanced years, everyone else in the room appeared to have adopted the song's philosophy without reservation—dextrously smoking, drinking, and eating while singing and dancing, as if life might not continue to be a cabaret after tonight. In front of the mantel, Benny Ryan and five women in their sixties, with arms linked on either side, high-strutted with precision.

"There's no people like show people," Theo said to Dan, who now wore a polyester raincoat buttoned to the neck that made him look like a flasher.

"WHAT? I'M WAITING FOR MAMA. SHE WANTS TO

GO HOME. THIS KIND OF THING DEPRESSES HER, I
GUESS."

"WHY DO YOU THINK I BECAME AN ACADEMIC?"
Theo bellowed.

"WHAT?"

"TAKE IT EASY, DAN."

There was another guest who, like Dan's mom, wsn't convinced
that life in a cabaret was worth living. In a chair shoved sideways
to the dining room wall, a lank freckled man with badly dyed
jet-black hair and a long morose rubbery face sat feeding olives to a
wooden dummy. He'd literally push the olives down the dummy's
throat. This was Theo's relative Buster McBride, the first ventriloquist to throw his voice on live television while drinking water.
Buster, catatonically shy, spoke only through his dummy, the
Latin lover Rudolph Fernando-Teeno—who, far from timid, ac-
costed every woman in range with machismo vaunts and gross
flattery. "Besa me, besa me, mi cariña. Your boobies are so booo-
tifull!"

"Hi, Buster," Theo said. "Hi, Rudy." He shook the dummy's
hand. "You like olives?"

Rudy stroked with tiny wooden hand his slick black lounge
lizard hair. "How else ees eet I geet my olive skin complexion,
muchacho?"

"Ah, of course." Theo laughed obligingly. "So how's life been,
Rudy? Fighting the women off?"

"Weeth dees wheep!" He slapped the tiny whip glued to his
other hand against his gaucho pants. "Dee weemons, dey lovvve
me!"

Two women from the chorus line walked through the dining
room then, circling the table to nibble at desserts. Rudy became
extremely agitated, bouncing about on McBride's knee and blowing kisses with his hands. "Kees mee, corazon. I got dee hots for
you," he cooed. The women made kissing noises back at him.
Buster McBride looked shyly away.

"Take it easy, Rudy." Theo patted the dummy's back with affection. He'd known him since he was a baby.

It was growing late. Theo walked down the long hallway, took
his bags from his childhood bed—still varnished with decals of

scenes from Shakespeare plays—and carried them back to the
foyer. Hearing sobs coming from his parent's room, he peeked in.
On the edge of their bed, he found Sweets Pudney comforting
Catherine Cassell, a large-boned woman with a flat broad face that
was now wet with tears. It struck him that he had few memories
of the former soap-opera star when she wasn't crying, either about
her disastrous love life (three husbands had run off with floozies
after robbing her blind), or her lost career (she'd never found
another role like that of the long-suffering mother in *The Salt of
the Earth*).

"I never even . . . regained . . . consciousness!" she heaved in
sobs, as Sweets rocked her in his arms. "Those fucking writers!"

"Honey," crooned Sweets. "That was five years ago. You got
to get over it. Hi, Theo."

"Theo, *sweetie!*" The big woman hauled him down to her other
side, and clutched him to her.

"What's the matter, Aunt Catherine?"

''She'll be all right." Sweets nodded. They all three rocked back
and forth together as the black man soothingly asked, "Now,
Cathy, didn't I hear you had a movie deal?"

"It's a *horror* film," she howled. "I'm a *cleaning lady,* and I'm
hacked to *pieces!*"

Sweets rocked her (and consequently Theo) in a gentle rhythm.
"Well, you got any lines?"

" 'Just 'What was that?' And 'Who's therrrrre?' " she wailed.
"Then he's at me *with the saw!*"

"Hey. You can do a lot with those lines, Can't you, Theo?"

"Sure you can," Theo agreed. "A lot."

After learning how someone named Hector or Chester had
given Catherine's chinchilla coat to someone named Mona or
Magda, Theo extricated himself from her embrace and made his
way to the library. There were not many books in it, but there
were a great many shelves of scripts, tapes, and records. The walls
too were covered with memorabilia of his parents' long careers in
"the business." Centered among the photos, posters, plaques, and
laminated reviews were Lorraine's Obie, Benny's two gold records, and a large happy oil painting of the three of them. The
artist had painted it one summer from a composite of snapshots

while Theo's mother was in New Haven at the Shubert, his father was in Miami at the Coconut Grove, and he was at camp, striking out in softball games. It had always seemed to him an apt symbol of their lives together.

Stepping inside the room to look at the painting, he saw two men seated on the couch. Across from them, on the television a young Cary Grant and Katharine Hepburn were tearing around silently (the sound was off) in a manic hysteria so extreme that in the real world they would have been forcibly subdued by tranquillizers. One of the men said, "Look at that timing." He pointed at Grant hyperbolically seething.

The other sucked ice from his glass, then spit it back. "A pro. There're no pros anymore."

"I don't call these people today stars."

"Me either." They watched in silence.

Theo couldn't remember the names of either of the men, which seemed to be the gist of their general beef with "the business."

The first one said, "So anyhow, I schlep to this reading. Four flights up. Place is a rat's nest. So anyhow, we start with this turkey. An hour later, we're still in Act One. The writer's fucking agent gets up and walks out. Act Two, it's midnight. His fucking *wife* leaves. Two A.M., we're still not done. I'd told him to cut the thing, we all did."

"They don't listen."

They watched Katharine Hepburn fall on her face.

"Beautiful," said the first. "Open audition for that Morris Schwinn piece of shit tomorrow. I hate those cattle calls. Be two thousand there easy."

"Easy. Who needs it?"

"Who needs it? . . . You going?"

"Yeah. You?"

"Yeah. Look at the reaction shot."

"Flawless. God, when it's good, there's nothing like it, is there?"

"Nothing."

Theo backed quietly away from the door. "Show biz," he said to himself. "Why won't you just admit that you love show people?" he heard Dr. Ko asking. "It's who you are. It's in your blood." Right, like a lot of other fatal diseases. It was true. No sooner had he escaped his parents than he'd taken up with Ford Rexford. Why couldn't he learn?

In the foyer, Theo's only real uncle, Arthur O'Ryan, the professional game show contestant who'd ended up in jail, leaned against the foyer wall by the breakfront, reading *Shakespeare's Clowns: Improvisation and Textuality.* "By Theodore S. Ryan, Ph.D.," he said benevolently to his nephew.

"Hi, Uncle Arthur. Thanks for reminding me."

Arthur was flabby of build, and his greenish white skin seemed never to have lost its prison pallor. "Long words," he said, patting the book.

"Yeah. You don't want to read that."

"Hey, bud, it's a habit. In the pen I read books two, three times, never got a handle on what the guy was talking about. Sigmund Freud, Carl Young, I read 'em. Lots of 'em. This one's about Shakespeare, hunh? Clowns? Milking laughs, comic bits, adding on business, that type thing?"

Theo said, "Exactly."

Arthur scratched his hair, a thinning washed-out replica of his younger brother Benny's. "I played Shakespeare once, twice. Should of stuck with legit, kept out of the TV racket, think? Take my advice, bud, don't ever go to prison. All right?"

Theo nodded. "All right."

"I was lucky, getting out before this AIDS thing. I'd be dead otherwise. I guess that's lucky. I still got nightmares from the Spics tearing up my ass."

It was no surprise that people tended to avoid his uncle Arthur at parties. Queasy, Theo said, "So you played Shakespeare?"

"The Forrest in Philly. Good story. They don't write 'em like that anymore. Played this guy that this hunchbacked king hires to bump off some little kids. His own nephews. Like me bumping you off."

Theo said, "Richard the Third."

"Yeah, Richard. Real nasty guy. Met a lot like him in the pen. One—big, mean one from Albany—used to claim he'd killed thirteen the cops didn't even know about."

"Did you believe him?"

Arthur set the book down beside the Yale diploma and the bronze tap shoes. He bared his teeth. "You know why these are false?" Theo shook his head. "He's why. Guy from Albany."

Theo said, "Gosh, I'm sorry. . . . Well, good to see you again, Arthur."

His uncle tapped the diploma. "What's this teaching deal like? Interesting?"

Theo thought. ". . . Yes. It's interesting and kind of peaceful, compared to show business."

"Peaceful's good. Not much dough though?"

Theo explained that nowadays many academics, even in English, earned substantial salaries, some in the six figures.

"How 'bout that!" Arthur picked the book up again, leafing through it. "I was a kid, I used to think about being a teacher. Funny, hunh? Kind of sounded like it'd be nice."

"I didn't know that." Theo touched the man's shapeless elbow. "I guess I inherited my vocation from you then."

The sweetness of Arthur's smile was a weak version of Theo's father's. "Think so?" he said. "That's a nice thought."

Above the musical racket, a woman screamed. It didn't sound like a joke. Theo heard people running in from the kitchen, and wondered if the portly man had fallen out of the window. He hurried towards the sound, and Arthur returned to *Shakespeare's Clowns: Improvisation and Textuality;* no doubt he'd heard worse screams back in the pen.

Ziti Klein was hopping up and down in the middle of the living room; her stretchy red bodice was pulled down to her midriff, her capacious breasts wildly jiggling. "Okay!" she shouted. "Where's the FUCK put this rubber mouse down my dress?"

About ten people shouted in unison, "WALLY!"

Even Benny Ryan felt moved to judge. "Wally, come on now, that's a little much!"

"Wally? WAAALLYYYYYY!" A general search ensued. Only Steve Weiner (transfixed by the Klein bosom), and Bette (asleep on the rug), failed to join in. But the magician in the red dinner jacket was nowhere to be seen.

"As usual, he's disappeared," announced Theo's mother finally. "Ziti, pull up your goddamn dress. Wally's gone."

"What an exit line," called the portly man from the window ledge. "Speaking of exits," Lorraine said bluntly. "It's past three in the morning. Stay if you like, folks, but I'm heading for the wings."

Benny hugged her from behind. "Nooooo. Dance with me. Come on, Rainie. Dance with me. Jack, play our song."

Bette's father ran to the piano and started beating out "Do the Duck!"

"Funny," trilled Lorraine.

Benny did his tight-lipped Bogart snarl. "You know the one I mean, Jack. If she can take it, so can I. Play it, Jack. Play 'Prom Queen.' "

Everyone shouted, " 'Prom Queen'!"

"Come on, Rainie." Benny Ryan danced towards his wife— sweaty and warm and sweet, smiling the smile that for a year or two in the mid '50s had caused young girls across the country to scream and tear at their hair.

"Leave me alone." Lorraine Page spun away from him.

"You're my dreeeeeam."

"Oh, okay, okay, for God's sake."

Everyone happily whistled as the sugary chords swelled into the familiar crescendo, and Theo's parents danced among their large noisy family, and Benny sang to his wife:

> You're my dreeeeeeam.
> You're my queeeeeen.
> Most beautiful girl
> The world's ever seeeeen.
> Da da deeeee. Da da deeeee. . . .

Theo nodded at Steve Weiner, who was urgently waving his watch. He thought about interrupting his parents' dance, he thought about waiting until it was over. But goodbyes were never easy. Benny would cry, Lorraine would rage between accusation and despair. For a moment, he stood in the hall by the door, bags in hand, watching the two of them, circled by "the family," seeing in their smooth and graceful, practiced turns, like a slow spiral of superimposed pictures, all the years of their dances together, seeing himself at three, at thirteen, at thirty-five—standing outside their circle, watching, as now.

Theo raised his hand quietly and waved goodbye. Their heads touching, black on gold, they didn't see him.

> You're my dreeeeam.
> You're my queeeeen.

And everything was the way it had always been.

IV

{Scene: London, and Other Parts of England}

CHAPTER

20

{Enter the Messenger, As Before}

This land of such dear souls, this dear dear land.

Richard II

ENGLAND WAS PARCHED. It steamed under a scorching sun that bleached the sylvan green from Windsor forest and turned the famous fields of Tilbury as dusty as a mesa in Taos. Theo Ryan had not been comfortable since his Iceland stopover. Not that he'd been particularly comfortable then, for they'd sat for hours, forbidden to leave the plane, while unspecified mechanical difficulties were investigated (and perhaps solved?). Nor could he have easily dislodged himself from the miserable seat anyhow, wedged as he was between a twitchy fat woman who drooled on his shoulder as she slept and a teenaged boy, hair shaved to a stubble, casually traveling abroad in neon green shorts and a Grateful Dead tank top. At Gatwick customs, eager dogs swarmed all over this boy's knapsack, and he was led by a policeman out of the lengthy queue where they all stood waiting to be eliminated as Irish would-be terrorists trying to sneak into England with explosives, or Third World would-be immigrants trying to sneak in with DNA bearing no familial relation to that of successful immigrants already living on the crowded island. An American woman in front of Theo expressed indignation at this Tory screening policy—less from liberal principles than from impatience at the length of the line, as far as he could tell.

Later Theo was to think back with nostalgia on the frigid interior of that plane, and with envy on the neon shorts of the underdressed drug smuggler. He himself, advised by such authorities as Frommer's and Jonas Marsh, and by a hundred films in which the sun never appeared to rise on the British Empire, had packed for drizzle and nippy fogs with sweaters, thick socks, his father's Burberry, and his mother's six-foot Aran Island scarf. All these he had now lugged for three weeks from one un-air-conditioned, historically resonant hotel to the next, as he moved about London in pursuit of cross-ventilation and significant sights.

For three unrelieved weeks, temperatures in the high nineties had hung upon the great city like a vast mildewed wool blanket. Londoners claimed that the heat wave wasn't a heat wave at all; quite the contrary, was quite a pleasant run of sunny weather; certainly nothing to get in a bother about—particularly if compared to the sticky summer of 1517 when, after a drought that had lasted from September to May, fifty thousand Londoners had died of the sweating sickness. Admittedly, 1517 did sound worse as summers go. Still, to Theo Ryan, three weeks of filthy haze and sodden humidity qualified as something that would send New Yorkers screaming into the streets with hatchets. He could almost forgive the elderly Viennese Josef Buzzy Middendorf for having left the country, abandoning his literary agency for an indefinite holiday.

For Theo had learned (when in a wilted, jet-lagged daze he had finally located the offices of Middendorf, Ltd.) that Rexford's agent had suddenly (as his young receptionist wistfully expressed it) "flown off, don't you know, to the Isle of Capri?" Nor had Mr. Middendorf left behind any manuscript from Ford, just the message that Theo must realize he was not the rightful owner of the play *Principles of Aesthetic Distance*, if in fact he had it. All Theo could do, then, was to keep pestering Middendorf's office until the agent returned and confessed Rexford's whereabouts. If in fact he knew them. Theo deduced that at any rate, Adolphus Mahan's wife, Amanda, the future producer of *Aesthetic Distance*, did not know where Ford was, or more to the point, where his manuscript was, since she'd obviously flown across the ocean to try to track it down; the receptionist had indiscreetly mentioned that Mrs. Mahan was at Claridge's and telephoning Middendorf, Ltd. twice a day, asking if they'd heard from Ford.

So there was nothing to do but wait and see. Theo, despite his threats to Bernie Bittermann, was not about to go randomly wandering in this heat through all of Cornwall in the hope of someday running into Ford and Jenny Harte by chance. At least, let such a desperate strategem be a last resort. Besides, maybe they too had left the country to escape the weather. Ford's tolerance for discomfort had always oscillated; at times he'd complain as bitterly about hammertoes and gingivitis as if he were dying of pancreatic cancer, but there had also been times (or so he'd told his biographer) when without a murmur he'd crawled through jungle brambles until blood glued his eye shut, or climbed over icy rocks until frostbite numbed his hand. Besides, maybe to a Texan this endless stretch of blank sky and blazing sun held all the comfort of home.

While Theo waited, he passed the time looking at London, and suffering its relentless sun. Whenever he was homesick for a familiar face, he found one at the Reading Room of the British Museum, where in the summer the long wooden tables were always three-quarters filled by American academics, a few of whom he could inevitably count on recognizing. In fact, the first day, when he went there to see the original of Walter Raleigh's wife's *Notebook*, he'd run into Vic Gantz. From Vic he'd discovered that Jonas Marsh was hiking with a friend through the Hebrides in emulation of Dr. Johnson, but would be back, as he'd put it to Vic, "in a fortnight, or bloody well near." Theo and Vic speculated about the identity of this "friend" (for frankly they hadn't thought of Jonas as the "friendly" sort), as they ate lunch together in an air-conditioned Indian restaurant near Russell Square. They were surrounded by other American scholars, all congratulating themselves on being in London where there were so many real bookstores, and so much legitimate theatre (a woman from L.S.U. raved, ironically, about a revival at the National of Rexford's *Her Pride of Place*), and all complaining about London's dreadful food, rudimentary plumbing, intimidating snobbery, high prices, thin mattresses, weak coffee, and rude crowds of (other types of) tourists.

Londoners themselves appeared impervious not only to these complaints from foreigners but to the heat as well, bustling about their business in suits and ties, dresses and hats, with their pale freckled faces lifted joyously to the brutal sun. At lunch hour, they lay down in the city's sweltering public parks as if on the beach at Blackpool. Even when the novelty paled and the sun did not, they carried cheerfully on, properly clad, indifferent to discomfort, ignoring pearls of sweat beading their lips—and all without so much as an ice cube in their scotch or a window fan in their airless offices. The only thing that appeared to distress them about the drought was the rationing of water for their flower gardens. Theo overheard many ingenious schemes for avoiding the scrutiny of Water Patrols who circled the city in helicopters in search of telltale sprays, swooping down to slap hefty fines on anyone caught with hose in hand. He noticed a Middendorf clerk siphoning H_2O out of the office water cooler into plastic jugs, and secretly succoring pots of geraniums. He saw his hotel manager, who'd complained bitterly about the American obsession with bathing, hosing down his terrace shrubs at three in the morning. Londoners would apparently give up their bathtubs before they gave up their roses. Otherwise, the weather seemed not to affect them. Their sangfroid amazed Theo, who lay naked and comatose each night under soaked towels in his hotel bed—with chairs braced in the sills to hold the windows open—as he listened appalled to crowds of merry Londoners below him, milling about outside pubs and wine bars.

Still, Theo was enjoying himself. To the young literary scholar, being in London was like walking around inside his own head, like living in a great sprawling book of all the poems and plays and novels he'd spent his life reading. Fiction was up every alley, history around every corner. Theo paced Raleigh's walk along the battlements of Bloody Tower. He stood where Raleigh had died, and placed his hand against the cold stone marker of the headless grave.

The first week, not even a brief faintness from heat stroke while climbing Hampstead Heath to Keats's house could dampen Theo's enthusiasm; nor the sight of Scottie Smith's name on the marquee of a West End theatre. The second week, neither a bee sting in

Blenheim, nor the theft in Stratford of his camera—deftly snipped from his shoulder at the very altar rail of the church where Shakespeare was buried—could keep him indoors (particularly given the stifling conditions of his room). But then, as he began his third week, exaltation began to flag. The London Underground abruptly called a general strike; in sympathy all the buses stopped where they were, and the high cost of taxis quickly played havoc with the academic's careful budget. Walking the hot streets, as his nose and his feet blistered and sweat soaked his shirt, gloom fell upon Theo's spirit.

He knew no one to call. He had had no answer to the note he'd written Dame Winifred Throckmorton. Jonas was still away, presumably tramping in handsewn shoes through the Highlands. And Vic Gantz had flown to Monte Carlo to catch a glimpse of his wife, Jane, who was there (with their son Nash), speaking on some phallocentric thing or other at the Joyce Conference. He'd had no mail except a long letter co-signed by his parents, and a long letter from Adolphus Mahan (enclosed with the manuscript of the Rexford biography and eight pages of—actually, very helpful—comments on it). The letter said that if he "just ran it through the typewriter one more time," it "really will fly as Part I of a Major Life. Very well done, Theo. It's alive. A high compliment. Do a last chapter, send me the revised draft, and the second half of the advance is yours. Take your time. Hope the play problem with Ford is resolving as well." (Mahan also wanted him to "give Amanda a ring at Claridge's.")

A third letter, Theo had opened greedily; it was from Rhodora (still subletting his house), but inside was only a Visa bill forwarded with a four-line note in which she described herself as "busy with the music thing," the weather back in Rome as "great," and which she signed "Love you lots." Theo felt lonelier and lonelier.

The hearty refusal of Londoners themselves to be hampered by the transportation strike (as they boated, biked, hiked, skated, and even pogo-sticked their way through the city) just made it worse. Although accustomed to solitary meals, his sojourns to unfamiliar restaurants had begun to make him melancholy too. Finally, exhausted by the blur of stimulus, by the anonymity of so many thousands of strangers pressing around him, worn out by his own lack of heartiness, he retired to his small dark hotel room, whose cracked wall was masked by terrible cardboard prints (one of a matador and one of gamboling springer spaniels), and whose thick flowered maroon wall-to-wall carpeting was ominously gritty to the feet. He spent an entire day there, lying on his bed drifting in and out of sleep. Then as he was headed to the toilet at the end of the hall, he stopped at a small bookcase filled with mostly grubby paperbacks, presumably left behind by decades of earlier guests. There between *Valley of the Dolls* and *Italian Made Easy*, he saw an old mildewed copy of a book he knew well: *Fortune's Favorite: A Life of Ralegh*, by Winifred Throckmorton. It was she who had brought Walter Raleigh so vibrantly to life that Theo had decided to write *Foolscap*. He took the discovery for a sign, and steeling himself to fight off his diffidence about imposing on strangers, he put through (after the loss of several ten-p coins to the bewildering pay phone in the hall), a trunk call to Barnet-on-Urswick in Devonshire. "Dame Winifred Throckmorton, please?"

"Yes? Yes?" The retired scholar's voice was piercing, and filled with swoops of tremulous warbles. "Of course it's you, Mr. Ryan. At the station, then, are you? Walk out the gate, you see it there?, turn left. No, my error, turn RIGHT, up the High . . . Oh. You're in London? Ah, not here at all then? . . . Terribly sorry, I took your note—too kind—to mean you were coming straight on. Misinterpretation of the text, ha ha! Nonsense, my fault entirely. Tomorrow then. Come along. Goodbye. . . . Pardon? Oh dear, expect he's rung off." And the phone clanked dead. Theo returned down the hall grinning; so much so that the young American woman clutching her robe as she made a nervous sprint from the bath to her room, took fright and broke into a trot.

Early in the morning, he made his way to Bedford Square, where a Georgian façade veiled the fin-de-siècle Hungarian opulence of Middendorf, Ltd. He was determined either to learn news of Ford or, leaving the city without it, go on himself to Cornwall after visiting Miss Throckmorton. He arrived at the agency just in time to help the receptionist, the Irish Miss Fitzhugh, push her bicycle up the steps and into the foyer. Theo had been on the premises so often that Miss Fitzhugh—a slender twenty-year-old with delicate fair skin and a tremendous quantity of eye makeup—was his oldest acquaintance in the city. And by now she'd warmed to him enough to take a flirtatiously caustic tone quite different even in accent from the stiff formality with which she answered the telephone.

"Hello, love," she waved. "Another grand and gorgeous day! Still not back yet from holiday, Mr. Middendorf, and no, I don't know when." She announced this as soon as Theo had stooped under the low door lintel and followed her into a fussily opulent waiting chamber dense with pink satin balloon curtains, peacock-bordered wallpaper, gilded chairs, and velvet ottomans. She added, "And I'm to tell you straight away, Mr. Ryan, if you won't be turning over this play script that belongs to Mr. Rexford—"

"Ah then, is it threats from himself now, Miss Fitzhugh?" Theo—unconsciously at first, and then increasingly for fun—had fallen into the habit of mimicking (or attempting to mimic—for he was quite inconsistent) the receptionist's Sligo brogue. "Well, then, Miss Fitzhugh, what? Gangland beatings? The Old Bailey?"

"Well, then . . ." She shrugged, apparently not having received instructions as to specific retaliations. "Well, you must then, that's all, isn't it?" She pushed up the sleeves of her thin red cardigan, exposing arms as white as the three large peonies in the amber glass vase beside her.

Theo leaned over the edge of her desk; it had an oriental look, black lacquered, with curved legs. He grinned at her. " 'Well then,' you're to tell Buzzy from me, before I'll do that, I'll eat every damned page of it first!" He scowled horribly. "Or I'll burn it."

"You'd never. Get on." In fact, Miss Fitzhugh preferred to think that he might; that Ryan's peculiar accent might mean he was one of those big-boned Scottish hotheads quite capable of stuffing an entire play script in his mouth and chewing it up. The notion appealed to her; frankly, she was bored by her job. She'd thought it'd be a lark to work for a theatrical agent, that she'd meet stars like Tom Cruise and Mel Gibson, but most of Mr. Middendorf's clients were old men in their forties, or worse. Or they were brainy sorts, stuck on themselves far more than on her, and (to judge from their conversation) much more interested in money than art. Where was their money, was just about all they ever said. Theo Ryan was young, good-looking, and treated her like a person. She smiled at him.

Theo, fairly certain by now that Buzzy Middendorf, unless ornately devious, really didn't know where the playwright was, smiled back: "You don't have even a phone number for Ford? I'll bet you do."

Miss Fitzhugh offered the mollification of a bigger smile. "My, and you've a head hard as rocks. Mr. Middendorf now, he says you're getting to be 'the *bone* of his existence.' " (The old theatrical agent, a native of Budapest, was famous for his cavalier contortions of English idioms, a trait which his young receptionist found as amusing as all British Islanders find anyone's inability to speak their language as well as they do.)

Theo rubbed at his sunburnt nose. "Listen. He told me on the phone I was a 'thorn around his neck.' "

"Oh, that's a new one." She laughed.

"Were you here when Ford came by in May? When he first got to England?"

"Oh, ay," she nodded, crossing her arms over her breasts as if to protect them in memory. "Just the once. Talked a streak, he did. I'll say this much for him, *sounds* a grand genius, doesn't he now?, Mr. Rexford does. And I've met plenty since coming here, don't."

"Plenty of geniuses?"

"It's them that says it." She wheeled sideways and answered the phone with pleasant indifference.

Theo prodded when she finished. "Ford talked a streak, and . . . ?"

"Had himself a bit of a nap, there on the sofa." She pointed at a soft Turkish-looking settee in a corner.

"Drunk?"

She tried not to smile, but failed. "Could be he'd had a pint."

"Could be he'd had a gallon." Theo flicked a rose-tinted crystal dangling from a Tiffany lamp shade. "Did he bring someone named Jenny Harte along? Blonde, American?"

Miss Fitzhugh shook her pencil at him. "Aren't you the nosy parker?"

Theo tried pulling rank. "I'm his official biographer. I know more about that man than he does himself."

It didn't work. "Except where he is," she said smugly.

Sinking on the settee, Theo sighed. "He may not know that either. Sometimes he doesn't."

Phones were ringing more often now; packages arrived by messengers with their trouser legs strapped for biking. Theo sat awhile watching Middendorf employees whisk in and out of the many doors that led to the waiting chamber. Most of the secretarial staff, like Miss Fitzhugh, were young, very attractive women.

Finally, he pushed himself up from the heap of soft cushions. "Miss Fitzhugh, have lunch with me?" He held out his hands. "A lonely stranger in a foreign land? Fellow Irishman?"

She looked at him, surprised into a blush that rose from her neck to her faintly freckled cheeks. "Well, I would really like that," she said. "But see, my bloke?—we're getting married—he comes round on his motorbike when I'm done here noontimes, and so we're after going out for a spot of something together. Come along with us?"

"No, it's you, or nothing. I'm off then," Theo said. "Don't miss me too much."

"Ah, I'll try my hardest. Back to the States?" She was disappointed.

"No, to Cornwall. . . . How big is Cornwall?"

"Never been. Only been here to London and home."

"I've got to get my play back, dammit!" Theo took down and angrily shook the signed photograph of Rexford ("Buzzy, Yours in debt, Ford"); it hung on the wall between photos of Noël Coward ("Mon petit Buzzzzz. Toujours, Noël") and T. S. Eliot ("To Josef, Regards, Tom"). Theo yelled at Ford's face, which was smirking at him in a maddening way. "I've come three thousand miles, you bastard!"

Stirred by the tall man's turmoil (which she attributed to blighted passion for this American blonde, Jenny Harte), Miss Fitzhugh made a sudden decision. Spinning about in her swivel chair, she took a flat package out of the file cabinet behind her. "Look here, Mr. Ryan. Don't you be telling a soul, but . . . This

just came for him. Have a look inside. Could be it'll give you a
hint-like where he's got off to."

Theo was around the desk beside her by the time she had tentatively slid a letter opener under the seal of the manila envelope.
He could now see that it was addressed to Ford Rexford at the
Middendorf agency. His heart spasmed so fast he had to squeeze
his eyes shut. When he opened them, he was still looking at what
he'd thought he had seen the receptionist riffling through: the
wrinkled copy of *Foolscap.*

"Damn! That's my play!"

"*Your* play?" Miss Fitzhugh looked skeptical. There was no
author listed on the cover page, nor in fact any title other than
"HISTORICAL PLAY." There was only a clerk's notation: "Return to Ford Rexford, c/o Middendorf." She tightened her grip
on the packet.

"Yes, mine!" Theo slapped his hand hard on her lacquered desk-
top. "What do you think I've been in here bugging you about for
weeks! Didn't I just say I wanted my play back? Look. Open it!
The first line. Isn't the character's name Raleigh? Doesn't it say,
"No need for hoarding now. I can be prodigal. As I was meant
to be. Light!"

Miss Fitzhugh flipped to the page. "No, it doesn't," she said.
"Nothing like."

"It doesn't?" He grabbed at the manuscript. "The bastard's
changed it then. What did he—" But Theo stopped. Clipped to
the cover was a note under the engraved letterhead of a firm of
eminent London producers. Its message turned his face as red as
the receptionist's sweater:

Ford dear fellow.

Where are you, rogue? Buzzy claims not to have a clue. Lying?
And why didn't you *see* me, when you dropped this thing off?

RE which: Many thanks, but must decline. Your young friend
may have talent, but given the subject matter, I'll pass. He's in over
his head. *Our* history, after all. Why so many of you Americans
want to muck about in it is a puzzlement. Really, you should
discourage him—put that positively—*En*-courage him to stick to

his own cabbage patch. As you do! Caught *Her Pride of Place* again Tuesday last. Sublime. Anything in the works for me?

W.F.D.

P.S. Sorry to let you down. You simply can't write plays like this anymore. Not in the twentieth century. As our beloved Buzzy would say, That's it in an eggshell.

"Give that back, Mr. Ryan!" Miss Fitzhugh and Theo engaged in a silent tug-of-war across the desk. "It's not addressed to you a'tall, now is it!"

"It's me he's talking about!" Theo hissed at her with such ferocity that she let go of the manuscript. His arm flung out and knocked over the Venetian glass vase, spilling water and peonies on piles of mail.

"Oh Jesus, Joseph, and Mary!" snarled Miss Fitzhugh as she snatched papers out of the water's path. "Well, don't be standing there!" she commanded in a sudden display of temper.

"All right, I won't." Theo turned briskly. "Sorry. Goodbye, Miss Fitzhugh." And, despite her shouts to return, he walked out the door of the glimmery gilted chamber, with his play and his letter of rejection tucked under his arm.

Three hours later he was on a train to Devonshire.

CHAPTER
21

{Enter a Soothsayer}

God, who is the author of all our tragedies, hath written out for us
and appointed us all the parts we are to play.

Sir Walter Raleigh

HOW DRAB AND MONOTONOUS were American trains compared
to this railway car with its wood-framed compartments and cozy
facing seats of worn plush. How empty would look American
highways after this array of villages and forests, towers and castles
and abbeys, parading past Theo's window without pause. Nature
here had grown more civilized, civilization more natural than at
home; there was none of the raw juxtaposition of wild mountains
and concrete shopping strips; time had smoothed the edges; the
scale could be comprehended. *Blue Guide* in hand, crouched near
the compartment's lowered glass, Theo followed his progress towards Devon. High over gold-grained plains, like a needle lancing
the clouds, he saw the soft yellow limestone spire of Salisbury
Cathedral, and later the medieval town of Shaftesbury, and then
the great houses near Yeovil in Sir Walter Raleigh country. There
he changed to the local train that would finally bring him to
Barnet-on-Urswick and Dame Winifred Throckmorton.

Theo felt grateful to the South-West Counties for distracting
him from the barbs of quotes that bored into his thoughts. "In
over his head. *Our* history, after all," the insufferable "W.F.D."
had said. Well, Mr. W.F.D., was ancient Egypt Shakespeare's
history? Had Marlowe grown up among the pampered Jades of
Asia? Theo snarled, vowing revenge.

On the other hand, these West End producers might know their business; he shouldn't dismiss their response out of hand. Or dammit, why shouldn't he? Hadn't Ford said Scottie Smith was wrong, when Broadway and the West End both idolized Scottie Smith! "Encourage him to stick to his own cabbage patch." Right! Were those producers sticking to theirs, when they mounted Rexford plays set in rural Texas? "You simply can't write plays like this in the twentieth century." Oh, you could *write* them. But could you get them produced? God knows, if it were a *real* Renaissance play they'd go crazy over it.

"In over his head!"

"Beg your pardon?" asked a portly gentleman, peering across at Theo around his folded *Times*. "Overhead? Yes, my case up there in the rack. Not disturbing you?"

Theo blushed. "No, I'm sorry, just thinking aloud."

"From the States, are you?"

Theo admitted it.

"Yes, well, we let you get away with that one." The portly man grinned, big square teeth under a bristly mustache.

Theo chuckled at what he took to be a joke about England's loss of the Revolutionary War, and, satisfied, the man disappeared again behind his newspaper.

No, thought the young American, as he watched a flock of sheep harried across a road by two small relentless dogs; no, he wasn't in over his head. At least he wasn't in over *Ford's* head. *Foolscap*, reread amid the clamor of Waterloo Station, was not as he remembered it. It was better. It wasn't that there were a huge number of changes from the draft Theo had seen tossed into the gold Lincoln back in Rome, but that each change rippled out into every part of the play — as when, after patient jiggling with strings of tiny electric bulbs, a Christmas tree suddenly lights up. He couldn't be angry. No, he *was* angry; but he was also impressed — and not just by how good Ford was, but how good *he*'d been shown to be himself. Didn't the people in this play now have the right to human voices?

But what about Ford? Should he pursue him to Cornwall, even though he now had in his possession the play, the thing he was ostensibly pursuing Ford for? And if he found him, what then? Oh, Theo had long imagined their meeting. He saw it sometimes on a foggy moor, a black wind whipping furze and heather against their legs as he and Ford fought atop jagged granite outcrops. He saw it sometimes on a barren coast, spumes of gray waves crashing high against chalk cliffs; and at the end of a narrow stone causeway that jutted into the sea—Rhodora standing in a black hooded cape like the French Lieutenant's Woman; while on the beach he and Ford slugged each other until Ford fell senseless in the foaming surf and had to be dragged out by his shirt. (It was always the same red-checked Pendleton shirt Ford had been wearing the day they'd met on Rhodora's Mountain.) At times, he'd make it Jenny Harte in the black cape, storm-swept and rain-drenched at the end of the jetty.

And occasionally, when the woman turned back from the sea, her face proved to be that of Maude Fletcher. This intrusion into the drama of revenge was disconcerting, since—while Ford's treachery against Rhodora, Jenny, and Theo himself was undeniable—he really had done nothing much to Maude except skip a few of her spiritual counseling sessions. It wasn't Ford's fault that Maude had preferred Herbie Crawford to Theo Ryan.

Well, then, it wasn't Theo's fault that Ford had run off with Jenny Harte, was it? Nor his business. What could he say, really, if they met? "Ford, here's a message from Rhodora," followed by a sock to the gut? Oh, he could tell Jenny: "Jenny, come home and finish your dissertation," but his advice was unlikely to be heeded. What would really happen? Theo imagined Ford leaning out of the half-door of a white stone cottage; resting his elbows on the sill. The door was painted bright blue, and inside the cottage a vase of blue flowers sat on a white mantel. He saw Ford (still in the wool checked shirt) slap his hands together and yell, "Theo! Jesus Fucking Christ! What are *you* doing here?! I'm glad to see you, big guy! Jenny, look who's here!"

So then, what's your response? thought Theo, knocking his fist so emphatically into his knee that his traveling companion gave him a troubled glance. "Ford, what I'm doing here is to tell you you've really pissed me off and let me down, and you've made Rhodora miserable, and you'll probably do the same to Jenny. You're a coward and a shit. That's what I'm here to tell you. So here's your play back; I hope you find an ending. And by the way, thanks for fixing up mine, and thanks for sending it to that producer. He didn't like it."

And he heard Ford say, "He didn't? Well, fuck him. He's wrong. Probably didn't read it anyhow."

Theo sighed aloud. This time the portly gentleman lowered his *Times* entirely. Theo excused himself and went out to stroll the corridor.

The train moved slowly through Dorset into the sun and Devonshire. Deep-green uplands unrolled behind yellow fields and clusters of stone farmhouses. In High Piddleminster, the man with the *Times* bid Theo goodbye. Then came Combe St. Mary. And then, at 5:07—precisely as promised by the timetable—a conductor passing by rapped on the glass of his compartment. "Here you are," he said, pointing. And there was Barnet-on-Urswick.

With its cobbled eaves and its trim fence, the reddish sandstone Victorian railway station (despite the absence of a tearoom, and the presence of a vending machine dispensing wretched-looking coffee in Styrofoam cups) looked so precisely like all the British village stations Theo had ever seen in movies that he half expected to come upon the decent adulterers from *Brief Encounter* hovering there in a tortured embrace, or Mrs. Miniver at the gate accepting her rose from the kindly stationmaster, or David Niven on the platform jollying the Immortal Battalion off to war. He saw no one who resembled any of them. Nor did he see anyone who resembled Dame Winifred Throckmorton, although when he'd called from London to tell her his arrival time, he had understood her to say she would meet the train. In fact, there was no one in the small waiting area except the ticket collector (who was absorbed in a wrestling match on the telly, and didn't look at all as if he might cultivate prize-winning roses as a sideline), and there was no one on the platform except two pimply teenaged boys in black vinyl jackets. They were sharing a single cigarette and a bottle of something wrapped in a paper bag, and didn't impress Theo as recruits for Military Immortality.

Also, while Dame Winifred had volunteered to arrange accommodations for him in a nearby inn, she hadn't mentioned which one. So, after a twenty-minute wait and an unsuccessful attempt to phone her, Theo picked up his bags, turned right out of the

gate, and crossed a little arched stone bridge over what he assumed
was the River Urswick. It was wide but shallow and so clear that
he could see trout quivering in the ripples above the rocks. He
watched them awhile, then started "up the High," as instructed.
The High was a very steep narrow street of slate cobbles deep
sunk in their bed. Shops, most of them gray or red stone, pressed
to the edges of the curbs, while second-story thatched dormers
reached across to neighbors on the other side.

When Theo reached the top, he sat down to catch his breath;
despite the blessedly cooler temperature here in the west, he'd
heated himself carrying the heavy luggage (he had with him everything he'd brought to England, which was considerably more than
he would ever bring again, particularly all the hard-covered
books). He rested beside a tall market-cross in the middle of what
he took to be the town square: before him an Elizabethan church;
on his left, the imposing King William Inn; on his right, the
smaller Nightingale. Little streets wound away in three directions;
no one of which, he now realized, Dame Winifred had specified as
hers. Rather than chance a mistake, he waited until a middle-aged
woman walking (or being pulled along by) an immense Great Dane
dog was hauled close enough for him to ask her if she could direct
him to "Lark Cottage."

Although unable to pause, the woman was able to help.
"Straight ahead," she wheezed. "Along Gate Row, at the corner,
can't miss it." She attempted a backward point but was jerked off
balance, and had time only to add before trotting away, "Saw her
just popping in at the station. Shan't be long, I expect."

"Dame Winifred Throckmorton?"

"Oh yes."

Gate Row ended in a narrow rounded street corner that curved
back down the hill. On one side was a half-timbered Tudor cottage
with fresh white plaster, green window trim, and gleaming black
thatched eaves a foot thick, clipped neatly over the dormers. A
plaque beside its door identified it as "The Heights"—quite accurately since one could from here glimpse the Urswick serpentin-
ing through the countryside below. Catty-cornered from "The
Heights" ran a low wall of uneven, mossy stones, behind which
grew a garden of such wild color and uncontrolled profusion that

the house it fronted could be seen only at the end of its brick walk. A slatted gate was hung between two squat stone pillars, each topped by a black orb. And nailed to this gate was a sign that said, "Lark Cottage." Opening the gate Theo accidentally leaned his hand against the top of one of the pillars. To his shock, the orb, which he'd assumed was iron, not only fell but bounced away into the street. He chased after what proved to be a painted rubber ball, nervously balanced it back on the pillar, and entered the yard.

From low silvery borders to lilacs clinging in clumps from the tops of walls, flowers grew everywhere—as if someone had randomly tossed great handfuls of seeds out the windows, mixing wild flowers, perennials, annuals, and even weeds. There seemed to be no pattern and no end to the colors: Blue delphiniums and orange poppies, purple irises, and gold achillea reached together for the sun. The whole place buzzed with delirious bees as Theo made his way past lavender foxglove and ruby-red peonies as high as his waist. Even on the path, little star-shaped daisies and nodding yellow pansies had pushed their way through cracks in the old bricks.

The small lopsided cottage itself was also of dark crumbly bricks, what little of it could be spotted behind gnarled vines of roses and clematis that climbed in a tangle over the rain gutters and onto a roof of hazardous-looking ancient red tiles. On either side of a faded black front door was a bow window with leaded-glass panels, the frames of which were also painted black. The door knocker, a brass bird with folded wings, looked, as it dangled from its one remaining screw, more like a duck hanging dead in a grocer's window than any lark for which the cottage might have been named. No one answered Theo's knock.

He had just returned to the gate when he heard a chinkling bell and looked up to see a very rusted-looking bicycle whirring towards him down the cobbled lane. Behind a wire basket crammed with packages, a stout bespectacled woman wobbled on the seat. It was undoubtedly his hostess, for her outfit was as out-of-control as her yard. She wore a plaid tam, a green tweed skirt, a black sweater, and a brown argyle vest over a red jersey. Her hair was gray and thick and stuck out bluntly from her chin line—rather like the sharply trimmed thatch on the nearby roof.

"Hallooo, Mr. Ryan?" she called in a high urgent way, as if she wanted Theo to catch her, and indeed she was barreling straight towards him awfully fast.

"Yes! Miss Throckmorton?"

She had passed him before her screeching brakes slowed her down enough to catch herself on a nearby postbox. Dismounting in a bustle of snagged hems and tangled sleeves, she headed back. "Do forgive me," she panted in her high piping voice. "Entirely muddled. *Not* the five forty-two then? But you've found your way, I see. Have you had your tea?"

"Not exactly, but . . . Dame Winifred?—"

"I've bought you some Devonshire clotted cream. Such a pleasure, Mr. Ryan." Pushing the bike back to the gate, she held out her hand, the fingers a little twisted with arthritis, and gave his an intense pumping. "You look very much as I thought you would. Quite tall and goldish. Elizabethan. Don't know how I knew." She looked up smiling at Theo, whose eyes looked even greener in his sun-browned face; his cotton shirt was creamy white and billowing, open at the throat, the sleeves rolled up on his long tan arms. She nodded at him happily. "You should have a beard, of course."

Close up Theo could see that, although very elderly, Miss Throckmorton's skin had a crinkled glow to it, with spots of pink on either side of a sharp nose, up and down which she continually nudged her glasses. He said, "I can't tell you how glad I am to meet you at last." He took the bicycle from her. "Thank you very much for letting me intrude on your schedule on such short notice."

Behind the wire-rimmed, loose-stemmed glasses, her hazel eyes were keen. "Mr. Ryan," she said, resting folded hands on a high-waisted stomach. "I have not so many visitors as you kindly suppose. And in my dotage, my schedule, apart from the—rather soon, I expect—necessity of expiring when called upon to do so, is entirely my own. Come in. . . . Here, let's just bring my bike. Watch that left pillar, the ball's a bit of a make-do. Actually, it always puts me in mind of Sir Walter Raleigh when it flies off. Fortune's tennis ball, you know." She stopped midway on the brick walk. "Oh my, the red peonies. Absolutely brilliant."

Theo looked around him again. "I have a little perennial border at home. But this is breathtaking. How have you managed in the drought?"

"Drought?" She looked momentarily puzzled. "Ah, that's *true*. It's been quite dry."

"Well, you're obviously quite a gardener, rain or not."

"Rubbish," she said, stooping to yank weeds (and a few columbines) from a bed of irises. "The ladies in Barnet pay collective calls ('not strong but by a faction,' you know), and speak of my garden as if of a dying invalid, urging me to pruning, mulching, and in particular, *thinning*. I'm afraid the poor woman from whom I bought 'Lark Cottage' can't bear to look in when she passes by. She sowed, and I failed to reap. In any case, many of the local ladies find me insufficiently quaint to make my eccentricity palatable." She threw the weeds over her shoulder.

"Everyone does appear to know you. A lady with a huge Great Dane told me you'd gone to the railway station."

"Ah. Mildred. 'The Heights.' " She pointed at the neat Tudor cottage across from her. "Such a snoop, but terribly impressed by my title."

"Yes, which do you prefer, Dame Winifred or Miss Throckmorton?"

She snatched the heads off a few chives. "Well, Throckmorton, I should think. My family called me 'Winnie,' which I detested as you might imagine. My old friends call me 'Freddie.' 'Dame Winifred,' yes, yes. Very sweet of the queen, but I would have preferred a pension a bit larger than the one Spenser was given five hundred years ago."

"You live on fifty pounds a year?" Theo blurted this out, then apologized for his nosiness.

"Heavens no. Joking. You Americans, quite generous in buying up my books year after year. Oh dear! Is all that luggage yours?"

Assuming that the source of her alarm was the thought that he might be planning a visit of eighteenth-century proportions, he quickly explained that he'd "overpacked," and that tomorrow he'd be on his way.

"Impossible," she told him, opening the door with a brisk prod of the bike tire. "I insist on taking you to Sherborne tomorrow.

Raleigh would never forgive you if you didn't see it. And the Abby Church. Sir Thomas Wyatt is buried there, of course, poor fellow. So foolish to chase after Anne Boleyn. I'm sure she led him on." Miss Throckmorton paused in the doorway, and raised her hands to her cheeks with a strangely romantic gentleness. " *'Noli me tangere.* For Caesar's I am, and wild for to hold, though I seem tame.' Marvelous!" She shook her head, and moved on. "But reckless. Just off to the left here. Mind the highboy. Looked *so* much smaller in my rooms at Oxford."

Theo squeezed down a small hall, stepped over a wood carton filled with scholarly journals, and followed her into a sitting room at the rear of the cottage. A glance out its rear window revealed a brick-walled back yard, more flowers, and a large wire cage on stilts with an immense (and angrily squawking) parrot in it.

Dame Winifred continued talking as she switched on two little tassled lamps. "And then, of course, Wyatt's harebrained son running about the countryside stirring up rebellion for Anne's daughter. Promptly loses *his* head. We may thank God Elizabeth had more sense, young as she was. Such a mess in here. You remember how the Council accused her: 'Wyatt wrote you treason.' Back her answer comes: 'A man may write what he will. Show me where I answered him.' Remarkable girl." The old woman stood, one arm half twisted out of her moth-pocked sweater, momentarily lost in contemplation of Elizabeth Tudor's savvy.

"Yes, may I just—"

"Dear me. Babbling. Put those bags down anywhere. Dreadful clutter, I know. Far too many books and not nearly enough shelves. Mind the cats. Tea? Oh dear!" She suddenly darted out of the room, and after the sound of banging kitchen pipes, Theo saw her through the window scampering across her backyard with a basin of water. When she reached the large wire cage, she flung the entire contents of this basin straight at the parrot. He immediately stopped his harangue, and began shaking out his wing feathers. A few more seconds and Miss Throckmorton was back in the sitting room, apologizing. "That was Orinoco. He has to be watered down," she said, apparently in explanation, though Theo had no idea why the parrot required this service. "Now, have a seat. I'll put on the kettle."

Miss Throckmorton's furnishings resembled her wardrobe and her garden: colorful, disorderly, and desperately in need of thinning. Most in evidence were the shelves, stacks, and boxes of books and records—both of every age, genre, and condition. But there were a great many other things (some extremely nice, some merely odd, and some better sent to the dump), all crammed so tightly together that Theo formed a very stately notion of the size of the retired don's former "rooms at Oxford." To eat his scorched scone, he had to clear a large tabby cat, the soundtrack to *Zorba the Greek*, and pounds of correspondence off the chintz loveseat, slide one foot under a porcelain coal bin, and balance his tea on a tiny whatnot table whose Chippendale proportions were marred by silver duct tape wrapped around two of the legs. Miss Throckmorton had explained over the telephone her inability to "put him up" in the cottage, and she had not exaggerated. There were so many books piled on her own bed, she now confessed, that she herself was sleeping on the couch in her study. This study (under eaves too angled for him to stand upright) she showed him at his request, although it turned out that she hadn't actually written the volumes which had so inspired him on that particular desk, nor indeed could he have seen it anyhow, so piled was it with more books, and yet another large cat.

She had three cats, all of them males with prizefighter faces, and each named for one of her famous manuscript discoveries. Tom (for Thomas Kyd), Kit (for Christopher Marlowe), and her favorite, a sleek black malevolent-looking creature named Water (Queen Elizabeth's nickname for Walter Raleigh). Over the next hours, Raleigh himself formed a large part of Dame Winifred's conversation, although Theo and she talked of many other subjects—their teaching and research, their agreements and disagreements with other scholars' theories. She showed Theo where and why he'd "gone wrong" in his Shakespeare book, and listened intently to his rebuttal before dismantling it. Throughout their talk, she neither asked for, nor offered, any personal information at all, and clearly assumed that his answer to her query "Why are you in England?" would be a library shelf number. He didn't disabuse her. "I came for the manuscript of a play," he said. "A modern play."

"Ah, yes, you teach contemporary drama as well." She nodded as if it were a foible of his youth. "I like very little of it. There is one. Your American Joshua Ford Rexford, I think actually quite good. Of course, he has no language, but that's hardly the man's fault in these monosyllabic times. And I am fond of the cinema," she added encouragingly. "*Doctor Zhivago, Duel in the Sun.* The big screen. Shake the superflux! Cast of thousands! Very Elizabethan. Don't you suppose Marlowe would have relished writing the script for *Spartacus*?"

As evening lingered in the slow summer sky, Dame Winifred talked of the Elizabethans as if she lived among them—and lived a racy life indeed there, brimming with lust and blood, piracy, plots, massacres, and murders. And in her talk the great courtier Walter Raleigh took center stage, as he had taken the leading role in her intellectual life for many decades. She spoke of him with such familiarity, such a range of pride, exasperation, and sorrow, that Theo realized that Raleigh had laid claim to Miss Throckmorton's heart as well. She was, in her way, she had long been, in love with Sir Walter Raleigh. And after all, whom might she have met in her bookish girlhood, or over her long Oxford years in the Bodleian Reading Room, who could match all that silver and swagger? Who could there be like that dangerous black-haired sailor with the double pearl in one ear and the lilt of Devon in his endless shimmer of words? Who else like that six-foot poet, scientist, warrior, historian, botanist, the scourge of Spain and discoverer of New Worlds? And perhaps most important of all to the old spinster was that the man had been so loving a husband to one Elizabeth Throckmorton, the lady-in-waiting for whom he gave up the favor (and the fortune) of the Virgin Queen. Fierce, loyal Bess Throckmorton, who carried her husband's embalmed head about with her in a red leather bag until the day she died.

Listening to Dame Winifred talk of Raleigh, hearing her quote from poetry he already knew by heart, hearing again the anecdotes with which he had lived for years—the young American came close to mentioning *Foolscap*—which he had, in fact, at that moment in his suitcase. But he didn't. And months later, he would remember how he'd almost told her, and would think how everything would have been different if he had.

"Are you then," he asked, as later that evening the two of them walked back towards town together, "descended from Elizabeth Throckmorton's family?"

"I am." She smiled, buttoning (in the wrong holes) a tweed jacket that did not look like the mate to her skirt. "Bustling, clever people they were, the Throckmortons, back in Tudor days. Decent men. But careful to change sides before the wind did. Unlike Raleigh, who was so sure he could change the wind itself. And so wrong."

" 'But stars may fall; nay, they must fall when they trouble the sphere wherein they abide.' "

She stopped, peering up at him. "Well, now, young man, you do know your Raleghagana quite well indeed. . . . Not much farther. Rest your arms a moment. The church over there, Early Perpendicular, of course, Norman font. The King William, coaching inn, Georgian. A bit dear, and the chops are tough. I've booked you into the Nightingale. Jacobean. Charles the First said to have hid here one night. Poor cowardly man, seems to have hid in half the inns in the country."

"Do they serve meals?"

"Expect I've starved you!" She patted various pockets until pulling from one a large watch on a ribbon. "Quarter past nine. Time is so terribly inconsistent, I find, the way it hurries on or stands still. Our market-cross, early fifteenth century, Saxon site. And our sky—" Lifting her chin towards the deep blue canopy of rolling clouds still gold-tinged even now, the old woman heaved a rapturous sigh that shook through her body and toppled her plaid tam unto the cobblestones.

"All English." Theo smiled, and picking back up his luggage, and her tam, took as deep a breath as she.

"Right then. Thank you, yes, my hat. Here we are. Hope it suits."

Theo looked up at the half-timbered front, at the painted sign of the nightingale hanging above the black nail-studded door. It suited perfectly. He even was given the room, up worn steep stairs, and around dark narrow corners, the room with open casements and carved canopy bed where Charles the First might have slept (if sleep he could—said the dramatizing proprietor—with Cromwell's army close on his heels).

In the "Spirits & Victuals Room" of the Nightingale, Theo and

Dame Winifred ate their late supper beneath a low black-beamed ceiling bowed under the weight of years and dark with centuries of soot. She confessed that she ate there nearly every night, finding cooking "a bore when it works, and a mess when it doesn't." When he saw that above the huge fireplace hung a small grimy painting of Sir Walter Raleigh, he was sure she came here for that reason too, and asked her if she thought whoever had put it there could have known that Spenser had called Raleigh "the summer's nightingale."

"I should like to think so, Theodore, but no. May I call you Theodore?"

"Please do," he said.

Hazardously sawing away at a thick lamb chop, she went on. "Fact is, a quarter of the shops in this area have his pictures in them. See his face on mugs, plates, jumpers, the lot." She speared the meat, which had flown off her plate after too vigorous a saw, back onto her fork. "Have more chips and sprouts. Potatoes, my weakness." She was in fact a voracious eater of everything available and finished off the heavy meal with two servings of batter pudding swimming in rich Devonshire cream.

With all the food, several pints of bitters, and the exertions of his journey, Theo was feeling very drowsy by now (it was eleven), and he occasionally lost track of his indefatigable companion's words. They were talking about Raleigh's epic poem, the ostensibly massive *Cynthia*, of which only fragments survived. She agreed that the fragments were all there had ever been; that unlike his steady friend Spenser, Raleigh was too easily distracted, too "flipperty-gibbety a bird" ever to have written a poem as long as he'd claimed he'd written; that in a word, he'd lied, "not the first time, and certainly not the last." It was then that Dame Winifred, wiping clots of cream from her sweater front, said something that jarred Theo to attention.

She said, "No sense looking for that poem. Total sham. What I do think the man wrote, Theodore, is a play." She smiled secretively, almost sheepishly, at him.

He stared at her a moment. ". . . You believe Raleigh wrote a play?"

"No one agrees, of course. Thought me utterly senile when they pensioned me off. My brains all broken, as poor Walter said of himself in a histrionic moment—one of far too many, the rascal."

"That's ridiculous. Your brains are—well, you should hear my colleague Jonas Marsh talk about your brains. He—"

"Ah, Marsh, Marsh. Yes. Excellent job editing the Congreve. Of course, I have a few quibbles, but—"

"See? I've never met anyone who so lives her work as you."

Dame Winifred placed her hand tentatively to her temple, as if to reasure herself that all was well inside. "I suppose I do 'live my work,' as you nicely put it. In these times, I find so many of the younger scholars do not. They live their careers. Which is, you know, rather different, isn't it?"

"Yes, it is." Two things should be said about Theo Ryan's emotions at the moment. First, he felt a strong affection for this old woman rise within him, and second, he felt a curiosity so intense about the possibility of a real Raleigh play, that it temporarily blocked from his thoughts the fact of his own Raleigh play. To that extent did his admiration for Dame Winifred's scholarship reach—if she thought something so, against all evidence, perhaps it was so. "But never performed?" he asked.

"Expect not. And a prose play. Not an early play, not when his little friends Kyd and Marlowe were scribbling them. But in the Tower, towards the end. Sixteen sixteen, even 'eighteen. Fourteen years the bird was caged, and forced to sit down at a desk. Had to write his way back onto the great stage. You know the man couldn't live without an audience. Look at the incredible quantity of prose he produced locked up."

"But LeFranc doesn't list anything resembling a play in Raleigh's canon. Wouldn't it have shown up in the *Remains*? Or been mentioned by the early biographers? I mean, he was such a cult figure early on, and there was so much copying of his manuscripts, and circulating, surely—"

"I think it was sent with his immediate effects—" She shuddered. "Including, dear God, the man's head—to his widow."

Theo sipped at his cold coffee. "Because of all his theatrical rhetoric? 'Our graves . . . drawn curtains when the play is done,' and the rest? His self-dramatizing? Therefore you think he was writing a play?"

"Oh, rubbish. I'm a scholar, man, not a psychoanalyst." Her eyes glittered behind the spectacles. "I think it because I have a letter from Elizabeth Throckmorton in which she says so."

Theo put the cup down. ". . . She says so?"

"In context, that construction is indicated."

"But it couldn't be an extant play."

Dame Winifred Elizabeth Throckmorton licked a last bit of cream from her spoon. "It might be."

"You've looked for a manuscript—?"

"Fifteen years. Eight years, since my retirement." Taking off her glasses, she rubbed tiredly at her eyes. "Frankly, Theodore, if I could find it, I could die quite contentedly, I think. I should know I'd made . . . a difference."

"Oh, how can you say that! When you've already made such a huge difference. You've given so much to other scholars. You've changed the field!" Theo was moved to touch her hand, which she acknowledged with a brisk pat.

"Yes, I suppose. But this, you see, is . . . rather special to me."

"But the likelihood of actually finding it at this point, Miss Throckmorton! It's impossible."

"Oh dear no," she said, and turned her eyes to the dark portrait of Raleigh above the fire. "I expect if he wants me to find it, I will."

CHAPTER

22

{The Manor Bourne}

All this was mine, and was taken from me unjustly.

Sir Walter Raleigh,
passing Sherborne on his way to the Tower

WHILE *Foolscap* hadn't been at the front of Theo's mind at dinner, he hadn't lain long in (possibly) Charles the First's high carved-oak bed before he started to think of it. And as he did, a thought began buzzing like a gnat around his head, keeping him from sleep. It came at first as a pleasant fantasy of revenge. What a fool he could make of Mr. W.F.D. The thought was next shrewdly disguised (even from himself) as an act of charity. Dame Winifred expected to find a play Raleigh had written in the Tower. She believed in a strange magical way that Raleigh wanted her to find it. She had been mocked for her belief. Old and slighted, she hadn't long to live and would die happier if she were proved right. But that there was such a play was, frankly, improbable. Just as unlikely the chance of finding it now even if it had existed.

Foolscap was about Sir Walter Raleigh writing a play about himself in the Tower. What if *Foolscap* had actually been Raleigh's play, the way Jonas Marsh had talked about what-if-Bolt-had-written-*A-Man-for-All-Seasons*-so-that . . . ? What a gift to Dame Winifred, what a revenge on her detractors!

"Americans shouldn't try this sort of thing," had said "W.F.D." "You simply can't write plays like this in the twentieth century."

All right, assume that London producer was right. In that case, it was unlikely that anyone would ever produce *Foolscap*. Well then, why not say it wasn't from this century? Why not say it was by the man who had first claimed America for England, five hundred years ago? As long as the characters in *Foolscap* were the creations of some twentieth-century nobody called Theo S. Ryan, they might never find themselves on a stage. But imagine their fates if their author were the great Elizabethan? Or even *might* be the great Elizabethan? Beyond doubt, if Dame Winifred accepted the authenticity of the play, a dozen other Raleigh scholars would deny it, if only from envy and contentiousness. And the controversy itself would be enough to lure producers. Maybe academic rivals would rush to the fray: Marston or Webster scholars might claim *Foolscap* for their author, or Bacon, or even . . . maybe *Shakespeare* scholars would wonder if it were just possible that, off in his Stratford retirement, the Bard had . . .

"Oh for God's sake," Theo muttered aloud. "You're out of your mind!" He turned over, yanking twisted sheets and comforter with him. What a stupid fantasy. Wait'll he told Jonas. It could never be done. It shouldn't be done. What a horrible thing to do to Dame Winifred, even if he could, which he couldn't. He could never fool her. And if he did, and got caught (which of course he would), his career would be over. His career? He'd probably go to jail. "You jerk," Theo snorted at himself, and pulled the feathery pillow over his head. Finally he fell asleep, trying to remember the name of the eighteenth-century man who'd plagiarized a Shakespeare play he'd called *Vortigern and Rowena*, and who'd seen it laughed off the stage opening night at the Drury Lane.

The next morning Theo chuckled over what he thought of as midnight mind-racing. Dame Winifred had collected him early at the Nightingale in a squat snub-nosed Hillman Imp so clawed with scratches that he wondered if it had been the victim of nail-wielding vandals. By eight, they were on their way in this vehicle to Dorset, where he was, to her gratification, suitably moved by his tour of Sherborne, despite the fact that so many alterations had been made in the manor house after King James took it away from the condemned Raleigh and made a present of it to his boyfriend. And to Theo the heraldic inscription above the immense alabaster fireplace, *Deo Non Fortuna* ("By God, not by Fortune"), sounded like the next tenants' slap at Raleigh's sense of his own grandiose destiny; or perhaps they'd meant it defensively—a public denial that they were vultures, battening on the decay of a better man. But Raleigh's dream was in Sherborne's design, still carved in the ceilings, still crouching in the stone roebucks upon the roof, and there were galleries and gardens where one could feel the great Elizabethan still in the air.

Thrilling in a different way was riding in Miss Throckmorton's old Imp up and down the B roads of the hilly Dorset countryside, for her driving bore, in its rash and myopic exuberance, all too striking a resemblance to that of Mr. Toad from *The Wind in the Willows*. Theo was continually slamming his foot into the floorboard as lorries rumbled towards them on what a flood of adrenaline insisted was the wrong side of the road. Moreover, many of these roads were so narrow that at their widest two cars could pass only if each veered halfway into the shouldering hedgerows—while at their narrowest a single car was thunked by bushy branches on both sides. High and brambly and unending, these hedgerows hid not only any view of the ostensibly lovely countryside but any ditches into which a tire might suddenly plummet. As far as Theo could tell, what the green and pleasant land of England looked like from a car's eye view was a solid green wall of—hedgerows.

Whatever the logistics of British driving, Dame Winifred had not mastered them. For one thing, she couldn't see (for she had broken one stem off her glasses, so that they kept falling into her lap). For another, she went too fast, and often on the wrong (that is, the right) side of the road. For another, she often went on the wrong road. And this despite the fact that by her own admission she had traveled between Barnet-on-Urswick and Sherborne "a thousand times." Obviously, thought Theo, never by the same route twice. "Sorry, my error," she would say, attempting last-minute jackknifing maneuvers. After piping shrilly, "Sheer stupidity!," she *backed up* in a fairly busy roundabout, and muttering

"I'd rather expected the B 3297 here," she shot off onto what she was sure was an unpaved lane, but which turned out, a mile of bumps and cow piles later, to be clearly posted as a footpath.

She had what might have been the good habit of beeping her horn, had she not been more likely to do it going down inclines than on the upgrades, when it might have been a useful warning to indignant tractors chugging over the crest, or flocks of intransigent sheep meandering around curves. "Right then," she would say, weaving in reverse backwards down the hill with hawthorn branches thwack, thwack, thwacking against the mirror outside Theo's door.

Throughout their trip, she was happy to fill him in about this possible lost play of Sir Walter Raleigh's, but during explanations of how she had traced Throckmorton papers to this place, or lost track of that trail, she occasionally lost track of the highway too. While fulminating against King James for throwing Bess Throckmorton out of Sherborne, she missed her turnoff for Wyatt's grave. An analysis of records of sale for Raleigh's sea charts—and she'd missed the town of Crewkerne, where she'd planned to show him a fifteenth-century grammar school. The story of how, after Raleigh's death, Bess had had to beg the king repeatedly to give her the books left behind in the Tower cell—and they'd run out of petrol.

Over lunch, Theo's guide decided upon "a scoot down to Budleigh" to show him the thatched farmhouse of Hayes-Barton where Raleigh had been born, and to let him "sniff the air" at the red-cliffed coast where Raleigh and his half-brother must have stood as boys, gazing out at an unmapped ocean that was to carry them off to glory, and in the end, in different ways, was to kill them. Miss Throckmorton parked a little closer to those cliffs than Theo would have preferred, and after some treacherous gear-grinding and tire-shredding, they were obliged to ask three stocky fishermen to help lift the rear wheel off a large rock.

Theo determined as he changed the tire to take a more active role in their travels. "If we are headed west," he therefore inquired as they set forth, "should the sun really be *behind* us?"

"Absolutely right, I'm muddled again." She grabbed at the spectacles hanging sideways on her nose, and shoved them in place.

"Just turn about then—" And with screaming tires, the little green Hillman Imp sluiced in and out of marshy meadow grass. "There now! One must keep one's eyes *skinned* to the road, mustn't one?"

Theo wholeheartedly agreed.

At the end of a terrifying search for her pocket watch, she announced, "It's only half past five. I think we have time for Bourne. And it's quite close to home. Let's just find the A thirty-five, shall we? We'll hurry along."

A glance at the speedometer suggested that Miss Throckmorton was already hurrying along at ninety-five miles an hour, but he decided that in the glaring sun his angle of vision must be deceiving. "Bourne?" he said, and slipped on the pair of sunglasses with Day-Glo green rims that he'd purchased in a hurry at Newark Airport.

"Bourne House. Seat of the Earl of Newbolt. Just the Devon side."

"Oh, yes. The Newbolt Library's there." (This was a famous private collection dating back to the 1660s.) "I've seen pictures of Bourne House."

"Lovely, isn't it?"

"We turn just ahead, I believe. The A thirty-five? Left, Miss Throckmorton. TURN LEFT!"

Tire squeals, and a burly fist shaken out the window of a passing dairy van. "Thank you very much. Exactly the road we want," said Dame Winifred. "So you see, Theodore, when Lady Raleigh was forced to go live with her Throckmorton relatives in West Horsley, she took with her what manuscripts, scientific instruments and so forth she'd managed to salvage from the jackals. And to make ends meet, she and Carew (their poor son Carew, of course) sold off Raleigh's effects bit by bit. Publishers were quite eager for the papers, and collectors for any souvenir. Carew even peddled medicinal receipts. 'In my father's hand,' he made sure to point out. Raleigh was, what would you say today?, a 'superstar.' People adored him."

"At times. He was booed at his trial."

"By scum." She brushed them away angrily. "And of course he went to the scaffold so magnificently. I quite agree that when the Stuarts killed Sir Walter Raleigh, they condemned themselves to death." Her grim face suggested that the Stuarts had gotten what they deserved.

"But some of these papers Lady Raleigh kept."

"Until the day she died. Eighty-two she was. Three years my senior." The old woman was quiet a moment, her crooked fingers gently patting the steering wheel. ". . . And when she did die, in sixteen forty-seven, a large lot of Raleigh's books (including many he'd looted from the Spanish in Cadiz) got bought by Francis Stanlow—"

"The first earl."

"Then just a young popinjay companion of Charles the First. When Charles the Second returned to the throne, he made this fellow Earl of Newbolt in gratitude—as you know—for the man's loyalty to his father. He also gave him Bourne Manor, after evicting the current tenant."

Theo said, "Home improvement was a rather chancy affair back in those days, wasn't it?"

"My dear," she snorted. "Survival was a rather chancy affair. If that pig Henry the Eighth wanted your abbey, he simply chopped off your head."

Dame Winifred had spent the eight years of her retirement tracing the dispersal of Raleigh's large library and his literary effects. She had deduced from her research that if there was a lost play, chances were it had been bundled in with the volumes bought by the first Earl of Newbolt. For, after a dissipated youth, this man had apparently turned into an insatiable reader, or at least an insatiable collector, of books, and by his middle years had become so obsessed with his bibliophilic hobby that his wife, the infamous Countess Charlotte, had been able to indulge in a series of love affairs (one of them the subject of a play by a famous Restoration wit), without the bookish earl ever noticing her late hours.

Dame Winifred's theory was still only a theory. Unfortunately, the catalogue prepared by the second earl's secretary had been destroyed in a fire set off by the fourth earl's fascination with the new theory of electricity. Luckily, at least three-quarters of the library (though not the fourth earl) had survived the accident. But without the catalogue there were no records of the original purchases of Raleigh's books. "Wasn't," Theo asked her, giving

his seatbelt a nervous check, "wasn't the Newbolt Collection catalogued again in seventeen eighty-five?"

"Quite right, Theodore," she gave his knee an approving tap.
"And again in eighteen-o-nine, eighteen seventy-one, and every
few decades or so since."

"And none turned up a Raleigh play."

"No. I've spent months at Bourne myself. Very kind of Horry
Stanlow—His Lordship. I've found eight printed volumes that
belonged to Sir Walter. But no more, and no manuscripts." She
turned and gave Theo a steely glare. "That doesn't mean there
aren't more left at Bourne."

"The road! The road!" he shouted, then dispensed with words,
and grabbed the wheel in time to avoid a startled cleric on a bicycle. "Remember: Eyes skinned to the road."

"There were two dozen sold, and only eight found," she said,
gripping the wheel.

On they sped to Bourne.

Back in the 1960s, when many of the Great Houses of Great
Britain had been auctioned for taxes, or put on the Trust to keep
their owners off the dole, or sold for exorbitant sums to innocent
rock stars, a few of the more enterprising survivors of the nobility
determined to save their ancestral seats by exploiting them as tourist attractions. They grasped the idea that, like rock stars, they
had something to offer: They had their privacy. They could trade
the fact of their aristocratic lives for the means to continue them.
And so rather than mourn a past of endless wealth, endless land,
and endless leisure, they looked to a future in which they could
package that past and sell it to those who envied it. Rather than
moon futilely back on feudal days when the peasants worked for
them for free, they would go to work for peasants, and charge for
it. Longleat led the way with its camel rides and hippos and the
bloodstained waistcoat in which Charles the First had been executed. Others followed.

Dame Winifred's friend Horatio (Horry) William St. Denis
Stanlow, ninth Earl of Newbolt, was the first of his family to enter
the tourist business, and by the time he did, competition had
stiffened. He owned in Bourne a magnificent estate (Tudor front,

Caroline wings, Capability Brown landscaping), plus the great library, a few good paintings, and some displayable knickknacks (Mary Queen of Scots' toothpick, a lock of Byron's hair, one of Queen Victoria's baby shoes), but he had little capital to promote these. Nor to his chagrin had he any especially illustrious or interestingly vile ancestors to trade in. No one had imprisoned royalty in the Lady Chapel or hacked a relative to death in the Long Gallery at Bourne. No one had composed immortal verse in its pavilion or committed a notorious crime in its topiary garden. True, his thrice-great-aunt had corresponded with Tennyson, and had written an unpublished novel about the first earl's unfaithful wife, Countess Charlotte, entitled *She Lived for Love,* but no one in the family had known about the book until after the aunt had died, and no one after that had been able to finish it.

As things turned out, however, young Horry Stanlow (who had failed to distinguish himself at Oxford in anything but two-man crew and dancing "The Twist") was a natural business man. He began with a small admission fee to the Bourne grounds, then a separate fee for the house, then guided tours, then tour books, then—for an extra pound—a tour book personally autographed by himself or his wife, the photogenic Countess Andrea (depending on which of them was on duty). By the time he was forty, he was a Baedeker starred attraction. But what had really inspired the ninth Earl of Newbolt to greatness was the jealousy of his neighbor and contemporary, the Marquess of Urswick, who'd rowed for Cambridge. Fifteen years ago, the bilious marquess (freezing to death in his nearby Norman castle) had sneered at Newbolt for "trafficking with the hoi polloi." Ten years ago, he had secretly installed his own ticket booth in his gateway, then a Tea Room in his stables, then a Dungeon of Medieval Torture Instruments in his armory passage. The Earl of Newbolt had retaliated with a Cafeteria in the tithe barn, a Petting Zoo beside the greenhouse, and a Costume Museum in the wine cellar. Both put in Souvenir Shoppes and sold postcards, T-shirts, Druidical crystals, and dolls of the wives of Henry the Eight.

And so it had gone on escalating through the years, as the earl and marquess sneaked over to each other's estates to count the tour buses in their expanded car parks, and to spy on new attractions. When Urswick imported a hundred miniature deer, New-bolt invested in two hundred free-roaming peacocks. When New-bolt claimed Elizabeth the First had eaten in his Banquet Hall, Urswick announced that Henry IV had slept in his Round Tower. As soon as there were medieval minstrels on the battlements and paddle boats in the moat of Urswick Castle, there were Shake-spearean actors in the forecourt and go-carts on the Palladian bridge of Bourne House.

Horry Stanlow had been happy to have Dame Winifred Throck-morton scrounging through his library day after day looking for Raleigh's play. In the first place he knew her. He'd attended a few of her lectures at Oxford, though not enough to do very well on his exams. Moreover, while at her research, she not only didn't bother the tourists, she was quite willing to answer their questions whenever they assumed she was stationed there to do so. In fact, the earl had offered to hire her as a regular. She knew more about the collection than its librarian, and certainly much more than the earl did. A lanky handsome man now in his early fifties, Stanlow was an excellent rider, angler, and ballroom dancer, but he'd never been much of a reader. None of the Stanlows had been, since the mid-eighteenth century.

That certainly didn't mean that it wouldn't make the ninth earl ecstatic if Dame Winifred should find on his premises an unknown play written by Sir Walter Raleigh. It would utterly destroy the Marquess of Urswick.

Theo was fairly certain they'd taken another wrong turn. Long after he'd seen the high ornamental chimneys of Bourne, they had failed to reach the manor itself, or anything that resembled a gatehouse, a formal drive, or even an informal drive. They seemed instead to be careening through an interminable meadowy forest, and although he knew that Inigo Jones, designer of Bourne Park, had been famous for his naturalism, these woods seemed both too wild and too big for anything planned by a human. In addition, he thought he had seen a buffalo about two miles back.

"Miss Throckmorton," he ventured. "Do you think it's possible that we turned before we reached the main entrance? That little dirt road was really small. And now, to tell you the truth, we don't appear to be on anything like a road at all."

"It is odd," she agreed, but kept going.

Theo's suspicions were confirmed when they skidded down a grassy hill and found themselves about fifty feet away from a glade of low trees at the foot of which sprawled three African lions. He pulled the emergency brake almost out of its casing, and the Hillman bucked to a stop. There looked to be a dry moat, presumably a deep one, around the glade, but he couldn't be sure. "Let's back up," he suggested.

Before they could do so, a tan jeep with an enclosed metal top roared up behind them, and its uniformed driver, lowering his window, screamed out it. *"How the bloody hell did you get in here?"*

Miss Throckmorton piped back at him. "We really have very little idea. Sorry. We're going to Bourne House."

"This isn't the way!"

"We'd rather concluded that," she admitted, replacing her glasses on her nose, and restarting the engine. "Could you direct us then?"

"Safari's not opened yet," the man went on, red-faced. "Public's not allowed." He looked around nervously at the male lion who had stood up with an amazingly loud growl and was now ambling to the edge of the glade.

"We understand that." She nodded sternly. "I'm Dame Winifred Throckmorton. I'm an acquaintance of the earl's. I've brought Professor Ryan to see the library."

"There's a dry moat around those lions, isn't there?" Theo pushed Dame Winifred back, and shouted past her. "THERE'S A MOAT?"

"Needs to be wider," the man yelled, and rolled up his window fast.

As if it had heard him, the lion crouched, twitched its rear, then leapt with no trouble over the ditch. He ran forward a few yards, stopped to look them over, then turned towards the jeep and growled at it.

"Jesus Christ! Back up, back up!" Theo shouted, unceremoniously grabbing Miss Throckmorton's hand on the clutch and shoving at it.

A foot at a time, the safari guard was lurching the jeep forward in short jerks, and using his motor to roar back at the beast.

"Too fascinating!" said Dame Winifred. "A game of territorial machismo. Challenge. Counterchallenge."

The lion raced towards the jeep, which scooted erratically backwards. Then the jeep revved its motor and raced towards the lion, which spun sideways, wheeled around, charged, and actually got its forepaws up on the hood. The guard's shouts of "*You bastard!*" could be heard through the closed windows. From their glade, the lady lions were on their feet and watching all this with interest.

Theo groaned. "I don't think this is a game!"

"Never seen anything like it!" Dame Winifred admitted with enthusiasm. "They're so very much like cats, aren't they? Simply immense ones."

By blasting his horn and bucking slowly forward, the safari guard was gradually maneuvering the lion back towards the ditch. Then all at once the animal appeared to lose interest completely, whether from real or feigned boredom it was impossible to say. At any rate, with the graceful disdain of a matador turning his back on a bull, it walked unhurriedly away from the jeep, jumped the ditch, and began in a flaunting manner to pace the perimeter. The concubines lay back down.

The safari guard, moving fast in reverse, rolled down enough of his window to shout at the Hillman as he went by, "Follow me!"

"Please!" Theo said.

The guard led them back to the service road, where he angrily jumped out of the jeep and asked them to notice that he was soaked in sweat from "bloomin' terror! That bastard thinks me jeep's after his bloody females!"

"Ah!" Dame Winifred nodded. "I see."

Banging his fist on a "No Trespassing" sign, the guard delivered a temperamental lecture on the dangers of muckin' about with lions. Then he calmed down and led the Hillman Imp around the border of the future safari park. From there they crossed a meadow, and passed alongside a lengthy watercourse in the middle of which sat an octagonal wire house where chimpanzees appeared to be watching television. At this point the safari driver slung his jeep in a circle, and motioned without slowing down that they should turn onto the gravel road ahead. "Quite right," shouted Miss Throckmorton, waving. "You've been most kind."

Finally Theo saw civilization. A small stone church. His companion pointed at it. "Saint Michael's." A Palladian bridge over the River Urswick and far down on the other bank a cottage with a boat shed nearby. Then he saw peacocks on landscaped lawns, and little Ionic temples set among orderly arrangements of ancient oaks, and then rising in front of them the great creamy expanse of Bourne House, with its double curving balustrades and marble steps and its symmetrical rows of forty mullioned windows. It was beautiful. It was closed.

"Drat." The elderly scholar looked at her guest. "Is it Tuesday?"

While astonishingly au courant with dates in the sixteenth century, Dame Winifred had a loose hold on the present. It was not only Tuesday, it was the first of July, and as she now recalled, the Stanlows were at Henley for the Royal Regatta. Even hardworking aristocrats must occasionally take a break.

While they stood beside the car coping with this setback, a thin young man on a go-cart roared out of an arched gate off the east wing. Strapped round his neck was a video camcorder. With a spray of gravel, he stopped beside them, took off his helmet, and shook out an abundance of resplendent red curls. "Hal-loo, Freddie." He smiled. "Looking for the *pater familius?* Bummer for you. Off to the races with Mum."

"*Pater familiae*," Dame Winifred corrected automatically, then introduced Lord William de Montpasson Stanlow, the earl-to-be. "Your Lordship," said Theo.

"Willie," said the teenager. "American? Awesome shades."

While asking Theo about his chances of getting into U.S.C. where he could major in movie-making, Lord William escorted them inside, through a forty-foot Palladian cube of fluted marble columns with gilt capitals, and a ceiling of painted cherubs in chariots. They walked along the carpet runners through roped-off waiting rooms and sitting rooms and dining rooms and state rooms and numberless other sorts of rooms. "A hundred fourteen all together," explained Willie, trained in the tour. "Course, *we're* all crammed in the East Wing." In the "Vanbrugh Chamber," they came upon two blue-jeaned young women sprawled on silk sofas watching MTV on a television hidden in a Chinese cabinet beneath what looked like a Constable landscape. These girls were introduced as Lady Caroline and Lady Anne, Willie's older sisters. The three Stanlow children were alone in the house (except for a skeletal staff of a dozen or so), and clearly enjoying the once-a-week opportunity to lounge about on furniture otherwise being stared at by hordes of tourists. During the brief polite chat, the two female teenagers—either because they had been sexually over-stimulated by too many lurid music videos, or because they rarely saw any live young males close up—stared at Theo with such undisguised if speechless lust that Miss Throckmorton asked them if they thought they'd met him before. This provoked explosive efforts to mask uncontrollable giggling, and the comment from Willie that his sisters were brain-dead.

After a few more questions about U.S.C., Willie left his two visitors in the library and hurried back outside to get some footage of his father's new zebras. He was making a documentary he called "To the Manner Bourne," which he planned to submit to his tutor at Eaton in place of his honors essay.

"I'm not sure that I approve." Dame Winifred frowned at the tall skinny boy. "To think clearly, one must write clearly . . . as I gather your father's tutor often told him, or as often as he attended his tutorials." She gave a sharp tug to her misbuttoned jacket. "Regrettably, those occasions must have been rare."

The son was unremorseful. "Now admit it, Freddie. You said Shakespeare would have been off to Hollywood in a shot. . . . Very-happy-to-have-met-you-Mr.-Ryan," he added with rote formality. Theo made him a present of the Day-Glo sunglasses. "Hey, totally super," said the future earl. "Anyone ever tell you, you look like Gary Cooper early on?"

"Well, actually, people do," Theo admitted. "Actually the playwright Ford Rexford told me that, and he knew Cooper."

This information won Willie over completely. "Ford Rexford wrote *Preacher's Boy*. It's one of my favorite movies."

"Did you ever see the play?"

"It was a play?"

"First," smiled Theo.

The Bourne library (Adam ceiling) was not quite as large as the main reading room of the Cavendish University Library, but the furnishings were much more handsome, and the collection of nine thousand books far more valuable. Theo touched illuminated manuscripts and first editions of everyone from Spenser to Austen. He looked at a Plutarch in which, according to Dame Winifred, the underscoring and the crabbed notes in the margins had been scribbled by Raleigh himself.

And as Theo traced his fingers over the coarse stained rag paper, the fantasy of Jonas Marsh's that had buzzed around his bed last night came back to him. And not as tentatively this time, but as a full-blown possibility bursting like a skyrocket inside his head. All during the ride back to Barnet-on-Urswick, he was so busy fighting with this thought that he scarcely noticed Dame Winifred's driving except when someone honked at her. Possibilities kept sparking in his brain all during their late supper together at the Nightingale, and didn't stop as he walked her home along Gate Row.

Moonlight glittered on the slate roofs and up from the cobblestones. Above them, the moon was full and large. "Lovely Cynthia," the old woman said. "And a lovely day too, Theodore."

"I'll never forget it . . . Miss Throckmorton, I have a proposal for—"

Suddenly, from "The Heights," a dog gave a deep howling bark. "Ah, there's Mildred, peeking round her curtain, I dare say." Dame Winifred pointed. "See her, up there?" She waved. "Mildred, good evening!" The light vanished from the dormer window.

By the gate of Lark Cottage, the black cat Water stretched himself slowly atop the stone wall, lashed his tail back and forth, then pounced down, and with a mew rubbed against Theo's pants leg. Dame Winifred snorted. "I should be honored if I were you. Wat doesn't much care for anyone, actually. A nasty, contemptuous creature." She leaned over and swept up the cat, who stuck a claw delicately into her hand. "As you see." Resting it on the high waist of her stomach, she scratched the twitching black ears.

Sticking his hands in his pockets, Theo began again. "I have a proposal. Would you consider letting me help you look for this Raleigh play? I have to go to London for a while, but otherwise I'm just at loose ends all summer, and if you wouldn't mind, I could come back next month, and maybe be of some use." The cat turned its head; the yellow eyes glinted at the American as insolently as if it knew exactly what he was considering.

Accept his help? Nothing would please Dame Winifred more. She was quite moved. She was delighted. And nothing could be easier than to lend him copies of her notes and computations and catalogues, and copies of all the architectural drawings made of Bourne House, at each successive stage of its history, beginning in the sixteenth century. They could make them in the morning at the photocopier's in Salisbury, for she insisted on driving him that far on his journey. They could even lunch together at the White Hart Inn where Raleigh had been arrested. Theo accepted with pleasure.

Then, "Good night. And thank you," he said.

"Good night, Theodore. I feel very, very excited about our prospects for success." She squeezed Wat to her breast. "Fresh blood. New possibilities. If a play exists, we shall find it."

"I think we will," he told her, reaching out his hand for hers. The black cat hissed at him.

Theo was too agitated to go back to his room. His long legs led him quickly down the High Street, arms swinging across his chest in a nervous flurry of motion. At the arched stone bridge, he paused and leaned over, gripping the ledge. Below him, the moon floated quietly on the black water of the Urswick. He took a long slow breath. "It's possible," he whispered.

In the months before he'd begun writing *Foolscap*, he had read over and over every extant word Raleigh had ever put to paper. As a scholar, he knew that there wasn't a phrase or allusion or syntactical construction in his play that couldn't have been written by Raleigh in 1618. But would anyone believe that it *had* been written by Raleigh in 1618? Would a great scholar like Dame

Winifred Throckmorton believe it? Oh, she would want to believe it. The Earl of Newbolt would want her to believe it. Was it possible that she could?

That Walter Raleigh was conceited enough, and imaginative enough, to make himself the hero of his own play, she could probably accept. That, once condemned to certain death, he would write so darkly about his enemies, would lie so extravagantly about his triumphs—that much she would probably not only accept, but relish. But would she believe it was good enough? Of course, it didn't have to be as good as the best of Raleigh. An old man, after all, debilitated, stressed; an only play. And great poets had written rotten plays before; look at Keats and Shelley.

Besides, it wasn't a rotten play. It was a good play. It deserved a chance. Dame Winifred deserved a chance. Oh, come on, Theo, be honest; you wouldn't be doing it for her. Well, what if he showed her his play and asked her to *help* him pass it off as Raleigh's? The two of them against the neglectful scholarly world. This appealing fantasy faded with an image of withering indignation on Miss Throckmorton's face. She'd be horrified if she knew he'd even thought about this! Even just as a hoax. Even just to see if he could. . . .

The sky spangled with stars above the dark stone houses of the village. Theo paced the bridge, and told himself he was crazy. "With intent to deceive." That made it forgery. A disgrace to scholarship. And that's what he was, wasn't he? A scholar. A teacher, a critic, a biographer. He wasn't a playwright. He wasn't a Ford Rexford. He'd often asked Ford why he kept writing, and the playwright had told him, "To stop all these goddamn people yammering in my head. To build them someplace better to live than the world they got." And another time he'd answered, "Why do you fuck? 'Cause it feels good." Of course, on different occasions Ford had given other answers: "To make a buck," and "To tell 'em Kilroy was here." But Theo suspected that the first two responses were the real ones. And while he'd felt them both himself while writing his play, he wasn't sure he had the stamina to feel them constantly. Then, so what if it was unlikely that anyone would ever produce *Foolscap*? So what if he never saw it on a stage?

Theo took coins from his pocket and jiggled them from one hand to the other. Face it, he thought. You aren't going to do it because you don't have the guts. You're not that wild. It's people like Ford, people like Walter Raleigh, who do things that crazy.

When they'd been working together on *Foolscap,* Ford had said of its hero, "Know what I love about Mr. Strut? The bet-it-all chutzpah of the guy. And you caught it in this thing, Theo, you did. Raleigh's boldness. Like when they come to arrest him so he quick takes these potions, goes into convulsions, foaming at the mouth, spouting gibberish. Drool in that long matted white hair. The guy cops an insanity plea. Right on the spot. Then when he's found out, he cites biblical precedence! 'Hey. King David did it, didn't he?' "

"It didn't work," Theo had reminded the playwright.

"He had a million schemes just as good. If I hadn't been held back—"

"*You* were held back, Ford?"

"Pusillanimity. Guilt. Sloth. Hootch and cooze. I'm riddled with neuroses. I don't kid myself. Dark of night, I don't. But if I'd had the balls to name my ship, the *Destiny*—I love it—"

"You too could have ended up on the scaffold."

"But oh Lord, how that guy could write a death scene! He even starts directing the fucking executioner: 'What dost thou fear? Strike, man, strike!' Bold, Theo. Think bold."

Yes, one of Raleigh's ships had been named *Destiny,* and another, *Revenge.* For destiny, for revenge.

Well, wouldn't it be interesting at least to find out if it were possible? And, of course, he'd *tell* her before she took any public step. "See how well you taught me Raleigh," he'd say.

Leaning over the bridge, Theo shook his head, smiling, and threw the coins in a spray of silver out into the Urswick.

Twenty minutes later the big American stood stooped in the red telephone box across the street from the Stag & Hart pub, speaking with an exhausted-sounding Jonas Marsh at his London hotel. "I called Vic and he said you got back this afternoon, Jonas. How was Scotland?"

"My feet are in a bucket of Epsom salts" was the answer. "How's the Aged D? With her now?"

"Dame Winifred? She's wonderful. Just what you'd expect."

"Didn't expect a thing. So, Ryan, you find Ford Rexford?" Marsh sounded preoccupied, perhaps by his feet.

"No, but I got back from him what I came for."

Marsh's tone was distinctly ironic. "Miss Harte? The sweet Corinna gone a-Maying, and obviously a-Juneing and Julying?"

"Jonas, come on. No! Listen, I need to talk to you about something important. How much do you know about transcriptions of sixteenth-, seventeenth-century manuscripts? I mean technically, orthographically?"

"A great deal."

"That's what I figured."

"A very great deal, frankly." Marsh was recovering his energy. "A damnable sight more than OUR NEW CHAIRMAN, Thorney the Swine-Faced Yahoo Toady, knows about medieval *anything!*"

"Yes, well, I've got a proposal for you, Jonas. Your idea about passing off a twentieth-century play as genuinely Jacobean."

"My idea about what?"

"You know, passing off *A Man for All Seasons.*"

"Bit late for that, isn't it?"

"Not that, but . . . Look, I don't want to talk about this on the phone, Jonas. Can we have lunch tomorrow? I could meet you at your hotel."

Jonas said that he wouldn't be in London tomorrow. It was his invariable habit to attend the Royal Regatta at Henley and he was "motoring" there in the morning.

"You've rented a car?"

"I own a car."

"In England?"

"It happens," said Marsh obliquely.

"Well, could I meet you at Henley then?" Theo was frightened that if he postponed this talk, he'd come to his senses and never have it.

"Something wrong, Ryan?" (It was a surprise to hear concern in his colleague's voice; Theo had never before associated what you might call relational emotions with Jonas Marsh.) "Something to do with this Rexford obsession?"

"Who said I was obsessed with Rexford?"

"Steve Weiner. We had lunch in New York. Inedible slop."

"How is Blabbermouth?"

"Miscegenation bound. La belle Jorvelle." Marsh cackled. "When that gosssip slithers up the tower of the Poodle-Fornicator Tupper, and into the long-lobed ear of Dina Sue-Wee Ludd, I hope to hear the howls across the Atlantic. Yap, soo-wee, soo-wee, yap, YAP!"

"Well, look, this play thing I need to talk to you about has got nothing to do with Rexford. It has to do with Winifred Throck-morton."

"Ah."

And so they arranged to meet at three the following afternoon in front of the Steward's Gate at the Henley Regatta. Marsh was attending with "a friend," who could provide tickets. After the races, they'd return to London together; meanwhile Marsh would reserve a room for Theo in his London hotel. "You'll prefer it to that scrofulous flea-trap you were in last week," Marsh predicted.

"It's not too expensive, is it, Jonas? I don't have your kind of money." (Whatever kind of money it was that Jonas Marsh had, which no one had ever figured out.)

"Don't worry about it. Cherrio, Ryan, ta ta, and *au revoir*. My feet are shriveling."

As it happened, Theo made one more phone call that night, not one he'd had the slightest thought of making until he was sitting with the half-dozen other patrons in the dark sleepy pub, the Stag & Hart, having what Ford Rexford used to call "the unwind whiskey." He was thinking about Ford, about how he'd felt when Ford had told him his play was good. How he'd felt those next few days working on it, learning from Ford.

There was a jukebox in the barroom between two video-game machines, and a pretty black-haired young woman in corduroy slacks kept playing the same bluesy song while she shot down planes on the video screen. She looked lonely, and the song sounded lonely. Involved as he was in his thoughts Theo might not have noticed the jukebox if he hadn't been thinking about Ford, and if the woman hadn't looked so sad. When he did faintly hear the singer's voice—a tough, smoky, voluptuous voice—he thought it sounded familiar only because it was a voice from the American South. But then he thought, she sounds like somebody. Who does she sound like? Then just as the song ended with a sad, sexy twang of a guitar chord, goosebumps prickled the hair on the back of his neck. He knew who it was. It was Rhodora.

"Excuse me?" He hurried over to the jukebox. "That song. Who was singing it?"

The woman looked up, startled, at the tall, sunburnt American. Then, "It's new," she said. "Country/Western. From the U.S. Joe likes 'em. They just changed these records today." She called over to the bartender, who was talking with two men about a soccer match. "Today, right, Joe? Jukebox feller come in today?"

"That's right," Joe said. "Come this noon."

" 'I Go On.' That's the name of it." The woman's sad hard-edged smile stayed on her face as she watched Theo.

He ran his finger down the columns of songs on the jukebox front until his hand stopped at the words "Rhodora Potts. 'I Go On.' " "Jesus, I knew it!" he said. "I know her!" According to the label, Rhodora had written the song herself. On the flip side was her version of "Dancing in the Streets," which he'd often heard her singing at Cherokee's with the Dead Indians. It was a Nashville label; it must be the little company that had wanted to record her back in the spring. And here she was in July on a jukebox in Barnet-on-Urswick, England. "God Almighty!" Theo said. "And she didn't change her name either. She always said she wouldn't. I know her," he repeated.

"Really?" the woman asked.

"Really." He lifted his whiskey glass in a toast to the jukebox.

The woman looked up a long instant into Theo's eyes. "Tell her from me I know how she feels."

Joe walked to their end of the bar. "Buck up, Steph," he grinned. "Could be worse. Not so bad as all that."

"Isn't it now?" she asked him.

Still shaking his head with the surprise of it, Theo pulled a chair over to the jukebox to listen to Rhodora sing "I Go On."

> Remember you?
> I don't want to, but I guess I do.

> You've gone on to love somebody new.
> I go on and on with missing you.
> Remember you?
> I don't want to, but I guess it's true.
> When I'm dreaming, you and I aren't through.
> I go on and on with kissing you.
> I go on and on and on.

As soon the song ended, Theo played the other side. Then he walked back out to the phone booth and called his home number in Rome, North Carolina.

A machine answered, sounding very clear from across the ocean, and very brief. "Hi, Theo Ryan's in England all summer. You wanna leave a message for Rhodora Potts, do it at the beep. Bye."

"Hi, Rhodora. It's Theo. Where are you? I just heard 'I Go On'! Goddammit, why didn't you tell me it was out! I'm in a little village in Devonshire, and it's on the jukebox. Congratulations! Well, I'll try you again later. I'll be here and there for a while. You can leave a message for me at Brown's Hotel in London, Okay?

"Look, I haven't found him. You still want me to?"

"Bye. Congratulations. I miss you. Bye."

Through the open window of the Stag & Hart, he could hear Rhodora's song starting again. He went back inside the pub and invited the young woman named Stephanie to join him for a drink.

Many drinks later, they walked together to her flat above a stationer's shop that hung out over the moonlit cobbles of the High. He kept thinking of Rhodora.

CHAPTER
23

{A Great Procession}

Tis better to be fortunate than wise.

Webster, The White Devil

IT WAS A HOT SUNNY DAY in Henley-on-Thames. The rain had finally arrived in the night, revived the flowers, then politely left. Crisp blue-and-white awnings fluttered on the Regatta pavilions. Light glittered on the river, mud glistened on the walkways. Theo Ryan and Jonas Marsh sat in their white chairs, chatting as they looked at the crowd.

"You'll never get away with it," said Marsh.

"But you told me—"

"Oh, yes, yes, Ryan, ink and paper, et cetera, can be managed."

"I'm telling you, that London producer didn't read my play. He rejected it on the subject matter. If he did glance at a page or two, he won't remember, and on the off chance he does, we'll get Ford—"

" 'We?' "

"—To say he'd gotten hold of the Raleigh manuscript right when it was found, and he'd sent a copy to the guy as a hoax: to see a producer's face when he realized he'd turned down a play by Sir Walter Raleigh! That sounds like something Ford would do. But I swear, Jonas, the man just flipped through a few pages. If that."

"I'm not talking about some idiot producer or—"

"What then? Ford?"

"Well, he certainly knows Raleigh didn't write it."

"He'll *love* the idea of fobbing off a forgery on the academy. He loves being 'bad.' "

Marsh crossed his legs, crisping the crease of his white trousers. "What if he gets bored, and decides to be 'bad' by exposing us?"

"I'll blackmail him into keeping his mouth shut. Besides, he's such a notorious liar, who'd believe him?"

"Beyond Rexford—"

"Don't say the play's not good enough, because you haven't even read it yet."

"I don't necessarily doubt you, Ryan."

"Is it the idea of doing it? The moral question? I know, I know. I mean, God knows, Jonas, I can't believe I'm—"

"The moral question is interesting, but arguable. It's *technically* that the thing is close to impossible. (A): The Bourne library is very carefully documented. Winifred Throckmorton knows every single—"

"I told you. We don't put it in the library. We don't even put it in the house. When you see the maps, you'll—"

"(B): The manuscript itself. You'll never get away with a holograph. A forgery of Raleigh's own foul papers would be spotted in minutes. Besides, the man's whoreson handwriting is unbearable."

"A fair copy then."

" 'Then'? 'If.' "

"Okay, okay. *If.*"

"It would have to be a transcript. And not by Raleigh's secretary either. Talbot's hand's too well known. An anonymous amanuensis. Early though. Sixteen twenties? . . . Family clerk? I don't know. Perhaps Mole can help."

"He can? How?"

"Please! Let me think about this. And don't talk to me about it anymore now, Ryan, will you? I have to read the play first, don't I? When it comes down to it, 'the play's the thing,' isn't it? If the play doesn't work, nothing works."

"But if you think the play can pull it off?—"

Marsh looked dubious. "I'll think about it. Now, we're here to bloody well enjoy ourselves. There's a hat!" He pointed at a short woman in pink silk who was entirely shaded by an enormous aquamarine hat with pink blossoms bunched at its band. "Givenchy, I expect."

The American academics sat back to analyze the Henley crowd. They agreed they had never before in their lives seen so many blue-eyed, pink-faced, well-off, well-dressed drunk people together in one soggy field. Of course, not everyone among the thousands gathered by the riverbanks was rich. Among the spectators in the public grandstand down the way, there must have been some who were pressed for cash. And maybe the parking attendants despaired of owning the cars they parked (though many of the Regatta venders were apparently aristocrats in disguise, keeping up old traditions of waiting on their peers for fun). Even among the upper crust who'd passed the Steward's Gate (through which—while not as narrow as the proverbial eye of the needle—all the well-heeled camels had entered), conceivably there were a few of shaky fortune: Theo overheard one elaborately frocked young woman fret to her friend, as they slopped daintily along the walkway, that if mud splashed her dress she was ruined, since she planned to return it to the shop in the morning and get her money back. Still—at least to Theo's eye—almost everybody at Henley looked rich as a lord, and in fact quite a lot of them were exactly that.

It was just as well that when they met, Jonas had bullied him into returning to the town center to buy a blazer and tie at a (horrendously expensive) men's store; for the Steward's Enclosure imposed prerequisites more immediately gleaned at a glance than inherited wealth. Male backs had to be encased in jackets, their necks surrounded by ties; female knees had to be covered by skirts. Moreover, officials stood posted at the gate, like sartorial Saint Peters, to check for interlopers. One inebriated woman attempted to circumvent this tiresome hemline rule by tugging her strapless minidress down below her kneecaps, but (still protesting that she *had* complied with the code as stated, and was after all planning to pin her jacket shut) she was firmly escorted from the sanctioned enclosure.

Nor was everyone at the races intoxicated; one assumed most

of the racers weren't, nor the band of the Grenadier Guards pumping out "Salute the Duke" from their gazebo; nor the row of nuns
who never left their bleacher on the top tier of the stands—and
were at times the only people in the stands. All day the beautiful
slender skulls, rowed by beautiful slender youth, flew up the flat
straight course from start to finish line, but watching them did not
seem to be a high (at least not a constant) priority except with the
nuns and a little group of Americans holding on to their frontline
positions in the canvas lawn chairs that stretched to the Thames.

Everyone else was promenading about the grounds, to see who
else was there and to show off their clothes to them. Or they were
at the Regatta Shop buying Regatta oven-mitts and ice buckets.
Or they were floating about the river in motor launches waving
at each other. But mostly they were squashed around congested
tables to which waiters rushed more and more flutes of champagne
and half-pints of Pimm's Cup. Mostly, they were out in the sun
from morn to noon to dusk, drinking as fast and hard as they
could. And mostly they were drunk.

Theo was himself still hung over from the night before in
Barnet—when he'd been surprised to wake up, with a banging
headache, not alone in the Nightingale, but in a flat, in bed, beside
someone named Stephanie, from whom he'd parted at dawn on
subdued if friendly terms. (She also had a horrible headache.)

It was therefore that Theo was particularly struck by the amount
of alcohol being consumed here at Henley, apparently without
effect on the imbibers.

"Yes, the remarkable thing," said Jonas Marsh, in blue blazer,
Harvard tie, and straw boater. "The thing to notice, Ryan, is that
these people are totally, totally blotto, and yet not a single one
has fallen on his, or her, face. They have tilted—"

"Remarkable tilts," agreed Theo, sipping his own Pimm's.
"That man in the maroon stripes—looks like he's counting the
gravel? I've been watching five minutes. He's hanging in there at
an amazing angle of list—"

"Tilted, but not toppled." Jonas nibbled at his tiny tea sand-
wich. "They are not sobbing in a maudlin way, or knocking each
other down, or even loosening their ties. They're still speaking in

complete sentences too. And there's not a vomiter among them.
And this when they are so drunk, if they were Americans, by now
they'd have their heads in a toilet bowl grunting like apes."

"I know the feeling," Theo said.

"And that, friend Ryan, is why England produced the greatest
empire the West has ever known. Self-respect. Discipline." The
Anglophilic Marsh stretched out his thin arms as if to embrace the
entire field of upper-crust sots. "What a relief to think there isn't
a Tupper or a Thorney for miles around! Or any of the other dolts
from the backward hills of Cavendish U!"

"Some of them aren't so bad," Theo protested.

Marsh's crossed leg shook furiously. "Not so BAD? What
would be bad? Orangutans? Our president, *General* Kaney, not
only thinks we should have gone to Vietnam, he thinks he's still
there. I don't know *where* old Mortimer and Lovell think they
are. Our provost is proud, imagine, PROUD, to be remembered
as 'the Bone-Cruncher'—"

Theo scooted his chair back from the kicking foot. "Well, come
on, at least Tupper okayed your running the London program
next year."

"Why, Ryan? Ask yourself why?"

"So what if they did it to get rid of you? At least you'll be here
in England where you like it so much."

Marsh's hands flew around his face after the invisible flies that
seemed to pursue him. "There may be a God," he admitted, and
turned back to admire Britain's finest on their feet.

And true, though wobbly, the whole privileged class was verti-
cal. They'd been at it all day, but at six o'clock they were still on
parade up and down in the mud: The women, in livid hats with
matching gloves, kept going while their high heels made little plop-
ping noises as they yanked them out of the sucking sludge. By
their sides, and a little to the patriarchal fore, strolled their men
in club jackets of broad cartoon-colored stripes with matching
beanies and ties that told everybody who they were. Stiffened with
drink, they carried on.

Theo Ryan and Jonas Marsh were on the premises by borrowed
privilege. They were not only in through the gate, but in under
the pink-and-white awning of the venerable Leander Club, off-

limits to all but members and their guests. They themselves were guests of Mr. "Mole" Fontwell, Esq., who had coxed the eights of Brasenose College, Oxford, to victory in the Thames Challenge Cup some thirty years, and pounds, ago. Mr. Fontwell was very short, dark, and nearsighted, and that, rather than christening, was no doubt the source of his being called "Mole." He was an old friend of Marsh's, who'd introduced him to Theo as a fellow Renaissance man, though not a professional. A "private" scholar. Since when Jonas had led Theo to meet Mr. Fontwell "back at the car," the car was a yellow Rolls, Theo translated "private scholar" to mean "rich amateur." Mr. Fontwell (wearing a yellow-and-black striped blazer with a pink tie) was a generous and convivial man, who instantly told Theo how much he'd admired his book on Shakespearean clowns, and added that he'd looked forward to their meeting since learning Marsh and Theo were colleagues. How Marsh and Mole had met was never explained, but apparently they'd known each other for some time; in fact it had been Mole with whom Jonas had been hiking in the Hebrides, and Mole with whom he'd "motored" to Henley, despite his insinuation that he himself owned a car. Mole's real first name was not disclosed.

Alone, Theo might have had trouble locating Fontwell's particular Rolls, as the entire parking lot (a cow pasture) had been packed with Rolls-Royces clumsily jockeying with Bentleys and Jaguars for space, and trying not to run over the tailgate parties. Here in this pasture had assembled quite a few people apparently not only with no urge to see the Regatta, but in no hurry to get anywhere near the course. Instead they were doing what the British love to do at the Season's poshest events: get all dressed up in formal clothes and have a picnic. So, just as they had done at Derby Day and Royal Ascot, at Lord's for the cricket and at Glyndebourne for the opera, here they were at Henley for the races, blinded by sun, besieged by bees, sitting on blankets beside their cars, having tea on the wet ground. Actually, not all of them were on the ground; some had surrounded their enormous cars with tables and chairs, silver services, and portable grills. Not many of them were having tea either. Champagne corks flew around the pasture as if anarchist snipers were hiding in the trees, trying to massacre as much of the upper class as they could manage.

It had taken the Americans and their escort a good while to return to the Steward's Gate, for they were waylaid en route by a gauntlet of boozy M.P.s, K.G.s, O.B.E.s, D.F.C.s, and assorted Esqs of Mole Fontwell's acquaintance. Their first stop was a gentleman in a cutaway who sat under a large umbrella and had a matching miniature umbrella shading his magnum of Mumm's. This man proved to be "one of the chaps" who'd been coxed thirty years ago by "little Mole," as he called the tiny Fontwell; and they were invited by him to share a bit of the bubbly. Another chap offered them Schloss Vollrad. Another, duck pâté with a decent hock. In fact, little Mole knew so many chaps, and all the chaps were so hospitable, that Theo and Jonas and Mole had all gotten "tiddly" even before they reached the Leander Club pavilion. It made the more startling the sight of so many grown men in bright pink beanies, pink ties, and pink socks, standing among so many pink balloons, pink flowers, and pink bunting in a pink tent. Pink was the Leander Club color, and they took it seriously. Their emblem, tiny pink hippopotami, was even on the boxers Mole was wearing at that moment (or so he said), and he directed them to the souvenir booth where they might purchase pairs of the same.

Mole Fontwell either had a remarkable number of friends, or everyone he knew was under that tent, for he certainly was on the most jovial terms with almost all of them. "Boaties, the lot," he explained. As they stood one another rounds of Pimm's, interspersed with quick darts out to the riverbank to catch the occasional Double Skulls or Prince Philip Challenge Cup finish, their joviality increased, until at six o'clock precisely, many of them began flirting in a loud-pitched way with anybody they found themselves mashed against in the press.

At the bar with Fontwell, Theo stood smiling at these sexual rites. From a nearby table a handsome woman kept winking at him and wriggling her fingers in a minuscule and lascivious variation on the royal handwave. Theo waved cheerfully back.

"Give it up, Charles!" Mole shouted to a laughing, red-jowled man who'd just had his hand removed from a woman's buttock by the woman to whom the buttock belonged. This man also wore a yellow-and-black striped blazer, which Theo now knew (from

Jonas Marsh, who'd begged him not to display his ignorance by asking anyone but Jonas himself for such information) to be the colors of Brasenose College, Oxford.

"Charles Blickers," Mole explained. "Good sport, really; gets a bit over the top at times. Distinguished himself his second year, won a bumper race at the White Horse. Got down twenty-two pints of Hall's best, with a brandy chaser. Woke up in hospital days later. Might have killed a smaller man."

"Even a large one."

"The brandy was the problem."

"Ah."

Blickers was now trying to impress another woman by tossing up strawberries, trying to catch them in his mouth, and only occasionally succeeding.

Theo yelled down at Mole Fontwell's beanie-topped head. "Do you happen to know the Earl of Newbolt? Wouldn't he have been up at Oxford about your time?" The large American squeezed quickly into an opening nearer the bar, and hauled Fontwell after him. "Just wonder if he's here today. I was told he would be."

"Couldn't say. Know Horry Stanlow, do you?"

"Oh, no. I was at his library yesterday."

"A stunner, isn't it? No, never knew Stanlow. Just a fresher when he took off. Went to Paris and won a dance contest, word was."

"Was he expelled?"

" 'Expelled'? . . . Ah, yes, 'expelled'—what you people call sent down. Couldn't say. He's certainly putting on an awf'lly good show at Bourne House now'days. No, my round. I insist."

This offer was a relief, since a while back, due to Mole's popularity, when Theo had passed the bartender a twenty-pound note to pay for a round of drinks, he'd been asked for an additional 50 p. The Royal Regatta at Henley was clearly not a cheap way to enjoy oneself.

Hugging their trays of Pimm's against the jostle, the two finally shouldered their way back to the table, which they found empty. When they'd left it, Jonas had been deep in conversation with an "antiques man" about current market conditions, and the two had gone off somewhere together. In fact, several of Mole's intimates seemed to share Jonas Marsh's interest in antiques, including one who "bought for Sotheby's," and another who "sold" for himself. Throughout the afternoon, Marsh and a series of these individuals kept whispering together in what struck Theo as a rather clandestine manner. Hoping for information, he asked Fontwell now, "You and Jonas are both interested in antiques?"

"Rabidly!" was the only answer he got. Then Fontwell suddenly clicked his glass against Theo's, and proposed a toast to Dame Winifred Throckmorton. "Jonas tells me you've just had a visit with the Great Tam, and that you're an admirer. I too." He rubbed his beanie. "At least now, through the rosy fog of time, I admired her most awf'lly. Hated her back when. To the Great Learned Tam!" He drank down a third of the potent amber punch. "Does she still wear that hid'jus old thing?"

"A plaid tam? Yes, but I don't know if it's the same one."

"I'm sure it is. Same bicycle, too, I suspect. What a dragon she was, absolutely terrified me."

"Her bike riding? Ever been in a *car* with her?" Theo held out his hands and shook them violently.

"I meant her brain," Mole said. "I took my D.Phil. with her positively glowering at me like the Medusa."

"You did! That's must have been something."

The little man tilted his head up at Theo. "Indeed."

"What was it on? Your dissertation."

"Oh, horribly boring. Jacobean scribal practices. Professional secretaries. Trial transcripts. That sort of thing. Old hat. Nothing theoretical and deconstructive like you Americans are up to. But I like piddling about, untying little knots. Wouldn't interest you at all, I'm sure."

Theo said, "You're wrong. I think it would interest me immensely."

Although almost literally in his cups, Mole Fontwell was quite cogent, as well as long-winded, as he affably answered all of Theo's questions about early-seventeenth-century "hands"; questions which narrowed to very specific inquiries about paper, ink, and cursive styles. They were eventually interrupted by a roar that shook the tent on the news that the Leander Club had won "easily" in the Queen Mother Challenge Cup with Charles Blickers's nephew rowing stroke. Shortly thereafter Blickers himself returned to the tent to stand a celebratory round, at the end of which Mole congratulated him and introduced Theo. When the hefty Britisher learned that Theo taught at Cavendish University, he leaned down (his well-featured face a scarlet blaze of broken blood vessels) and clapped the American on the shoulder. "Astonishin'. Friend of mine went off there to teach, you know; South Carolina, is it?"

"North."

"Righto. Paid him an astonishin' 'mount of money. As a salary, I mean. You must know him, Herbie Crawford. Just saw him in the loo, now where the devil did he get to?" Blickers weaved to his considerable height, and began searching the crowd.

"Herbert Crawford, the historian?" said Theo.

"Astonishin' 'mount," said Blickers. "Wonder what he does with it? Expect he gives it all away. Remember, Moley, when he gave that old Welsh woman that did our shirts fifty quid for Christmas?"

Theo hoped they were talking about two different people. "Herbert Crawford, the Marxist historian who teaches at Cavendish University? He's here at Henley?"

"Somewhere sloshed, Thatcher-bashing, I expect. Up at school, he was quite the tough; always in that filthy black rollneck pullover, the Cockney bit, man of the people, strewing the quad with leaflets. Remember the marijuana crumpets he passed round at crew table, Moley?"

"Vividly."

"Always off boozing with the town scrubbers," Blickers said. "Good man, though. We won our blades together at Eights Week. Right, Moley?" He grabbed the little man by the neck and choked him affectionately. "Gave our lovely cox quite a dunking, didn't we? Remember?"

"Vividly."

"Well, he's about somewhere. Very-nice-to-have-met-you-Mr.-Ryan." Off Blickers lurched, disappearing into the swarm, though Theo identified his whereabouts by a woman's sudden squeal of "Stop that, Charles!"

"Crawford's left Oxford, then?" asked Mole. As a private

scholar, he obviously didn't keep up with even the hottest academic gossip.

"Yes," Theo hissed. "I suppose he's back in England for the summer. What's he doing at the Royal Regatta? He's supposed to be a Marxist!"

Mole laughed. "You Americans are so . . ." He searched his Pimm's Cup for a word. ". . . earnest."

In a while, Jonas Marsh returned to bring Theo back with him to watch Harvard race against Trinity. So leaving Mole and his friends in the midst of a drunken roundelay of some obscurely scatological ditty, the two hurried outside. There, leaning from their lawn chairs nearly into the Thames, they cheered on the Crimson crew so ardently that bemused eyebrows (rather affectionately bemused eyebrows) were raised by the Britishers seated around them, and one said to his neighbor, "Americans."

Theo shouted defiantly louder. "GO! GO! GO!" Jonas, with his typical intensity, corkscrewed in his seat, and appeared to be stroking along with the scullers. "FIGHT FIERCELY!" he screamed. Bow to bow with their opponents, the Harvard crew shot past in a flurry of oars, their young faces contorted with strain. "GO, CRIMSON, GO!!"

"STROKE, BLOKES, STROKE!" a voice shouted behind him. "For God, for Country, and for Harvard!"

This misquotation of Theo's alma mater's motto turned his head around, causing him to miss Harvard's half-a-length victory, and to see instead the unwelcome sight of Herbert Crawford approaching across the grass. So Blickers had been right; Theo had been hoping the man was too drunk to have recognized himself in a mirror, much less an old college chum in the loo. With Crawford was someone who looked like, someone who *was*, Maude Fletcher.

Behind them walked a sweet-looking stooped elderly couple, both with canes in their outside hands, and their inner arms linked. The old man wore a pink beanie and the woman a hat that looked like a fistful of orange mums. As for Maude Fletcher, she appeared to have shucked her clerical collar along with her virtue, and looked disgustingly happy in a bright silk print dress. And as for Crawford: While sporting the only black leather jacket in sight, he had bent his principles to a white shirt and, of all things, a pink Leander tie.

"So much for your theory, Jonas," Theo muttered. "About never running into anybody from Cavendish. There're two right there."

Still spasming from his efforts to row on the Harvard crew while seated in a lounge chair, Marsh looked where Theo was pointing. "Oh. Who are they?" he asked.

"Herbert Crawford and Maude Fletcher, dammit."

"Know of him. Don't know her." (Marsh was not a campus socializer.) "He looks youngish to have written eight books."

"Eight? Crawford's written *eight* books?"

"Brilliant, frankly. The four I read."

"Well, that's just fantastic," sighed Theo.

Almost worse than Maude and Herbert's presence was the evident delight in their waves when they recognized their colleague in the crowd. Gently depositing the old couple in adjoining chairs, they hurried over. Maude even kissed him, on the cheek.

"Well done for our side!" beamed Crawford, referring apparently to Harvard's victory. All American colleges were the same to him?

"Sky Masterson!" Maude also beamed. "What a great surprise! Jorvelle wrote me you were over here!"

"Yes, I am. I didn't know you were. Hello, Herbie."

"Pal!" Crawford gave him a palm-first, tilted handshake, presumably (like his accent) radical activist in nature. " 'Aven't seen you since we rocked 'em and socked 'em, Ryan, in the great dark days of the strike h'again the Tyrant Tupper."

Maude nudged him. "Oh, Herb, you saw him in *Guys and Dolls*!"

"H'i never saw a soul on that stage but you, love," grinned the despicable man. (He still hadn't gotten his teeth capped.)

Theo introduced Jonas Marsh, and the four exchanged Cavendish news for a bit. Buddy Tupper was still in the wane, and Claudia Pratt the ascendancy, in the aftershock of the Bleecker Strike. The English Department had hit Number Ten in a national poll. As a result, Jorvelle Wakefield had gotten (another) raise, to keep her from going to Yale. They reminisced about *Guys and*

Dolls, and about the strike. Jonas Marsh had ignored both at the time, and did so now.

"So what brings you two here to Henley?" Theo asked, thinly smiling. "Planning to organize a vendors' strike?"

"We probably should," Maude said. "What are *you* doing here?"

"Observing the Scene," Theo said. "The privileged at play." He looked pointedly at Crawford's pink tie. "Leander Club?" he asked.

"Can you believe it?" Maude laughed. "Herb actually rowed once upon a time. I'm serious."

"So I just heard from a former crewmate of yours, Charles Blickers."

Herb shrugged off his old skill, or his exposure as one of the hated upper class, with an apologetic grin.

Maude hugged Crawford's waist. "They say he was pretty good, skinny as he looks."

Theo couldn't stop himself. "Oh, is that why you need such a long lap pool in Rome, Herb? Keep your oar in?"

"Ya bastard!" Crawford punched his shoulder with a playful poke. "We h'all 'ave our stinkin' pasts to live with, right? Surprised you know old Blickers. Man boasted he never set foot in the Bod his whole time at university. Bloody believable too. Good fellow, though."

"Certainly impressive drinking habits. So, Maude?" Theo turned to her. She looked a little thinner; the hair longer, black curls behind her ears. "Plans for next year yet?"

Crawford answered for her. "Yah knew her rotten department and the Bone-Cruncher gave her the boot? Sod 'em all. Well, we showed 'em what the workers can do, didn't we, Maudie?"

"You showed them." Maudie smiled at him with unmistakable affection, if not adoration.

What the "worker," Herbert Crawford (endowed chair of History at a six-figure "salary"—apparently redundant), had done was to tell the Cavendish administration that Reverend Dr. Fletcher stayed, or he went: "They put Maudie back, or I'd bloody well go to Santa Cruz at twice the pay and the sun on my face. Not renewing a woman's bleedin' contract because of 'er political principles! A woman already with a book in print, damn decent reviews, and those dim-wit snooze-os in Religious Studies couldn't muster a fuckin' monograph among 'em."

"Good for you, Crawford!" suddenly shouted the traitor Jonas Marsh, swinging his straw boater wildly. "If Cavendish threw those cretinous FUNDIS back in the benighted ooze they crawled out of, maybe our redneck youth could learn that while they did DESCEND from the apes, they are NOT required to stop there!"

Crawford stared at the handsome, twitching Marsh, then he slapped him on the back of his blazer. "Right!" he bellowed. "Well said, mate!"

"Bugger Tupper!" Marsh added for good measure.

Crawford now grabbed Marsh's hand, and shook it. "Let's all go have a drink together to buggering bloody Tupper. I'll just tell the Ma and Da." And off he went, with high, loose-gaited steps, to kneel beside the meek old couple, who nodded obediently at everything he was saying to them.

"Could I speak to you, Maude? Excuse us, Jonas." Theo practically yanked her aside, and walked her along the river's edge. Then, staring at her, he shook his head. "I don't understand what you're doing."

"What do you mean?" She looked honestly puzzled.

"Coming over here with him. He's married."

Now she looked not only puzzled but offended.

"Do you know what you're getting into?"

Her cheeks pinkened. "Just a *second*, Theo, okay!"

"I'm sorry, Maude, but I feel like, from the play, we got to know each other pretty well, and I like you a lot. I know it's none of my business what you do, but . . ." He gave out, and stared at her.

"Oh, Theo." She looked up at the tall young man so long and so seriously that he lowered his eyes. Finally she said, "Herb's wife's in the process of divorcing him."

". . . Ah."

". . . I love him. Okay? . . ."

Theo looked out over the Thames, then back at her. ". . . Okay," he said. Inside him, he heard her singing on the stage back in Rome: "I'll know, and I won't stop to ask, is it right, am I wise. . . ." Because this certainly didn't look particularly wise. "Well, I hope it works out."

"Me too." She smiled. "You know, a lot of guys I dated before Herb were either scared of me because I was a priest—like I was a witch or something—or they actively disliked *any* woman being a priest, or they wanted to get into sort of sicko things because I *was* a priest. But Herb doesn't care one way or the other. It's just my job to him. He's an atheist. It's kind of a relief."

"A Marxist and a priest?" Theo said. "What are you gonna do, try to convert each other?"

"Well, I know I'm going to try." She grinned.

"Look . . ." Theo rubbed his neck, then his head, then made an effort to return her smile.

Her voice brightened. "So. . . . How 'bout you? You look great. 'Course, that's the first thing I ever heard about you, before I even met you: Theo Ryan, best-looking eligible man at Cavendish."

"Fat lot of good it did me."

"I'll take that remark as a great compliment," she said, and squeezed his hand. Then she leaned around him, calling, "We'll catch up!" Crawford was standing beside Jonas, waving her over. The historian did a silly jig, and blew her a kiss with both hands outstretched. Maude took Theo's arm. "You were looking for Ford last time we talked. Did you ever find him?"

"No," Theo said. "I guess you heard."

"That he left Rhodora? Yes. Jorvelle told me."

"Supposedly he and Jenny Harte are in Cornwall together."

"What about Rhodora? What do you hear from her?"

"She's got a record out."

"Really! That's wonderful. I keep feeling like I've met Rhodora. You and Ford both talked about her so much. You think they'll get back together?"

"I hope not. And God knows what's going to happen to Jenny. Or already has."

Maude tapped his arm. "You worry about a lot of people, Theo."

". . . I guess."

"You guess!" Drawing him back towards the others, she gave

his hand a swing. "Let's talk about *Guys and Dolls.* I think we were good."

"Pretty good."

"Pretty damn good. I had a postcard from Bill and Joel; they said Iggy's thinking of *Hello, Dolly!* for January." She stopped, and turned to him. "Theo, it's going to be a rough year for me, coming back this way with Herb, well, railroading them, and with us living together. My department'll treat me like I've got a scarlet letter sewn to my breast. I can just see them scurrying past, hugging the opposite wall. So I'm counting on you and the gang to pull me through. Can I?" She brushed a black curl behind her ear. "Friends?"

Theo made a wry face. "Well . . . it wasn't what I had in mind."

"I know." She took his hands and smiling up at him, sang a line from their duet, "But—" And she sang it. "You'll know when your love comes along . . . et cetera, Sky."

He pressed her hands together, then let them go. ". . . All right, Sister Sarah. You can count on protection from the civilians."

"Civilians?"

Together they headed back towards the bright pink-striped tents. "That's what show-biz people like my parents called everybody who wasn't in the 'business.' 'Civilians.' And anybody who was, was 'family.' "

{Accepts a Favor}

Illiterate him, I say, quite from your memory.
Sheridan, The Rivals

BACK IN LONDON, the heat wave had been swept off by rain, and the blue English summer sky rolled with billowy clouds. Theo found Brown's Hotel both the most pleasant and the most expensive place he'd ever stayed. "Don't worry about it," counseled Jonas Marsh. "Put it on tick. I'll advance you the money." "Advance on what?" Theo fretted, but Jonas just wagged his finger impatiently and said, "Give me your idiotic play, then leave me alone."

Late the following afternoon, in black tie and dinner jacket, Marsh walked into the hotel bar where Theo sat nervously twisting shreds of cocktail napkins into a chain. Marsh dropped the script of *Foolscap* on the table, slapped it, and glared without a word at his colleague.

"Well?" Theo asked.

Marsh snatched at his bow tie as if to yank it off. Then he jabbed both fists into his cheeks, pushing out a raspy sigh.

"What? Jonas, come on!"

"It's possible," said Marsh, and sat down.

It was one of the best compliments Theo had ever received. Marsh cut off his attempts to say so by adding, "What *isn't* possible, Ryan, is for you to sit in Mole's box at a Royal Performance wearing that corduroy suit. Execrable! Have you no evening clothes?"

"None."

The dapper Marsh spluttered noisily. "God is so goddamn perverse. He sends Walter Raleigh to the scafford wearing ruff and cloak, velvet waistcoat, satin doublet, silk stockings, and taffeta breeches. And then He gives the gift not only of Raleigh's looks but of Raleigh's voice NOT to a man like me!" He made a sweeping gesture down the black silk and satin of his suit. "But to a whoreson creature like you who doesn't even own a dinner jacket! Well, quick, you'll have to rent one."

"But can you do it, Jonas? Can you fake the manuscript?"

Marsh stared at his elegant long fingers as if he were furious at them. "That puny gift," he said, "I do have."

"Great!"

"More accurately, I should say that Mole and I can do it."

"Mole? You want to tell Mole Fontwell?"

"I've told him already. We've been discussing it at length."

"You *have?* Jonas, you should have asked me. Can you trust him?"

Muscles twitched in Marsh's handsome face. "In fourteen years, I've seen no reason not to."

Theo thought this over. It had become clear to him, when the three of them had driven back to London in the yellow Rolls, that Marsh and Fontwell knew each other well: Not only had Marsh obviously been a frequent visitor to Fontwell's home in Kent (where the "private scholar" seemed occasionally to live with his mother and three sisters), but they reminisced together about past junkets up the Nile and down the Rhine and across the Aegean, and also mentioned plans for an upcoming barge trip in the Loire Valley. In addition, Marsh was now sharing Fontwell's suite (which appeared to be of a rather permanent nature) at Brown's Hotel. It had naturally passed through Theo's mind that the two men were (in Tara Bridges' phrase about fellow Thespians Bill Robey and Joel Elliott) "more than best friends, if you know what I mean." Nothing was ever said or done by Marsh or Fontwell to confirm this possibility, and it struck Theo as sad and impressive that they'd had to sustain the relationship over such a long distance for so many years, and under the limits of summers and holidays. At least he'd never seen Mole in Rome, North Carolina. But then no one had ever seen the inside of Jonas Marsh's home either, and perhaps that was the reason why. Not that anyone would *care,* Theo was thinking when Marsh stood up and curtly remarked, "Together, or not at all, Ryan."

Quickly, Theo nodded. "Oh, of course, if you think so. It's fine. But he should understand that there probably won't be any, well, money in this. I mean, we won't *own Foolscap.* If we pull it off, I suppose it will end up belonging to Newbolt, with, I hope, some bequest going to Miss Throckmorton. In fact, Jonas, I can't pay you either."

With a scratch of his luxuriant hair, Marsh smiled. "With your writer's eye for detail, it can't have entirely escaped your notice that poverty is not one of Mole's vices. Or mine. We wouldn't do it for money. We'd do it to see if it can be done." He tapped the script. "You of course have your own reasons. Now, give us a while to study this line by line. You'll have to make changes. Once we're sure of the internal evidence, then we'll come up with a plan for the external. Your research about placement, et cetera. This is going to take time, you realize that? The faked takes even more time than the original. At least successful fakes do. Of course there was the Frenchman who forged a letter from Mary Magdalene in a snap, but he did it in French, on French paper, and even the bloody Frogs smelled a rat."

Theo wasn't sure if he should ask, but he did. "Jonas, please don't be insulted. But have you ever done anything like this before?"

Marsh whipped a handkerchief out of his coat breast pocket so violently that Theo thought he might be going to slap him across the face with it. But all the thin man did was blow his nose with an explosive high sneeze.

"God bless you."

"I've caught a blasted cold in that damnable rain!"

Hurriedly, Theo added, "It's just that you seem to know so much about literary forgeries."

Marsh twisted his nose angrily in the handkerchief. "I know a VERY great deal about literary everything. It's my PROFES-SION. And it appalls me that most of our cretinous Cavendish colleagues are disgustingly unaware that it IS a profession! Why,

Vic Gantz just told me on the phone, last week at the Joyce Conference they passed out a questionnaire, to JOYCE SPECIALISTS, asking how many of them had read, quote, 'SOME PART OF' *Finnegans Wake*! The bloody man only published three novels in his drunken life, and JOYCE SPECIALISTS are being polled about whether they've managed to read PART of one of them!"

"Well, Jonas, I have to confess that—"

But Marsh was on his feet, and had the mesmerized attention of two middle-aged ladies at a corner table. "When the dolts in Ludd Hall have skimmed the major texts in their FIELD, they consider themselves well ahead of the game. By GOD, if a dentist knew as little of teeth as most literary critics know of literature—leave scholarship aside, as that's gone the way of the DODO—why, I'd never let that man inside my mouth! *ACHEWW!*" Another twist to his nose, and Marsh sat abruptly back down, jabbing the handkerchief in his pocket.

"God bless you," Theo said again. "Could I get you maybe a brandy?"

"No." Marsh thrummed his fingers on the script. "Now, do we do this or do we not?"

"Then you think we *can* do it?"

"Think we can successfully deceive Dame Winifred Throckmorton?"

Theo frowned into his empty beer glass. "You don't have to put it like that. She wants more than anything in the world to find this play."

Marsh jerked his hands in an impatient flurry. "She wants to find *Raleigh's* play. There is a considerable difference, which you would prefer to forget. Forgery is an art, Ryan, not a delusion. True, Chatterton went off the deep end and swilled arsenic at seventeen. But he was *caught*. I do not want us to be caught. Nor to expose ourselves by vulgar boasts. When Michelangelo fobbed off his 'Sleeping Eros' on Cardinal Riario as an ancient Roman masterpiece, he could not resist bragging that he'd done it. That's pride, Ryan. Forging artists can never own their art. If your pride requires the authority of authorship, then give this up right now."

"I don't want to be caught."

"Of course you do. You and Mole both do and don't want Dame Winifred to see through this. From my point of view, it's unambivalent challenge. May the better scholar win. And I intend to do this with my point of view the commanding one. Now, let's call round, and see if we can find you some decent rags. Allow me." Marsh dropped a handful of coins on the table. "I don't suppose you brought evening pumps along on this trip, did you? Or even black shoes?"

Thanks to Jonas and Mole, life in London in the week following Henley was proving far less lonely. During the days, while they pored over *Foolscap* in their suite (Jonas wrapped in a blanket with a vaporizer beside him), Theo kept himself hard at work in his own room. He was revising his draft of the Rexford biography. In this effort, he was spurred on less by guilt than by the lure of the second half of Mahan and Son's advance. Another practical motivation was the suspicion (heartily agreed to by Jonas) that if Norman Bridges had said his promotion to full professor might depend upon his producing a second book, then under the new Thorney regime, he'd probably need the whole Rexford trilogy, if not the Pulitzer Prize, to avoid teaching remedial reading at 8:00 A.M. on Saturdays for the rest of his career.

But as Theo worked on the biography, he was relieved to discover that Adolphus Mahan—however tainted his compliments by the desire to secure *Principles of Aesthetic Distance* for his wife, Amanda—had been right to praise this draft: There was a book here. And not a bad book, either. God knows, a third of Ford Rexford's life was more life than most people ever had. And the beginning of the story, plenty to start with. It was not an especially happy beginning. Texas in the dust bowl depression. Ford's mother, married too young to a man she didn't love—timid, dreamy, unhappy, quickly broken by the loss in infancy of two children, and dead herself when the boy was ten. Ford's father, son of a drunk, self-taught minister of a merciless God—astringent, cruel, hard as the land and raging against the imperfections of the people living on it, raging mostly against the son he'd named Joshua. Reading back over Ford's childhood, Theo felt his anger at the adult begin to loosen and fall away.

Meanwhile, not only were his days busy, his nights soon filled up as well. The mantelpiece of Mole's (or Jonas and Mole's) suite at Brown's was lined with invitations and tickets to this or that, and the two men kindly included him in a number of their evenings out. For Jonas, armed with tissues, sprays, pills, and syrups, did not allow his cold to keep him from bloody well enjoying London—not after the cultural deprivations of FUNDIVILLE, as he referred to the "outrageously misnamed" town of Rome, N.C.

Determined, over their objections, to pay his share in these outings, and finding himself near the end of his traveler's checks, Theo telephoned his parents in Manhattan, and asked them to wire him two thousand dollars, which he promised to pay back in the fall by cashing in one of his frugal C.D.s. Although they'd often offered, even tried to force him, he had declined for many years to accept any money from them, and he was touched now by the obvious pleasure it gave them to say yes. In their own way.

HIS FATHER: "Hey, Old Bear, sure you don't need more? Three, four thousand? I'm loaded."

HIS MOTHER: "It's news to me, unless you mean drunk. And he hasn't told us what he needs *two* for! Are you in trouble, Theo?"

HIS FATHER: "Pooh's not in trouble, Rainie. He's having a blast!"

HIS MOTHER: "How would we know? Has he written, has he called?"

HIS FATHER: "Aren't you, Pooh? Having a ball? By George, I loved England. The good old Palladium. 'Everybody do the duck, hey, hey.' Jerry Lee was supposed to headline, but he got in that sex mess with his cousin. Great town! 'A foggy day in London town.' Met any girls?"

HIS MOTHER: "Benny, please shut up. Theo, you aren't in the hospital, are you?"

"Rainie, for Christ sake, why do you always have to expect the worst?"

"Why? Because I married you, that's why. Somebody has to worry, somebody has to *think!*"

"Mom. Dad."

"Rainie, sometimes I really wish you'd stop assuming I'm stupid."

"*Assuming?*"

"Dad! Mom! This is a transatlantic call."

HIS MOTHER: "So? I told you, call collect."

"Listen, you two. I'm not sick, I'm not in trouble, I'm not even trying to find Ford anymore—"

HIS MOTHER: "Good riddance."

HIS FATHER: "Well, now, if you think the man needs you, Old Bear. That piece in the *Times* Sunday must have really hurt."

"What piece?"

"You didn't see it?" (It had never occurred to Theo's parents that everybody in the world didn't read the Arts Section of the *New York Times* every morning of their lives.) "I'll send it to you. It said Ford Rexford was washed up, how *Out of Bounds* hadn't been any good, and how he hadn't written anything else since then, and sort of suggesting he never would. 'Washed up!' Boy, I know how it feels when they turn on you like that."

Fury flared in Theo. "Miserable petty little scorpions! Well, he doesn't give a fuck what they think. And he never reads the paper anyhow. He thought I was joking when I told him George Bush was president. Jesus, that makes me mad!"

HIS MOTHER: "Theo, don't start brooding. You've gotten yourself obsessed with this man's problems."

" 'Obsessed'? Have you been talking to Steve Weiner?"

"You're going to get my ulcers. Just tell yourself to have a good time, and DO it!"

"I'm having a very nice time, Mom. In fact I'm going out so much, I need to buy some decent clothes."

"Why didn't you say so! It's like Sweets says, you look like an angel, and dress like a bum."

"Oh, Rainie, why do you tell him things like that?"

"Mom, Dad. How is everybody? Uncle Arthur, Cathy, Sweets?"

HIS FATHER: "Great!"

HIS MOTHER: "Crazy."

"And you two are fine?"

"Sweetheart, I told you my servants for hire business has sort of petered out in this downswing? Well, your father and I have taken a stupid singing job—don't ask me why—"

HIS FATHER: "It'll be fun!"

HIS MOTHER: "On a lousy cruise ship. With bunk beds! In the tropics in July!"

HIS FATHER: "I've never been to Central America. The Panama Canal, hey! That's a great American achievement in engineering. I'll be damn proud to see it, I'll tell you."

"Dad, I'm not sure this is a good time to go to Panama."

HIS MOTHER: "What can I tell you? We love to scare ourselves. We love to be miserable. That's why we got married."

"Rainie, I know you think you're joking but—"

"Joking? Ha!"

"Goodbye, Mom. Goodbye, Dad."

"So now your son's a comedian too, Benny. Theo, are you eating plenty of fresh fruit? . . ."

They wired the money the next day. With it, Theo was able to trade in his quickly rented "rags" for elegant rags of his own. And in them, he went with his new collaborators to theatres, to auctions, to teas, to the Garrick Club, and to a great many pubs. Here he met a great many friends of the gregarious Mole, including a few of the chaps previously encountered at the Henley Regatta. Frequently these friends had been up at Oxford together, and despite the passage of time, their years in school loomed large in their conversation, especially after several rounds of drinks. Indeed, their years then, as their evenings now, appeared to have pretty much consisted of rounds of drinks. At least their stories of college life often ran an alcoholic course—almost invariably coupled with infantile physical pranks.

Theo (who, with only moderate lapses, had spent his Yale years studying as hard as he could) was a little surprised to hear these well-educated men (well placed now in business, the arts, and even the government) talk as if not only their happiest, but their *only* memories of Oxford were of drunken binges and Three Stooges–like high jinks: He heard them fondly remember the time when one had hung by his ankles from Folly Bridge; when two others had smashed all the furniture in So-and-so's rooms; when several had gone punt-jousting on the Isis and broken most of their ribs.

He listened to them lovingly puzzle over old mysteries: Had X really set fire to the porter's lodge? Had Y been the one who'd cemented the statue of the Virgin Mary into the urinal and put it in the Senior Common Room where it hadn't been noticed by the dons for a week? Had Z actually mailed a pig's penis to So-and-so's fiancée?

Learning of Theo's acquaintanceship with Dame Winifred Throckmorton, they told him (at least three times, and with discrepancies) "the Throckmorton copper story," which involved her having absentmindedly biked away from the front of Blackwell's (or the police station) on a bicycle belonging to a female (or male) police officer, who gave pursuit on foot and was struck in the face by Dame's Winifred's book bag (or umbrella) while attempting to retrieve the bike. He also heard "the Throckmorton Parson's Pleasure story," which involved Dame Winifred's apparent enthusiasm for punting, and her failure while out on the Cherwell with an American (or Canadian) woman, to disempunt rather than pass a nude male swimming hole known as Parson's Pleasure; instead she had carried on straight past several elderly, naked male academics, ignoring their screeched shouts to "Keep Away!" and cheerfully greeting three (or more) by name.

Theo received the same satisfaction to his repeated "Is that true?" as he'd always gotten asking the same question of Ford Rexford.

Because of the Cavendish connection, he was occasionally asked about Herbert Crawford's salary (high), his lakeside chalet (large), and the woman he'd chucked his wife for (everything a man could wish). Did he still affect a Cockney accent, black leather, proletarian sympathies? (Yes, yes, yes.) He also heard a number of stories about Crawford's undergraduate career at Oxford, and while the inbred lingo left him slightly at a loss as to the specifics of the man's achievements, there was little doubt that to take a First in History, a Blue in Boats, the Newdigate Prize, and the virginity of a Master's daughter was to distinguish oneself. To add to these, such triumphs as organizing sit-ins, hanging the North Vietnamese flag from the Magdalen bell tower, running up a £360 bill for cigarettes and scotch at the college buttery, crashing a Commem Ball disguised as the deputy ambassador of Venezuela, and using

the 1968 Long Vac to get himself arrested in Chicago at the Democratic convention—was to conclude that Herbert Crawford had
been destined from his youth for glory of one sort or another, if
not inevitably the authorship-of-eight-books sort. Obviously the
celebrity historian had gone from rowing eights to writing eights
without a dropped stroke, and if the brave, the brash, and the
brilliant deserved the fair, then Herbie Crawford deserved Maude
Fletcher. And with that consolation, Theo admitted to himself
that it was time to give up the last flicker of the fantasy that she
was the one he was waiting for. For the truth was he already knew,
had known without wanting to know for a long time, that it wasn't
Maude he'd been waiting for anyhow.

He heard from Rhodora on the Fourth of July. To celebrate the
holiday, he had taught Mole and six of his friends the American
sport of baseball in Hyde Park. (Jonas, who claimed to be ignorant
of the pastime, and content to remain so, sat in a lawn chair
nearby, blowing his nose and reading Raleigh's *Essays and Observations.*) It was satisfying to Theo, having listened to so many
hours of obfuscatory chitchat from these men about cricket rules,
to be able to say things like "No, you can't run if the ball's foul,
but if it's a pop-up, you can, as long as you tag after it's caught,
as long as you aren't picked off." The Britishers were very good
sports about it.

After this game Theo returned to Brown's, sweaty and cheerful,
to find a package that had been expressed to him from North
Carolina by Rhodora. It contained her new record single, a Blue
Ridge Mountains bumper sticker, a Cavendish T-shirt, a little U.S.
flag, a plastic beer mug from Cherokee's bar, and an eight-by-
ten studio photo of Rhodora herself, inscribed "I Love You,
T. Schneider Ryan. Rhodora." With these souvenirs was a note
in her large looping handwriting.

So you don't forget where you belong.
    Thanks for calling. That was nice, hearing your old voice. Your
house is fine, if you're worrying. I hired a cleaning lady. I'm running all over creation with this damn record thing, and signed so
many papers I'm getting a wart on my knuckle! Flying up to NYC (!!)
tomorrow to shoot a music video! I guess I've got to thank that

bastard Ford for something. He kept telling me I could make it. And I wouldn't ever even have written "I Go On" if he hadn't messed up my mind so bad. Right?

Tell him to get fucked. (I'm sure he is.)

Never mind, let him alone. I guess I'm getting him out of my system. Kind of like a real bad bug? One morning, you wake up and tell yourself, "Get on with your life, looks like you're gonna live."

How you doing, friend? You forget Ford too, hear? Just finish the damn book without him. The asshole can't even remember his stupid life anyhow. Just don't you put me in a goddamn footnote or I'll kill you.

Happy Fourth of July. America, love it or leave it, but don't stay gone too long. Come on home. I miss us talking.

Love, Rhodora

(Can you believe it, first, the damn record co. won't sign up the Dead Indians and hires me this new band—okay, so maybe Ford was right. They weren't so hot, but they're sweet guys. Anyhow, then they tried to make me change my name to Rhodora Rayne! I told them it stays Potts.)

P.S. You got some pretty yellow roses out back.

That night, Theo arranged Rhodora's gifts on his mantelpiece, placing her photograph between the small American flag and the record jacket. Her song hadn't been on any of the jukeboxes in any of the pubs he'd gone to lately, but he always checked. Whenever he'd passed record stores, he'd checked them as well, and had found the single in the two that had "Country/Western" sections. He'd also checked *Billboard*, excited to see "I Go On" not only #26 on the Country/Western chart, but #43 on the Pop/Rock. He became so fretful that night thinking about Rhodora's career that he called his machine in Rome to tell her to be careful about signing papers, and to get a good agent if she didn't have one. To get a good business manager. To get Bernie Bittermann. Still unsatisfied, in the morning he called his father to tell *him* to call Bittermann about Rhodora, to see if the two were already in touch, and to suggest some agents if she needed one.

"Which one is this Rhodora?" his mother kept asking. "This isn't the woman priest Steve was talking about?"

"Obviously not, Mom. Obviously, she's a singer."

"Who can tell with hillbillies? She could be both."

"Well, she's not. And she's not a hillbilly. Dad, she's on *Billboard*'s Country/Western chart."

"You're kidding! Where?"

"Twenty-six."

"On her first record?"

"Yes, and it's only been out a few weeks. Forty-three on Pop/Rock."

"Crossing over!" Benny Ryan whistled into the phone. "And she hasn't got an agent?! They'll eat her alive."

"I know. Have Bernie put you two in touch, okay, Dad, talk to her?"

"He should talk to her now at three A.M. in the morning?"

"Oh, Jesus, Mom, I'm sorry! I forgot what time it was there. I'm a little revved."

"Theo, are you on drugs?"

"Oh, Rainie, Pooh's just trying to do a good deed."

"At noon, it might be a good deed. At three A.M., it sounds more like drugs. That woman you lived with who taught art, I always thought she was on drugs. Thank God that's over."

"Mom, have you ever liked anybody I've lived with?"

"Of course I have. I was crazy about every one of the boys you roomed with those first years at Yale."

"Funny, Mom. And Francie didn't take drugs. She didn't even drink coffee."

"I knew there was something odd about her."

If there was a drug involved, it kept Theo awake most of the next night too, and left him resolved—while he was in the process of giving people up—to let go of Ford Rexford's unfinished play. He took it out of his suitcase and reread *Aesthetic Distance,* seeing now without anger how clearly, and with what affection, Ford had caught the young drama professor and the young southern singer. With what wonder he had seen the strength of Rhodora's gifts. Of course, the character wasn't Rhodora really, and the young professor wasn't really him, and it certainly wasn't the two of them together, since they had never been together. Not the way the characters in this play, *Aesthetic Distance*, seemed so . . . inevitable.

Ford should finish it. It was a play just calling out for an ending. Who was he, Theo, to hold back Ford Rexford's creation all these weeks? Who was he to try to punish Ford?

This change in feeling about the play grew out of the same softening taking place in him as he'd been working to edit his biography of Ford Rexford's youth. As he'd been back with the child Ford in that hot sterile Texas town, back into the shabby ugliness of the spare house, in the grain of whose every surface wind had bored dust too deep to clean, back with the grubbing and scrimping and fighting the intractable earth for food. He'd been with Ford watching the angry despair of the rancher who'd shoveled his dead frozen calves into a pit, watching the arrest of the farmer who'd killed a banker who'd taken away his farm. He'd been with Ford off eating supper in the homes of the Mexicans who were scapegoats for the ranchers' and the farmers' and the bankers' own poverty, for their powerless war against the unrelenting, unending land.

Here in his London room, looking at the boy long ago in Texas, Theo forgave the man. Looking at the world that the boy had seen in Bowie, and looking at the way the man had turned that world into *The Valley of the Shadow*, into *Preacher's Boy* and *The Long Way Home, Desert Slow Dance*, and all the other plays, Theo found himself feeling again his love for the person who'd had the gift, and the heart, to imagine them. Sixteen full-length plays. Twenty-two one-acts. Ford Rexford washed up? Never. The trickle seeping from the smallest eddy of such an ocean of talent could flood whatever dried-up critic had written that article dismissing his future.

In this mood, early the next day, Theo mailed Adolphus Mahan two hundred revised pages of the biography, then he walked over to the Middendorf Agency with *Principles of Aesthetic Distance* under his arm. He expected to meet there with an angry harangue from Miss Fitzhugh for having run off with the other script the way he had, but he hoped to set things straight by giving her Ford's play.

In fact, the receptionist was angry, but, as it turned out, more because she hadn't been able to find him for eight days than about property stolen from Middendorf, Inc. (She herself stole the odd stamp, cut flower, and note pad all the time.) "So there you are, and bad luck to you, Mr. Ryan!" Flush with rouge and temper, Miss Fitzhugh stood behind her lacquered desk, arms crossed over her red satin blouse. The glass vase he'd knocked over had obviously escaped breaking, since it was back in place with three orchids in it.

"I come on my knees. Metaphorically." He stepped aside to let an immaculately dressed young man (no doubt an agent) escort an older man in jeans (an actor Theo recognized from the movies) through the rococo lobby. Business was busy today, phones ringing, doors opening and shutting as quickly as those on the set of a French farce.

Theo smiled. Miss Fitzhugh scowled. He changed approach, and attempted a formal tone. "Is Mr. Middendorf in?"

"That he's not," she snapped. "And for you to go checking out of your hotel without a word! I've phoned a good dozen searching." She picked up a small stack of memos. "There's—"

"I'm staying at Brown's."

She stopped. "Are you now?" It was clear from her derisive grimace that this possibility hadn't occurred to her. "Aren't you the swell! Well, you might have told someone."

"Look, Miss Fitzhugh, I'm sorry I skipped out with the play. But it did belong to me. Forgive me?"

"I've been in a terrible fret."

"Forgive me? Fellow Irish?" He held out his hand, with a hopeful smile. She shook her head ruefully, but accepted the offered hand, and started to say something when Theo interrupted again. "Mr. Middendorf must be back by now from Capri?"

She glanced at one of the doors. "I'm not at liberty to say." (Perhaps she'd been reprimanded for being too free with information.)

"Well, he'll be glad to know I've brought Ford's—" He held

up his folder, but she waved it impatiently away by shaking the handful of memo notes at him.

"Now, you listen." She pushed up her sleeves, a sign of her seriousness. "Miss Harte's in a state, she is. And all this week, coming and calling and coming and calling, trying to find you before she leaves—"

"Jenny Harte? She's in London? Is Ford?"

Miss Fitzhugh thrust the notes into his hand. "She phoned not an hour ago from her hotel. She's flying back to the States this very day, and postponed it twice now already, and all because of wanting to talk to yourself. I'll ring her up and say you're coming." She reached for a telephone eagerly, still under the romantic impression that passion for Jenny Harte had driven Theo to pursue the young woman and Rexford across the Atlantic.

"She's not with Ford?"

Miss Fitzhugh leaned towards him, motioning him closer for privacy. "Ay, Mr. Rexford's driven her off, I'll wager, upset as she is. And buying her off as well, is what I'm thinking, sending her here with drafts to pay and no money left in his account but what Mr. Middendorf put there out of his own pocket." Whatever hopes the Middendorf agency might have had of drilling discretion into their young Irish receptionist would have been dashed had they overheard this indignant torrent rush past her beautifully painted lips.

Theo was horrified. "What did Jenny *say?*"

"What need had she to say a word, herself with those dark circles under her eyes and spooky-like with her narves all gone to pieces." Miss Fitzhugh acted out a state of overwrought grief by trembling and clasping her hands to her face. "And her not speaking a mean word against him neither."

Still clutching the folder, Theo ran towards the door, dodging gilded chairs and the impatient clients who waited in them, leafing without a glance through magazines. "Tell Jenny I'm in a taxi on my way. And, Miss Fitzhugh, *thank you.*"

The receptionist called to him. "Don't be blaming her, Mr. Ryan. It's you bloody men what do it to girls."

"Too too true," laughed an elegant woman on the brocaded settee.

CHAPTER
25

{Sound Retreat, Afar Off}

It is my last mirth in this world. Do not grudge it to me.
When I come to the sad parting, you shall see me grave enough.

Sir Walter Raleigh, when warned against levity on the scaffold

JENNY HARTE, in jeans and sweater, her luggage beside her, sat in an ugly armchair in the small, poorly lit lobby of her hotel, the first one she'd come to when she'd walked out of the train station three days earlier. And it had been only three days, not a week. (The Irish exaggerate.) Just as Miss Fitzhugh had inflated the time Jenny had been in London, she'd overstated the havoc wrought on the young woman's face. Jenny looked tired, and she looked unhappy, but otherwise she looked the same as when Theo had seen her last, that May afternoon on the Cavendish campus. Her hair the same blonde, her eyes the same clean blue, and in her movements the same clear, resilient, unmistakably American imperviousness to experience. She had not, Theo thought with relief, been so damaged by whatever had happened with Ford that the pain was left on her face.

With too deliberate cheer she bounced out of the chair and waited for him to come over to her. Then she said with excessive brightness, "Thanks for getting here."

"Oh, Jenny." Theo pulled her to him, hugging her. At that, she burst into tears. "It's all right," he murmured at her, and held her head against him while she cried, until she pulled away, quickly wiping her eyes with the backs of her hands.

"Oh boy," she said, sniffling with a little laugh. "Oh boy, excuse me. It just hit me when I saw you. Somebody from home. I'm okay. I'm glad you got here; I have to go in"—she looked at her watch—"in half an hour."

"Home?"

"To Charlotte. My parents just retired there from Minneapolis." She laughed again, sharply. "Just don't tell me I made a mistake, all right?" Turning, she flung herself back into the armchair. "I don't need any more lectures. I've had plenty from them."

"All right." Theo sat down across from her. "Where's Ford?"

As far as Jenny Harte knew, Ford was still in Cornwall—at the cottage they'd rented in a town on Port Isaac Bay, south of the Arthurian castle at Tintagal. And as far as she knew, he was still drinking. He'd been drinking for a month. He hadn't asked her to leave, nor had he left her, nor struck her, "or anything else my parents may think." She'd left him, and had wanted to leave him long before she finally did. When, or even if, he'd noticed that she'd actually gone, she couldn't say. She'd told him she was leaving, and he'd given her a letter for the Middendorf agency, for money out of his account to pay her plane fare home. But then he'd disappeared again; so she'd hired a taxi to take her to the nearest train station.

In the past weeks, Ford had disappeared a lot. Sometimes he stayed in his "study" for days, drinking; then he wandered through the house in the middle of the night, making long-distance phone calls, knocking into things and breaking them, "talking crazy junk at nobody." Sometimes he went away for days, driving a rented Jaguar convertible around the countryside, either by himself or with "local weirdos" he picked up in pubs. This was the second car he'd rented; he's smashed the rear-end of the first one by backing into a stone wall outside a pub. Sometimes he'd brought these local strangers to the house; other times they had carried him back there from whatever pub they'd met him in. Usually, they stayed, sitting in the front room drinking until they passed out, or they got in a fight with Ford and left, or he threw them out. One of them had broken Ford's nose. The police had come to the house. All this Jenny related with a kind of puzzled matter-of-factness, as if she were summarizing the plot of a play whose tone had taken a peculiar turn and confused her.

Theo lifted his head from his hands. "Oh, Jesus. For a month? Why didn't you call Middendorf? Or Bernie. Somebody. Don't you know how frantic they were?"

"He didn't want anybody to know where he was." She shrugged. "Look, I thought it would go away. Plus, I guess I thought I could handle it. I was never around anything like this before. It was . . . pretty bad."

In researching Ford's biography, Theo had of course heard from many sources stories about such prolonged binges. Twice they'd ended with the playwright hospitalized. Even Ford himself described these episodes as "scary serious shit," "soul holes," "muzzle-in-the-mouth time." But the last one—when he'd shot at his now ex-wife and fled to Tilting Rock—had been more than two years ago. After Rhodora had moved in with him, the drinking hadn't stopped, but the binges had. Under her flat-out refusal to tolerate it ("I'm not hanging around watching some chickenshit asshole guzzling poison so he can kill himself without admitting it"), then, even the drinking had tapered off—at least until the last few months. But in retrospect, Theo could see there'd been warning signs of another outbreak: the broken collarbone, the pint bottle hidden in the glove compartment, the Lincoln crashed and the arrest by the Rome police, the sudden bolt to England, the break with Rhodora. Had Ford, as Rhodora theorized, been "running scared" from marriage with her? Had that fear started the binge?

"Was Ford drunk when you two left Rome together? Did you *plan* this or what?"

Jenny Harte admitted that they both had been drinking, that in fact she'd had to drive the Lincoln most of the way to Atlanta because Ford had passed out in the backseat. And that, no, they "hadn't exactly planned it."

"You just left, drove to Atlanta, and took a plane to England? Just like that?" Theo tried to keep his voice calm. "Let's don't even talk about that you were supposed to be grading papers for my course, and I had—"

"I feel very bad about that."

"Let's don't even talk about your dissertation—"

"Well, actually, I worked on it." This struck her as humorous.

"Let's talk about your life, Jenny, for Christ's sake."

She bounced in the armchair, pulling her legs under his, hands squeezing her knees. "I was always so damn good! Good kid, good student, neat room, papers on time. I wanted to do something wild, not responsible, not planned, not—"

"Well, I'll say you managed that."

She sighed at him. "Please? No lecture."

Theo rubbed his head hard, crossed his arms. "Fine. So he was drunk from day one."

"Not all that much at first. The first couple of weeks were great. I mean it. He even helped me with my work. We fished, played cards; I did things that were fun, for a change. We went exploring Cornwall. He taught me how to see things. Really see things." She looked at Theo, leaning over her crossed legs. "You know what I mean?"

"Yes, I know." He massaged his eyes.

A middle-aged couple, Americans, waved at Jenny as they entered the lobby, ladened with cameras, guidebooks, and shopping bags. They stopped to ask why she hadn't left for the airport; was anything wrong?

"They've been nice," Jenny said blandly as the couple started up the dark carpeted stairs. "Look, Ford was fun, you know? He really was. . . . Then all of a sudden . . ." She pulled her knees towards her chest, rocking them.

"I wish you'd called."

"He got so he wasn't, you know, even *there*, he wasn't rational."

"Yes. . . ."

"I mean, sometimes he'd say he felt rotten I'd gotten messed up in it, for me to go home, and on and on, but I wanted to help. I mean, Theo, the man *was* a great writer."

"What about his writing?"

She shook her head. "I mean, he'd do maybe a page, then he'd tear it up. One time he dumped a bunch of paper in a wastebasket, threw whiskey on it, and set it on fire. I think that was a big part of the problem. . . . Anyhow, I couldn't handle it." She waved her hands as if brushing off memory. "No way."

"Jenny, if you'd only come to talk to me before you did this! Couldn't you tell he wasn't the kind of man to throw your life away on?"

She shook her head with annoyed impatience. "I never wanted to throw my life away on him. Are you kidding? I thought it would last the summer. I mean, I always planned on being back at Cavendish in the fall. I'm teaching! I'm on the last chapter of my dissertation. I knew it was just an affair. He's had hundreds. I knew that."

Her tone shocked Theo. "Didn't you know Ford was getting married in a month!"

"Right! Obviously he was serious." Her look was so contemptuous Theo blinked. Then, pulling her hands through her hair, Jenny stretched out her legs. "I really don't think you can ask me to feel responsible for that."

"That's not—"

She glanced at her bright-colored watch. "I'm sorry. I've got to get to Heathrow. All I wanted to—"

"I'll find a cab and take you."

"No, thanks anyhow. The Middendorf agency's sending a taxi for me. They've been really nice. All I wanted to say is, somebody ought to do something about Ford. His family or somebody. And you're the only person I know who knows him, so . . ." Taking her plane ticket and passport from her purse, she checked them, put them back. Then she handed Theo a piece of paper with an address and phone number on it. "That's where he is. Was."

Theo rubbed slowly at his knees. "Damn it. I should have given Middendorf Ford's manuscript soon as I got here. Maybe he would have gone back to work then."

Jenny looked puzzled. "What manuscript?"

"*Principles of Aesthetic Distance.* Christ, the critics trash *Out of Bounds.* Then his wife throws his computer out the window. So he loses *A Waste of Spirit* too. Then I act like an asshole, hold on to his new play—"

"What are you talking about?" The young woman stood up,

pulling on a short suede jacket. "Ford's got *Aesthetic Distance* and *Waste of Spirit* both. With him. They're just not finished. That's what I've been saying. That's the problem. Pretty ironic, hunh? Here I've been analyzing the endings of plays, even a Rexford play, then here I was watching him not be able to finish one. It's so ironic, I hate to think I'm leaving because I don't think he *will* finish. Pretty awful thing to think about yourself."

Flushed, Theo stood too, jamming his hands in his pants pockets. "Well, I'm sure you'll get a good publishable chapter out of the episode."

Her eyes widened, quickly wettening. "That's not what I meant. That's not why I came here with him."

"Jenny, I'm sorry." He touched her shoulder. "I apologize. I know it isn't why you came. You came because, well . . . there's nobody like him. And you left because he's impossible. I know that. But you're wrong about *Aesthetic Distance. I've* got his only copy." Theo pointed at the folder on the table beside the chair. "That's it, right there."

The tears vanished as rapidly as they'd appeared, leaving her eyes the same clean blue. "I'm telling you, Theo. He's got two or three copies of both of those plays. I mean, he wouldn't let me read them, but I've seen the manuscripts when he was working. He locks them up in that trunk of his. The one you shipped him from Tilting Rock."

Theo told her she must be mistaken. Then the memory of Ford's voice rushed to his ear, from that April evening back in Rome as they'd left the Pit 'n Grill, when he'd fretted about giving Ford *Foolscap.* How Ford had said, "I don't lose plays, kid."

"He used to joke about it," Jenny was saying with animated interest, as if Ford Rexford the playwright had no connection to the man with whom she'd lived for two apparently horrific months. "About how his agent and producers were going nuts because I guess you'd told them how great *Aesthetic Distance* was, and you'd convinced them it was finished and all. I remember two or three times he said, you know the way he talks, 'The three B's'—that's what he called them, Bittermann, Middendorf, and Amanda Mahan: Bern, Buzz, and the Bitch—'the three B's had their fangs an inch from my poor tired backside, then Theo throws them this great big make-believe bone, and I slip under the fence while they're fighting over it.' It used to crack him up."

Hearing Ford's voice, even in her flat paraphrase, Theo now believed it was true. So that had all been a lie about Ford's ex-wife destroying *A Waste of Spirit*. All a lie, Ford's telling Bittermann that he'd left his only copy of *Aesthetic Distance* back in Tilting Rock; all a lie, telling Adolphus and Amanda Mahan that Buzzy Middendorf had the only copy; telling Middendorf that Theo had the only copy.

And Theo had played right into it, because he thought he *did* have the only copy. He'd told everybody he did, told everybody he would withhold it too, until Ford returned *his* script. He'd made the lie work, since while hardly anyone believed Ford anymore, there was no reason to doubt his scrupulous, indignant biographer. All a lie, all a joke. No, Theo told himself, a delaying tactic until Ford could finish. Or a cover-up, because he couldn't.

Theo stared at the young blonde woman. "He can't finish the plays."

She ducked her head under her purse strap, pulling the bag to her side. "Who could, drinking like that?"

"Maybe that's why he's drinking like that, Jenny."

"It doesn't help."

"No . . ."

She made a face, sensible, dismissive. "All myths to the contrary, the talent's not in the bottle, and the talent sure doesn't justify the bottle either. When Ford Rexford drinks, he's just a drunk." Spotting a taxi driver looking in the hotel door, she waved at him.

Theo picked up her suitcases. "Did you tell anybody at Middendorf's?"

"Where he is? No. And not about the drinking either."

"That Ford has the plays? Did you tell anybody that *Aesthetic Distance* isn't finished? The Mahans or Bernie. Nobody? You're sure?"

She shook her head. "Who would ask *me*?"

"Well, don't."

She gave a defensive shrug.

After Theo helped the driver carry Jenny Harte's luggage to the taxi, he leaned into the back seat to tell her goodbye. "I'm sorry it was so rough."

"Me too," she said. "Do I look sadder but wiser? That's how I feel."

"You look like you'll be fine."

She nodded, not doubting it herself.

No one answered the phone at the Cornwall number Jenny had given him. He kept calling until two in the morning. Cornwall was a long way off. Even by American distances. Theo drove there early the next day in a rented "budget car," having declined Mole Fontwell's offer to lend him the Rolls.

"Now find out," Jonas nagged, "exactly what Ford told this Mr. W.F.D., and make sure he understands that *Foolscap*—"

"I know what to say," Theo reassured him. "We don't have to worry about Ford." This remark was met by a maniacal laugh from the fretful Marsh.

"Or drive you in the Rolls myself?" asked Mole, his small dark face full of solicitude. "It'd be an honor to be of assistance to Ford Rexford; I admire his work awf'lly. Jonas and I saw *Her Pride of Place* just last month. Overwhelming. And you say he helped you with *Foolscap*, which you know I think absolutely splendid. Very generous of him."

"Yes, he's very generous." Theo smiled. "Immoderate in every sense. . . . In a way, *Foolscap* is as much his as mine."

"Elizabethan," Mole said, buttering his toast at the elegant little table wheeled in each morning by a Brown's waiter. "Much prefer the old Elizabethan attitude of crib and share the lot, as Dame Winifred used to say, to all that Romantic pride of authorship, don't you know. Bit much, the sole solitary original 'Artist,' proclaiming Self in every line." The private scholar deftly cracked open his boiled egg. "When a writer's life becomes the sole subject matter of the work, the life begins swamping the work, and then substituting for it, and then—"

"And THEN, sooner or later, we get Thomas Wolfe!" Jonas Marsh suddenly exclaimed, furiously spraying a decongestant up his nose. "We get one well-done if minor novel BY, and seven hundred huge biographies ABOUT, F. Scott Fitzgerald—all of them telling us he was infatuated with his wife and couldn't hold his liquor. And I'm certain *your* biography will perpetuate Ford 'Great Original' Rexford as yet another irresistibly soused Romantic."

"Well, now," Fontwell said, "the original Romantics cannot really be described as soused—"

"Bugger the Romantics!" Marsh blew his nose furiously. "Infantile narcissists mooning and moaning to their daffodils and clouds and their filthy sheep. BAH BAH Wordsworth-less!" The slender man leapt onto the blue chintz couch in front of the mantel, clutched his hands spasmodically, and shouted in a palsied warble:

> God, said I, be my help and stay secure.
> I'll think of the leechgatherer on the lonely moor!

" 'Thoughts too deep for tears'!" Marsh spluttered on. "Thoughts too deep for *thought!*"

Despite the kind offer of Fontwell and Marsh to accompany him, Theo had felt he should go to Cornwall alone, and certainly (nervous as he was about British roads) not in a borrowed Rolls-Royce. So he left them there in their suite, with Marsh (to whom all the world was clearly a classroom) charging the Romantics with glamorizing the neuroses of the artist into a signature of the seriousness of the art. This "everyone's thrilled by Van Gogh's sliced-off ear" theory had led, he insisted, straight to Hemingway's writing sophomoric world-weary claptrap when he was young and sentimental macho rubbish when he was old. "Stay on the motorways," Jonas suddenly paused in his diatribe long enough to advise. "You can go ninety miles an hour, easily. The M-Four to Bristol, the M-Five to Exeter. Then head west. Maxwell Perkins has a lot to answer for, making all those ME ME ME chauvinist adolescents synonymous with the modern American novel. And that 'Aw shucks, I'm jest a natural born genius' promo of Rexford's! Really! See you soon, Ryan."

Theo had obediently gone on the motorways, and had gone ninety miles an hour too, though not easily. It was the heading west that had taken all the time. Hour after hour into the sun, into Devon again, rattled by winds on the Dartmoor hills, across the Cornish moors, the landscape wilder and less settled than any other he'd traveled through in England. He'd driven two hundred and fifty miles when he finally saw, far off on the horizon, late afternoon light glistening on the choppy waves of Port Isaac Bay.

He'd come too late. Ford wasn't there.

It was a small gray town, and with the directions Jenny had given him, it wasn't hard to find the cottage. It sat in a grove of low gnarled apple trees atop a hill overlooking the bay. A farmhouse really, it looked as dark and primitive as the land. The moss-stained stone sides sloped unevenly, the bedraggled thatched roof sagged. In the hilly yard was an odd assortment of furniture, like the unbought remains of a tag sale—a thin mattress, a broken rocker, an ugly set of andirons. When Theo parked on the dirt road that led to a dangerously tilted barn behind the house, a dog raced barking towards his car. Then a short, gray-bearded man in rubber boots and dirty ribbed sweater came out of the open door, calling to the dog. He carried a large pail and a mop. This man, the owner of the property, was, he finally explained after prodding, in the process of cleaning the house, having evicted the tenant, Ford Rexford, two days earlier.

"But I've just driven all the way from London," Theo told him, walking stiffly across the stone-strewn grass, kicking to stretch the cramps from his legs.

"Missed him," the old man said with no evident regret.

"Ford Rexford is . . . I'm his . . . close friend. I was told he was ill."

"Ay." The man nodded with a sour look, tossing the dirty water from the pail into the yard. "'Tis ill he should be, from the lot of whiskey bottles I've carted off. And a madman besides. 'Out ye go,' says I. 'I'll not have the carryings on,' says I, 'what I've heard tell of up and down this town.'" Disgusted, the man slapped the mop against the stone steps. "And if you're here looking for his young wife, she left him a week Friday. A taxi come from Trebarwith and carried her off with her traps. Andrew Simpson the postman saw 'em go."

"Ah, well, yes, I realize that." Theo held out his hand, which the farmer begrudgingly took. "I'm Theo Ryan."

"Thomas," said the old man, leaving Theo to guess that he meant not his Christian but his family name.

"Mr. Thomas, I spoke with, ah, Mrs. Rexford in London. She asked me to come see what I could do. Mr. Rexford hasn't been well."

"Well enough to eat a great huge pig and send its fat up my chimney," the man mysteriously protested.

"I beg your pardon?"

Slowly Theo lured out of the landlord, an odd combination of garrulity and parsimonious silences, that the immediate cause of the eviction had been the report (confirmed by eyewitness testimony) that Ford, in league with one "Daniel Llangbi, a bad 'un from Wales," had "kidnapped" the local vicar, brought him to the farmhouse at gunpoint (who'd lent them the hunting rifle was still unknown), where the American had not only made this priest listen to obscenities about the Bible, but had torn pages out of the Holy Book and used them to light a fire in the front room. It was in this fireplace that Ford had roasted an entire spitted pig (origins suspiciously undetermined, and perhaps tied to the hunting rifle). It wasn't clear to Theo whether the old landlord was more incensed by the kidnapping, the blasphemy, the presence on his premises of a Welshman, or the greasy mess splattered all over his whitewashed walls. But incensed he was, and had given the playwright notice the next morning.

"Did the vicar press charges? Is Mister Rexford in jail?"

"No more he's not," complained the farmer. "Father Mabyn denied it to the magistrate's face, and may God forgive him for the lie. Told how he'd gone off with 'em of his free will, when his own housekeeper saw him marched out the vestry door with his hands high over his head! Shut yer mouth, Liz, damn ye!" (This to the spotted dog, with a nonchalant kick in her direction, which she ignored.) "But the story come out in the Black Prince that same night, what with Daniel Llangbi bragging on how they'd done it to any would listen. So my wife says, 'Out he goes, rent or no!' I give him his notice next morn."

"But where did Mister Rexford go?"

"Drove off." Thomas gestured with the mop in the general direction of the rest of England.

"Drove off? Where? Where are all his things?"

"Don't know. Father Mabyn come in his housekeeper's husband's lorry and fetched this big black trunk he had." The old man struggled with himself, then added, "I'll not deny Mister Rexford paid up handsome for damages." More facial contortions accompanied an angry wringing of the mop. "I'll not deny he had an open hand."

This admitted, Mr. Thomas seemed to think he had fulfilled all obligations, for he turned back through the doorway. But Theo hurried after him, entering the low, rough-plastered room, where there were indeed fresh grease stains on the walls and on the wide stone hearth. In fact, neatly displayed on a wood-planked table lay the damaging exhibits of a few sizable charred bones and several burnt pages of the Old Testament. What furniture there was, was dark and large and roughly made. The whole place, stripped and scrubbed, smelled of ammonia. It was, at least potentially, a very pleasant space, but there was nothing personal in it now. Theo, receiving reluctant permission to look around, followed the narrow stone-slabbed hall past a bedroom and into the little room that must have been Ford's "study"—and the reason he'd rented the house. There was a table pushed up against the casement windows. The windows opened westward, out over the hills to the sea.

"I've cleaned," growled Thomas unnecessarily; the room now was scoured and spare as a monk's. There was nothing in it but the few pieces of furniture.

Unlatching the windows, Theo leaned out, watching the low twisted apple trees bending to the wind. At the edge of the sky, the sun rose a last moment on the waves, then slipped down into the water, turning the low clouds red.

"Were there no papers, Mr. Thomas?" Theo asked the landlord, who'd followed him suspiciously from room to room. "Typed papers, or notebooks, anything like that? He was a writer."

"Took off. Or burnt."

"You burned his papers?" Theo turned sharply.

The old man thrust his beard out with a defensive truculence. "Not I, lest he'd throwed them in the rubbish. He now, he burnt whatever he took a mind to. The police come one time on account of the smoke where he'd lit up half my woodpile with the flue shut. 'Give him notice while our barn still stands,' says my wife to me." After another internal quarrel, Mr. Thomas opened the top drawer of a wobbly dresser, and took from it a dog-eared book with a broken spine. "Left this book here under the bed."

It was a cheap, small-print collection of the plays of Shakespeare, published in 1907 and inscribed in a faint, laboriously uniform hand as having been "Presented to Lavinia Birch, Winner of the Eighth Grade Essay Prize, Bowie, Texas, June 10, 1916." Some of the brittle pages had been patched with tape, now dry and yellow; others had come loose from the binding. On the frontispiece, someone had drawn glasses around Shakespeare's eyes.

"I'll take this to him," Theo said. "It belonged to his mother."

Father James Mabyn, Anglo-Catholic vicar of Saint Agnes Church, was a bald, middle-aged, overweight man with a wonderful smile and green fervent eyes that grew even greener when Theo introduced himself as a friend of Ford Rexford's. In the little graveyard of the church to which Mr. Thomas had directed him, Theo found the vicar down on his hands and knees doing a charcoal stone rubbing of a half-buried tombstone. Brushing at his black cassock, Mabyn scrambled to his feet, offered his hand, then retracted it when he saw how sooty it was. He explained that he was taking impressions of the older grave markings before salt and wind wore them away, erasing from memory those who had lain for centuries beneath them. " 'Unswept stone besmeared with sluttish time,' he added cheerfully, kneeling to wipe his hands on the grass. "So you're Theo Ryan. A pleasure. My word! Just as Ford described you. What a pity you missed him. It might have helped. I'm afraid he's gone. I never met the young woman staying with him, but I gather she'd left earlier."

"Yes, I spoke with Jenny. Do you know where he went?"

"I think, now this is sheer hypothesis, I think he went to Stratford."

"On Avon?"

"I think so. He said, 'I want to go shoot the'—is it 'wind'?"

"Shoot the breeze?"

"That's right. 'I want to go shoot the breeze with Will.' I'm assuming from the context he meant Shakespeare." With a grunt, the fat priest gathered up the paraphernalia from his rubbings. "Cup of tea? What am I saying? Stay to supper. I dare say you're famished after your drive. All the way from London? Stay the night." And talking in this hospitable way, Father Mabyn led Theo through the scattered tumble of graves to the vicarage, where he had little trouble persuading the exhausted American to accept both food and lodging, postponing the long trip back to London until morning.

Throughout a very large, opulent meal in a very small, shabby dining room (served by an elderly housekeeper who was the evident cause of the vicar's plumpness—for she forced heaping platters upon him as if he were something she was fattening for Christmas), Father Mabyn talked of Ford, whose plays he obviously both knew and loved, and whose soul he'd resorted to praying over—all else having failed. For they'd had many "all-nighters" during Ford's six weeks in town; usually initiated when the playwright reeled drunk into the church or came banging on the vicarage door, demanding ("in a thoroughly obnoxious manner, I grant you") to debate with the priest issues of faith already settled to Mabyn's entire satisfaction before the Middle Ages began. "Oh my word, he'd positively shake the roof with it. Existence of God, omnipotent good, presence of evil, original sin, all that sort of thing. In a rage against imperfection. Poor Mrs. Roberts here was certain he'd murder me one night; expected to stumble over me stabbed like Beckett at the altar. Isn't that right, Mrs. Roberts?" Mrs. Roberts, squeezing an extra stuffed cabbage onto the vicar's plate, gave a defiant nod to testify that indeed she had suspected exactly that.

The kidnapping then had been only the last of numerous such encounters, and yes it had been a real kidnapping: "In the sense, you see, that Ford was terrifically tight when he burst in with the rifle," said Mahan, delicately lifting a sole fillet from its bones. "And in that frame of mind where contradiction was like a match to petrol. He's such a *believer*," Mabyn paused with a broccoli flower speared on his fork. "Naturally drove him mad to hear me say so. His father must have been a very mean-hearted man. One of those ministers who think God so hates the world He hires on sadists to help Him condemn it.

"Yes, Ford wanted intensely to shock me by tossing Leviticus into the fire. Like a nasty little schoolboy. But, uhhh, being obliged to dine on raw whiskey and black burnt pork! That, now, Theo, was a bad shock." The vicar shuddered, patted the napkin tucked into his clerical collar, and returned to his stuffed cabbage.

"And this Daniel somebody?" Theo asked.

"Llangbi. Oh, a would-be poet, our banker's son. Worshipped Ford, and egged him on. The village atheist. You know the type. I'm sure you have them in the States."

Theo wasn't sure that they did anymore. "But Mr. Thomas evicted Ford because of this 'kidnapping'?" he asked.

"A sanctimonious churl, I'm afraid. His wife put him up to it. Mrs. Roberts, roast beef looks lovely. Still, I'll wager it cost Thomas a horrific struggle, greedy as he is. Charging Ford four hundred pounds a month for that wretched farm! And booted out his own son-in-law to do it, too. On the other hand, I grant you, Ford did rather make a mess of the place. My impression is, he was ready to go in any case. I sensed the . . . young woman and he had . . . had parted company."

"Yes, they have. It sounds as if his drinking really got out of hand again." Theo attempted in vain to stop Mrs. Roberts from adding the fifth slab of roast beef to his plate. "Thank you. . . . Do you know if he was working on a play here?"

Mabyn poured Theo a glass of wine. "Well, again just my impression. I don't think it was going well. No, not well. But he talked about writing in general with great passion. He can talk, can't he! He'd talk all night. I confess, I rather lost a lot of sleep. He told me, by the way, that you were a marvelous writer yourself."

"He's very generous," Theo said.

"Fond of you. . . . Thank you, Mrs. Roberts. We're fine now."

"Custard coming," she threatened as she left.

The vicar pulled the napkin out of his collar and scrubbed pleasurably at his mouth. "Very fond of you. And, let's see, ah, an American Indian name. 'Pawnee,' yes, Pawnee."

"His son, younger son."

"I see. And someone called Rhodora. Spoke of her with great admiration. A singer. With Indians, I believe. Cherokee Indians?"

Theo held his hand near the warmth of the candle. "Not exactly. . . . Did he say anything about Rhodora personally?"

Mabyn searched the ceiling for the memory. "That she'd left him? Is that right?"

"Ford said she'd left *him?*"

"I believe so. Declined to marry him? Perhaps I misunderstood."

Folding his napkin, Theo sighed. "Oh, Lord. . . ."

The custard was followed by coffee, the coffee by port wine and cheese. Theo asked about Ford's army trunk. "His manuscripts are in it—or used to be. I'd hate for—"

"Safe and sound. He asked me to have it shipped for him to London, care of Midden-something, I believe."

The two agreed that, instead, Theo would take the trunk to London in the hatchback of his rented car. "Such sad and intriguing stories," the vicar said, picking up crumbs of Stilton with a moistened forefinger.

"Of his life?"

"The poor fellow did not have an easy young time of it, did he?"

"No. He said to me once, 'Maybe God can't change the past, but *I* can.' That's what he called the plays, alternatives to reality. 'I can't cope,' he said, 'but I can create. Re-creation's the best revenge.' "

Mabyn smiled. "The real life sounds fantastical itself. Just the tales of that old trunk! Imagine having to hide in it all night from Mafia casino owners. Really, what a life Ford's led, compared to mine. Well, compared to most, I'd wager. But, of course, I needn't tell his biographer that, need I?"

Theo laughed out loud. "Actually, I hadn't heard anything about the Mafia."

"No? In Las Vegas?" Father Mabyn proceeded with enthusiasm to tell the convoluted, and undoubtedly entirely fabricated saga, a few episodes of which Ford had clearly lifted from *Desert Slow Dance.*

Theo looked across the little table at the plump, red-cheeked priest. "You liked Ford a lot, didn't you?"

Mabyn's kind smile spread over his face. "I did. I will be proud to tell my grandchildren someday. . . . Yes, yes, Mrs. Roberts, if I ever manage to find a wife in time to have any; needn't look so pointedly. . . . I will tell my grandchildren with pride that I, an undistinguished cleric in an insignificant little town, was kidnapped one day by the great American playwright, Joshua Ford Rexford. I only wish . . ." The vicar put down his fork and knife, and looked with surprising sadness across at Theo. "I wish God had given it to me to have been of some help to him. That I'd been, well, clever enough, or deep enough, to help. He is a very unhappy man. Almost in despair, I think; for all his marvelous love of life." Mabyn reached out his hand. "Please. I hope you won't consider it presumptuous of me to say that, a comparative stranger. To someone who, well, who loves him so deeply as I know you do."

". . . No." Theo shook his head. "And I'm very glad he met you."

"There is," the vicar said, "*I* believe, at least—there is more real goodness in the world than people think. And less real greatness. God gave Ford (and how Ford kicks at the thought), God gave him that rare rift of great talent." Mabyn held up his pudgy fingers, tracing them slowly across the air, much as he had rubbed the fading words of the stone in the churchyard. "And I believe, as his friend 'Will' said—abandoning all pretense of Christian humility, we must admit—'Not marble, nor the gilded monuments/ Of princes, shall outlive this powerful rime.' " The vicar's fervent green eyes gleamed in the candlelight. "I believe Ford Rexford will last like that. Whether he knows it or not."

Theo rubbed his hair. "Oh, he knows it. How could he not? The jackass can read. . . . Knowing doesn't seem to help much, though, does it? I mean, with this life."

"Oh, this life. No, so far he has royally messed up this life." The vicar peered into his glass as if the temporal world were in there with the port. "But fortunately, he is mistaken about its limits, too." He raised his wine glass. "To Ford Rexford! 'Here's dirt in your eye, partner!' "

"Mud." Theo toasted Ford.

The next morning Father Mabyn helped wedge the large trunk into the back of the car. "Tell him he's in my prayers," said the vicar.

"If I find him, I will." Theo shook hands through the open

window. "And if he calls, tell him I want to see him. Thank you, Father James. I hope we'll meet again." The American grinned. "In this life, I mean."

"Whenever."

Theo reached London late that afternoon. He drove to Brown's and had the footlocker carried up to his room. He didn't enter the hotel. After he returned the rental car, he walked to the nearest Underground station, passing on the way a bookstore in whose window a clerk was stacking dozens of copies of Ford Rexford plays. He was surprised by this prominence, but attributed it to the success of the revival of *Her Pride of Place.*

Then, waiting for the tube to take him to the Middendorf agency, he saw seated on a bench a young man in jeans who was reading a paperback of *Proof Through the Night.* An acting student, Theo decided.

It was not until he was standing in the crowded train, jostled in the rush-hour press, that he learned the true cause of all the interest. He looked down and saw the front page of the newspaper held by a woman seated near him. In a lower column, a headline said:

JOSHUA FORD REXFORD DEAD
AMERICAN PLAYWRIGHT KILLED IN AUTO CRASH

The words separated into letters, the letters broke apart into slashes of ink, disconnected, nonsensical. As long as he could keep them from coming back together, as long as he could stop the letters from joining into language, they wouldn't mean anything, they wouldn't be words and so they couldn't be true.

CHAPTER

26

{Exit the Guardsman}

Time and death call me away.

*Sir Walter Raleigh, in a letter
to his wife*

IT SOUNDED SO MUCH LIKE A FORD STORY, and after all so few of those were true. Why should this one be any different? Later, Theo would remember that he'd even thought, Stupid joke, Ford; this is in very poor taste. He would remember that he'd thought, Rhodora, you don't believe this, do you? Besides, the newspapers told the tale in such inconsistent ways; and wasn't that also typical of Ford fabrications? According to an early report, an Italian sports car convertible had smashed after midnight into the embankment of a bridge in the center of Stratford-on-Avon. According to a later report, the convertible was a Jaguar and it had crashed through a fence, diving into the Avon River at 11:05 P.M. One paper said Ford had drowned. Another said he'd died of a broken neck. Two alleged that he'd been drinking heavily prior to the accident; a third didn't mention alcohol. The fact that he hadn't used his seat belt was stressed by some; the fact that he wasn't wearing shoes struck others as particularly interesting.

Only an evening tabloid had a picture of the twisted wreckage of the convertible being pulled from the water. Only the *Times*, which said almost nothing about the accident itself, cited correctly the number of Ford's Tonys and Pulitzers, the number of his plays, the number of his wives. But the one thing that every paper claimed, however many newsstands Theo walked to, block after block, hour after hour, was that Joshua Ford Rexford, the American playwright, was dead. He had died late last night in an automobile crash in Stratford-on-Avon, England; alone, barefoot, in his sixty-sixth year. That much they agreed on.

The messages handed to Theo by the desk clerk at Brown's made the same nonsensical claim. No matter how long he sat in the dark by his hotel room window, resting his feet on the black army trunk; no matter into how many arrangements on the scratched surface of the trunk he moved the small pieces of note paper, their messages persisted in this idea that Ford was not alive. The Middendorf agency believed it; Jonas and Mole believed it; from across the whole breadth of the ocean, Adolphus Mahan and Theo's parents and Steve Weiner all appeared to believe it was true. There was even a message saying Bernie Bittermann was already on a plane to London, and with him was Ford's older sister, Ruth, who (Theo knew) had never before in her seventy-two years left Texas; they were coming to claim the body, which suggested strongly that they both believed Ford was dead. The fact that the BBC wanted Theo Ryan to call them back implied the same belief. Only Rexford's official biographer declined to accept this latest story of Ford's as any more factual than the thousands he'd already heard.

That night Theo not only didn't return the calls, he didn't make any of his own—because as long as he didn't talk to Rhodora, as long as no message came from her, what everyone else was saying wasn't true. Finally, however, he did answer the persistent knocking at his door, and accepted condolences from Jonas and Mole, pretending to agree with them that Ford was dead. When they said they'd ordered dinner to be sent up to him, he promised to eat it. When they told him there would be a "Special Report" on Rexford's death at 11:30 that night, he even turned on the television, and heard the BBC commentator add new plot twists to this preposterous tale of Rexford's Last Evening Alive. It all sounded just like Ford.

The story was that yesterday the playwright ("highly inebriated, according to a number of witnesses") had attended a performance in Stratford by the Royal Shakespeare Company of *Antony and*

Cleopatra. Wearing jeans and a tuxedo jacket with ruffled shirt, he'd gone backstage at the second intermission, signed autographs for the Queen's maids, Iras and Charmian, and visited Cleopatra in her dressing room. (Fifteen years ago Cleopatra and he had had an affair, when she was starring in the London premiere of *Maiden Name;* this was not mentioned in the interview by the BBC.) The star cried beautifully, and regretted that she hadn't asked Ford to surrender the pint of scotch visible in his jacket pocket when he'd stumbled while trying on her pharaonic headgear. What had the playwright talked about with her? About old times, and Shakespeare. About how Shakespeare had "done everything right."

BBC: "Artistically?"

STAR: "Financially, actually. About Shakespeare's owning stock in his own company, then retiring and investing in real estate. Of course, I know Ford meant artistically as well. He loved Shakespeare so. Quoted it for hours when I knew him first. He loved this play in particular." (Here, more beautiful tears, and an averted face, backlighting the profile.)

The next interview was with a young male actor, who'd played multiple walk-ons in this production of *Antony and Cleopatra,* and whose "only excuse" for letting Ford go on stage in his place for his last role ("the Guardsman") was that he was "so awed and overwhelmed and, well, thrilled to meet Mr. Rexford that I suppose I allowed him to talk me into it." The young man's only excuse for confessing all this on national television was blazingly evident to every other actor in the business. With a vivacious solemnity, he described how Ford had glanced at the few lines, repeated them successfully, donned the military tunic, hefted his lance, strapped on his helmet, and entered the play near its tragic climax, which, in fact, it was the guard's small duty to help initiate:

{ENTER A GUARDSMAN}

Guardsman: Here is a rural fellow
   That will not be denied your Highness' presence:
   He brings you figs.
Cleopatra: Let him come in.

{EXIT GUARDSMAN}

The audience had no idea that the unshaven, stiffly upright and somewhat bowlegged supernumerary making this announcement to the captive Queen and her maids, was, according to the BBC commentator, "thought by many to have been for his time the greatest living playwright in the English language." A few people who'd sat in the front rows that night were to dine out on the fact that they'd thought they'd recognized Ford Rexford, or had at least suspected something out of the ordinary. But they hadn't; although one woman had noticed how extraordinarily blue the guard's eyes were, and she was to think of those eyes over the years whenever she saw a Rexford play. Of course, Cleopatra, Iras, and Charmian had known immediately that this guardsman was not the guardsman they'd expected, but other than the slightest startled flutter of their lashes, they'd treated him exactly the same as any other palace nobody. All they wanted from him was the asp in the basket of figs.

{ENTER GUARDSMAN, WITH CLOWN BRINGING IN A BASKET}

Guardsman: This is the man.
Cleopatra: Avoid, and leave him.

{EXIT GUARDSMAN}

In his younger days, slim and handsome, Ford Rexford had appeared in a few of his own plays, and a few of his movies. He loved acting—a chance to be everybody and do everything—as anyone who'd ever lived around him was well aware. This last role of his, a walk-on, a spear-carrier, a member of the chorus, was just the kind of joke Ford liked to play. Then to change back into his jeans and make a present of his boots to the young actor, who held them up for the BBC camera: "When he took his socks off, he was very upset that his, well, that his feet had gotten old," said the young actor. "He kept staring at them, and said mine would look that way too some day." The young actor smiled to indicate the improbability of age ever assaulting him. And then to be overheard by a policeman as he stood outside the church where Shakespeare was buried, singing "Amazing Grace." And then with a meteoric leap to fly off a road into the river of the Swan of Avon—they were all good Ford scenes too. But to die there? To break his neck and die?

The BBC special report ended with a few quickly filmed tributary sound-bites from British theatrical luminaries, in which the words "great genius," "tragic loss," and "deeply shocked" appeared often. A celebrated playwright who, Theo knew, utterly despised Ford (and vice versa) sonorously intoned the final bite: "The voice of a giant is silenced, and the stages of all the world are a little darker tonight." Theo heard Ford beside him in the room snort: "A *little* darker? You prick!"

These tributes were followed by a three-minute montage of photos of Ford, stills from his plays, shots from his movies, film footage of him loping up to podiums to accept prizes, or hopping out of limousines with beautiful women. Obviously, Rexford had warranted one of those preplanned obituaries, and they'd had their file all ready to roll, for there was old news coverage of him at civil rights marches and presidential conventions, as well as homier footage from an earlier PBS documentary. As a voice-over to this montage, they'd chosen (because of the circumstances) to have the actress who'd played Cleopatra that night reciting part of one of her speeches about the dead Antony. She had a lovely voice.

> For his bounty,
> There was no winter in't, an autumn 'twas
> That grew the more by reaping: his delights
> Were dolphin-like, they show'd his back above
> The element they lived in. . . .

Ford in New York, pacing rehearsal stages; Ford at his ranch in Texas, leaning over a corral rail with some Mexican friends, admiring horses. Years ago in Tilting Rock, Ford sitting in his armchair with his feet on the black army trunk, a pencil and pad of paper in his hand. The last photograph of the playwright was the most famous one, the 1949 cover of *Life,* a black-and-white portrait of a lanky young cowboy in workshirt and jeans, grinning at the camera, sure and eager, as beautiful as a movie star; behind him the great scenery of the western sky.

Think you there was, or might be, such a man
As this I dream'd of?

And the BBC signed off.

Within the week, Theo was to hear from various sources that there'd been disgruntlement in the theatrical community from Americans who'd happened at the time to be in London regarding the BBC's tribute (which was re-aired over the next few days). The decision to use a British actress reciting Shakespeare, rather than an American reciting Rexford himself, was taken as a national slight. So was the decision (the BBC denied that it was a decision) to solicit testimonials exclusively from British luminaries, rather than from the disgruntled Americans, who felt they had more to say about Ford Rexford, and more right to say it, than any foreigner possibly could. As a matter of fact, none of these compatriots had known Ford nearly as intimately as the British actress, who'd slept with him for eight weeks. As for Theo, he felt sure Ford would have loved having Shakespeare's Cleopatra sing his swan song, and wouldn't have cared at all to hear what Amanda Mahan and Scottie Smith (two of the disgruntled Americans who chanced to be in London) had to say about the tragic loss of his great genius.

Within the week, Theo Ryan had admitted as a fact unsusceptible to revision that Ford was dead. He'd had, of course, to act upon the premise long before that, while his heart was still sealed against it. He had obligations and responsibilities that required the premise. The next day he'd had to accept the sympathy of his parents and friends. He'd had to offer sympathy to other people; some of whom, like Pawnee Rexford, wouldn't admit they needed it. He'd had to decline to turn over *Principles of Aesthetic Distance* either to Amanda Mahan or to Buzzy Middendorf (who'd finally returned from Capri, or had at least admitted he was back); he gave as his reason for withholding the play "legal questions regarding the estate." He'd had to hear Adolphus Mahan pretend to be grieved for a decent amount of transatlantic time before saying that he wanted Theo's permission to submit for prepublication serial rights, chapter one of the Rexford biography to *The New*

Yorker and chapter two to *Vanity Fair.* (Mahan pointed out in a polite way the courtesy of his request, since he didn't need Theo's permission, as by their contract first serial rights were reserved to the publisher.)

That afternoon Theo had had to meet with Bernie Bittermann as soon as the latter had arrived at his London hotel, to learn officially what he'd pretty much suspected, that he was to be Ford's literary executor. He'd had to go down lists of names with Bernie to be sure everyone who should have been called had been called. Theo knew that Bernie, the most organized man alive, had not forgotten any conceivable name—from Ford's first wife to Jenny Harte—or any detail of the playwright's liabilities or assets, but they went over it all anyhow. He'd already had his first argument with Bernie, too, over the contents of the army trunk: He'd argued that, as literary executor, he and he alone would examine and catalogue the papers in the trunk. He would do it as soon as he felt capable of it, but he wasn't capable of it today. Ford had left him "authority for the disposal of all manuscripts, correspondence, and other papers at the discretion of said executor," and that's exactly what that trunk was full of—papers. "I'll go to the mat," Theo threatened, towering over the business manager. " 'At the discretion of said executor'—that's what it says." With a snarled "I told Ford not to put it like that," Bittermann finally yielded. "All right, all right, for now. You're upset, we're all upset."

Bittermann was the trustee of the estate, and Pawnee was the heir. Already, the accountant was fretting that Pawnee, a heavily mortgaged small-time rancher, would refuse the inheritance, and that his older brother, Josh junior, a millionaire real estate developer, would sue for half. It was that night, after he had returned from the Stratford mortuary with Bittermann and Ford's sister, while Bernie was griping as he always had about Ford's impracticality, if not perversity, in not anticipating a fight by his older son over the will, that the crack began to open in the seal around Theo's heart. That's what it felt like, like a sharp, scary, painful crack in his breastbone, splintering a space in the bone through which the fact could slip.

He'd looked into Ford's face on the table in the mortuary, and

Ford wasn't there anymore. As he touched the cold blue lips, Theo heard Hamlet's line, "That skull had a tongue in it, and could sing once." And for hours, driving back to London, sitting in the hotel room, the line stuck fast in his mind, over and over: "And could sing once, and could sing once, and could sing once."

Bittermann, short and bald, red-eyed and still in the wrinkled suit he'd worn on the plane, stomped endlessly in methodical squares around the hotel sitting room, complaining about Ford's having so stupidly killed himself. "I knew this would happen, sooner or later, I knew it. I knew it. 'You keep this up, Ford, and sooner or later, you'll end up dead,' I told him. 'You'll die and you'll leave a mess.' How many times did I say that to him, Theo? A hundred, a thousand? Thirty-two years I said it to him."

"I know, Bernie. You tried your best."

"What best? He's dead." Bittermann began to cry.

The tears ran from the accountant's nose, not his eyes, and seeing that, the crack in Theo wrenched a little wider.

Miss Ruth Rexford, small and thin, dressed in a cheap, unfashionable black suit, sat on the edge of the couch in the corner of the room, her purse in her lap. Timid and dislocated by all the unfamiliarity, she spoke willingly whenever addressed, did whatever Bittermann asked her to, and otherwise waited patiently until she could go back home to Bowie. She looked like what she was: a very old unmarried nurse from a rural Texas town.

"Sure you don't want anything to eat, Miss Ruth?" Theo kept asking her. "You sure about that tea? I remember when I visited you in Bowie, you made me such a nice meal, and we had iced tea."

"I'm just fine, thank you, honey." She folded her hands on the purse.

"You were so helpful to me on that first trip, showing me where Ford had grown up and gone to school and all."

"Well, he called me up, and he said would I take you 'round, Theo. I recollect how he wanted you to see Mama's grave, didn't he?"

"That's right." Theo sat down beside her. ". . . He talked to me about how you'd raised him after your mother died. He talked about you a lot, you know, Miss Ruth." (Theo wondered if she had any idea that Ford was still talking about her this very night at the National Theater where *Her Pride of Place* was playing.)

She turned the old purse on her lap, crossing her hands over it. "Well, he was so skinny when he was little. . . . 'Honey, the wind's gonna blow you away.' That's what I used to tell him." Straight-backed, bony, old, Miss Rexford looked over at Theo, and he saw in her mouth the sweetness of Ford's smile. "First time I tell him that, he says to me, 'And I'll fly and fly and fly! I'll fly right up in them stars and eat 'em up.' Ain't that something? I still remember that."

Theo looked out the hotel window at the stars. "Maybe he did," he said. "I wouldn't be surprised." The crack in his breast broke apart then, and he believed that Ford was gone.

Believing it, he could call Rhodora. He knew Bernie Bittermann had already reached her in New York where she was filming her video, and had told her before she had had to hear it on the news. So she'd known. Still, the first thing Rhodora said to Theo was, "Okay, I guess it's true, isn't it? Goddamn bastard, breaking my heart all over again."

The next thing she said was, "Now you listen to me. I promised him he'd be buried in Bowie, Texas, with his mama's family. I already told Bernie this, and he give me some shit about it wasn't practical, about cremating him and bringing the ashes to Bowie. I didn't tell Ford I'd dump his damn ashes in Bowie, I told him I'd see to it he was *buried* there. I gave him my promise, hear? So all those artsy types can have their big memorial New York shindig for him whenever they want to. Ford won't give a shit. What he *wants* is his body in the ground in Bowie, Texas. Now, can you handle this, Theo? Because if you can't, I'm hanging up and calling the airport right this minute."

"I can handle it."

"You let Bernie Bittermann bring Ford home in some goddamn little screw-top urn, and I swear, the sight of me coming at you's gonna be the last thing you see. You hear me?"

"I hear you. I'll talk to Ford's sister. She's right here in the next room. It's her decision."

"Bernie's dragged Ruth all the way over there? Jesus Christ, poor old thing. Where's Pawnee?"

"He wouldn't come."

"If he knew how much like his daddy he is, he'd plow his dumb-ass car into a bridge too. Put Ruth on the phone."

"Okay, let me get her. Look, are you going to go to Bowie, Rhodora?"

"I said I would, didn't I? Hell, if the asshole hadn't dumped me, I'd of had to cart him to Bowie myself. I'll see you there."

"Me? They don't need me to come to Texas."

"Oh, sugar. *You* need you to come. Don't you know that yet? He's broken your goddamn heart too."

It was true.

V

{Scene: Various Stages}

CHAPTER
27

{Interlude}

Oh, you hard hearts. You cruel men of Rome.
Knew you not Pompey?

Julius Caesar

MEANWHILE back in Rome, high above his kingdom of Cavendish, the provost, Dean Buddy Tupper, Jr. was sniffing the political atmosphere. He had his nose to the ground, he told himself, pressing that bulbous organ to the plate-glass window of his office suite. War was in his nostrils, and he opened them to suck it in. War between him and Dean Claudia Pratt. Ever since he'd lost yardage over the Bleecker strike, that bleeding-heart woman had been trying a quarterback sneak right up the middle into the end zone of his job. He knew that; for all her wishy-washy jabber about "cooperation" and "compromise." He knew there were meetings going on that he wasn't asked to, phone calls being made, a funny kind of coolness in the air on the top floors of Coolidge Building that had nothing to do with the air conditioning.

Well, let Pratt go for it, thought Tupper, roughing his gray flattop. She'd never get past the Bone-Cruncher, that's for damn sure. Let her sidle up to the trustees, and take the other deans off to Asheville for rabbit-food lunches. Let her get down and suck the faculty's whatevers, and fill them so full of themselves they figured they could walk all over the administration. Look at her, down there right now, heading out of Bleecker Dining Hall with a bunch of hangers-on, including the "chairperson" of so-called Cultural Studies, probably down there planning some more of those courses about runaway slave journals and old TV sitcoms and "Powerful Genders," or whatever the hell they called that one. Let her. She'd never budge Buddy Tupper. He still held the fort. He gave its wall a satisfactory pound with his big-knuckled fist.

As a matter of fact, Dean Tupper admitted, he was having a pretty good week. Nobody had quit, died, sued, or asked for a raise. The students who'd tried to get back the land Cavendish sat on for the Cherokee Indians had just had their case thrown out of court. A childless textiles king (who'd already had an embolism removed from his leg, a tumor taken out of his colon, and pig valves sewn onto his heart) had just told Tupper that he was leaving his alma mater, Cavendish U, twenty-one million dollars, unrestricted.

Yes, the Bone-Cruncher had lost a few, but he'd scored some big ones too. Of course, it still rankled that the damn Limey Commie Crawford had outflanked him on the so-called Reverend Maude Fletcher business. The whole History Department had run in here squealing like cats with their balls in a mousetrap as soon as Crawford had pulled that "I'll go to bloody Santa Cruz" crap on them. "Herb's made us number five in the nation! Number five in the nation!" the chairman kept shrieking at him. "Do something, Buddy!" Not that he had relished busting the chops of Religious Studies (two of whom were ordained ministers of God—not that that meant squat anymore; the Fletcher woman was an ordained minister herself!).

But he'd had to do it. Let's face it, Religious Studies wasn't number five in the nation, or even on the charts, and no insecticide king had ever given them anything near thirty-five million dollars either. They were as poor as the apostles, and a lot less interesting to other people. Naturally, they were pretty hot under the collar about renewing the Whore of Babylon's contract after they'd fired her, but he'd thrown them a new tenure slot, a few teaching fellowships, and a couple of computers, and they'd gone for it, four to two. At least Religious Studies had the satisfaction of knowing they were trying to make Fletcher's life in the department hell, even if they couldn't manage to get her stripped of her collar, or whatever you call dishonorable discharge from the church. He'd heard rumors that Claudia Pratt even went to one of those big parties Crawford and Fletcher kept throwing (why not, with their salaries!) at his lakeside chalet. An engagement party! Little late to be talking about getting engaged, wasn't it? He'd heard a lot of Cavendish faculty were at that party. Spineless suckbutts.

So, okay, he'd lost that battle. But there were compensations. 'Erbie Crawford might be here, but he wouldn't be in Santa Cruz. Look at Waldo College, Cavendish's once proud rival; they'd not only been taken over by the Japanese, they'd just had their whole Economics Department bought out from under them by some evangelical university in the Midwest. Thinking of Waldo College was always a comfort to Dean Buddy Tupper, Jr. After all, at least he still had a core curriculum and grades. He wasn't losing celebrities. He didn't have the Yellow Peril for a board of trustees.

There were more immediate consolations too. For the past five days, President Irwin Kaney hadn't been doddering in and out of Tupper's bathroom (where lately he'd been not only forgetting to flush the toilet, but forgetting to unzip his trousers before he used it). Thank the Lord, Kaney's middle-aged daughter had taken the general off to West Point for a reunion of other old soldiers who'd mentally faded away. Good luck to her, growled the provost; I hope she packed her daddy a big supply of jumbo Pampers in the back of that Cadillac.

Over in the loony bin of Romance Languages, Professors Torres and Montemaggio had dropped their suits against each other, once their respective eyeball and finger had healed; so the public relations director wouldn't have to deal with the embarrassment of a trial. According to Tupper's sources, right in the middle of some poor soul's Ph.D. orals, they'd decided to make up, and had started to cry and hug and even kiss. (Two grown men, but what can you expect with names like that?)

Plus, some nutcase in the Physics Department had just found out he'd won the Nobel Prize, so if Physics *was* building a bomb over there, at least one of them probably knew how. The Nobel Prize meant outside grants. Tupper loved outside grants; the university could skim fifty-five to sixty percent off the top for what went down on the books as administrative costs. (Hell, he'd heard Yale skimmed sixty-*five* percent, but then they'd been at it longer.)

Plus, that star anthropology professor that they'd found out was pulling down two full (very full) salaries, one from Cavendish and the other from a well-known Ivy League university? Well, Tupper'd had a satisfying talk with that Ivy League university, and an even more satisfying blowout with the career bigamist (who might in fact be a real bigamist, since he appeared to have a few Ivy League girlfriends that his Cavendish wife knew nothing about). This guy's moonlight hayride was coming to an end.

And that junior who'd said he was suing Cavendish because his faculty adviser had sexually harassed him? He'd settled out of court. Maybe he was sick of trying to explain how, against his will, a six-one, hundred-and-ninety-pound, twenty-year-old male on the varsity ski team had gotten himself tied to a bedpost, un-dressed, and spanked by a short, skinny, fifty-seven-year-old Classics professor. Yes, a pretty good week. The football coach had just told the provost there were two promising Peach Bowl prospects in the freshman class, and both of them already knew how to read.

Besides, summers were always easier. Students were easier then. They were either under-the-gun undergraduates making up courses they'd farted around and flunked in the spring, or they were decent outsiders trying to get ahead in the world. Why, Tupper's own wife, Rosemary, had taken summer school courses for twelve years running, just to get out of the house; and she knew more about Etruscan art and the anatomy of sea urchins than any woman needed to know. The faculty was easier in sum-mer too. Most of the tenured celebrities, who gave Tupper so much trouble during the regular term, shot out of Rome so fast in May it looked as if Hannibal's elephants were chasing them down the streets. As soon as they got their spring grades from whoever had done the grading for them, they turned them in, in exchange for their colossal checks, and off they flew. The dean of the summer school always had to scramble to find graduate stu-dents who'd rather teach his courses for peanuts than go back home; Cavendish faculty stars sure couldn't be bothered to show a little team spirit and play secondary by filling in with a section of Expos. or Western Civ. No, they'd rather hop a jet to some library in London, or conference in Paris (why did mathematicians need to go to Paris?), or seminar in Honolulu (what did Hawaii have to do with biochemistry?), and bill Tupper for their plane tickets. They never seemed to go places they could *drive* to, like Charlotte or Atlanta, either.

Here was a stack of Ludd Hall receipts from old Fruchaff right now, thick enough to choke a goat. (Smelled like she'd spilled an ashtray and a bottle of Cherry Herring on them too.) Jane Nash-Gantz: helicopter from Nice to Monte Carlo. "Plenary Speaker—Ovidian Joyce: Hermaphroditic Transformations." What in God's blue heaven did that have to do with what she'd been hired for? Hadn't her vita said her training was in American poetry? Well, pardon Dr. Tupper for asking, but as far as he knew, James Joyce wasn't an American, or a hermaphrodite either. And Jorvelle Wakefield: round-trip coach to Amsterdam. After what she'd gotten out of Cavendish with that Yale bluff of hers, why didn't she buy her own damn plane? What'd she need to research seventeenth-century Dutch West Indies shipping records for? Hadn't Norman said that woman taught *novels?*

And, Crap Above, Dina Sue was going to have a shit fit if these rumors about Wakefield were true. He'd already had to pour a slug of Jack Daniels down her throat over Gash-Nantz's, or whatever her name was, lecturing on Emily Dickinson's clitty. But if his cousin found out that her other Ludd Chair was planning to marry a white man over Thanksgiving break, he'd have to put the fat old bag on lithium. Dina Sue was definitely for separate-but-equal, no getting around it. Poor old Norman had practically had to lick her toes for a month to get her to go for Wakefield in the first place. Well, the provost sighed, he'd calm her down somehow. He had to: His cousin's money was one of his aces in his showdown poker game with Claudia Pratt. That, and the fact that Mrs. Ludd was Ubal Cavendish's granddaughter, and the fact that she couldn't stand Claudia. Dina Sue didn't like liberals any more than she liked mixed marriages.

Now, the truth was (despite the assumptions of people like Jonas Marsh), it didn't really matter to Dean Buddy Tupper whether Jorvelle Wakefield married Steve Weiner or not. The

provost was a sexist, and a nationalist, an antimodernist, antiso-
cialist, and antipacifist. But he had nothing against blacks per se;
they were good athletes, and that made them all right with the
Bone-Cruncher. His brand of racism had more to do with geogra-
phy than color. In general, foreigners rubbed him the wrong way.
So if anything, Tupper's question was why would a North Carolina girl like Jorvelle Wakefield want to marry a New York Jew?
Actually, he'd liked Jorvelle; he'd liked going head to head in their
scrimmages over salary. At least, he'd liked her until he'd seen her
out there on that Bleecker picket line in May; Weiner'd probably
recruited her for that socialist malarky anyhow—the way they
do. Well, there'd be snow on the hills of hell before that smart-ass
Weiner ever got to be chairman of the English Department. That
was one blessing.

Tupper sat down behind his gargantuan desk to count his others. Things were shaping up pretty nicely over in Ludd Hall.
Marcus Thorney wasn't going to give him a lick of trouble; he had
the man's pecker in his pocket, and they both were real comfortable with that. Thorney was a different kind of gutless from Norman; he wasn't going to fret and nag and appease and backtrack
and flip-flop. Thorney didn't *care,* and that was going to make
things a whole lot easier. He was going to let Tupper do all the
hardball playing, and then he'd carry all the hard news back to
Ludd Hall, saying, sorry, there was nothing he could do about
the raise or the promotion or the tenure or whatever. Fine. The
provost loved hardball. He pulled a #1 pencil out of a trophy cup
and made some notes.

1: No promotion for John Hood; if the Miltonist was going to
wimp out of going to London just because his mother had lung
cancer, then he could wait for that full professorship till he was
ready to give Cavendish one hundred percent.

2: Only the minimum raise for the maniac Jonas Marsh; maybe
he'd take the hint and leave. Meanwhile, a few more letters like
that last one to the *Chronicle of Higher Education* about their
South African stocks, and Marsh would be over there in London
trying to make ends meet on half pay.

3: No tenure for this young Critical Theory guy. There was too
much theory in that department as it was. Tupper didn't mind a

little flimflam; look, people had to earn a living somehow, and this kind of gobbledygook was harmless. But the English Department was getting out of hand. What about this hotshot visitor they'd brought in to teach a Milton course, and all the kids had done was spend the entire term with their individual letter presses, every one of them typesetting their own printing of *Paradise Lost,* letter by letter. "I bet they *know* it," was this celebrity nut's comment when interviewed by the *Cougar Gazette.*

And 4: No tenure for this Rice, Early American, either. English already had four Americanists, and by God if at least one of them didn't know something about the "Early" stuff, they ought to all be fired. Sure, Rice was Thorney's little pal, but Thorney would only put up a pro forma fight. That'd be a nice change from Norman's endless wheedling.

Speaking of Norman, there was Effie Fruchaff, that sarcastic old secretary he was always making excuses for, despite rumors that she was drinking on the job. She must have been there since Mabel Chiddick's day, plus she refused to learn how to use E Mail. And Marcus Thorney didn't want her. Fine. A new broom sweeps clean. She was already way past mandatory retirement anyhow. No prob. 5: Fire Fruchaff.

Speaking of retirement, there was this thing about old Woodrow Mortimer and Davey Lovell suddenly deciding to call it quits and go off and live together in a senior citizens community in Boca Raton, Florida. The provost wondered momentarily if the two little southern widowers had gone gay in their old age. Or maybe they'd always been funny. Hadn't their wives died about the same time? Maybe Mortimer and Lovell had murdered them so they could spend their twilight years together. Tupper chuckled, giving the bronzed football on his desk a spin. He was just kidding. Besides, he'd never had anything against gays per se, as long as they kept their hands to themselves. Hell, he'd seen a couple of football players pork each other in the shower once. Good athletes, too. Tupper was all for personal privacy: A man's sexual preference was between him and his wife . . . or whatever.

But Mortimer and Lovell leaving. This could be trouble. The English Department would want to hang on to those two freed-up tenure slots, and there was that new faction over in Ludd Hall who wouldn't want to use them on something tried and true like what Mortimer and Lovell had done with Romantic Poetry and Victorian Novels. (What they'd done, for forty years, was have their classes go down the rows, each reading aloud a page of Dickens or a stanza of Shelley, until the bell rang.) No, that faction might try an end-run with those tenure slots, go for some radical feminist or psychoanalytic theorist or specialist in Native American folktales and drive-in horror movies. Of course, the best thing to do, money-wise now, would be just to collapse two slots as soon as Mortimer and Lovell retired, and pull the funds back into the kitty. That would take care of the added tenure slot he'd promised Religious Studies, and he could get the French Department off his back by giving them the other one.

Dean Tupper was spinning the football by thwacking its tip with his middle finger as he mused on these options, when his secretary buzzed him that Norman Bridges was out there wanting to see him.

Norman Bridges (former department head, and recent recipient of a Ludd Chair) looked as if he might have just gotten back from the beach. Everything that was visible was burnt to a crisp, including his feet, on which he wore rubber thongs that didn't really go with his seersucker suit. He made a sharp hissing noise through his teeth when he sat down too, and moved forward so that only the edge of his buttocks touched the chair.

"Norm, good to see you. Been to the beach?" The provost came around his desk, bulldozing his swivel chair into the wall behind him.

Bridges hissed again when Tupper shook his hand in Bone-Cruncher fashion. "Not really," he said.

Not really? Why couldn't people just say yes or no? "Well, you sure fried your hash somewhere. Put on a little weight too." Tupper socked himself hard in his thick flat stomach. *Whack!* "Regular exercise, Norm. There's not enough of it around this place. When the Grim Reaper comes for me, I'm going out fit and trim." *Whack!*

Bridges agreed that it was better to die healthy, and then explained that he'd acquired his frankly painful sunburn by falling asleep in his bathing trunks at the Hillcrest Country Club swimming pool. His wife, Tara, had forgotten that she was supposed to meet him there at eleven in the morning. Instead she'd driven to Asheville to buy a videotape of *Hello, Dolly!*, and he had waked up at four that afternoon in the state he was now in.

Tupper guffawed. "Tara's stopped the clock on her love life for a couple of days, I guess."

There was no response from Bridges to this manly jocularity, other than a weak smile. In fact, Tara had stopped the clock on their love life for a couple of decades now.

"Well, Norm. You tell me." Tupper slapped his thick thighs as if to show it could be done if you weren't stupid enough to boil yourself like a lobster. "How does it feel to be a free man on a year's sabbatical *and* a Ludd Chair when you come back?"

"Yes, it's a wonderful honor. I was very touched that the department felt moved to, and naturally Dina Sue, and of course you and Claudia and—"

With a smack of his hands together, Tupper cut off Bridges's gratitude before it meandered through every name on campus. "So! What brings you here? You're supposed to be on vacation, and what I here tell is, you're over in Ludd Hall before the janitor can get there and unlock the johns."

Bridges cleared his throat. "The fact is, Buddy, well, I was on campus, and I thought I'd drop by because, em, em, I wanted to talk to you about something."

Yeah, obviously. Why couldn't people stop beating around the bush? "So, talk." Tupper swung his rear-end onto his desk edge, picked up the football, and practiced a throwing position. "But I don't want to hear another word from you about John Hood's promotion."

Bridges opened his mouth, but when the provost aimed the football at it, he shut it again. Then he pulled his shirt loose from his lubricated chest, and said, "It's Theo Ryan. I know he's made an appointment to see you tomorrow. He's here in Rome—"

"I kind of figured he's here in Rome if he's made an appointment to see me, Norm. But don't talk to me about Ryan or anybody else in that faction. What's he want to see me about?" Tupper couldn't resist a scouting report before a game.

"Well, I don't know if you knew this, but Ford Rexford died last week."

"Heard it on TV. Heard he plowed into some river over there

in England." So much for Ryan's promise to get Cavendish on the theatrical map with a world premiere of a Ford Rexford play. Well, but let's be fair, Tupper thought, as he watched Bridges wriggle at the edge of his seat rambling on about Rexford's death. Let's be fair. Thanks to Ryan, Cavendish (well, Doug Spitz) wasn't going to be paying that juvenile escapee from the Betty Ford Center, that wild-spending nutcase Scottie Smith, a hundred and fifty thousand dollars a year to bankrupt the Spitz Center. Thanks to Ryan, they'd instead hired this other director, Barbara Sanchez, who'd asked for eighty and settled for seventy-six. 'Course, she looked like a, a, a Chicano, Hispanic, whatever you were supposed to call a Mex these days. But actually Barb was a pretty decent sort. Said she'd played basketball at Texas State. Even had a Ph.D.; the board liked that. Good vita. Won a couple of awards. Good interviews. Doug Spitz was impressed. Even that little power-crazy twerp Thayer Iddesleigh didn't get too bent out of shape, after she'd said she didn't see why he shouldn't go on directing the two C.F.D.C. musicals every year himself. Not at all a bad appointment for Tupper to sign up while there was all this flak in the air. The world would see Claudia Pratt wasn't the only one scoring affirmative action points. Besides, better Sanchez than some off-center oddball like Scottie Smith who'd be roaming the streets of Rome looking for boy prostitutes. Tupper wondered if there were any.

The provost had plenty of time for his musings while Norman Bridges dithered his detouring way through the details of Rexford's fatal accident. "So Theo himself, with, of course, the family, flew the body to Bowie, Texas. I forgot to say that Rexford had grown up there. I remember his talking about—he came to my house once for dinner. This was last November, I think—"

Tupper slammed the football down on his desk. "Norm! I'm sorry the man's dead. What's the point?"

"Yes, it's a terrible loss to the American theatre, a terrible—"

"Norman."

Bridges winced as his back scraped the chair when he pulled away from the big Bulova watch Dean Tupper had stuck in his face. "I'll get right to the point," the plump professor said. The provost cupped his palms, wildly gesturing as if he wanted Bridges to come on and fight him. He'd started to think maybe he'd have to hit that buzzer under his desk, so his secretary could get on the intercom and say the governor was on line one.

The point. It was that Theo Ryan had been appointed (Bridges noted parenthetically that he'd predicted this) literary executor of the Rexford estate. This was a great honor for Cavendish. It could well mean that Cavendish would one day house the Joshua Ford Rexford papers (the way Bridges had always hoped). As literary executor, there were a million things that Theo Ryan needed to do now. Plus, Mahan and Son (very distinguished publishers) were eager to push up the publication of volume one of Ryan's biography of the now dead playwright (it was a big book, and would bring honor to the English Department). The point was that, in addition to all this, Theo Ryan was in a distraught state (he had been a close friend of Rexford's, very close), and needed to get away.

"I thought he *was* away," Tupper interjected. "I thought he'd gone to London with the rest of my damn faculty that couldn't get a boondoggle to Tahiti or the Riviera."

Well, yes, Ryan had been in London, but he'd flown to Texas for the funeral, and then come back here to Rome.

The provost scratched at his flattop. "I heard he'd sublet his house to a Country/Western singer. My secretary told me the local press was over there trying to get an interview with her. You know the one. Can't think of her name right now. My son got her autograph at the Boone Civic Center."

"How is Henry?" Bridges politely asked.

"Don't talk to me about Henry." Tupper's youngest son had been a source of baffled disappointment long before declining to go out for varsity football, trading his (unused) telescopic-lensed deer rifle for an electric guitar, and his Philip Morris stock shares for a red alligator jacket with white birds all over the back. "And don't bother calling him Henry Tupper either. He's changed his name to Snow Williams." The provost suddenly remembered that Norman didn't even know where his own son *was* half the time, and probably didn't want to find out. Tupper shouldn't complain. "Kids!" he offered as a gesture of solidarity.

"Rhodora Potts," said Bridges. "The singer's name. Very nice young woman. I was never really clear on the particulars of her relationship with Ford Rexford. She went with Theo to Texas. It was a private service. There'll be a memorial in New York in the fall. I'm not that much of a fan of country music myself, but—"

"You're all over the backfield again, Norm." Tupper made a snaky movement with his arm. "You're losing me."

With a sigh, Bridges patted his heart, and plunged in. "Theo Ryan wants to take next year off. I think he deserves a paid leave." Having begun, Bridges plowed ahead, unencouraged by the expression on the provost's face. "I realize he's not due for a leave till year after next, and he had that ACLS grant, but he's worked hard for the department. This time would be important to him."

"He's scheduled to teach."

"There's a fifth-year graduate student who's taught for us, and T.A.'ed Theo's survey course twice already. 'Sophocles to Rexford.' Jenny Harte's her name. She could take it over for the fall." Bridges thought it best not to get into Jenny Harte's own relationship with Ford Rexford, which had, frankly, been a shocking disappointment to the former chairman, on both sides. He went on explaining how this course could be shifted, and that course postponed.

Tupper took a stroll around his wall-to-wall carpet. Then he held up a palm in a stop sign. His voice sounded almost benevolent. "Norm, what does this have to do with you? This isn't your prob anymore. If anybody should be coming to me about this, besides Ryan, it's Marcus Thorney. He's chairman."

With a wince, Bridges eased himself off the seat. "Well, Buddy, I guess I felt that Marcus might not, em, em, necessarily, all things considered, be the strongest advocate for Theo, and—"

"That's for damn sure," Tupper conceded. "Norm, you got to give this up. You just about had a nervous breakdown when you *were* chair—"

"Well, not really."

"And I don't notice you fussing and fretting at me any less now that you're *not!*"

Norman Bridges looked sadly down at his red blistered feet in their rubber thongs. He supposed it was true. He couldn't keep away from Ludd Hall, even in the summer, when it was practically deserted. Maybe he'd lived in, and for, the department so long, maybe he was like a, like a convict who couldn't adjust to freedom. At home, at his desk alone with Walt Whitman, with his daughter off stuffing envelopes in the next room, with Tara off at dance class and voice lessons and terrifying shopping sprees, he found himself still nervously reaching for that Almond Joy. At home, with no phones ringing, no Effie Fruchaff bullying him, no junior faculty in tears, no professor in a huff, maybe he didn't know what to do with himself anymore.

"Relax, Norm," the provost advised. "Play some tennis. Pump some iron. Go fishing."

Bridges had never pumped any iron, or caught any fish in his life. "I know. . . . But, but—" He squeezed his hands together hard, and was sorry he'd done so. "But I just want to be sure you realize, Buddy, that Theo Ryan deserves—"

"Ryan doesn't 'deserve' squat till fall after next."

"And maybe we should keep in mind that, after all, the world being what it is—perhaps an earlier generation of scholars, like ourselves, when teaching figured more prominently—still, public recognition, and national—"

The provost wheeled on the plump sunburnt professor, and glared.

Bridges took a breath. "And parenthetically, Buddy, you might think of this. The board of trustees will care much, much more about Cavendish's getting the Ford Rexford papers," he took another breath, "than they will about whether Theo Ryan or Jenny Harte teaches English one twenty-four next year. And Theo is going to decide where the papers go."

Dean Tupper looked appraisingly at Norman Bridges; well, finally, the man had gotten to the point. He smiled, and rapped his ring twice on the desk top. "Norm, I appreciate your taking the time to come talk to me about this. I'll think it over after I see Ryan, and after I talk to Marcus. Let me walk you out."

"Thank you, Buddy." Norman Bridges smiled; not for long, because it hurt. "It's good to see you." He'd been dealing with Tupper for twenty years, ten as chairman; he knew the provost wouldn't "think it over" after talking to anybody. He knew the provost had already decided to give Theo Ryan the paid leave; he always rapped his ring like that when the answer was going to be yes. And if Tupper said yes, Marcus Thorney wouldn't say no.

Out in the cavernous waiting room, Bridges, by a dextrous twist, escaped being slapped on the back by the Bone-Cruncher; he nodded at the people standing around, pretending not to notice that they were staring at his feet. Back he gingerly walked to Ludd Hall, passing the door to the chairman's office with a wistful sigh. Then he turned back again, and peeked inside to see if Effie Fruchaff was at her desk. Maybe she'd like to go over to the Forum for a cup of coffee and a cinnamon roll.

Then maybe he'd give Theo another call, and, well, just offer a little advice on what perhaps Theo should, and on the other hand it might be better not to, say in his meetings tomorrow with Marcus Thorney and the provost. Then maybe he could try just once more with Marcus about John Hood's promotion. After all, the department wanted to do the right thing. . . . By everyone. . . . Didn't they?

Buddy Tupper, Jr. certainly felt like slapping somebody. Claudia Pratt was right there in his waiting room, laughing it up with his assistant provost, and his secretary! Even his own secretary was laughing! When they saw him staring at them, they all stopped, like a choral director had cut them off in midnote, and started busily shuffling the papers in their hands. Turning on his heel, Tupper shouldered his way back through his office door, and slammed it. Their giggling voices started again, fainter from the other side. Right! Go ahead, he told them; forget who made you who you are. Take your best shot, Pratt! Georgia Tech couldn't push me back when I was crawling in the snow and mud with a broken hand; and, lady, neither can you. The provost rubbed his thick neck while he surveyed the trophies in his office at the top of Coolidge Building. Nobody, but nobody, was going to get his job away from the Bone-Cruncher.

In this determined prediction, Buddy Tupper proved right. He was to remain provost at Cavendish until he retired. Dean Claudia Pratt was to be catapulted by the trustees right over the defensive line of that lower position, and to do her victory dance under the goalpost as the university's first woman president.

CHAPTER

28

{Throws Down a Glove}

King: What do you call the play?
Hamlet: "The Mousetrap."

"Yes, AUTUMN, autumn," Mole Fontwell exclaimed as fields flew
by the car window in a golden blur. " 'Season of mists, and mellow
fruitfulness, / Close bosom-friend of the maturing sun.' Now, really, Jonas, that's awf'lly good."

"Bloody competitive Krauts!" Marsh downshifted, flooring the
Rolls in order to pass a Mercedes with German plates that didn't
want to be passed.

"You must give Keats top marks for 'Autumn.' Mustn't he,
Theo?"

"Well," Marsh snarled. "Bleats is better than Whatworth, Dol-
tridge, and Jelly. That much I'll give you. Let's see, we're now
thirty-seven miles from Salisbury, so we should be there in
approximately—"

"Five minutes," suggested Theo from the capacious leathery
backseat of the yellow Rolls-Royce.

"Isn't he a demon?" Mole cheerfully agreed. Jonas Marsh clearly
took his own advice, and drove the major motorways at "ninety
miles an hour, easily." On the other hand, he was a far better
driver than Dame Winifred Throckmorton had been, or than
Mole, who loved to talk and liked to look at people, even those
in the back seat, when he did so.

It was the seventh of September. Theo Ryan was again in England, on his way with his friends to Devon, to Dame Winifred Throckmorton and the great estate of the Earl of Newbolt. With them in the car was a locked attaché case; in the case were two leather-bound books printed in the early seventeenth century, along with one folio miscellany written in a seventeenth-century hand. The printed books really had been printed in the seventeenth century.

That he should be in this car, with these men, and these books, felt to Theo both destined and yet impossible to connect with the arrangements of his past life. In early September, for example, he was always in Rome, North Carolina, preparing to teach his fall classes. He was always in his house near the campus, everything in its familiar place, every day nearly the same. For years at a time, he'd gone nearly nowhere; yet here in one summer he'd flown twice to England, twice to New York, and once, for a single day, all the way to Texas; and there were new people in his life who were changing it in disconcerting ways. For years at a time, he hadn't written anything at all, and now, since spring. . . .

"We'll stay the night in Honiton, at the Crown and Mitre," Marsh called over his shoulder. "Drive to Bourne once it's good and dark. The vicar should tottle out of Saint Michael's the minute evening prayers say Amen. You didn't forget those torches, did you, Mole?"

"No, nor the tool kit. You needn't keep fussing so."

"Planning is not 'fussing.'" Marsh passed an immense shipping lorry on whose side were painted gargantuan boxes of tea biscuits, shortbreads, cookies, and cakes, and below them the huge letters "FONTWELL'S. OF COURSE." As Marsh went flying by, he beeped the horn in a merry rhythm, earning quite a scowl from the startled driver. "Ah, Grandpapá!" he waved at the truck. "Bless him, Mole."

"Bless you, Grandpa," Mole agreeably called out the window. "And you're not 'planning.' For the last two months we were planning. He really worked feverishly while you were in the States, Theo."

"Yes, you've both done an incredible job."

"Now he's fussing. Is he so fussy in Rome?"

"Worse." Theo yawned. "But I'm not feeling very calm myself."

"Well, I feel quite exhilarated," said Mole, his black eyes glittering beneath the dark bang of hair that kept falling into them. "And confident. The skiff will be where I left it, the key will be where the vicar left it, and the chest will be where time has left it for the proverbial lo these many centuries."

Jonas twitched at the wheel. "And where it may sit for a few bloody more if we're not right about their pulling out that choir stall."

"How can they shore up a wall without removing what's in front of it?" Mole settled cheerfully in his seat, and reopened his book. "Right then. On we go. Now, which would you chaps rather hear, more 'Autumn,' or 'Grecian Urn'?"

"Alexander Pope," growled Marsh.

" 'Autumn' it is."

"Please! No more bah-bah oozy-woozy John bloody Bleats!"

Theo leaned his head back against the soft leather, while in the front seat of the speeding car Jonas and Mole returned convivially to arguing the merits of the Romantic poets. He closed his eyes and thought about the last two months.

Two months exactly since Ford's death. And death had certainly not put an end to the demands the man made on anybody foolish enough to love him, or the chaos and pain or for that matter the plain downright irritation and discomfort he could cause.

"I can't believe we're doing this!" Bernie Bittermann had complained to Theo and Ruth Rexford across the entire Atlantic Ocean, jolted out of his characteristic patience by all the disruptions of his tranquil habits.

"It's been a nightmare," he'd moaned to Theo's parents, who'd rushed to Kennedy to be with their son for the short span of his stopover, and to pick up their plane tickets for Miami, where they were to start their Panamanian cruise ship jobs. "Benny, Lorraine, don't go," Bittermann had gloomily advised them. "There's bad luck in the air."

"They'll never get here, it's a disaster," the accountant had groaned for hours in the Dallas airport before they'd finally located first Rhodora, then (two flights later than he'd told them) Pawnee Rexford.

"I knew it, I knew it. We're crashing!" Bittermann had whimpered nonstop in the little rattling private plane that had flown the five passengers and the casket through an electrifying thunderstorm to Bowie, Texas.

"The heat!" he'd griped when he'd crawled out of the limousine at the cemetery. "The dust! It's all over you in a second! *Here*'s where Ford had to make us bring him from five thousand miles away? There's nothing here! There's a thousand miles of dirt here!" And he'd turned to tell Ford's first wife (who, with her husband, had been driven over from the next county by their granddaughter), "Ford was always a terrible driver."

"I haven't seen him in forty-some years," the woman replied. "But Sam here thought we oughta come for Ruth's sake."

Pawnee Rexford, son of the third wife, a taller, darker replica of his young father, kicked his boot through some of that dirt. "I told you fuckin' Josh wouldn't fuckin' show," he said, in reference to his half brother, son of the second wife. He put his sunglasses back on, and pulled a pack of cigarettes from the pocket of his suede vest. "Let's get this shit over with. Where'd that fuckin' preacher go?"

Rhodora jerked her own sunglasses off. Her legs like fast scissors below the black minidress, she strode over, grabbed Pawnee's arm, and shook him. "Get it together, you hear me? Stop talking like trash 'round Miss Ruth and her friends before I crack open your goddamn head."

"You're not my mother, so don't fuckin' give me orders."

"That's enough, Pawnee." Theo pushed between him and Rhodora.

"She's the same age I am! Can you believe my fuckin' father, man?"

Sweat poured from Bernie Bittermann's bald head. His jacket was soaking wet, and red dust stuck to his face. "Why, why are you doing this to me?" he asked the sky or the grave or the endless plain of dirt.

As Theo stood in that bare, windswept cemetery, watching the red dusty earth trickle down the sides of Ford's grave, a breeze suddenly blew against the back of his neck and dried the sweat there so it stung him. He slapped at the sweat, and with the slap he heard:

"Mark me."

"What?"

It was Ford's voice. "Mark me."

Theo turned around; no one was behind him. Everyone else stood staring into the dusty hole, listening to the singsong of the minister. Theo closed his eyes.

"I am thy spirit's father," Ford said. "Doomed to walk—"

Cut it out, thought Theo, opened his eyes, and saw Ford on the other side of the cemetery, leaning against a tombstone. "Stop waving at me."

Bernie Bittermann looked at Theo. "What'd you say?"

"Nothing."

Ford laughed. "It's called beckoning, kid. I'm beckoning you. That's what I was doing all along."

Theo thought, You're scaring me.

"That's a start," he heard Ford say, but when he glanced over at the tombstone, there was no one there.

After the ceremony the funeral party split up. In the middle of it, (despite its extreme brevity) Pawnee had kicked a path back to the limousine and leaned against it, chain-smoking. The travelers gave Miss Ruth her first moment of relief in days by telling her good-bye. They then flew back to Dallas and told each other goodbye. (Well, Pawnee didn't exactly say goodbye, but he did lift his hand, and even apologized to Rhodora for "taking it out on you instead of the Fuck in the coffin.") Hunch-shouldered, he walked off onto his plane while Bernie Bittermann was trying, again, to explain to him that he'd inherited several million dollars. Pawnee left for Santa Fe.

"It's in the genes, it's got to be in the genes," Bernie muttered. He shook Theo's hand, said, "If you're not lying the way *he* did, if you've actually got that play *Aesthetic Distance*, you've got to hand it over, Theo. There're contractual obligations involved here. Even if what there is of it is a miserable mess, which I'm already sure is the case, so don't think you'll be disappointing me. Ford had lost hold, Theo, we have to face that."

"Not you, Bernie. I don't want to hear you gave up on him."

"I know I've missed my plane," said Bernie and left for New York.

Rhodora put her arms around Theo, and the two stayed that way a long time, standing there by the airport security check, crowds streaming on both sides around them like a current. Some of the travelers glared at them annoyed, but others looked kindly at the young couple quietly hugging.

"I love you. Hang on," Rhodora said, and she left for Nashville.

Theo went home to North Carolina. There were two things he had to do there. One was to try to persuade his new chairman, Marcus Thorney, and the provost, Buddy Tupper, to let him take a year's paid leave a year before Cavendish owed him one. He wasn't sure he could do it. He wasn't sure he could do the other thing either; or that he should. But in the airport, realizing that even Bernie Bittermann had lost faith in Ford, Theo had made a vow. He had to at least try to do something. He had to try to write the last half of the last act of *Principles of Aesthetic Distance*. He had to try to make people believe that Ford Rexford had left behind him at his death a finished play.

Tupper and Thorney were easier about the leave than Theo had thought they'd be. The play was even harder. To work on it, he'd locked himself inside the lodge at Tilting Rock, high above the winding kudzu-tangled road at the top of "Rhodora's Mountain." Rhodora had never tried to sell the chalet, or even rent it; the cleaning woman whom Theo had hired in May had kept coming once a week to air it out, dust off the furniture, and, it appeared, polish off the contents of the freezer, the liquor cabinet, and the woodpile. The place smelled stale, but was otherwise the same, just empty.

Rhodora hadn't understood why Theo'd wanted to go there while she was in Nashville. They'd argued about it in the Dallas airport. He told her he had a lot of work to do on the biography, that the chalet would be the best place to do it; it was convenient, free, and isolated; he liked it there this time of year, with the summer sky filled with shooting stars.

"Remember, Rhodora, how he'd sit on the porch and watch those stars in the summer?"

Rhodora flung her black-and-gold jacket over her shoulder. "Umhm. And I remember how he fell off it drunk and I had to lug him to the car and cart him to the hospital with a broken collarbone. But you go ahead, get over it however you got to." She unhooked the key from a silver ring and gave it to him.

Theo had told himself that he needed to hide out in Tilting Rock because he didn't want to risk anybody's learning (including Rhodora) that he was trying to finish Ford's play. And he didn't want to talk to people while he was doing it. His friends at Cavendish had been kind and sympathetic (including Maude Fletcher, with whom he'd had lunch several times since his return). But he didn't want to talk about Ford now. He wanted to talk *to* Ford. The truth was he needed all the help from Ford he could get, and he figured the playwright might be hanging around the lodge—might be in the porch rocker with his feet up on the rail, or at the oak door of the desk he called Sharon, or squatting by the fireplace beneath the yellow pine beams of the big vaulted living room. He might be skipping all over the barn roof, or dancing around on the pond. He might be sitting up in a bough of Lavinia, the slim white birch outside his study window that he'd named after his mother. But there was no sight or sound of the dead playwright anywhere around, at least none that Theo could sense.

True to their word, Federal Express had flown the black army locker to Asheville by the time Theo'd arrived at the airport. "Anything that involves his work, you should always bill the estate," Bernie Bittermann had said, and when Theo saw the shipping costs he'd been glad to know it. His last plane ticket had already done in his Visa card. "Ford, you're killing me," he'd muttered, lugging the scratched and dinted old trunk up the porch steps of the lodge. He'd brought in his groceries and two cases of beer. Then he'd hauled out from the study Rexford's lumpy, stained, cigarette-scarred writing chair, Chester. He'd built a fire, sat down, and opened the trunk.

The next three days had been spent methodically sorting out the papers; a trunk full of them, scrambled as if Ford had jumped around in there like a child in a pile of leaves. And the trunk would be only the first part of Ford's pack-ratting to put in order. Theo knew that the playwright, with ridiculous claims of being "responsible for Bernie's sake," had tossed every scrap of paper he'd ever written on (including unidentified phone numbers), and every piece of mail he'd received (including junk circulars) into file cabinets (not in the files, just in the cabinets). And when these were filled, he'd dumped the contents into cardboard boxes that were still stacked against walls at the ranch in Mexico, at the house in Florida, and maybe (if his fourth wife hadn't thrown them away) in the penthouse in New York. All waiting for Theo Ryan to sort them out. But, then, it was what Theo had been trained to do. And the process had a peaceful, soothing satisfaction to it. So, for days, he drank the beers and stacked the papers in rows around the chair.

The papers in the trunk were the ones Ford most cared about. A few dozen old letters. And the rest, his plays. Handwritten plays, typed plays, galleys of plays, notes on characters, lists of place names and titles and dates. There were opening scenes that stopped in midline. There were paragraphs describing sets, sketches of plots, scraps of paper with single phrases on them; mysterious, disconnected sentences like "She sleeps where she can see the moon." And, "Billy: Hell, honey, only time will tell. Ava: Most likely, tell a lie."

Also in the trunk were the original manuscripts of Rexford's sixteen three-act plays and his twenty-two one-act plays, as well as innumerable revised versions of many of these, and revisions of the revisions. He'd apparently never stopped making changes. He'd reworked lines, whole scenes, in plays that had been per-formed for decades in standardized editions. In fact, he'd scribbled rewrites in the printed texts themselves; had sometimes scrawled "Cut" or "Blew it" across the page. It was troubling. Such author-ity had the printed word for a scholar like Theo, such familiar inevitability had the official version, that Ford's changes upset and confused him. Did even Ford have the right to change Miss Ra-chel's final monologue, after she'd been saying it one set way, all over the world, for thirty years? After Theo, and hundreds of thousands of others, had been reading it one set way? As literary executor, should he insist that these changes be incorporated into new productions, new editions, or not? It was very troubling.

And what about *A Waste of Spirit*? For, yes, as Jenny Harte had claimed, there was a partial manuscript of that play extant. It was in the trunk, as were two copies of *Aesthetic Distance*, the same unfinished text as Theo had in his suitcase, but each with dozens of penciled changes, and one with a scrawled, elliptical outline for several possible endings.

The problem with *A Waste of Spirit* wasn't that it was incomplete, however, but that it wasn't any good. It was so bad it was almost impossible to believe Ford had had anything to do with it, much less that he hadn't *known* it wasn't any good. At least Theo thought it wasn't. But had he any right to suppress it because he thought so, and because Ford had bequeathed him "authority for the disposal of all manuscripts, correspondence, and other papers at the discretion of said executor"? Maybe Ford would want him to do what he'd claimed his fourth wife *had* done—thrown *A Waste of Spirit* away. After all, he had said it was gone for good, whereas he'd never said that about *Aesthetic Distance*. With this thought, Theo actually got out of the chair, walked over to the wide fireplace, and held the *Waste of Spirit* manuscript near the burning logs. But he couldn't do it. Adolphus Mahan had been right: He of all people couldn't destroy a Rexford text.

Oh sure, Theo, he told himself, setting the script down on one of his neat stacks of papers. Sure. You're willing to *forge* things right and left, but you're too scrupulous a scholar to throw away something that *should* have been thrown away?

Taking a beer out on the porch, he sat in Ford's rocker and looked out over the mountains and black pines at the sky of stars. A soft summer wind was cool in his hair. "What?" he said.

Silence.

"Okay, *what*? Burn it?"

"That bad, hunh, big guy?" Ford said.

". . . Yeah." The sound of his own voice startled Theo. He rocked forward out of the chair, and stood to look out from the porch.

The stars winked in the trees. "Must of suspected it when I came up with a title like *A Waste of Spirit*, hunh?"

"You can laugh." Theo shook his head, rolled the cold bottle against his temple; then he sat back down in the rocker.

Ford said, "So save my ass. Give the manuscript to Cavendish with the rest of the stuff. Stick it with something boring. Like Bernie's letters. One of these days, some graduate student'll get a job out of it. You'd like that, wouldn't you?"

"Yes, I would." Theo sipped his beer, rocking.

The stars all twinkled. "Hey kid. How'd you like *Aesthetic Distance?*"

"As good as the best."

"I wrote it for you."

"I don't think of it *as* me. Or Rhodora. I think of it as Billy and Ava."

"Whatever. She's still the one." The night was quiet.

". . . Why didn't you finish it?"

Quiet. In the high black boughs of the pines, stars hid blinking, and starlight sparkled the tips of the dark needles.

". . . Ford?"

No sound.

". . . Ford? . . . Do you want me to finish it for you?"

The pine trees shivered when the soft-blowing wind suddenly moved through them over the mountains.

Then Theo heard in the wind what the playwright had said to him long ago, when Ford had asked for a last line for *Foolscap,* and Theo had answered, "Me?" "Is Marlowe in the kitchen?" the wind said.

Setting the beer down beside the rocker, Theo leaned out over the porch rail and let the breeze slip inside his shirt. "But which ending? You've got all these endings."

In the soft soughing sound of the wind, Theo heard the word, "Choose." The word rushed through the porch and off into the dark woods. "Choose."

Theo called out, ". . . Ford, are you there?"

"So long, kid."

"Ford, don't go."

One of the summer's shooting stars arched out of its sphere and fell through the sky.

The next day Theo called Dr. Ko's office. She wouldn't be back from vacation for a week. He wasn't sure he really wanted to hear what she might say about "ghosts" anyhow. The return of the repressed. Projections. Externalized grief, Oedipal guilt, and all the rest.

That evening he went to check his house in Rome. Rhodora's things crowded colorfully on shelves and counters in every room: the bright sheen of her clothes in his closet, the mysterious alchemy of her salves and potions in his bathroom. There were pink geraniums on the kitchen table. And there, on the bed, was her blue quilt. . . . And there, in the rocker by the fireplace, solid palpable flesh, was Ford Rexford, his muddy boots propped on the white bricks. "You're doing pretty good, kid," he said. "I knew if I could get you over to England, break the pattern, I could pull you through your stall-out."

Theo shouted, "Don't you dare! You're claiming you did all those rotten things to me on purpose to save me! Bullshit!" Shaking his finger, he muttered, "Look, you're not real. You're just a projection of my grief. Repressed Oedipal guilt."

"Repressed?" Ford laughed. "Who are you kidding? Not repressed enough!"

Theo strode into the kitchen, where he found Ford doing knee bends by the window. "Okay, okay," the playwright was saying, "maybe I wasn't thinking of saving you at the time. But it's like art, kid. It's like me. It doesn't have to be real. It just has to be true."

Theo jerked a can of beer out of the refrigerator and slammed the door. "You knew I had to go wandering all over England? Sure."

Ford appeared to be pretending to do bar exercises in a ballet class. "I knew," he said, "here was one incredibly good-looking, talented, dead person."

"You should talk, Ford! You made a hash of your whole life, trashed everybody who loved you, and now you *are* dead."

"Don't rub it in. Don't think I like being dead. Believe me, it's no illusion."

Theo sipped his beer. "No," he agreed, "death's a fact."

"Well, fact's no excuse for fiction," the playwright said. "I was always clear about that. What I never quite got straight was: Art's no excuse for life." He sprang upward in a parody of a flamboyant dancer's leap, and disappeared.

*　　*　　*

To hear Ford out at the lodge walking the night, to be shooting the breeze in his own house with Ford this way, was disturbing to Theo. So disturbing that, on Saturday when he was back in Rome at Cavendish, on his way to the library, and he happened to see Maude Fletcher hurrying up the steps of Wilton Chapel, he followed her inside to talk with her. He found her preparing the altar for the next day's service, and so he sat waiting until she'd finished. She wore her black clerical collar and blazer, and worked with a solemnity in her face that made Theo realize in a way he hadn't before that she was someone for whom her vocation, her priesthood, was literally that—a calling.

"Maude," he said, as soon as they were seated together in a pew of the empty chapel. "What do you tell people if they say they're seeing ghosts? I don't mean the church's official position, but *you*, what do you say? What would you tell me if I said, well, that Ford's been talking to me the past few weeks. . . ." Theo looked carefully at Maude; there was nothing skeptical or bemused in her eyes; she was just listening. "I mean," he went on, "the voice isn't inside my head. Well, maybe it is, of course, but it doesn't *sound* like it. I'm sure you'll say, I'm all upset about Ford's death, and I'm just projecting—"

Maude nodded. "I'm sure you *are* upset. But maybe that makes it easier for you to hear Ford. . . ."

"You mean, you think I could be hearing him? I don't just *believe* I'm hearing him?"

She pointed at the cross hanging above the altar. "Hey, far be it from me to talk against belief, right? Or life after death. You said you hear his voice. So I guess what I'd ask you is, What's Ford saying to you? Is he saying helpful things?" Maude smiled. "I have a professional interest in Ford's spiritual outcome. He and I spent a lot of hours working on his soul. Is he a good ghost, or a bad one?"

"Ordinarily I'd feel really stupid, talking like this." Theo looked around the wood-arched chapel. "But I think Ford wants. . . . I think basically he's trying to help me make some choices."

"About what, your work?"

"Yes, that, and some, well, personal. . . . Oh, never mind."

She looked with an earnest thoughtfulness for a long while into Theo's eyes. Then she said, "My advice is, Listen to him."

Two weeks later, when Rhodora returned from Nashville, Theo asked her to come and stay with him in New York. She said yes.

Three weeks later, when Dr. Theodore Ryan, Rexford's literary executor, dropped Rhodora off at her new agent's, he was as happy as he'd ever been. Accompanied by Bernard Bittermann, trustee of Rexford's estate, he went to show the cover of the manuscript of *Principles of Aesthetic Distance* to Morris Schwinn and Amanda Mahan, Rexford's longtime producers, in their 44th Street offices. At this meeting, Theo let Bernie do the arguing. He'd promised he would. And as Bernie had promised him in the delicatessen before they went up to see those producers, the argument was not especially pleasant. After all, Bernie had been extremely upset himself the night before, after he'd read the letter from Ford that Theo had brought with him to New York. The letter was more in the nature of a contractual obligation, really; neatly typed (by Theo, for Ford, on Ford's typewriter), and carelessly signed (by Theo, for Ford, in Ford's enormous, uptilted, unreadable signature); in it the playwright stipulated that the premiere performance of *Principles of Aesthetic Distance* be directed by Barbara Sanchez and be staged for a minimum run of two weeks at the Spitz Center for the Performing Arts, Cavendish University, Rome, North Carolina. All subsequent performances elsewhere would note in their programs that the play had premiered there.

When Theo had called Jenny Harte to tell her he'd found a completed manuscript of *Aesthetic Distance* that Ford must have finished after she left Cornwall, along with instructions about premiering it at Cavendish, she was happy to hear it, and not at all suspicious.

But Theo wasn't surprised to encounter arguments. He had even argued with himself about this letter; about forging it, that is. On the other hand, he'd reminded himself that he was only typing out a verbal contract to which Ford had actually been a party. He was only writing down exactly what Ford had promised him he would do; Ford had, after all, told Theo he could make this pledge to Dean Buddy Tupper, Jr. as part of the plan to stop Cavendish from hiring Scottie Smith. Ford did, after all, want Barbara Sanchez to direct. Except for the obstacle of being dead, Ford would have signed the letter himself.

But it wasn't especially surprising that the producers did what the business manager had predicted. Exploded. Shouted and pounded. Sulked and spoke ill of the dead. It never occurred to anyone that Ford *hadn't* left behind this insane stipulation. It sounded just like him to them. Now, this letter didn't tell Schwinn and Mahan they weren't to be the producers, or weren't to have the profits, or weren't to move the play anywhere they wanted to after those first two weeks. And it was true that they always tried out plays somewhere beyond the reach of Manhattan critics anyhow, and that they'd always had to fight with Ford about theatres, casts, designers, and directors. The producers didn't even particularly mind the choice of Barbara Sanchez.

What they minded was the implication that the choice wasn't theirs to make. They minded very much being told they *had* to premiere a play of theirs anywhere, much less the Spitz Center, a place they'd never heard of, much less in North Carolina, a state so far beyond the reach of Manhattan critics that the critics might not even bother sneaking down to see it on the sly. The producers found it hard to say, without popping tendons and gagging on spittle, how very, very much they minded it.

"Rome's no farther than Louisville. You've done tryouts there," said Bittermann mildly.

"Everybody *knows* Louisville," shrieked Amanda Mahan. She was as handsome as her husband, Adolphus, or would have been if her face hadn't been so distorted with rage—something the publisher never allowed to happen to his face.

"Ford's out of his mind," screamed Morris Schwinn, who was as short and ugly as his partner was tall and striking.

"Nobody knew Louisville till somebody did a play there," Bittermann replied with a calm smile.

"Ford doesn't have a legal leg to stand on," Amanda yelled. Both producers had apparently forgotten that Ford was dead. "I'm sick and tired of these stunts of his."

"Let's look at it this way," Bittermann suggested. "You've never seen the Spitz Center—"

"Spitz?! What is this Spitz?!" Schwinn spluttered.

"Maybe it's a great space, Morris. You don't know."

"It's a great space," Theo said. The producers turned and glowered at the tall young man in his impeccable English suit, as if he'd wandered in from Times Square without any clothes on at all.

Bittermann was soothing. "Theo says Ford loved the space. Now, second thing, you haven't read the play."

Theo held it up; they eyed it greedily.

"Maybe Barbara Sanchez is perfect for it," the accountant went on.

"Ford thought she'd be perfect for it," Theo said.

"Third thing." Bittermann took the manuscript from Theo and splayed open the pages with his thumb. "Who knew for a while there, that there *was* a play? Who knew you'd ever get it out of Ford?" This much the producers had to admit, and did so with disgusted nods. Bittermann nodded back at them. "I'll be honest with you, until Theo told me he was coming up here with a completed manuscript, I was figuring Ford had stalled us again."

"It certainly wouldn't be the first time," Schwinn told his partner; no news to her. He angrily yanked at his belt. "I still think when he told us he had to fly back to Florida to *get* Act Three of *Out of Bounds,* he really flew down there and *wrote* it. I always thought that."

"Don't mention *Out of Bounds,*" sighed Amanda Mahan. "Eight hundred thousand dollars, and, poof, over, dead, gone in a night."

Bittermann shrugged. "It'll earn out," he predicted. "You know how many calls from the West Coast about Ford I took yesterday? Thirty-nine, that's how many calls, and that's one day."

The producers looked at each other shrewdly. Then they looked at the wall. It was covered with posters of Ford Rexford plays in which they owned a share of the film rights.

"Now, thanks to Theo, we've got a new play." The accountant waved the manuscript in front of them, then returned it to Theo, who returned it to his briefcase.

Amanda crossed her jeweled arms tightly across her breasts. "Now we're on the subject, Theo," she smiled nastily, "why didn't you give the script to me a month ago? Buzzy Middendorf told me distinctly—"

Theo said, "Ford didn't feel ready to let go of it—"

Schwinn yelled, "*Two years* ago, we advanced Ford—"

Bernie held up a mild hand. "The point is, now we've got the play. I read it last night. I say it's a good play."

This stopped both the producers, and Theo. The accountant was not an effusive man. "Good" from him was raving hysterics from Frank Rich. He nodded at them that, yes, they'd heard him right. Then he said, "Morris. Amanda. You want to talk legal, we can do that. We can bring in the lawyers. Theo here as literary executor has his say." Schwinn and Mahan glared at Theo. "As trustee, I've got my say. As heir, Pawnee's got his say. You've met Pawnee."

The thought of Pawnee Rexford having his say sank Schwinn and Mahan into their leather chairs. They'd been in Sardi's, opening night of *Out of Bounds,* when Pawnee had knocked his father into a table crowded with champagne glasses.

Bittermann let the memory linger. Then he sat down across from them, methodically folding his glasses into their plastic case. "So we can do the lawyers. Or . . ." He slipped the case into his jacket pocket, and tapped it to be sure it was there. "Or we can tell ourselves, This is Ford's last play. This is the way he wants it. Maybe this way isn't so bad. Maybe we'll read his play, we'll go look at this Spitz Center, we'll go talk to Barbara Sanchez. Maybe we made not such a small amount of money in the past, thanks to Ford Rexford, and it wouldn't maybe kill us to do something he asked us, that, could be, it's a good thing anyhow. Could be, it even makes us some more money. I for one would prefer we do things that way, like old friends. . . ."

Morris Schwinn's homely face quivered. "I can't believe Ford's gone."

"Neither can I." Bittermann patted the producer's shoulder in sympathy. "Well, I've said my say. So. Is it a deal?" He waited with his customary patience.

The producers looked at each other like bidding bridge partners who'd played together a long time, then they turned as one to Bittermann.

"The Spitz gets no producing credit," said Mrs. Mahan.

"No royalties on first run or subsidiaries," said Schwinn.

"No say in production," said Mahan. "We get fifty percent on ticket sales for the two weeks we're there."

"Twenty-five, off the top. But they won't ask rent," said Bittermann. "And the Spitz gets a token on subsidiary. Five percent."

Schwinn and Mahan: "Two and a half of the net. College and community—amateur rights only."

Bittermann: "Three of the gross. Is it a deal?"

In the end Schwinn and Mahan and Bittermann and Ryan agreed that it was a deal. Theo opened his briefcase and handed the producers each a neatly bound copy of the manuscript of *Principles of Aesthetic Distance*. They forced themselves to look up from the pages long enough to say goodbye.

That afternoon Theo watched Rhodora rehearse a music video.

That night he flew back to England. On the plane, Ford hogged the seat beside him, his elbows greedily spreading over the armrests.

"Tell you the truth," Ford said, "I'm jealous as spit. But I didn't have the guts for her. Hope you do."

Theo kept writing on his legal pad. "His art was a kind of salvation for him, and a curse. He could turn the human failure into plays, save himself by creating, the way he couldn't save himself with people."

Ford slapped the page of words. "Biographers!" he snorted. Then he stepped into the aisle, running his hand through Theo's hair as he crawled past him. "Okay, I'm out of here. I'm history!" He laughed, then gave Theo a slow salute, his hand falling gracefully open beside his tilted head. "Remember me, okay, kid?"

The shape wavered, faded, was gone.

"All my life, Ford," Theo whispered. "All my life."

"Ryan! Wake up! We're in Honiton."

"Poor old chap, quite gone, isn't he?"

A door slammed. Theo sat up in terror; he didn't know why it was dark, or where he was, or who was talking to him. "Oh," he

said, gave his face a rub, and looked around him. His hip hurt
from where the edge of the attaché case had gouged into it. He
was in the back seat of the yellow Rolls. The Rolls was in the
inner court of a white Georgian coaching inn called, according to
the sign at the archway, the Crown and Mitre. A crunchy noise
came from the graveled courtyard. Jonas Marsh was out there
doing a brisk set of jumping-jacks. Beside him Mole Fontwell was
deliciously stretching his short arms up to the full autumn moon.

Theo crawled out of the car, and rubbed at his thighs. "We're
in Honiton?"

"Astute as ever, Ryan!" Marsh started jogging in fast erratic
little circles. "Let's check in, let's eat, and then—" He did a knee
bend. "The game's afoot!"

"I guess I nodded off," admitted Theo.

The affable Mole Fontwell patted his arm. " 'Was it a vision, or
a waking dream? Fled is that music:—Do I wake or sleep?' "

Jonas Marsh clapped his hands wildly to his ears, and did an
odd leaping dance in the moonlight.

CHAPTER

29

{Enter Two or Three Lords}

If this were played upon a stage now, I could condemn it as an improbable fiction.

Twelfth Night

THE TIDES OF FORTUNE wax and wane at the whim of a goddess less constant than the moon. Those who paddle furiously after them may find themselves swept out to sea one moment, washed up on shore the next; those who swim against the tides usually drown. But the agile few who can float on the waves are known as fortune's favorites. Such a one was Sir Francis Stanlow. This Devonshire gentleman, whom Charles the Second was to make first Earl of Newbolt, happened always to be at the right place at the right time with the right people. And when the tide was turning the right place into the wrong one, he always hopped back to dry sand. His serendipitous jumps were never calculated. Francis Stanlow wasn't shrewd; far brighter men than he had sunk in the depths of their own ambition. Nor was he cautious, or especially decisive or particularly in the know. He was simply lucky, as his family before him had been. On this natural gift, and the jealousy it wrought in a neighbor of Stanlow's, hung the whole *Foolscap* scheme concocted by Fontwell and Marsh, and explained to their fellow conspirator as soon as he'd returned from America.

The forgery was beautiful: There it was, "*Writ by Sr. Walt. R. in Bloody Tower & preserv'd by Lady Ralegh his Wife after his martyrdom. Called by him Foolscap, A Short Comedie.*" In

crabbed italic script, in ink that (according to Mole, who appeared
to have reason to know) was proof against the microchemical tests
to which it would be subjected, the play was written on the blank
folio sheets of a genuine hand-stitched, vellum-bound, slender Jacobean commonplace book—a miscellany of a few favorite poems
and homiletic apothegms collected by some early seventeenth-
century admirer who'd luckily lost interest in the hobby early on,
and left a good two-thirds of the pages just waiting for something
to be written on them. Fontwell's grandpa (himself a collector—
"ignorant and indiscriminate, I must admit," said Mole) had
picked up the book in a Brighton junk shop for a few guineas back
in 1904, and it had sat in the Fontwell attic until Mole had found
it there (luckily, after he'd left Oxford, or he might have "shown
it off, don't you know, to Dame Winifred"). If they'd had to buy
the volume from a current dealer, or steal one, or fake one, they
probably would have been caught. Even the great Thomas Wise
had been caught, after years of excising the blank end papers from
manuscripts in the British Museum, and forging things on them.
But this book was safe. And Fontwell was donating it "to the
cause." When Theo protested at his generosity, Marsh explained
that (a) they were enjoying themselves, (b) they could sell, for
"you'd be surprised how much," the front pages scribbled with
Jacobean ditties and wise sayings that had been undetectably removed from the folio.

The question was—where to put the book? From the start
they'd agreed that the earl's library was out; had such a volume
been in the Newbolt collection, someone would have found it.
Indeed, hiding it anywhere in Bourne House was not only risky,
but problematic. For centuries, the occupants themselves had
combed the place for treasures and had had plenty of opportunities
to do so. Moreover the Stanlows had always been regrettably neat
and given to home improvements; they'd kept Bourne in excellent
repair, from 1660 on been the first in the county with the newest
modern conveniences. So their walls had been continually opened
for ducts and pipes, pulleys and wires; their floors restored, their
ceilings renovated, their attics tidied. Besides, what rationale could
the forgers offer for their simply wandering around and immediately stumbling over the manuscript? They needed instead for

Dame Winifred to discover it in a particular place because there was an historical reason for it to be there. Theo had promised her he would *research* the matter. Let's say he had—actually, Marsh and Fontwell had done most of it—and had found out. . . .

. . . Just what they'd concocted: a plausible provenance for when and why and how the book might have been separated from its owner Francis Stanlow, first Earl of Newbolt, and left by one Robert Dawbney, who hated him, in the small stone chapel of Saint Michael's, on the banks of the Urswick, on the grounds of Bourne. Left there unnoticed for more than three hundred years, tossed with some old prayer books in a little discarded chest. The chest wedged behind a choir stall where Mole Fontwell (on the last of his three rconnoitering expeditions) had discovered it when squirming his small body into the (unrestored, unrenovated, and untidy) nooks and crannies of the old church.

"Well, it sounds a little complicated," Theo had told them.

"It's simple, really," Mole had claimed, seated on the Turkish carpet in his suite at Brown's, with books piled high around him like a child's fort. "With the useful advantage of being true, and of Dame Winifred's knowing that it's true. It's a question of, well, fortune: The Stanlows have always backed the right horse. The poor Dawbneys of Urswick have always backed the wrong, and always despised the Stanlows for never noticing how everything they had, all they were, they owed to the Dawbney curse. It goes quite back to that." And the private scholar proceeded in his affable, long-winded way to pull Theo forward from the beginning of this great rivalry to the moment when a Dawbney ransacked a Stanlow's home, pocketed a number of his valuables, and then hid one of them, Raleigh's play, in Saint Michael's chapel—or so the forgers planned to propose, and indeed had almost come to believe it themselves.

Mole began, "The Dawbneys tried to be kingmakers. The Stanlows let themselves be made by kings. They were lucky from the start."

When Henry Tudor landed in Wales, a sheriff named Stanlow had been waiting in the surf to welcome him. Soon after, at Bosworth Field, young Stanlow happened to wrap his chain-and-ball around the raised mace of a Yorkist about to knock off Henry's head. In that chain was twined the family's fortunate future. Henry VIII gave Squire Stanlow's son a Devonshire convent, after shooing the nuns out. It was five miles from Bourne Manor, a property of the ancient Dawbney dukes of Urswick (one of the nuns was a Dawbney herself), and that proximity gave to the first Stanlow the fantasy of someday living at Bourne.

The next Stanlow, a fervent Protestant, happened to be smuggling wool to the Netherlands when Bloody Mary's officials went to Devon to arrest him. His good-looking son Sir Thomas happened to be winning a superb game of tennis when Queen Elizabeth (who admired looks and talent) dropped by the courts one day. Thomas happened to be still extremely good-looking (and quite a bit wealthier) when James the First came to the throne. James dubbed him a baron, after groping briefly at his breeches at a crowded Whitehall masque, while Stanlow was under the happy misimpression that he was being fondled by the infamous beauty Frances Howard. Time after time, it was as if Hamlet had been thinking of Stanlows when he said, "Our indiscretion sometimes serves us well, / When our deep plots do pall."

Sir Thomas had one son, Francis, whose mother happened to be friends with the homophilic James's neglected queen. And so the boy had fallen into the company of little Charles Stuart. While everyone else (including, from the Tower, Sir Walter Raleigh) was fawning over Charles's older brother, the Prince of Wales, Sir Francis Stanlow and the shy stammering Charles were becoming bosom buddies. When to everyone else's horror the Prince of Wales suddenly dropped dead, the two boys were still bosom buddies, and Sir Francis was soon to be really rich. After the king dropped dead as well, he became the second richest man in east Devon. Not as rich as the great lord of both Urswick Castle and Bourne Manor, but richer than any Stanlow before him had ever been. And now a baron.

Having added a forecourt to Stanlow Lodge, and a coat of arms to its ceilings, the new baron rode off on his new horse to the Short Parliament, arriving a day after Charles the First had put an end to it. When the Long Parliament decided to put an end to Charles the First, Lord Francis rallied to the king's cause, and at

Naseby bent over to fiddle with his spurs just as a Roundhead musket ball shot past him and killed the man behind. At Langport, he distinguished himself against the New Model Army by getting flattened by a flying horse (a cannonball had exploded under it), thereby becoming the very last Royalist to retreat the field. While Fairfax and Cromwell burned Bridgewater, besieged Sherborne, and ransacked Stanlow Lodge, Baron Stanlow was up north at his uncle's house, recovering from his broken leg, and thumbing through the books he'd just bought from Sir Walter Raleigh's son Carew.

The Royal tide quickly ebbed, leaving many high and dry. But as Charles the First stepped onto the scaffold in London, Francis Stanlow stepped onto a boat to France, where the future Charles the Second embraced him warmly, read the letters he'd brought, and vowed that if ever he should reign in England, his poor father's faithful friend would receive his just reward. Eleven years later, this genuine gratitude was not to stop the Merry Monarch (and a considerable number of his Cavalier pals) from sleeping with Francis's wife, the alluring Countess Charlotte, but it was to bestow on the unsuspecting cuckold the earldom of Newbolt and the magnificent manor of Bourne. There Francis lived to a peaceful old age, happily adding to the books he'd retrieved from the ramshackle Stanlow Lodge, and so lucky a man that he never once noticed his wife's infidelity, not even when he saw a play about it on the London stage.

Now contrast this happy Stanlow rise out of the Welsh surf—said Mole Fontwell from his pile of books—with the churning sea in which the unlucky Dawbneys had flailed since a Norman D'Aubiney came over with William the Conqueror and was promptly killed by a Saxon arrow at the battle of Hastings. That man's son fell off the top of the round tower before finishing Urswick Castle; his granddaughter was murdered by her lover, and his great-grandson was butchered in Cyprus on the Third Crusade. If there was a black plague, a Dawbney was sure to catch it. If there was a rebellion, a Dawbney was certain to be on the losing side. They backed Matilda against Stephen, and Simon de Montfort against Edward I. Made dukes by Edward the III, they were attainted by Henry IV. They went down to defeat with the

Lancastrians at Tewksbury, and with the Yorkists at Bosworth Field. A Dawbney told Henry VIII to his face that he'd go to hell if he divorced Catherine of Aragon, and a Dawbney helped try to put Lady Jane Grey on the throne. Dawbneys supported Mary under Edward, and Elizabeth under Mary, and under Elizabeth one of them became so besotted with the imprisoned Queen of Scots that he carried her miniature about with him in a silk purse; it was confiscated, and so was Urswick Castle, although the temperate Elizabeth gave the latter back to him when he got out of the Tower.

Dawbneys had lost and regained their titles and lands so many times they took pride in the fact that not a single generation had escaped the block since John of Bourne, Duke of Urswick, had attempted to rescue Richard II from his Pomfret prison. The family had spent so much time in the Tower, they almost thought of it as a town house. In fact, Robert Dawbney had been in there for annoying King James at the same time that Sir Walter Raleigh used to hoe in his prison herb garden in the mornings and write in his cell at night. Might it not be assumed (why not?, said Mole) that Raleigh had even mentioned to this teenaged nobleman that he was writing a play?

Now, to their other natural instincts for disaster, Mole explained, the odd Dawbney added a self-flagellating penchant for religiosity either so devout or so mule-headed that four of them had been exiled, several assassinated, and two burned at the stake, while not a single one had ever recanted. They were always rushing off into crusades, convents, mysticism, and heresies; inevitably Catholic when it was better to be Protestant, and of course, vice versa. It should therefore come as no surprise that during the reign of Charles I, this Robert Dawbney, Earl of Bourne (they'd been demoted from the dukedom again) converted to radical Protestantism at the height of the High Church days of Laud. He'd seen the light while in the Tower, which was at the time full of aristocratic radical Protestants. All too publicly denouncing the "hellish popery" of archbishop and king, Dawbney removed the stained-glass windows from the family chapel of Saint Michael's, installed a plain pulpit and a radical minister. The Parliamentarian earl was soon warned for refusing to bow at the name of Jesus, and his minister was soon arrested for refusing to move the communion table to the east side of the chancel and rail it off. Next, carrying even Dawbneyism to an extreme, "Mad Rob" (as he was understandably called), read out in the House of Lords an attack on king and bishop by the Puritan William Prynne, for which the author himself had already had first the tips, then the stumps of his ears cut off, and both his cheeks branded. When Mad Rob had a £3000 fine slapped on him, naturally he refused to pay it. He was escorted to the Tower by none other than his Devonshire neighbor, that "popish toad," Francis Stanlow.

Then suddenly the tide turned again. The Earl of Bourne was out of the Tower, the Archbishop of Canterbury was in, and the king was on the run. It looked as if, in Oliver Cromwell, the Dawbneys had backed a winner at last. Robert went to war for the right to see God as he chose, and stop other people from doing the same. And despite the bad luck of being "shot in the cods" at Langport and losing an eye at Tiverton, the rebellious earl did indeed live to squint at a flag of victory flying from the round tower of Urswick Castle. He had the further satisfaction of looting that Royalist stronghold, Stanlow Lodge, and removing from it a number of morally lax artifacts, among them a particular book with a play in it. (Everything up to and including the sacking of Stanlow Lodge by Robert Dawbney was recorded in history. Anything about a book with a play in it was not.)

In general, the Puritan earl considered plays the evil weapons of Satan (he had Prynne's diatribe against the theatre, "The Players' Scourge, or Actor's Tragedie," read from the plain wood pulpit of Saint Michael's), but *this* play not only talked about how the rotten Stuarts were ruining England, this play was written by that Great Parliament Man, that Noble Martyr to Stuart tyranny, Sir Walter Raleigh himself, whom Mad Rob had actually met in the Tower, and whom he had idolized ever since. Even the lewdness of a few scenes of this play (one of them shockingly insinuating that the author might have had carnal knowledge of the Virgin Queen) could not shake Rob's hero-worshiop of Raleigh, nor his determination that a Stuart-loving Stanlow had no right to such a relic.

For eleven years, a patch on his eye and a truss on his groin, the earl enjoyed the stern pleasures of life in the Commonwealth.

He harassed closet Catholics; he went to Ireland and killed a lot of the natives; he read the Bible out loud to his sons every day, hour after unappreciated hour; towards the end, he even met Milton (who'd written so much propaganda for the Commonwealth by then, that he couldn't even see out of one eye).

Of course Mad Rob should have known it couldn't last. Of course, being a Dawbney, he didn't. The Commonwealth fell, and with it radical purity. Those who had been all for Levelling when they were on the rise, became all for the Status Quo after they'd gotten there. In the end, the rich did not much care for the notion of common wealth, and the poor never did get to vote. The net result of the Revolution was to privilege wealth as well as title ("Hear, hear! for Grandpa's tea biscuits," said Mole), and as often as possible to see that wealth and title were the same ("Grandma's pa was a viscount," said Mole).

So Charles II came home to cheers and revelry and the officers of the New Model Army went back to being alehouse keepers. The body of Cromwell was dug up, hanged at Tyburn, and his warty head stuck on a pike atop Westminister Hall, where it remained for twenty-five years to remind the people of England that the "Late Troubles" were over.

Actually, Mad Rob was not as unlucky as he felt, hiding out in Saint Michael's and expecting the worst. His minister had fled to America, his sons had become Cavaliers (just to get away from him). Some of his friends had recently had their bowels and sex organs cut off and burned in front of their eyes (if they were looking), after being briefly hanged and permanently quartered. But thanks to the Act of Indemnity and Oblivion, all that Dawbney got was the latter. He might have endured the oblivion, too, had it not been coupled with the unbearable news that the parvenu (and undoubtedly closet Catholic) Francis Stanlow, now Earl of Newbolt, was from this day forth the owner of Bourne Manor, where some Dawbney or other had lived since cranky Duke Mortimer had thrown his entire family out of the main castle in 1395. Bourne! Where Dawbneys had lived when Stanlows were herding pigs through the marshes of Wales! It was literally unbearable news; the old limping, squinting descendant of Norman nobility, of Plantagenet diehards, of five hundred years of Royal disfavor, died of apoplectic chagrin the minute he heard it.

(That Robert Dawbney had hidden himself in Saint Michael's and had expired there were historic facts; it was also a fact that he'd hidden looted property of the Stanlows in the church, presumably out of jealous spite. That the Stanlows had failed to recover a particular piece of that property was another piece of Fontwellian fiction, or as he preferred to call it, an hypothesis.)

The Dawbneys were never to get Bourne House back, nor were they ever to regain the title of duke. Still, even under the handicap of their congenital lucklessness, they managed to keep Urswick Castle, and eventually Queen Anne reelevated one as far as a marquess. And Marquess of Urswick a Dawbney remained (despite their inability to get along with any of the Hanoverans and few of the Windsors) until the present day. For a while—with monarchs unable to turn to the scaffold to solve their political quarrels—the family even grew quite populous; but World War I took care of that.

During the Restoration, the Stanlows restored Saint Michael's to High Anglicanism, installing lovely stained-glass windows, a handsome choir screen, and a pulpit ornately carved with Saint Michael slaying the dragon (of radical Prostestantism). They had Bourne House completely redesigned by Inigo Jones to the Caroline perfection it still enjoyed. The Dawbney arms were chiseled off every surface on which they could be found, and replaced by the Newbolt crest with its motto, *"Gratius Rege"* (Thanks to the king). "Simply put," said Jonas Marsh, "and damnably true." The Dawbney motto *"Meo Volente"* ("By my will") was equally accurate; they'd self-destructed at every conceivable opportunity.

And so to the present day, when Gordon Dawbney, rowing for Cambridge, slipped his oarlock and was defeated by Horry Stanlow, rowing for Oxford, when that same Dawbney, spying from his round tower, saw the first tourist bus pull into Bourne, the House of Urswick continued to believe that every ill-gotten gain of the House of Newbolt was rightfully theirs. Not that they could get hold of them. Centuries ago now, the popish toad Francis Stanlow had even taken back all the valuables that Mad Rob had once looted from his lodge. Or so both families believed. But then they didn't know about the Raleigh manuscript. Yet.

"Stroke, stroke, steady now," whispered Mole Fontwell from the stern of the little wooden rowing skiff where he sat with both steering lines in hand. "Theo. Oar up a sec. You're over-rowing Jonas."

"YES!" Marsh panted. "Sit back there on your buttocks, Mole! Who'd you think you are, the bloody captain of the *Pinafore*?"

"He's got the rudder," Theo wheezed. "This current's pretty strong."

"He's COXING for Brasenose again, off in his Lilliputian brain! We're not in a RACE! It *is* midnight. I wouldn't say this godforsaken stretch of the Urswick was JAMMED with boats tonight, would you?!"

Mole steered them portward, towards the huge dark shadow of a willow tree that bent into the river. "If you keep shouting like that," he said pleasantly, "we might as well have simply driven up to the church door, waving in at the vicarage as we went past the window."

"We should have!" Marsh gasped, flinging backwards as his oar popped out of the water and sprayed his elegant trousers.

Mole pulled briskly on his guideline. "Here we are. Starboard, starboard. Backstroke, Theo, please. More, more. Mind that bough. Mind— Oh, Jonas! Well, if you won't listen!"

The three conspirators hopped ashore, right beside the church.

Indeed, Saint Michael's was so close to the Urswick that in earlier days people had come by river to its services. No one did any more; in fact, not all that many came to Saint Michael's by any means. The church was now fairly down on its luck, no longer being subsidized by family dukes, or by popish coffers, or by the state, nor even helped out much any more by the earls of Newbolt, who from 1660 to 1919 had held the gift of its "living" (i.e., the right to hand out its ministry, *cum* comfortable income, to any ordained body they pleased). But in these secular democratic times Saint Michael's had to pay the price of independence, and rely on its own parishioners, with a sideline in baked goods, innocent gambling devices, and the odd tourist buying a postcard or rubbing a brass. It was all the church could do to keep its doors open, much less repair them whenever they needed it. And the whole place needed repair, more and more so as centuries took their crumbling toll; but if it hadn't been for the Countess Andrea's hosting that fund-raiser in the Bourne House Costume Museum, they wouldn't even have been able to pay the contractor to do something about the "serious structural jeopardy" he'd said the supports of the chancel were in. "If these walls come down on your choir, don't say you weren't forewarned," he'd told Mr. Brakeshaw, terrifying the old rector with nightmares of screaming mutilated boys crawling out of the rubble next Sunday, and their parents bringing suit the day after. The rector had phoned the contractor in the morning, agreed to his terms, and begged him to start work as soon as possible.

"Norman arch," said Jonas Marsh, shining his flashlight on it until Theo grabbed his arm.

The key was under the urn of geraniums from which Mole had seen Mr. Brakeshaw take it after a flustered search through all his many pockets, presumably for his own key. Inside, the small ancient stone chapel smelled cool and spicy. The stone faces of medieval Dawbneys glared open-eyed at the interlopers, as if startled by the darting lights. In their crannied tombs, Stanlow couples in wooden ruffs leaned on their elbows, watching the three men tiptoe up the steps and into the sanctuary.

"Now just hold the torches," Mole instructed them. "When I get there, you lower the books down the back of the stall. For God's sake, don't drop them on my head."

"You've got your gloves?" Marsh's hiss echoed eerily against the old vaulted stones.

"For the hundredth time, yes." Mole Fontwell lay down on his belly in front of the draped altar, and then slithered off into darkness, as if—or so the dead Puritan Mad Rob might have thought—his prostration before an altar, that idolatrous emblem of High Church popery, had transformed him on the spot into the Serpent Lucifer.

Marsh hissed after him. "Be sure you really cake them in the dust."

"All right?" called Theo, after Mole had gotten the loose panel off the rear side of the stalls, and crawled beneath them. A muffled affirmation reverberated from under the choir seats.

Marsh paced the alter. "I bet the chest is locked after all."

"Jonas, he got it open the last time he was here."

"I bet he'll chip it."

"All right, Mole?" Theo called.

"All right."

Jonas and Theo stared at the stained-glass windows, dead and black now, at the dead Dawbneys and dead Stanlows, at the risen Christ painted on a banner behind the organ, at each other.

"Got it," came the spooky sound of Mole's voice. "Wonderful! What a bit of luck!"

"What! What!" The two Americans crouched over the back of the choirstall but couldn't see a thing in the tiny wedge of space.

"There's a *coin* in here. Didn't spot it before. Wedged in a corner hinge. Looks like. . . . No. Yes, wait! Good Lord, looks like Elizabeth!"

Jonas wagged his flashlight frantically. "Get it!"

"Not bloody likely," called the disembodied voice. "It stays right where it is. Better for us. Right, then, pass down the books."

Suddenly a hideous *whack* banged against a side window. "CHRIST!" Theo gasped, as Marsh flattened himself against the altar. They shut off their flashlights and listened to their panicked breath awhile.

No one charged in with a gun or a warrant.

Finally, there was another thwack, then a noise like BBs hitting the stained glass. "Rain," Theo finally whispered. "It's raining hard. Must have been a tree branch in the wind."

"Perfect," Marsh growled. "We row back to the whoreson car in the whoreson rain! It'll be pneumonia for me this time."

"Books?" Mole was calling, a little impatiently.

So, slowly and carefully, Theo lowered behind the stall first the two small, perfectly genuine 1604 Books of Common Prayer. They'd also been donated by Mole, who'd declined to say what he'd paid for them, except "Not awf'lly much, really." After seeing that enormous truck go by shouting FONTWELL'S. OF COURSE, Theo wasn't sure what "not awf'lly much" might mean to the biscuit heir. But they were ordinary prayer books, run-of-the-mill editions that any Anglican church would be always buying and losing and replacing, and discarding as doctrine changed and new editions appeared (as, for example, in 1660). There were, or had been, thousands of copies like those two prayer books.

The other book was one of a kind.

With a last rub of the soft scratched leather against his chest, Theo passed down the thin folio containing his play. No, he thought, as the twine slid slowly through his hands. No, not my play. Not Ford's. Not Jonas's and Mole's. *Foolscap*, a Short Comedie, writ by Sr. Walt. Ralegh in Bloody Tower.

"Good luck," he said.

And he relinquished it.

CHAPTER
30

{Enter Baſtard}

There be requisite effectually to act the art of cony-catching
three several parties: the setter, the verser, and the barnacle.

Robert Greene, A Notable Discovery of Cozenage

NO GRATITUDE was ever received with more blushing modesty
than Dame Winifred Throckmorton's gratitude to Messieurs Fontwell, Ryan, and Marsh (as she'd gaily introduced those three
younger men to her neighbor Mildred by shouting up to "The
Heights' " thatched window from the lane below): "Guests of
mine. Messieurs Fontwell, Ryan, and Marsh," the old scholar had
shrilled, and the bedroom curtains of "The Heights" had pulled
immediately shut.

Time and again, Dame Winifred had told her three visitors that
she couldn't be more grateful, and each time had sent a flush of
shame up Theo's neck. She was grateful for Ryan's evident happiness in seeing her again, for Marsh's admiring (indeed, startlingly
emphatic) praise of her work, and for Fontwell's kindly telling her
she hadn't changed a bit since Oxford (he meant it, too; in fact, he
later joked that he'd recognized the egg stain on her misbuttoned,
moth-pocked sweater vest). But far beyond these pleasantries, the
old retired academic was grateful for their *belief*. For their willing-
ness to believe that there might be, or even that there might once
have been, a Raleigh play. For their faith that she wasn't as off
her head as everyone else seemed to suspect. After all, these three
men were by no means, as she informed them, "brainless bump-

kins off the common roads." They were trained scholars; she'd read books by two of them ("A few quibbles of course, but on the whole, sound, Mr. Marsh"), and she had personally trained the third—the only one who hadn't gone into the business, as it happened; for which failure she'd occasionally blamed herself, and occasionally the Fontwell Biscuit Company.

Time and again she'd said how touched she was by all the work they'd put in over these last months to master the background, and analyze the possibility of such a manuscript's existence. It was marvelous that they wanted to give over the next whole two weeks to working with her, and had taken lodgings right here in the village in order to be at hand. Theodore Ryan was clearly a man of his word, not like so many young people who simply said nice things to be polite and then forgot about them. Scarlet by now, Theo wanted to run from the room, abandoning the whole ridiculous scheme; in a way, it hadn't been real until now, and the reality was *awful*. It didn't help when Dame Winifred confessed that she felt a little ashamed of herself for having suspected that Theo would never even return to Barnet-on-Urswick, particularly after she'd received a postcard from him in America, saying that he'd been called away by a friend's sudden death. But how wrong to doubt the tall, large-boned, tawny young man (so Elizabethan-looking, really); for it proved that his friend had been Rexford the American playwright, who in fact had died. And Theo Ryan had returned to "Lark Cottage," and had brought his colleagues, just as he'd said he would.

They'd suddenly arrived at her (broken) gate, squeezed their way through the now seedy flower stalks, and rapped at her dangling brass door knocker, which came off in Marsh's vigorous hand. She brewed them tea, but forgot to serve it. She poured grayish chocolate cookies out of a box, and scooped them back on the plate when, hard as lead, they thudded off the table. She threw a cloth over Orinoco, who screamed "Kiss arse!" and worse, every time Jonas Marsh came clicking and cooing near his cage; leading her to wonder again about her parrot's previous owners. Jonas Marsh said they had a theory. She told them, "Sit," which, after dislodging the cats Tom, Kit, and Wat, they managed to do. Then she folded her hands on her high stomach, placed her feet on a cassock (her very old toe stuck out of the top of one slipper), and commanded, "Speak." Mole was to say that night, as they walked back to the King William Inn, that her high-pitched order had reminded him too vividly of their encounters at Oxford nearly thirty years earlier, and had given him on the spot a terrific stomachache.

She listened to them, often with her eyes closed, for an hour. (Theo thought she might have gone to sleep, but Mole knew better.) From time to time, she asked a question, or corrected a fact, but otherwise she quietly listened, periodically scratching a foot with her exposed toe, or cleaning an ear with the stem of her glasses, then running the stem through the thick gray thatch of her hair. Jonas did most of the talking, as Theo was in a moral torture, and Mole appeared to have developed a stammer that tangled his tongue every time Miss Throckmorton stared at him over her glasses and said something like "*Not* sixteen sixty-one. The Act of Uniformity; 'sixty-two, of course." Or, "You're muddling Naseby with Marston Moor, Archibald." (This was Theo's first inkling of Mole Fontwell's true Christian name; the disclosure shed light on the man's unwillingness to reveal it.)

Finally, Jonas finished, and Mole (who'd added biting his fingernails to his stuttering), stammered, "It seems at least possible, that is . . ."

Jonas took over, scowling at both his companions. "The point is: If Mad Rob did pilfer a Raleigh manuscript from Stanlow Lodge when they sacked the place, who's to say Francis ever got it bloody back?"

"I'm thoroughly ashamed!" Dame Winifred clapped her hands together, and Mole froze in motionless terror, like, thought Theo, well, rather like a mole. "Always took as my hypothesis," she went on, "that the manuscript had reached Bourne House. Never doubted it; the fascinating allure of the fire, I expect. And of course, other Raleigh books *were* there. Sheer stupidity!" She gave her temple the sharp reprimand of a slap.

Jonas Marsh reassured her, "It may *be* at Bourne, ma'am, if it exists. We only suggest that someone consider the possibility that old Dawbney pocketed it—" He pantomimed sneakily slipping something inside his beautiful jacket. "—and kept it. We only suggest that someone research the collection at Urswick Castle with that in mind."

This was as far as the conspirators had planned to cast their lure; any closer and a wary old trout like Dame Winifred might spot the line; she would have to swim to it herself. With a grimace, she said, "The Dawbneys do have books, but— Oh dear, I've forgotten your tea!" What she poured into their cups was teeth-achingly cold, and (as Jonas later shuddered) acidic enough to tan plates of rhinoceros hide. She drank hers down without seeming to notice a problem, then continued, "But I've had the privilege of examining the Dawbney collection, and I must tell you it now consists largely of Victorian sermons and modern murder thrillers. They were obliged to sell their library in seventeen fifty-five. Gaming houses, card debts, rake's progress, I'm afraid. The auction was catalogued, as I'm surprised you didn't discover in your research, Archibald."

Mole squirmed. "Well, we meant, what if that puh, puh, particular volume had been mispuh, puh, placed, you see, buh, buh-fore—"

Jonas kicked Mole's ankle, and Theo threw in, "Before the sale. We know there are no records of such a discovery at Urswick, but since the family has lived there since—"

"The Conquest," the old scholar supplied. "And the Dawbneys *are* rather—" She glanced about her own cluttered sitting room. "—rather slack. I myself had the pleasure of stumbling across some very nice first editions of Dickens for them in a box of old issues of *Punch*, which the marquess sold, I gather, in order to build that awful 'Chamber of Medieval Tortures.' So ghoulishly popular with the young."

"Don't allow it! Stretch the brats on the rack!" suggested Jonas Marsh, with a pounding of the tea table that sent the black cat leaping from the back of Theo's chair across his lap. "Screw a few little feet inside the Iron Boot, and I bet they'll soon stop drooling after horror dungeons!"

"No doubt," conceded Dame Winifred. ". . . But I'm just thinking . . ." She smoothed the pleats of her green tweed skirt over a rip she'd noticed. ". . . There is another possibility. If in fact Robert Dawbney confiscated—and because of their shared imprisonment was particularly attached to—a manuscript by Raleigh . . ."

The three men waited with flat expressions.

She swam slowly closer. "Perhaps you weren't aware of this. It is rather obscure. But there is evidence that Lord Dawbney—despite being pardoned, I must say generously, too, by 'Indemnity and Oblivion'—had to be *forced* to return the Stanlow possessions he'd confiscated. Indeed, after the Restoration, he carried on so in public with his slanders against the king's private life (quite factual, but still), that a warrant went out for his arrest. As I recollect, he escaped the sheriff's men disguised as a lunatic—"

"That wouldn't have been hard," Theo noted.

"Indeed not. And hid himself in what had been the Dawbney family chapel. Saint Michael's. Ironical, I always thought, for such a Puritan to seek, you might say, sanctuary." Dame Winifred paused, closed her eyes, and considered this. Her tongue bounced about inside her mouth as if it were looking for something, then the keen old eyes popped suddenly open, and she added, "Yes, might have kept such a relic as a Raleigh play right there with him. Died there of a stroke. Buried under the nave, west aisle." Tapping the teaspoon against her cheek, she said, "Yes, there is Saint Michael's. One might suggest it as another possibility."

"But no records or rumors about such a thing in the church history?" Jonas asked with a skeptical frown.

"None whatsoever," she admitted. "Moreover, I've had many conversations about my Raleigh theory with the rector of Saint Michael's. Mr. Brakeshaw. He prides himself—with insufficient cause, I fear—on his knowledge of the Civil Wars, and he would have vaunted such a fascinating connection, I'm sure, had he ever come across the rumor." Dame Winifred smiled with a blink of her wry hazel eyes. "Mr. Brakeshaw thinks me a dotty old woman, and I think him a pompous and patronizing old man." She shrugged. "Still, I make every effort to be civil. And I shall assume so does he; though frankly he might try a bit harder. Still, I suppose, better a man who quotes Marvell and tells me it's Milton, than a man who doesn't quote Marvell at all."

Jonas Marsh politely sucked at the edge of his cookie. "Either's better than a man who quotes a lot of Wordsworth and Keats," he muttered.

"We might have a look at Saint Michael's. Make some inquiries," ventured Theo quietly. "I understand it's small, which certainly can't be said for Urswick Castle."

Mole recited the speech they had planned for him. "We shouldn't leap to ku, ku, conclusions. If Robert Dawbney had it, and that's simply speculation, Robert's home is where we should look for its truh, traces. That seems to me obvious."

Dame Winifred flung her feet off the cassock, stood, and shook her glasses at the small dark man perched on a stool by her hearth. "Archibald, your work was always diligent, thorough, and reasonably accurate. But a bit, as I recall, cautious. A little . . . obvious, is that fair?" She rapped her spectacles on his shoulder. "Facts are cattle. Theory is a bird." Her bent fingers fluttered skyward. "One must *leap*, in order to soar."

"YES!" said Jonas Marsh, biting sharply into the rock-hard cookie, and instantly regretting it.

They made their plans over mixed grills at the Nightingale (Miss Throckmorton declined to eat the chops at the King William, where the three men were staying. Jonas had rejected the Nightingale's accommodations; he preferred Georgian coaching inns to the "daub and wattle, stoop and shiver paddocks" of earlier hostelries). It was decided to split up: Ryan and Throckmorton would take Saint Michael's church. Marsh and Fontwell would take Urswick Castle. Mole shared with Gordon Dawbney, Marquess of Urswick, membership in the Garrick Club, which should help. Besides, Dame Winifred confessed that the irascible marquess had "turned her out of the house" after learning of her prior friendship with the ninth earl of Newbolt, and after hearing from an eavesdropping butler that she had made "unfavorable remarks" about his library as compared to that of Horry Stanlow at Bourne House. "Quite right, too," she said.

"It seems pretty ungrateful, after you'd pointed out those first editions for the marquess," Theo said.

"Theodore," she said, hacking away at her pork. "There are those who simply cannot forgive a favor. . . . And those who never forget one."

Theo kept his eyes guiltily fixed on his plate.

And so, one golden autumn day after the next, Marsh and Fontwell drove the yellow Rolls under the dog-toothed gateway into

Urswick Castle, where they'd been very graciously received by the marquess, after telling him that Dame Winifred Throckmorton believed a play by Sir Walter Raleigh was lost somewhere at the house of his great rival, but that *they* believed it might be right here on Dawbney property. The marquess even offered to put them up while they searched, but as Jonas now had a cold, and as the guest rooms of the Norman castle were icy even in September, they declined with thanks.

When he wasn't overseeing the construction of his new "Frontierland" amusement park, Gordon Dawbney, a stocky ginger-haired man of fifty and a passionate hunter, was busy, now that the summer tourist trade had thinned, trying to kill pheasants while not killing either straggling American toddlers or any of his expensive miniature deer. So he was unable to help personally with the search. But he instructed the staff to show his visitors every courtesy.

For twelve days, the two men happily toured the towers and turrets of Urswick, pretending to search for the lost manuscript. They looked in the Duke's Great Hall, the Earl's Small Hall, the kitchens and even the library, where Mole read a good Agatha Christie and Jonas found a nicely bound Wilkie Collins. They strolled stone corridors thick with racks of antlers, and in galleries studied the portraits of Dawbneys who'd been stabbed by their lovers, expired of the plague, burned at the stake, and died in innumerable other unpleasant ways fighting on the losing side in fields across the land. They examined the cabinets containing the heretical version of the Bible one Dawbney had defiantly taken to the block, and the little model of Urswick Castle one had nostalgically whittled in the Tower. They felt the nicks on the long sword with which John of Bourne had attempted to rescue Richard II. They stared at the oak beam rafter from which a love-crazed Victorian Dawbney had hanged himself with a velvet drapery tassel.

One afternoon, they climbed the round tower, tapped about for hidden recesses in the "Henry IV Apartments," and had a picnic on the battlements. Another day, they peeked inside the crusader's arrow chest in the armory passage (now the Dungeon of Medieval Torture Instruments). At trestle tables in the Tea Room they wrote postcards they'd bought in the Souvenir Shoppe. They circled the moat in the paddle boats, enjoyed pleasant talks with the medieval minstrels, and sympathized with the weary staff who'd just heard that next summer they were all going to have to wear fourteenth-century costumes and act out the Peasants' Revolt in front of D'Aubiney Keep.

Every day they left early enough to visit all the antique shops in the area, where they found what Mole described to Theo as "terrifically nice little things," and which certainly looked as if they might be. Ranging far and fast, they bought thick bolts of table lace in Honiton, and great clumps of crockery in Lyme Regis. Then every night, over Nightingale chops, Marsh and Fontwell reported back to the other team their lack of success at the castle.

In their searches, they said, they *had* discovered a number of objects the Marquess of Urswick hadn't known he had—some of them (including a Norman two-handed battle-ax) quite valuable. They'd come across an Elizabethan printing press in the secret "priest-hole" behind the chimney of the Great Hall; they'd unearthed a well-thumbed *Lady Chatterley's Lover* and a mint condition *Essay on Miracles* inscribed by Cardinal Newman himself. But they hadn't found anything resembling a Raleigh manuscript, or for that matter any book at all predating 1755, anywhere in the great pile of Urswick stone. Still, the two men cheerfully promised Dame Winifred to carry on, their faith in the existence of a Raleigh play undiminished.

Theo spent his evenings either with them, or in his room working on the Rexford biography, or at the Stag & Hart listening to Rhodora's songs on the jukebox. The young woman named Stephanie whom he'd met there never returned, and when Theo finally asked the bartender about her, he was told that she'd "patched up her break-off with her fiancé" (the source of her sorrow when Theo had met her) and moved into his flat in Ottery St. Mary. Theo said he was glad to hear it.

His days he spent with Miss Throckmorton, and (as long as he didn't think about the implications of the forgery) he enjoyed them greatly. Despite their disparity in age and background, they never seemed to run out of conversation. They shared the Renaissance, and that was ample and luxurious meeting ground.

Each morning it was a sight to see (and Mildred saw it from her spy post in "The Heights") the drivers of the two teams—Miss Throckmorton in her Hillman Imp and Jonas Marsh in the yellow Rolls—as they revved their motors in the Barnet town center, and shot off down the High, scattering pebbles and pedestrians. As the Rolls zoomed to Urswick Castle, the Imp bucketed past Bourne House, and along the river road to Saint Michael's Church. There the rector, Mr. Steven Brakeshaw, was not nearly as receptive to the Theory as the Marquess of Urswick had proved. Mr. Brakeshaw had heard for years about Dame Winifred's search for Raleigh relics, and placed no credence either in her ideas or her qualifications to pursue them. In fact, being quite ignorant of literary matters, he really didn't much believe that Dame Winifred had made those earlier "famous discoveries" (as they were locally called) for which she'd (somehow) been dubbed a Dame Commander of the British Empire. The sinewy stooped old parson didn't really much believe that any woman had ever done, or was capable of doing, anything, whether famous or not, worthy of his attention.

On Theo's tenth daily visit to Saint Michael's with Miss Throckmorton, the rector had taken him aside, and whispered to him about "unmarried women of a certain age," and whether it was wise to indulge them too far in their (he waggled his bushy eyebrows in Dame Winifred's direction) "fancies." Although Brakeshaw was himself an unmarried man of a certain age, he was a widower—with years of experience in not indulging female vagaries: He'd kept a tight guard on his wife's fancies with great success until she'd managed to escape him by dying of a rapid brain tumor a few years ago.

"Balmy," Brakeshaw confided to the young American. "Whole notion of this Raleigh business is balmy." He pointed across the nave. "She's been at it ever since she moved to Devon."

The retired scholar looked to be at it right now, or at least to be asking Mad Rob Dawbney about it, for she was down on her knees in the west aisle, her hand holding her tam on, with her ear pressed close to that Puritan earl's brass marker.

"Dame Winifred, really!" called the rector across the length of pews. "Dame Winifred!" (Though Low Church by birth, he was hopelessly Royalist by inclination, and loved the sound of a title, even if [somehow] connected with a woman.) "You would do well to recall the words of Charles the First. 'I beseech you, in the bowels of Christ, think it possible you may be mistaken?"

One may doubt whether King Charles would have found it amusing to discover on his tongue words actually spoken by Oliver Cromwell, his successor and executioner, but Miss Throckmorton certainly thought it worth a belly laugh. Brakeshaw, of course, attributed her guffaws not to his misquote but to her compulsive hysteria over "this Raleigh business." With surreptitious head motions, he urged Theo to take notice. "Sad thing," he sighed. "Not certain she shouldn't *see* someone." The rector ostentatiously straightened the rack of brochures ("A Short History of Saint Michael's on Urswick" by Steven R. Brakeshaw, M.A., Rector) on sale for 35p each by the south door. He added, "If a great man like Raleigh had written a play, some man or other would have discovered the fact by now. And it wouldn't be here in Saint Michael's. It would be in some great library."

"Not necessarily," said Theo, taking the hint and buying a brochure, plunking his coins into the slotted box. "Things go astray. And remember how long Raleigh was in prison, and how he died."

"Yes, yes," Brakeshaw nodded importantly. "Elizabeth executed him over the Scottish succession business. He died an atheist, you know."

"Hmm." Confronted with this thick wall of inaccuracies, Theo choked down the urge to point out that Raleigh had died a devout Christian, executed by James; he decided to bypass history, and to stress random luck. "It's quite possible to find very rare, and valuable, manuscripts where you least expect them. They found the Boswell papers in a croquet case. And, think about it a minute." Theo walked with the rector up the center aisle of the ancient chapel, into whose stone slates were inset mosaic Latin words for the Christian virtues, pausing on PATIENTIA. He said solemnly, "Miss Throckmorton, as you know, is a world-renowned Renaissance scholar."

Brakeshaw stopped in midstep (ironically with his foot on SAPIENTIA), and mentally attempted to reject, or suppress, the idea of Dame Winifred's being a world-renowned anything, even deluded fanatic, when he himself was not renowned as far as the edge of the county—if last Sunday's attendance at Saint Michael's was any indication. "Retired schoolteachers get these fancies," he stubbornly muttered.

"But just suppose," Theo urged. "Admittedly, it's unlikely, but for a moment, just suppose that's she's *not* mistaken about this play. Suppose a great literary discovery *should* be made here; can you imagine what it would do for your church's reputation?" Theo waved his arms around the dilapidated nave of little Saint Michael's with such enthusiastic conjurations that the Reverend Brakeshaw suddenly saw the small space transformed into a vast cathedral with magnificent ribbed vaulting, soaring pillars of marbles, and rich alabaster fonts. He suddenly saw a steady stream of pilgrims flooding down the aisles, each paying at least 50p to view the Raleigh manuscript. He saw television interviews, and his name on a brochure: "*RALEIGH'S LOST PLAY* by Steven R. Brakeshaw, M.A., Rector of Saint Michael's on Urswick."

These thoughts, as can happen with visions, began to turn the rector's mind around. While he continued to give Miss Throck-morton and Theo only begrudging encouragement, and denied them permission to search the premises except in his presence, or to examine the old church records in any methodical way—still, conversion, fed by greed and jealousy, was growing like a weed inside him. He himself started, in the odd leisure moment, to look about, to poke a tentative broom under the confessional or shine a torch along the rafters of the crypt (terrifying a few rats, and himself). And whenever he saw Dame Winifred pausing some-where to scribble notes, he'd rush to the spot as soon as she left it, and try to imagine what those notes might have said. Brakeshaw also instructed the young, affluent contractor in charge of the upcoming restoration to keep an eye out for "well, anything" he should come across. "Like old church property, odds and ends. Old books, that sort of item."

The contractor, who was always in a hurry, gave a quick ruth-less look around the crumbling church. "Listen here," he growled. "Miss Throckmorton's been narking at me seven years about old books and like, ever since I started with the earl's renovations at Bourne House, so I don't need telling to keep a lookout for her."

"For her? Ah ha," said Brakeshaw with a tap to his beaked

nose. "Should by some fluke anything antique-ish come to light in Saint Michael's, of course you will bring it to *me*." The last word was significantly stressed by the rector's repeated rapping on his chest, as if he'd lapsed into the Catholic practice of mea culpas.

"Right-cher-are, Rev," muttered this disrespectful youth, who then zipped off in his Alfa-Romeo to give a neighboring town an estimate on what he would charge to save their medieval Guild Hall before it was too late.

The day after the major work of restoration began at Saint Michael's, Messieurs Fontwell, Ryan, and Marsh bid a temporary farewell to Dame Winifred. They had decided it would be better if they weren't in the vicinity of Barnet-on-Urswick when what they called "the discovery" occurred. But the reasons they gave for their leaving happened also to be true: Theo had to work on the Rexford biography. Mole had to give one of his sisters away in marriage. Jonas had to return to London to begin orientation for the Cavendish Year Abroad students. "God help me," he groaned to Dame Winifred during their final supper at the Nightingale. "As into my cultural care come a dozen shrewd and simpering southern belles, and a dozen lobotomized libidinous young studs with thick shaved necks and bright pink feet each the size of a half-grown pig."

"He loves teaching," Mole said.

"Thought so." Miss Throckmorton nodded.

Mole called on the waiter for another bottle of wine. "Dame Winifred, we'll keep on. In a month or so, we'll come back and tackle Buh, Buh, Bourne House with you."

Jonas said, "Perhaps we should look into inventories of dowry articles that left Bourne when daughters married out. Or perhaps—"

"Dear me, dear me," the elderly woman muttered, as she sawed wildly at her meat. "Sometimes suspect I've led you kind gentlemen off on a dreadful fool's journey. Chimera, whole thing. Wild goose."

"Ma'am," said Jonas, kicking under the table the lamb chop that had flown off her plate. "Ma'am, remember the Lost Colony. If Raleigh could lose *that*, he could lose a play. And what's been lost, can be found."

"Ah, if only that were true, my dear Mr. Marsh," she replied,

hewing through her remaining chop. "As you'll recall, there were
five hundred thousand manuscripts in the great library of Alexandria. They were all burnt to soot." The old woman noisily sighed,
as if that loss, sixteen centuries old, was still raw and shocking to
her. "We know," she resumed, swatting bread crumbs from her
vest, "the titles of more than one hundred and ten plays by Sophocles, and have only—" She turned quickly. "—How many left to
us, Archibald?"

Mole glanced with wild consternation at Jonas and Theo, neither of whom could, or would, help him. "Puh, puh, plays of
Sophocles? . . . I think . . . seven?" he stammered hopefully.

"Exactly, only seven. And only seven by Aeschylus. And many,
many as doubtless marvelous as those, Mr. Marsh, gone forever.
I should myself love to see far more of the editorial insights of
Aristophanes of Byzantium than I know I shall." The homely old
woman put down her fork and knife quietly. "For Time is a very
careless custodian of our little human history. . . ." And with a
sad grimace, she opened her hand, letting the image of irrevocable
loss fall through her withered fingers like sand.

"Bu, bu, but Raleigh's not an ancient Greek," said Mole Fontwell with warmth. "And, my word, you've made great Renaissance discoveries before."

Theo said, "And will again, sooner or later."

"Sooner, then." Dame Winifred smiled. "Later, I trust I shall
be making far more . . . wonderful discoveries." She tapped the
general vicinity of her high stomach, causing, back at the King
William Inn that night, a great deal of agitated discussion among
the three men as to whether her gesture, following such an ominously mysterious remark, referred to some terminal cancer or
fatal heart condition, or, on the other hand, had simply resulted
from indigestion after so much fatty grilled meat.

Further agitation followed. The moral unease that had festered
in Theo for weeks burst forth, and he confessed to "having second
thoughts" about playing this kind of a hoax on Miss Throckmorton at all.

He was, he told his friends, unable to go through with it. Each
day when the two of them had arrived at Saint Michael's, she'd
knelt quietly in a back pew for five minutes or so; her tam bent

down to the rail of the pew's back, her glasses slipped onto the edge of her praying hands, her old face squeezed with thoughtful struggle. And this sight had troubled Theo deeply. She'd told him once, as he helped her to her feet, that he shouldn't suppose she was praying to find the manuscript (which was just what he'd supposed). Rather, she was praying to be freed from the burden of wanting to find the manuscript in order to justify herself. "Regrettably," she confessed, "one does not retire as easily from ambition, envy, pride, and vengefulness, as one does from Oxford, where those emotions are so richly nurtured."

The elderly woman's words upset Theo more and more, and led finally to his outburst to Jonas and Mole about his "second thoughts." He felt, he said, that any good they might do by making Dame Winifred (and her detractors) believe she'd found a Raleigh play was not worth the risk of her pain (not to mention her contempt for them) if she saw through the forgery. Theo's collaborators strongly disagreed, and a long fight ensued.

Jonas said, "It's too late for second thoughts, or third or fifth or last." He spoke from the floor of the King William bedroom where he was doing sit-ups, his toes braced under a bureau. "*Foolscap* is no longer ours to disclaim, or—" He swiveled, hands behind his head, and looked at Theo. "Or to claim. Right, Mole?"

Mole glanced over from the bed, where he lay, in plaid bathrobe and slippers, biting his nails. "Umhm," he said.

"Well, I say we stop here. I for one feel like a real bastard." Theo held up the neat folders Jonas Marsh had organized for the approaching Cavendish London program. "We're teachers, we're scholars, Jonas! How can we pretend any good can come of forgery?"

"Any GOOD?" Jonas grunted through two more sit-ups, then crawled to his feet, tenderly rubbing his stomach. "To the Romans who forged the memoirs of Dares, that fabricated Trojan soldier, and Dictys, that equally suspicious combatant on the Greek side, we owe, don't we, the story of Troilus and Cressida? Is that not good? To Carlo Sigonio who in fifteen eighty-two forged the *Consolatio* of Cicero, we owe all the consolation it provided during the two hundred years before it was discovered to be a fake. That's good. The medieval poems poor bonkers Chatterton forged are good medieval poems." He swung his arms from side to side. "I could go on."

"Please don't," called Mole. "They were all found out."

"Your play," said Jonas, "is a very good play. No matter who or how many wrote it, or when they happened to do so. All that is simply how scholars earn a living by pissing out territory and then bickering over it."

Mole sighed, chewing on a cuticle. "Well, I say I'm glad we're doing it, if for no other reason than the Reverend Brakeshaw's condescension to Dame Winifred. It's awf'lly infuriating. We'll show him up properly!"

"There is that," Theo admitted.

Jonas said, "Ryan, we've gone too far to stop. You agreed that once I undertook this, no more questions. Didn't you make that pledge? Didn't you? Yes, you did. Well, we're going ahead. *I'm* going ahead, and you two sentimental cowardly lions are coming with me." He glowered at them until they lowered their eyes, then returned to his exercises.

"Theo," Mole said sweetly. "No sense in us fussing. With the construction going on, we couldn't get *Foolscap* out of there now if we tried."

"Ridiculous to think of it!" Jonas curled up like a hedgehog and began rolling back and forth on his back.

"And I'd *like* her to have this last triumph," Mole went on. "After the way they've all written her off."

Jonas spluttered. "Now, be honest, Mole! *You* want the triumph of tricking your old teacher!"

"That's not fair!" The small man sat up, brushing the black bangs from his forehead. "Oh, I do suppose I would like her to see I did have more, don't you know, imagination, and, all right, daring, than she suspected."

Theo picked up one of Dame Winifred's books, *Puritanism and the Early Modern Theatre*, from Mole's stack of research materials. "I think he wants Miss Throckmorton to triumph too, Jonas. And it's true; look how the search has invigorated her."

"Hasn't it!" Mole knelt up on the bed, exclaiming, " 'How dull it is to pause, to make an end, / To rust unburnished, not to shine in use!' "

"Mole!" Jonas Marsh warned.

" 'Made weak by time and fate, but strong in will/To strive, to seek, to find, and not to yield.' "

"My GOD," shouted Jonas, running to clap his hand over Mole's mouth. "He's started on the Victorians! Worse, worse than Bleats and Jelly."

Mole removed the hand, and said, "It's Fortune's call, Theo. Either Dame Winifred believes it's real, or she doesn't. Either they find the manuscript or they don't." And settling into his pillow, he picked up his anthology of British poetry. "Tennyson, anyone?"

"I still feel like a bastard," Theo sighed. "All right. Here's the deal. If it looks as if she's going to make a public statement that could embarrass her later, then we tell her privately. All right?"

Jonas kicked at the bed leg. "She'd be the first to admit that if she *does* get fooled, she *deserved* to get fooled."

"That's the deal, Jonas."

Jonas raised his eyebrows, growled, shook his head, yanked at his hair, and nodded.

CHAPTER
31

{General Alarum}

For the love of the lie itself.

Sir Francis Bacon

THE CONSTRUCTION workers found the manuscript two weeks later. It was far from the first of their finds. Saint Michael's had been left structurally unrestored for so long that at almost every blow of the sledgehammer, every prise of the claw, there tumbled out, if not old treasure, at least antiquated trash. Among a dump heap of other debris, the crew unearthed an embroidered hawking glove, a pewter candlestick, an eighteenth-century sheep clipper, a rotted cope with gold threads, and a black biretta green with mold. They came across assorted bones (some of them human), and assorted bits of iron, glass, and crockery (most of it not as old as everyone hoped). Behind the great drawers of an armoire for clerical vestments, they found a 1702 edition of Izaak Walton's *The Compleat Angler,* lost there perhaps by some fishing enthusiast of a minister who'd rushed from his favorite bank of the Urswick just in time to throw down rod and creel, and fling on chasuble, alb, and stole.

Used as a leveler in the bracing legs of the pulpit steps they found two high Anglican tomes: *A Safeway to Salvation* by William Chillingworth, chaplain to the Royalist Army, and a 1627 collection of seven sermons on the divine rights of kings by John Cosins, rector of Brancepeth. The symbology of the use to which these particular books had been put greatly amused Dame Winifred, for reasons Mr. Brakeshaw could not fathom (even when she gave him a hint: "Royalists used as levelers for a Puritan pulpit, ho ho?"), and which he therefore dismissed as further hysteria.

To the great happiness of its rector, Saint Michael's proved to have hoarded symbols more transparently valuable than irony. Secreted under the stones of the sacristy was a small cache of high sacramental implements, vessels for the host and holy oil, including a gold ampulla, a eucharistic pyx, and a scribonium with sapphires in it. Even though, before anyone else saw it, one of the masons had pocketed a little monstrance (either because it contained somebody's sanctified finger bone, or because it was solid silver and sprinkled with pearls), the three remaining antiques sent Mr. Brakeshaw into a delerium. Like a gambling addict on a roll in Reno, he now expected King Tut's tomb every day; he looked for tax chests packed with Spanish gold in the bell tower, and the Holy Grail under a pew. Workers complained that they could scarcely tug on a crowbar without tripping over the old parson; he shoved his head into any cavity they created before they could even pull out their hammers, and the crowds he was inviting in to watch their work made it impossible for them to do any.

After the visiting bishop was beaned by a piece of falling plaster, and the Earl of Newbolt fell in a hole where he'd expected the altar steps, the contractor (raising the specter of million-pound lawsuits) convinced the rector to ban these guest parties, but only a lack of more ready cash (and the Countess of Newbolt's reluctance to supply it) kept Mr. Brakeshaw from telling the crew to dismantle the entire church stone by numbered stone, and look for another Sutton Hoo underneath.

Brakeshaw was not cooled even by any embarrassment he'd felt at having erroneously told the local paper that the hidden altar objects were Jacobean Anglican, buried under the sacristy just before the Civil War. When corrected by Dame Winifred in front of a pimply teenaged reporter (the objects were early Tudor Catholic, secreted when Henry VIII had snatched the nearby convent from its Dawbney abbess), Brakeshaw was entirely unshaken, and said, "These are matters for men who are experts in these matters. It remains a question of some debate."

It was not until September 29 that the little Tudor chest, its lid a carving of Saint Michael standing with his foot on a dead dragon's head, was discovered when the west choir stall was temporarily removed. Inside this chest were two 1604 prayer books, an Elizabethan shilling, and a bound folio containing a manuscript of a play called *Foolscap*. That the discovery was made on the church's own name day, Michaelmas, the Feast of Saint Michael and All the Angels, struck some as a miracle and others as just a coincidence. That the organist was practicing (or trying to, with half the organ draped in drop cloths) a Magnificat by another Elizabethan, William Byrd (who'd undoubtedly even met Raleigh), struck at least the organist as proof that he was deeply attuned to great spiritual forces from the past. That the psalm for the day was 139, *Domine probasti*, "Oh Lord thou hast searched me out and known me. Thou knowst my down-sitting and my up-rising; thou understandest my thoughts long before," caused Theo Ryan to break out into a sweat when he saw it on the morning service program (where Dame Winifred Throckmorton had jotted the exact time and date on which she'd opened the vellum commonplace book).

Summoned by her telephone call, Theo had rushed back to Devon as soon as Mole and he had tracked down Jonas and as soon as Jonas finished flogging twenty-five Cavendish undergraduates through the National Portrait Gallery (where the Armada portrait of Raleigh seemed to stare at Theo with cynical reproach). By the time the three arrived at Saint Michael's on Urswick, so had the press.

At 9:45 that morning, the chest had been brought straight over by the contractor to Dame Winifred, who happened then to be at her prayers in the back of the nave, having just arrived at the church. By chance, Mr. Brakeshaw wasn't there; after morning prayers, he (and a hired security guard) had taken the ampulla, pyx, and scribonium to London, and he wasn't scheduled to return until evening. But the young contractor would have brought anything with books in it to Dame Winifred anyhow; he'd known her for years from Bourne House, and though she was in his opinion "loop-de-loop," he liked her, and he didn't like the rector. He'd liked her enough to be concerned by her behavior when she opened the thin bound folio. Her breath caught, color left her face. Carefully but quickly she turned the pages, front to back, tilted them to the light, held the glass of her spectacles close to the ink.

She swayed slightly in the pew, just once, then she sat there upright and entirely motionless, her eyes closed, not speaking, not responding to the contractor's asking if she were all right, not moving in any way at all except that finally a spill of tears fell from the corner of her eye; one dropped into the dust on the book's vellum cover.

The date of the discovery, Dame Winifred was too skeptical to take as miraculous, but she did tell Theo that it felt like a wry sign from God (and from Raleigh, if God and Raleigh were on speaking terms) that on September 29, her hand should first open that folio, and first see the words, "Writ by Sr. Walt. R. in Bloody Tower & preserv'd by Lady Ralegh his Wife after his martyrdom. Called by him Foolscap, A Short Comedie." For Saint Michael's name day had always been significant in Dame Winifred's life; Michaelmas was the first day of term at Oxford where she'd spent so many decades, and Michaelmas was her birthday, her eightieth.

By evening the little stone chapel by the river Urswick was fuller than it had been in many a sadly secular year. The (very few) parishioners who'd come by regular habit to pray, and the few more who'd come because it was a Holy Feast Day, were amazed to see what looked like a party going on in their house of worship. Even more amazed when he arrived in a taxi was the Reverend Steven Brakeshaw, whose heart at first almost went up in flames at the envious supposition that his part-time curate had drawn a crowd like this for an evensong prayer service. The photogenic Earl and Countess of Newbolt, both in lovely cashmere suits, were there with their four children (including Willie Stanlow, the earl-to-be, who filmed the whole scene with his camcorder). The Marquess of Dawbney (in torn pullover, stained corduroys, and enormous wellingtons) was there with his three springer spaniels tied to a tree outside. The construction crew was there, lounging by the riverbank, eating Big Macs from the new McDonald's in the next town. The rector spotted Dame Winifred Throckmorton there with the big American and his peculiar friends. They were chatting with the *London Times.* And the BBC.

When the rector found out *why* they were all there, he quickly scooted to the vestry, changed into his newest surplice, did the best he could to cover his scalp with the few strands of hair left to him, and returned to be interviewed. In slow sonorous tones, he told the BBC that it was he who'd first put Dame Winifred Throckmorton onto the possibility of there having been a Raleigh manuscript hidden somewhere on the premises of Saint Michael's; he then launched into a garbled anecdote in which Raleigh's "heretical wife Carew" and "Catholic terrorists" figured prominently. Dame Winifred's exasperated sideline snorts at this historical mishmash, the rector took to be hyperventilation from emotional upheaval, and he instructed the old scholar to sit down and put her head between her legs.

Asked by the BBC whether he believed the manuscript to be a genuine Raleigh play, Mr. Brakeshaw (who hadn't clapped eyes on it) said he hadn't a doubt in the world.

Dame Winifred was not nearly as forthcoming about the play's authenticity. "It's certainly not in Raleigh's hand," she said. "It looks like a secretarial transcription in the style of sixteen twenty or thirty. It is possible it is a copy of a Raleigh original, one which the family (or others) had made for themselves sometime after Raleigh's death. But of course, I couldn't possibly say, without further study." She went on to explain why and how she'd spent a decade looking for such a play, and why and how this might, or might not, be it. She paused, squinting into the lights. "I'm sorry, young man? I'm afraid I don't quite follow your, your hieroglyphics — "

The youthful BBC reporter was making all sorts of rapid gestures at Dame Winifred, telling her via these facial contortions and hand signals to face the camera, smile, speak louder, speak faster, lower her voice, hold up the book, come to a conclusion. Willie Stanlow filmed the BBC filming her, and did a close-up of her shaking her finger at their camera, piping, "Young man, stand still! You're muddling me with all your whirring about."

The BBC decided to leave these remarks in the segment they

aired; it sounded so quintessentially like what they'd decided to say she was: "A legendary Oxford figure, a scholar from the old golden days of textual criticism, famous for her brilliance, and cherished by generations of Oxonians for her high spirits and unconventionality."

To Reverend Brakeshaw's chagrin, the news showed a nice shot of Saint Michael's, but gave not a single second's worth of his own interview; instead there was a clip of a former student of Dame Winifred's, now an illustrious gray-haired Renaissance professor at Cambridge. He said that if Dame Winifred were to tell him *Ralph Roister Doister* was by Sir Walter Raleigh, he wasn't sure but what he'd believe her. So if she said this *Foolscap* was Raleigh's, by God it was Raleigh's.

But that was exactly what she wasn't saying, at least not yet. Dame Winifred told the press that she wouldn't say it *wasn't* by Raleigh, but neither could she commit herself beyond doubt to say that it was. Theo never took his eyes from her face, but though an excellent reader, he couldn't interpret her expression.

"Dear Freddie! Good for you!" cooed the svelte, blonde Andie Stanlow, Countess of Newbolt, as she bent to kiss the old scholar's cheek.

"Dear, dear Freddie! *Very* good for you" crooned the svelte, ruddy Horry Stanlow, Earl of Newbolt, as he bowed to kiss the old scholar's hand, and to remove from it the vellum folio. He walked out of Saint Michael's with the manuscript under his arm, and did it with such an assumption of baronial privilege that no one stopped him. The Marquess of Urswick would have tried, but he'd had the congenital bad luck to be outside trying to breakup a fight between his three spaniels and the rector's bulldog while Stanlow was in the church. Dame Winifred even went home to Bourne with the Stanlows, so they could lock *Foolscap* in his temperature-controlled library safe. It was hard, Jonas Marsh later noted, to say who was made more apoplectic by the news that Newbolt had commandeered the great literary find—Brakeshaw or the Marquess of Urswick. Both of them helplessly tangled in the moil of leashed dogs, they shouted repeatedly that the earl should be stopped and brought back. ("And shot!" the marquess added. "Bloody Stanlows!") No one obeyed them.

While Dame Winifred appeared reluctant to make up her mind about the authorship of *Foolscap,* other interested parties were less so. Over the next week, while Theo, Jonas, and Mole waited fretfully by their London phones, photostats of the play were made, and then the thin folio volume was subjected to a battery of tests by a battery of impartial experts brought to Bourne House for that purpose. As far as technical criteria went, the text passed (or as Theo said, Mole and Jonas passed) with a resounding cry of "genuinely Jacobean." But which Jacobean? The great Raleigh or not? Far more than they had anticipated, the fact that Dame Winifred Throckmorton thought it *might* be by Raleigh was enough to set off other scholars one way or the other. The debate began the day the discovery made the front page of the *Times*—on both sides of the Atlantic. In the months to come, when copies of *Foolscap* began circulating, the grove of academe blazed with a heated controversy whose flame would burn for years.

Absolutement oui, said one eminent expert, from France. "No way," said another, from California. "Unmistakably Raleigh," affirmed a committee of six officers of an international Renaissance society. Five members immediately resigned in protest. "Not a very good play, but it is Raleigh's," claimed the illustrious gray-haired Renaissance professor at Cambridge; "Brilliant, but it is not Raleigh's," rebutted an equally illustrious gray-haired professor at Oxford. A scholar in Scotland was convinced that *Foolscap* was a forgery from the Commonwealth period, possibly by William Davenant, designed to enhance the reputation of Raleigh as an ur antimonarchist revolutionary. "Idiotic," said his colleagues.

A few of the Baconians (so called because they believed Sir Francis Bacon had written all of Shakespeare's plays) thought Bacon had written *Foolscap* as well. Several who were sure the Earl of Oxford was Shakespeare, were equally sure he was also the Raleigh who'd written *Foolscap.* The post-Baconians (convinced that *Hamlet* was Edward de Vere's autobiography) attempted to demonstrate that Raleigh in *Foolscap* was none other than that same melancholy Dane de Vere. The Marloweans (who believed that young Christopher Marlowe had not gotten killed in a knife fight after all, but had gone into hiding and written all of Shakespeare's plays instead of any more of his own) were unanimous in *not* believing that Marlowe had written *Foolscap*. The text lacked that *je ne sais quoi* that was Marlowe (and Marlowe pretending to be Shakespeare). And as for the Raleigheans (who believed that Sir Walter Raleigh had written all of Shakespeare's plays), they broke into terrible factions over whether or not to claim *Foolscap* (either for Raleigh as Raleigh, or Raleigh as Shakespeare, or neither); heated remarks were made in haste, not repented at leisure, and finally the society's annual banquet had to be postponed until a time when enough members were willing to sit down next to each other to make it possible to serve the meal in one building.

Jane Nash-Gantz was asked her opinion of *Foolscap* on the *Today Show*, where she was supposed to be talking, with three other preeminently successful career/family women, about "Long-Distance Marriage." Her opinion was: Who cared which Dead White European Male had written *Foolscap*? "I mean, do we really *care*?" She certainly didn't. Now if they'd found a new Jacobean play by a *woman* . . .

Two female assistant professors in New Haven, both up for tenure, fell into a shouting match during a conference panel, with one backing Elizabeth Carey, Viscountess of Falkland, as the author of *Foolscap,* and the other pushing the notion that Lady Raleigh had written it herself after her husband's execution. Their public fight quickly became so famous that the two young women were offered high-paying full professorships at the same California university; on discovering which, Yale tenured them both.

Through all this academic hoopla, no announcement of any sort came from Dame Winifred, who spent her days in the Bourne library studying the play, and her nights working with a computer analysis of the vocabulary of Raleigh's *History of the World*. But long before the spread of what came to be called "The *Foolscap* Question," indeed by October 10, Horry Stanlow, the ninth Earl of Newbolt, had not only declared the manuscript authentically Raleigh's, he'd declared it definitely his (and had shown a freshly inked copyright form to prove it). At the same time, he'd announced his intention to have the contents of the play professionally produced on the London stage, while the manuscript itself was to be enshrined in the great Newbolt Collection at Bourne

House. The earl said that *Foolscap* belonged to him because he was a direct descendent of the Francis Stanlow who'd bought it from Sir Walter Raleigh's son. He cited Dame Winifred's articles on the subject.

By October 14, Gordon Dawbney, Marquess of Urswick, had filed an injunction against Horry Stanlow enjoining him from doing anything with either the dramatic contents or the physical artifact of *Foolscap*. The marquess said *Foolscap* was his, because he was a direct descendant of the Robert Dawbney who'd befriended Raleigh in the Tower, and had obviously attempted to preserve Raleigh's play from Royalist destruction by hiding it in Saint Michael's, where it had somehow been misplaced, mixed in with some discarded prayer books, and lost for centuries behind the choir stall. He cited Dame Winifred's essay on Mad Rob Dawbney, the Puritan earl.

A second suit was threatened by the theatrical producers to whom Stanlow had already optioned *Foolscap* as soon as they heard they couldn't proceed with production because they'd bought the rights to something from someone who didn't have the right to sell them.

The Urswick camp scored heavily when the private Tudor travel chest in which the volume had been found proved to be in fact embossed on its latch with the Dawbney imprese, *Meo Volente*. (This freakish coincidence turned Mole Fontwell an alarming hue of green when he heard it. It was as if, he said—entirely spooked—everything really *had* happened just as he'd imagined it.)

The Newbolt camp fought back by producing the very receipt of sale to Francis Stanlow for "books, volumes, & papers that belonged to my late father," signed by Carew Ralegh.

The marquess then produced records proving that when Mad Rob Dawbney had died in Saint Michael's, he'd been hiding out there and had with him a sealskin chest; court records proved that Dawbney had refused to relinquish property taken from Stanlow Lodge, some of which was kept in a sealskin chest and included "gilt jugs, hangings of imagery, a striking clock, and divers books of great value."

The earl retaliated with a copy of a letter from Raleigh's friend, the great scientist Thomas Harriott, to Bess Throckmorton in which "a bundle of plaies belonging to yr. late husban" was mentioned.

The Earl of Newbolt and the Marquess of Urswick grew so engrossed in their battle, they were slow to notice any new foe on the field. Then Newbolt was suddenly served with a warrant for having stolen property belonging to the Church of England. A valuable manuscript, said the warrant, had been illegally removed from Saint Michael's Church, in whose possession it had been for more than three hundred years. No matter (said the Church) who had left the book in the church, no matter what family may have built the church, no matter what other family may have handed out the rectorship to whomever they pleased for a few hundred years. None had any rights now in the church *in situ* or any otherwise. The book was found in the church, had been in the church a very long time, clearly *belonged* to the church. And the church claimed it, just as it claimed the 1604 prayer books, and the fifteenth-century gold ampulla. When he filed his suit, by "church" Mr. Brakeshaw meant Saint Michael's-on-Urswick. When the bishop told Mr. Brakeshaw to step aside and let the church handle this—by "church," the bishop meant the capital "C" *Church*. The Church which paid the rector's salary and owned the house he lived in.

By the time that capital "C" Church finished skimming its take off the top of the Sotheby's auction of the altar objects to the British Museum, and the books to a private collector, little Saint Michael's got only 30p on the pound. Mr. Brakeshaw was told by his bishop that the Church was graciously generous to give Saint Michael's that much, and for that much Mr. Brakeshaw would of course offer daily prayers of thanksgiving with a grateful heart.

It took two months of this wrangling before the three major parties (earl, marquess, and Church), in a protracted conference, with their solicitors present, agreed to postpone their disagreement in order to capitalize on the current press attention the play was getting because of "the *Foolscap* Question," before the chariot of Fame moved on to stir up the next flurry of dust. They therefore decided to allow the producers to whom Stanlow had optioned the work to move ahead with their production. Any profits would be held in escrow until the question of the ownership of *Foolscap* could be settled.

From London the three forgers followed all of this in the papers. Jonas and Mole were delighted by the great brouhaha. Each new academic battle, each new aristocratic challenge, set them happily pounding with their palms on the breakfast table at Brown's. "By God, we did it!" said Jonas, and rubbed his face in a joyful frenzy. "Ryan, congratulations!"

"Well done! Well done!" Mole pumped Theo's hand with both of his.

But Theo was still waiting.

And Dame Winifred was still declining to say anything more than "It certainly sounds like Walter Raleigh, doesn't it, Theo?"

CHAPTER
32

{They All Enter the Circle}

I have a long journey and must bid the company farewell.

Sir Walter Raleigh, on the scaffold

"SCOTTIE SMITH?!" Theo gagged. "They've hired Scottie Smith to direct *Foolscap*?"

"Shh shh shh!" The theatrical agent Josef "Buzzy" Middendorf, an ebullient, vain, and foppish man of seventy, wiggled his small pink ringed fingers to shush the big American.

"Buzzy, are you serious?"

"It's vonderful," the agent said in his carefully maintained Bavarian accent. "Scottie izz one of my clients. I flew in on the dead eye from New York to make the deal. My appearance, forgive it. I'm sweating like a dog. To tell you the truth, I'm on death's bed." Middendorf coughed into a paisley handkerchief, and asked his receptionist, Miss Fitzhugh, if she happened to have any "old Vics." With a wink at Theo, she reached into a drawer of her black lacquered desk and found her employer some cough drops.

It was the middle of November. Theo had come to the agency to discuss the Rexford estate, but in the small talk that followed his business meeting with Buzzy, the subject of *Foolscap* had naturally come up—because, on Theo's recommendation, the Earl of Newbolt had engaged Middendorf to represent that play. Lord Stanlow—while quite up-to-date on many things, from ballroom dancing to crowd-management in Bourne's new self-serve restaurant—knew so little about the theatre that he'd expressed his desire to have either Richard Burton, James Mason, or Laurence Olivier play Sir Walter Raleigh in *Foolscap*. The sad news that all three of these fine actors had passed away unsettled the earl, and he made his subsequent suggestions with a wistful tentativeness that the play's producers found too easy to ignore. Thus, on his son Willie's urging, Lord Stanlow had turned to Theo Ryan for "theatrical advice"; Theo had sent him to Middendorf, and as a result the young American was in on the play's progress. For example, he met the five British producers of *Foolscap* soon after they'd optioned it. His first response was relief that none of them had anything to do with "W.F.D.," the producer to whom Ford had sent "The Raleigh Play" last spring—from whom nothing was ever heard, confirming Theo's hypothesis that the man had never looked at the script. His second response was surprise that every one of these producers was younger than Theo was.

The five producers, who had been in the Footlights Club at Cambridge together, were a little difficult to distinguish from one another, except that three were male and two were female, and except that the one named Cynthia Lewis-Bristol disagreed with everything, and the one named Polo Burr paid for everything, carrying so many hundreds of pounds loose in the pockets of his vicuña Italian overcoat that Jonas Marsh decided he was a yuppie organized crime racketeer. (Mr. Burr was flattered when he heard this.) The five producers were all in their early thirties; they all had rich hair and wore rich clothes, and cared very much about what they ate, and where they ate it. Like their American cohorts, they were all very involved with their personal fitness, and discussed issues like binding-fibers, natural endorphins, and their psycho-ecology in a self-confident talkative manner.

But that they knew much more about show business than the Earl of Newbolt himself, Theo would have doubted, had he not been told that two of them had already been vice-presidents of British film corporations, and the other three had already produced a musical based on the entire forty novels of Balzac's *La Comédie humaine*, which was soon to open in the West End. These five handsome young people had told the earl they were full of daring ideas and good contacts, and that seemed to clinch their qualifications for producing *Foolscap*. (Apart, of course, from their being absolutely mad about the play, and one of the women's being a cousin of "Andie" Stanlow, the Countess of Newbolt.)

The contacts part proved true; they had the entire play read out by old Footlights friends of theirs in the Mayfair sitting room of Polo's great-aunt, and while this ancient creature and friends of hers dozed off occasionally during the reading, they awakened at the conclusion and wrote out checks totaling £75,000. As soon as they did so, the relatives (and their friends) of the other producers all wanted to be backers of *Foolscap* too, and they wrote out more checks, and soon there were plenty of checks with which to put on the play. The producers even announced that there was Hollywood interest in the project, and at that news, even more checks came in. As for the ideas, Polo Burr's idea of trying to cast Robin Williams as Raleigh and Madonna as Queen Elizabeth was admittedly daring, but to his disappointment, the two stars passed on the project. (Cynthia Lewis-Bristol had told him they would, and should.) Horribly enough, his second idea, to get Scottie Smith to direct the play, worked out. And that was what Theo was just learning from Buzzy Middendorf beneath the Klimt frieze in the opulent fin-de-siècle waiting room of the London agency.

"Scottie had his show finished at the Barbicon, and he meets Mr. Burr, and he likes Mr. Burr—" Middendorf shrugged as if to say this is how the world works, and Theo thought, I bet!, for Polo Burr looked exactly as one might suppose a young man would who was called "Polo." The old pink, plump little agent straightened a Kokoschka *Kunstschau* poster, as he went on to explain, "Scottie didn't want to be haggled, and these boys and girls didn't haggle; well, the Lewis-Bristol one haggled some. I gave them a ball-point figure, just off the top of my hat. Outrageous, this figure. They don't blink an eye. Out they wrote the first check, just like that. We ironed it up in one day. Miss Fitzhugh, my darling, help my poor eyes!"

Theo glared down at the agent, who was now tilted over, squeezing eye drops handed him by his receptionist into his bloodshot eyes. "But do they know how to produce?" the American said.

"So what is it? Producing is writing checks," said Middendorf, tears running from his eyes. "When pinch comes to shove."

Theo shook his head. "It's their judgment. I don't think Scottie Smith's at all a good choice to direct *Foolscap*. Not at all."

"Theo, excuse me, but there's not a moment's element of truth in what you say. He is perfect." Middendorf finished with the eye drops, and took the antihistamine Miss Fitzhugh was holding out. "He loves this play. He's been at it twenty-four hours a day, twelve days a week. Working with the designers. Casting. Don't forget, he pulpited to fame doing Shakespeare. And this is close."

"Well," shrugged the author of *Foolscap*. "I wouldn't go that far."

"You're kind to take the interest, Theo. But I tell you Smith's smart as a button. This *Foolscap* is going to be a hit. Already I can smell the crowd mulling about. Now, tell me—" Middendorf suddenly opened his cerise silk jacket, and patted his stomach. "Am I fatter than you saw me last?"

Miss Fitzhugh grinned again at Theo behind the agent's back. "Tell him he looks grand," she advised.

"Thinner. I would definitely say so." Theo nodded politely. Buzzy Middendorf had always seemed equally overweight to him.

"No, I am fat. I've gouged myself in America, that's why I'm fat. I should join weight lifters. I was never fat before. But Miss Fitzhugh—" He trotted around the desk and kissed her hand. "—will put me on a terrible diet, and make me thin again. She winds me around her little clock, Theo."

"Come along with you, Mr. Middendorf," the receptionist laughed, deftly removing her fingers from his clasp. "I never."

"Theo, you must tell me!" Middendorf squeezed the young man's large hand. "Where iz der play of yours?"

"What play?" But immediately Theo realized that of course Buzzy (and everyone else he'd gone yelling to about Ford's stealing his play) was wondering where and what that play might be. Well, he asked himself; what might it be? It couldn't be *Foolscap*. It couldn't be *Aesthetic Distance*. It had to be something new.

Middendorf wriggled his short fat fingers as if he were going to tickle Theo. "You and Ford were writing a play, you said. He took it away. I want to read that play. You have it back?"

Theo thought for a moment, then smiled. "Yes, I have it. But it needs a lot of work."

"About what is it?"

"I can't tell you."

For now, that was certainly true. But it occurred to Theo that he'd think of something. Why not? Maybe there was more than one play in him after all.

Miss Fitzhugh was saying, "I.C.M. on line two, Mr. Middendorf."

The agent hurried towards one of the doors off the waiting room. "Hugs to Bernie. My hat goes out to him. All those movie sales for Ford! And such a shame Ford can't enjoy the money. How he spent money! Like a fish! Theo, I want to see that play. Bye-bye."

"About Scottie Smith, Buzzy—"

But Middendorf slipped away back to his satin-stuffed office without further response to Theo's concerns about Scottie Smith. After all, as far as the agent knew, Theo had no connection to *Foolscap*, other than the useful one of having recommended his agency to the Earl of Newbolt. But even if he had known that Theo was the author, he would have still slipped away without listening. Authors counted for little in the packages Josef Middendorf was famous for tying together; on *Foolscap*, for example, he represented the script, the director, five of the actors, two of the designers, and he owned ten percent of the theatre in which the play was going to be performed. Knowing how to tie knots, and how to slip out of them, had made him the most successful theatrical agent in town.

To this theatre, near Leicester Square, Theo began going to watch Scottie Smith direct *Foolscap*. He went, as a child might keep riding a Ferris wheel that made him sick every time, but from the top of which, the world was beautiful. First of all, he had trouble getting into the theatre. Scottie Smith's assistant told him the rehearsals were closed to outsiders. Only the intervention of the Earl of Newbolt forced the director to make an exception in Theo's case. Second, he was as invisible once he did get inside as if he'd stayed out on the sidewalk. While he'd been convinced that he'd long ago done the emotional work necessary to give up *Foolscap* as his own, he quickly discovered during these early rehearsals that this was by no means entirely the case; he was often in a

torment at having to sit there ignored, unable to correct the misinterpretation of his meaning or the misreading of his lines. He
would have to bite his lip to avoid calling out things like "Raleigh's
being ironic there!" or "That line has to be said to seduce the
queen, not to *whine* at her: 'I am a hawk tied to your glove, but
bred for higher flying. Loosen me, and see.'"

On the other hand, nothing could have kept Theo away from
the thrill of seeing his characters incarnate, hearing their words
in human flesh. Nothing, not even Scottie Smith, could kill that
pleasure.

Scottie Smith was no older than his five producers, and no bigger than Thayer Iddesleigh (a fact that Iddy, back home in Rome
in his black silk Bob Fosse pajamas, might have been pleased to
hear), but unlike the Cavendish band director, the famous Scottie
Smith knew better than to emulate the styles of past great ones,
and he dressed like no other director before him, except possibly
Sarah Bernhardt. For the *Foolscap* rehearsals he wore white knee
pants, and a quilted black jacket as iridescent as an oil spill. He
also wore red wooden clogs that sounded like slamming shutters
as he skidded down the aisle towards the stage without so much
as a glance in Theo's direction, and shouted at the actors, "Good
morning, you abstracts and brief chronicles of the time! Hi ho,
it's off to WORK we skiddle!"

But, then, the news from Buzzy Middendorf that Theo was not
only the earl's adviser but also Ford Rexford's literary executor
(with say in who would ever get a chance to direct any revivals of
any Rexford plays) reached Smith. Suddenly he noticed Theo
seated in the empty auditorium. Having seen him, he took to
waving at coffee breaks, and then to inviting Professor Ryan to
comment as a Renaissance scholar on textual ambiguities in *Foolscap*. "I'd be happy to," said Theo, and showed up the next morning with a twenty-page list of suggestions. "Pow! Zap! What a
LOT!" said Smith, who tended to talk at times like a comic book,
and at other times like essays in *Diacritics*.

It had been immediately clear that Scottie Smith had no memory
of Theo from that horrible (and admittedly crowded) playwriting
workshop so many years ago, no memory at all of Theo's having
submitted a play anything like the one Smith now so worshipfully

referred to as "Raleigh's last testament." He did say that from the first moment he'd read *Foolscap* he had felt as if he'd known the play forever, but he'd attributed that feeling to the "spine-jabbing alchemy of individuated genius and cultural familiarity that means masterpiece." This was the way Smith talked when he wasn't talking like Action Comics. Critics loved him. Academics loved him too because he was always consulting them about textual accuracy, and would make half-a-dozen long-distance phone calls to Shakespeare scholars to decide, for instance, whether, in *Othello,* he should go with Desdemona's saying, "Then Lord have mercy on me," as in Quarto 1, or instead he should have her say, "O Heaven have mercy on me," as in the Folio.

"Ah," Theo said to Smith, during one of the coffee breaks. "This is how you do it then. You do nothing to the words, and absolutely anything you want to with everything else."

"You got it!" Smith smiled.

"But that only works with plays whose texts have the power of their canonical status."

"That's a lot of power." Smith smiled. It was his claim that the text of a master (like Shakespeare, or Raleigh) was inviolate, and the director's contribution "merely conceptual" — a "merely" with which he certainly ran, setting *Othello* on a riverboat, with Iago as the Interlocutor in a minstrel show; and staging *Hamlet* (of which he'd allowed not a single syllable to be cut) as a saga of Nazi collaboration in Denmark, with Fortinbras's army as the Allied invasion.

As a result, Theo found himself in the bizarre position of suggesting a large cut in *Foolscap,* only to have the director accuse him of blasphemy. The further irony was that last year this particular scene had been one that Theo had insisted on keeping for its thematic relevance, despite Ford's telling him, "Lose it. It won't play, kid." Now, hearing the scene on the stage, Theo felt compelled to suggest to Scottie Smith that it didn't play, only to be told by the director that it was a "crucial link in the thematic grid."

The actress playing Elizabeth happened to be the R.S.C. star who'd been Cleopatra in Stratford the night Rexford died. (In fact, a number of times at rehearsal breaks, in Theo's hearing, she told

the story of Ford's final night, always beautifully.) Buzzy Middendorf had talked this woman (also his client) into taking the part
in *Foolscap*, although Elizabeth didn't come on until Act II, and
even when she did, she wasn't quite sure what she came on *as*. "If
this is sixteen eighteen, I've been dead for fifteen years," she kept
telling Smith.

"Don't be so literal," he advised her.

"Am I a ghost, or what?"

"You're a memory, darling."

"A flashback?"

"No, no, NO. A thought."

"I'm a thought? How do I play a thought?"

"Not so *fleshily*," he suggested.

Scottie Smith and the actress were not getting along. One day,
he stopped rehearsal and told her bluntly, "You're not giving me
what I want."

"I'm giving you what you *get*." The great actress, hands ominously on hip bones, shouted it into the dark theatre. "What *exactly* is your objection?"

"That you're playing Elizabeth with all the cynical ennui of
Mother Courage in a brothel."

"Ah. . . . What would you know about *women* in a brothel?"

Smith smirked. "Don't be bitchy." Down the aisle he came
clattering in his clogs. "I want the repression, the insecurity as
well as the ballsy power. I want sexual fear. Let's remember *why*
Elizabeth was called the VIRGIN queen, can we? I know it's a
stretch for you, darling, but try to think back to whenever you
were one—say, aged nine or ten?"

"That's it!" The actress's script flew all over the stage. It took
Buzzy Middendorf two days to reconcile the two.

During the weeks of rehearsal, Smith became quite friendly with
Theo, and even invited him to sit in on concept-strategy sessions,
as he called them: What this meant was a session where his strategy
was to tell everyone else how he'd arrived at a concept, and then
showed them the set they'd have to build to go with it. "Everyone"
did not include the actors, who were best left out of creative deci-
sions. The director's concept for *Foolscap* was not, of course, to
stage it where it took place, in the Tower of London in 1617, with

flashbacks to represent Raleigh's restagings (and rewritings) of his past. Instead, Smith had wanted (as always) something hot and now. He'd toyed for a while with the notion of playing Raleigh as a type of Solzhenitsyn in a Siberian gulag. He explained why to the roomful of what he called "Foolscappers." Four of the five producers listened to him as reverently as they did to their cassettes of New Age spiritual counseling. The fifth, Cynthia Lewis-Bristol, said periodically, "I'm not following you," in a tone that implied she didn't care to, either.

Smith sat on (not in) his chair at the head of the conference table: "I thought, after all," he said, "Raleigh was an *author*, condemned for his ideas. The writer-as-political-dissident imprisoned, even executed, for challenging the state. It has deep contemporary resonance." But Smith (as a great believer in the "readiness is all," or the "hot and now") confessed that on further thought he'd seen "a grando problemo," and had ultimately decided that the gulag was an idea whose time had come and gone. "Torturing writers has an early eighties feel to it," he told the producers.

Cynthia Lewis-Bristol said, "I'm not following you."

Nowadays, Smith explained, with a playwright president of Czechoslovakia, and Russian poets judging beauty contests in Moscow, and even South Africa trying to improve its PR, really, where could he set *Foolscap* as a prison for dissenting writers, except maybe China or Cuba?

"I don't see Raleigh as Chinese," said Cynthia Lewis-Bristol, a little too wryly, for one of her co-producers felt compelled to warn her with a pointed finger against (presumably) further sarcasm.

"Or Cuban especially," Cynthia added, undeterred.

Scottie Smith thought about this awhile. "Cuba. Orinoco. Raleigh does say . . . what is it, about the Indians?"

Theo called from his seat off to the side, " 'I could have been King of the Indians. My name still lives among them.' "

Smith yanked on his spiky hair as if trying to make himself taller. "Zounds! Wowie!" he said. "I'm impressed, Dr. Ryan. How'd you get to know this play so well so fast?"

"He's got a photogenic memory," Buzzy Middendorf suggested.

"Dr. Ryan, what do you think of Cuba?"

"Not much."

The director clicked his little red clogs together. "You're right. The more I think about Cuba, the more I see Spider Woman and Evita plastered all over it." No, Smith continued, the artist politicized was as passé as the artist problematized. The nineties were going to "interiorize the artist," existential depression and aesthetic decadence and apocalyptic anticipation were going to turn the artist back on himself in the old fifties fashion, but new and hot. The real prison was of course individuation itself; the death sentence, the inescapable solipsistic center and circumference of reality was going to be! . . .

And here, Scottie whipped off the cloth cover from a box on the big table, and revealed a scale model of a set. It looked like (with all its electric circuits and complex machinery) the inside of a space capsule. But what it was, according to Scottie Smith, was the inside of Sir Walter Raleigh's brain.

And it was there—with all the characters who played Raleigh's different memories color-coded to match the neurons that had sparked them off—it was there, in that brilliant Renaissance brain, that *Foolscap* was to take place. We would literally see Raleigh's thoughts.

". . . No comments?" asked Smith, tapping his silver nose-stud as he glanced around the quiet room.

Only Cynthia Lewis-Bristol had the guts to ask how the actor playing Raleigh (a very famous actor) was supposed to be inside his own brain, because the notion of this star's doing a voice-over was not going to fly.

Smith said that Cynthia's was a fascinating metaphysical question, wasn't it? Perhaps we were all inside our own brains, and nowhere else. Perhaps reality was only those electric synapses we called words, hm?, and images, hm?

Cynthia Lewis-Bristol said, "I'm not following you at all."

Polo Burr had to agree with her. "But Raleigh imagines his own execution. And I think we should *show* it. I mean it. The ax, the head and all. We need blood."

Smith smiled. " 'Raleigh *imagines* his own execution,' yesindeedydo. And where do you imagine things?" The director ran the fingers of both hands skipping quickly all over his head. "Inside the brain."

Cynthia Lewis-Bristol said, "Then why shouldn't the audience simply save the price of the ticket, stay home and *imagine Foolscap*? Inside their brains."

"Because they have no imaginations!" Smith leapt up and down. "They need to be ZAPPED, POW! If they weren't numb, it wouldn't take *Chain Saw Massacre* to make them jump."

"So the set's a brain . . .," mused Polo Burr. "Or rather . . ." (He began to get into it.) "Wouldn't you say, not a brain, but a *mind*?"

"Good, good," Smith patted him. "Bingo! Interiority. Believe me, it's nineties. The critics will love it." Smith did a Groucho Marx–like looping stare around the table, but failed to notice (or at least to be affected by) the look on Theo Ryan's face. "Other comments? . . . Oh, my dears," the director said. "I can't tell you how much I *love* working with long-dead authors. Give me Shakespeare. Give me Raleigh. You never have to listen to their bitching. God, if we had the author of *Foolscap* to put up with, he'd probably be having fits right now because we wouldn't get out our hammer and nails and reproduce the boring old Tower of London for him, and stick everyone in ruffs and hose. And frankly, beloveds, if we did that, we'd all go right down the loot-and-laurel draino." Smith held the wide arms of his iridescent jacket out like a prophet. "And, correct me if I'm wrong, but loot and laurel is what we're here for. We all want to be King of the Indians forever, don't we?"

The following year, when the nineties began and *Foolscap* opened, the critics loved it. Scottie Smith won two awards in London for best director, and then the year after that he won three more in New York, including the Tony.

In the playwriting category, Sir Walter Raleigh wasn't eligible. And of course neither was Theo Ryan.

CHAPTER

33

{Exeunt All But . . .}

Even such is Time which takes in trust
Our youth, our joys, and all we have,
And pays us but with age and dust:
Who in the dark and silent grave,
When we have wandered all our ways,
Shuts up the story of our days.

Sir Walter Raleigh

THREE MONTHS had passed since the discovery of *Foolscap* in Saint Michael's Church, one month since the five producers had optioned it and hired Scottie Smith to direct it, and only a week since the three rival claimants to its ownership (earl, marquess, and Church) had, in the Christmas spirit, agreed to a final settlement. Rehearsals were still in progress. Theo had just returned to England to attend them. The week before, he'd flown to North Carolina to serve as best man at the wedding of Steve Weiner and Jorvelle Wakefield. From London, Jonas had sent his regrets, and a Georgian sterling tea service.

The two Cavendish professors were married in Greensboro, and Maude Fletcher performed the ceremony. Neither Jorvelle's mother nor Steve's father looked very happy at all (and both predicted that, had their spouses been alive, they would have refused to come), but "Time, time, time," Theo's mother advised them cheerfully, and maybe time would help.

Maybe time would help the look in the eyes of Jane Nash-Gantz, too. For, to the professed astonishment of the international academic community, Vic Gantz had suddenly left his wife. One evening, after they'd returned home from a party, he'd simply handed her his lawyer's card, and suggested she get one of her own. "Vic?" everyone said. He had not only left her, but left their son, Nash, whom he'd raised so devotedly, and left Cavendish, which he'd served so diligently, and (apparently) was planning to marry a young woman who taught at the state college in New Jersey where he'd taken a job. "Vic?" everyone said. Not only that, he was suing Jane for alimony.

"And he charges *me* with mental cruelty!" Jane, stylishly dressed as ever for the wedding, but looking as if she'd been starved and bruised, hugged Theo, lured her son away from Jorvelle's cousins, and roared off with him to drive back to the airport. She yelled out the window of her Mercedes. "Vic told me, all his life, all he ever wanted to do was *leave* New Jersey! See what I get for arranging it!"

Also at Jorvelle and Steve's wedding, Lorraine Page and Rhodora Potts met for the first time, and to Theo's astonishment, the two women seemed to like each other, or at least to find endless topics to talk about together—from makeup under stage lights to the aggravatingly slow pace of Benny and Theo Ryan—during the entire flight back to New York.

After meetings there with Adolphus Mahan, with Bernie Bittermann, and with the SoHo director Barbara Sanchez, Theo flew to London, where he learned that under the terms of their new contract, the Earl of Newbolt, the Marquess of Urswick, and the Church of England were to share equally in all profits from productions of Raleigh's *Foolscap*, and from the auctioning of its original manuscript. (The highest bid came from a private museum in Los Angeles, where the thin vellum folio was soon to be locked in a glass case between a first edition of Raleigh's *History of the World* and a lock of Milton's hair.) By a special stipulation insisted upon by Horace Stanlow, Earl of Newbolt, and finally reluctantly agreed to by the others, Dame Winifred Throckmorton was to receive one-quarter of all those profits, since (as the earl generously pointed out) there never would have been a Raleigh play if she hadn't been so determined to find it.

The earl's comment was true, too.

Not that Dame Winifred had ever officially said that *Foolscap was* a Raleigh play. And now, the day of Theo's return, she'd written letters to the earl, and to a number of Renaissance newsletters, and to the London *Times,* saying quite the opposite: that she did *not* believe the author of *Foolscap* was Sir Walter Raleigh, or any other Jacobean with whom she was familiar; indeed, she rather suspected that *Foolscap* might be a modern forgery.

Absolutely no one agreed with Dame Winifred Throckmorton.

In fact, her position struck some as perverse, and others as evidence of senility, or at least a failing grasp of modern scholarly techniques. She declined to comment further on her views, just as—whenever asked about the newest attribution of the play proposed by some other academic (the Davenant theory, for example, or the Elizabeth Carey theory)—she would usually smile, and say something like "Ingenious," or "Dear me, how very funny."

So, when, a week following her letter to the *Times,* she telephoned Theo in London, and invited him (if he had no other plans) to spend Christmas Eve with her, the American wondered if finally she wanted to bring up openly the question of the play's authenticity with him. "Deny it!" commanded Jonas Marsh. "You got what you wanted. She never took an erroneous public stand." Jonas and Mole were leaving to spend Christmas at the Fontwell family home, and Theo had come over to Brown's to see them off.

"I won't answer a direct question with a lie," Theo told him.

"What curious distinctions you make," Jonas said.

"Tell her Merry Christmas." Mole's kind smile stayed at the window of the yellow Rolls until it turned the corner.

And so it was with uneasiness that Theo left his Russell Square B&B on the morning of December 24. He traveled by train over the same route that had first brought him to Barnet-on-Urswick, then he hiked that afternoon up the steep cobbles of Gate Row, and past the tangled yard of "Lark Cottage," on whose door now hung a Christmas wreath, with its plaid bow askew and white porcelain birds clinging upside down by their wire toes to the sweet-smelling circle of pine.

His uneasiness grew when Miss Throckmorton, wearing a sprig of holly in her hair, sat with her feet up in her chair by the fire, and talked for hours of medieval Yuletide rituals, and of Tudor Christmas carols and Victorian Christmas dinners, and of everything in the world but *Foolscap.* There was something in her hazel

eyes, keen under the drooping folds of old skin, that made it hard
for the young academic to look at her. And he was fairly certain
he knew what the look was. So in a way it was almost a relief
when she suddenly put down her teacup, shooed the black cat
Wat off her plaid tam, pulled the cap down on her head (crushing
the holly), and said in a stern voice: "Several months ago, you had
a theory for me, Theodore. Now I have one for you. Come with
me, please."

Christmas Eve. A brusque afternoon, a sky like flint. On the
grounds of Bourne House, or rather in the river Urswick which
bordered the grounds of Bourne, floated a punt, near a spot where
on the reedy banks, hidden by willows and the massive gray trunk
of a medieval oak, there rose the small stone bell tower of a little
stone church that had belonged—at least the ground it stood on
had belonged, like the house and the banks of the river—for three
hundred years to the earls of Newbolt, and for six hundred years
before that to the dukes of Urswick.

Dame Winifred and Theo were in the punt; the stout old woman
standing on the platform deck of the long flat shallow boat, pushing it along near the bank with her unwieldy punting pole; out of
the sky, large, lazy snow flakes wandered down and melted into
the river. The two were making their way to Saint Michael's
Church, having rented the punt from a riverside quay a mile back.
And Dame Winifred's theory had to do with the fact that on a
cloudy afternoon this past September, her neighbor Mildred (of
"The Heights") had seen Mr. Archibald Fontwell renting a skiff
from that same quay, *two days before* his alleged arrival in Devonshire with his friends. Moreover, this nosy neighbor had later
wheedled out of her nephew, who rented the boats, that he'd seen
Mr. Fontwell, with two other men, rowing about in the rain in
the little skiff near Saint Michael's, *at midnight* on the night before
they'd called on Dame Winifred to offer her their theory about
Mad Rob Dawbney and a lost Raleigh play.

Mildred had told her neighbor with gusto that she'd thought it
extremely suspicious that any one should be out on a river in the
rain at midnight. Her idea was that Miss Throckmorton's three
male guests were sex murderers, who had already disposed of one

slaughtered carcass in the Urswick, and who were likely to do the same to two defenseless women living alone in, respectively, "The Heights" and "Lark Cottage," with only a Great Dane, three cats, and a parrot to protect them from rape and dismemberment.

Now, Mildred was always imagining that people other than herself were up to no good—usually of a violent, vile and sadistic nature. Miss Throckmorton therefore had paid no attention to her neighbor's accusations against her three visitors. But in retrospect, in conjunction with other assumptions she'd been obliged to make, she'd come to wonder if Mildred for once in her life of criminal fancies had been partially right. Not that the three men were murderers, of course, but . . .

All that said, Miss Throckmorton rested from her punting, and, staring straight at the large American seated uncomfortably in the bow, piped at him with a foreboding frown on her face, "With that in mind; I think, Theo, there may be something that you need to say to me. Is that fair to suppose?"

Theo looked up at her a long moment. There was no sense in asking if she meant something about *Foolscap*, because he knew she did. So finally he met her hard unblinking gaze, and answered, ". . . Yes, that's fair."

She was relentless. "And?"

Theo said, "Yes. . . . You're right."

"That's why you were in the boat just here?"

"Yes."

"Because you . . ."

Obviously, she wouldn't rest until she forced him to *say* it. "Yes, I came by the Urswick here to the church. I put the manuscript behind the choir stall. Please understand, Jonas and Mole were only . . . accidentally involved."

Dame Winifred took a long breath. Her look was undeniably skeptical. ". . . I see."

"My reasons were not all bad. I . . ." He faltered to a stop under her dry-eyed glare.

Her eyes blinked against a snowflake. "I am very angry," the old scholar said. "And I am profoundly disappointed."

"I know. I ask your forgiveness."

"Rubbish! Ask yourself forgiveness! You have betrayed, not

me, and not the fools who have made all this squabbling, greedy fuss over the thing! You have betrayed your *profession*. You of all people, Theodore! Where *any* reason—" Her thin quavering voice rose. "*Any* reason but the undeviated pursuit of truth is a 'bad' reason! And I will be no party to it!" She took up her punting pole and began vigorously to push them along in silence.

After a while he asked, "Did you first suspect because of what your neighbor said?"

She snorted in disgust. "Certainly not. Nor, initially, I confess, did I doubt the technical authenticity of the manuscript. With which, I dare say, your friend Archibald Fontwell had considerable 'accidental' connection. You may tell him, yes, I underestimated him, as no doubt he wished to prove.

"I wanted very much for it to be real, so much I almost . . . But in the end I knew it wasn't by Walter Raleigh because I know Walter Raleigh . . . apparently better than a great many other people. It has always distressed me to discover that the world is not wiser than I." She shook her head. "It leaves one with such a . . . wobbly feeling."

Theo asked her if she'd never considered the manuscript might be Raleigh's.

The stout old woman sighed. "No. I very nearly believed it was his. . . . I have no idea who wrote it. But I think nineteenth century or later. Am I right? Whoever wrote it loved and understood the man."

"I wrote it," Theo said.

Letting the boat float along again near the bank, Dame Winifred pulled her punting pole out of the water, and rested it against her misbuttoned tweed jacket. Snowflakes landed like little stars on her plaid tam. ". . . Ah," she said quietly, and bowed her head to Theo. "I congratulate you."

". . . Thank you. Though I'm not sure how you mean it."

"I mean, the play is not dishonest, simply because its author was." Dame Winifred fished about in her tweed jacket for some gloves, but could find only one, into which she poked her hand. "Then *Foolscap* belongs to you. . . . Well, you certainly have as much right to it as those who say they own it because they think some relative of theirs made off with a copy three hundred years ago. What do they think a play is? Pieces of paper? A most peculiar idea of what art is about!"

Theo thought how oddly like Ford Rexford she sounded then—when who could imagine two more different people?

She went on. "Why don't you claim *Foolscap* now? I expect it would make *you* famous, given that everyone is so certain that somebody else famous must have written it all these centuries ago. Or was that the plan all along?"

Theo blushed furiously. "No! Could you possibly believe me, Miss Throckmorton, that I don't, that I never wanted the fame, and not just because it would come connected with the forgery."

She sneered. "The way the world is these days, so successful a forgery would doubtless enhance rather than harm your reputation."

"Do you believe me? I did it for a lot of reasons, I guess, but fame wasn't one of them. Unless you mean the play. I did want fame for the play, I suppose, for its characters. But not for me. Anonymity is fine with me." He lifted his head from his hands. "But I will understand if you feel you are bound to expose me, Miss Throckmorton, I'll certainly understand, but—"

She peered at him over her glasses. "I have no intentions of 'exposing' you. Or Mr. Marsh. Or Mr. Fontwell. And don't bother to talk any more rubbish about their 'accidental involvement' at me. No, I've taken my stand. I've said this play is not by Raleigh, and not of the period. No one believes me. So be it. Let them let enjoy their battles. Better to have idiots quarreling over the literary output of Walter Raleigh and Francis Bacon than idiots burning each other over whether holy wafers turn into God in the priest's hand, halfway down our gullets, or not at all. And that's what intellectuals were doing in Raleigh and Bacon's day. Progress, I suppose."

Theo said, "You won't tell the earl to stop the performance?"

"Why should I? Some of the money will go to Saint Michael's." She pointed at the small stone church, now directly across from them. "Some to Newbolt's library, and some to me, for the library I'd like established in *my* name when I'm gone. You see, I lack your thirst for anonymity, Theodore, though I struggle against the snare of ambition daily. Your little secret pride is that you

know you wrote *Foolscap*. Mine is that I know Raleigh didn't, and
have publicly stated that I know it. And someday, someone will
realize that I was absolutely right." With jerks, she wrenched the
punting pole out of the mud in which it was stuck. "In the meantime, it's a fine play, and I think all fine plays should be performed. Whoever wrote them."

Theo reached forward and held out his hand. "Thank you."

"Why?" She scowled at him. "I trust your conscience is not
entirely salved by the news that you are not to be exposed."

"No. Believe me, I've felt a great, great deal of guilt about this."

"Good!" They punted along, bumping against dark roots of
trees that reached down into the river. "If you want to be a playwright, Theodore, then be a playwright, without all this cork-
screwing about."

Distracted, Dame Winifred neglectd to pull the end of her pole
out of the muddy riverbed at the conclusion of her otherwise
energetic stoke. The pole stuck in the mud, and stayed where
it was. The punt proceeded downstream, rapidly increasing the
distance between her hands (clasping the top of the pole) and her
feet (planted on the stern of the boat), as her stout, tweed-clad
form quickly stretched to an acutely diagonal position over the
water.

"Let go of the pole! Let go of the pole!" Theo shouted, scrambling towards her. But too late. Miss Throckmorton clung
until her feet in their sturdy oxblood brogans slid from the platform; then in slowest motion the punt eased itself out from under
them, and shot away. In the instant which invariably feels eternal
to its participants, Theo, tumbling back to the boat's stern, leaned
out to grab at Dame Winifred while she swung scrabbling at the
top of the wildly weaving pole like a stout bear treed in a sapling
by ravenous hounds. Then down she crashed, smacking her head
against the long low punt. And on billowing tweeds she was swept
unconscious out into the deep quick midstream current of the
Urswick.

Theo was later to say that he possibly owed Dame Winifred's
life to all those miserable summers his parents had shipped him
off to camp so they could work the summer-stock circuits without
him. For as a result, he was an excellent swimmer, and able to tow

the stout woman to shore so quickly in his Red Cross cross-chest carry-hold that, despite her advanced age and the coldness of the day, she recovered her breath only seconds after he pulled her up on the bank, and (although shivering and blue about the lips) was strong enough to be able to slap at him and say, "For heaven's sake! Stop paddling me like bread dough, Theodore!"

By the time Theo found Mr. Brakeshaw, and the rector raced back with a doctor from Little Bourne, Miss Throckmorton was protesting that she was perfectly well, and in a great hurry to return home before the shops closed. She'd invited Theodore to her home for Christmas dinner, and had just now realized that she'd forgotten to buy anything to fix him.

"Ridiculous woman should be in hospital," the rector muttered at Theo. "She's old. She should listen to Milton: Time's winged chariot is hurrying near."

Miss Throckmorton sat up on the couch in the rectory living room where they'd tucked her under a half-dozen blankets. "Marvell, man, MARVELL!"

Mr. Brakeshaw smiled down on her sympathetically.

On Christmas morning, the world was white, and so clean and crisp that its newness hurt the eyes. Having stayed the night in Barnet, Theo attended Saint Michael's morning service with Dame Winifred. There in a pew near the tombs of Dawbneys and Stanlows, she sang tidings of comfort and joy in her high shrill voice with a smile on her face so infectious that Theo began laughing as he sang too; he in his beautiful voice, Dame Winifred Throckmorton beside him unconcernedly off-key.

> Who would not love thee,
> Loving us so dearly?
> Oh come let us adore him.
> Oh come let us adore him.

"In the beginning," pompously intoned the rector Steven Brakeshaw from the pulpit, "was the Word, and the Word was with God, and the Word was God. . . . And the Word was made flesh, and dwelt among us . . . full of grace and truth."

As Dame Winifred told Theo on their drive home, she was

struck today with the wonderful fact that it didn't matter that Steven Brakeshaw was neither very graceful, nor very gracious, nor very bright. It didn't matter a bit to the grace or the truth of the words he read. And they had to accept, hard as it might be, that it didn't matter to God's love of Steven Brakeshaw either. "Or—and dear me, this is even more difficult, I confess—it doesn't matter to God's command that *we* love Mr. Steven Brakeshaw, M.A., as well. Or at least make a valiant if unsuccessful effort to do so, and then not even congratulate ourselves for having made the effort. Quite a rigorous challenge. I continue to struggle with it."

She smiled sweetly at the rector as they left the church, and kept smiling when he quoted Herbert at her and told her it was Donne.

As Theo drove the Hillman Imp into Gate Row (for he'd persuaded Dame Winifred that his years in the Appalachian mountains had made him an expert on snow driving), they saw a yellow Rolls-Royce parked in front of "Lark Cottage." Waiting patiently inside it was a middle-aged, uniformed driver. Theo had met the man once before, when he'd brought Mole's sisters to London to shop for the eldest girl's wedding. Now, the chauffeur took out of the bonnet of the Rolls two large hampers (labeled as perishables) from the store Fortnum and Mason. These he presented to Dame Winifred as a Christmas gift sent to her with the best wishes of Archibald Fontwell. Then he took out of the backseat a small soft pine Christmas tree and a box of Christmas ornaments that looked to Theo like Victorian antiques. These, he said, were a present to Theo Ryan from Jonas Marsh.

The driver declined Miss Throckmorton's invitation to stay to dinner, explaining that Mr. Fontwell had given him the car so he could visit with his daughter who lived just over in Otterey St. Mary. "Merry Christmas then," the old woman told him with a cheerful wave as he slowly maneuvered the Rolls around the curve beside "The Heights."

In the wicker hampers were all the makings of a Christmas dinner, already prepared and needing only to be heated. "That much I think I can successfully accomplish," Dame Winifred said.

"No, please, allow me. Would you?" said Theo. "You sit here by the fire and read."

"Dear me. How dreadful to invite you here, no food, prove you a forger, nearly drown you, turn you into a kitchen skivvy." She tried to struggle out of all her blankets. "And why, in any case—and I hope you'll allow me to say this—has such an extremely handsome young man as yourself no lover with whom to spend the holiday? 'Youth's a stuff will not endure.' On that you may rely."

Theo pressed her shoulders softly back into the chair. "Please, stay there. . . . Well, I am in love, Miss Throckmorton." He nodded at her. "But there've been complications."

She looked up at him, her glasses half off her thin nose. "My sense is that love is rather simple. Though the participants—I judge—are always getting themselves into these complicated fixes. Where is this young person? In America?"

"Yes. Actually, I'm meeting her in New York for New Year's. She's singing there."

"Ah, a singer. That's good, Theodore." The old scholar's voice grew drowsy. " 'And certain stars shot madly from their spheres/ To hear the sea maid's music.' "

"She sings Country/Western songs. Do you know what that means?"

One hazel eye slowly opened. "I loved Hank Williams's lyrics before you were born." The eye fluttered close. Theo tucked her blanket over her, and unable to resist the warmth, she nestled her head into the corner of the high-backed chair and soon was gently snoring.

Out of the beautifully wrapped hampers came a feast. Theo served it, course by course, at a tea table in front of the fire, and in the corner he set up the little Christmas tree with its angels playing their horns and cymbals to the glory of the day. He found a record of Renaissance Christmas music and put it on her (very good, he discovered) stereo.

> Ding dong! Merrily on high
> in heaven the bells are ringing.

With great pleasure, Theo and Dame Winifred spent Christmas together. They ate celery soup with Stilton. And then they ate potted crab and quail eggs. They drank wine and ate roasted goose with sage and onion stuffing and leek pie and scalloped oysters.

> Ding dong! Verily the sky
> is riven with angels singing. Gloria.

"I think we have done Archibald's gift proud," said Miss Throckmorton finally, patting her high stomach, and wiping her brow with her napkin.

"There's more," Theo smiled, and returned from the kitchen with marzipan and gooseberry fool and a Maderia cake and a bottle of claret.

> Shining beyond the frosty weather.
> Bright as sun and moon together.

The fire burned low, and the bright sun slanted lower off the white Devonshire hills.

> People look East and sing today.
> Love the Star is on the way.

Dame Winifred raised her claret to Theo. "To *Foolscap*," she said.

"To Walter Raleigh."

"It is in fact a better play than I think Sir Walter would have written."

"Oh—"

"—I don't mean it's as good as other things he wrote. I'm sorry, I don't think it is."

Theo smiled at her, and poured her another glass of wine.

"I meant, Theodore, he was not a playwright by . . . nature. His genius flew about blowing trumpets a bit more bombastically than suits a play. Even a play so—shrewdly—full of self. You caught it wonderfully, that exasperating selfishness kicking up a fuss in so generous and brave a soul. I will tell you something else, too. There's a line at the end, when he's imagining the death so soon to come. I think perhaps that is what I hate most to lose as truly Raleigh's, for its faith gave me comfort. It made me feel—oddly, in a way his own remarks hadn't—that his piety on the scaffold was not just another great performance. It made me feel the author really did die quite graced with faith."

"I hope so too," Theo said, and quoted the lines he knew she meant, the final one added by Ford.

> Shut tight the book. For now night calls. And soon
> Destiny on a sharp wind will sail me safely home.

"Yes," the old scholar said. " 'Will sail me safely home.' " She pointed her finger at him. "You are a good playwright, Theodore Ryan."

The American shook his head. "I had the best playwright I know in the world to help me."

"You mean your study of Shakespeare, of course."

Theo smiled.

Epilogue

ONE APRIL NIGHT, exactly two years after that faculty meeting at which he'd been thinking of endings to other people's plays, Theodore Ryan, now full professor of English at Cavendish University, co-director of the Spitz Center, and curator of its Winifred Throckmorton Memorial Library of Theatre Arts, stood in the wings of the Grand Ole Opry in Nashville, Tennessee. He stood there with Rhodora Potts, waiting with her for her cue to go on in the first show. Around them, performers moved about deftly in the vast, bustling backstage space. Autograph-seekers hovered near their favorite stars. Troops of clog dancers in short flounced polka-dotted skirts whispered together as they casually stretched their legs behind their backs. In fringe and satin colors, lanky singers chatted with their relatives and fiddled with their guitar frets.

Theo looked at all of them with affection.

"Darlin', you mind watching from here?" Rhodora held on to his shoulder as she checked the high thin heel of her glittering shoe.

"Me?" He smiled. "I've been backstage since I was born. I'm a behind-the-scenes kind of guy."

"You love the craziness," Rhodora said. "Nobody made you

go to all those rehearsals last fall." (She meant rehearsals of the original production of *Principles of Aesthetic Distance*, staged by Barbara Sanchez, the other co-director of the Spitz Center.) "Nobody makes you fly to London every time there's a cast change in *Foolscap*."

"It's business," Theo said. "One-quarter of the profits of *Foolscap* go straight into Dame Winifred's memorial library. I have a practical stake in its outcome. And *you* get the royalties on *Aesthetic Distance*."

"Don't kid me. You love the craziness." Rhodora took his arm, and they walked towards the front of the wings, to the edge of the side curtains.

Theo waved at her lead guitarist—one of the musicians who'd replaced the Dead Indians. "Okay," he said. "I love the craziness. But second show, okay if I hide in the dressing room and work? I promised Buzzy a revised last act by next week."

Rhodora nodded, stroking his arm, but peering past him at the show onstage. She looked pale against the red folds of the great swagged curtains, and her bare shoulders were shivering. "You sure my eye-liner's all right?" she asked, and tilted her chin up at him, turning her head from side to side.

"I'm sure. Hold still." Leaning over, he brushed her black shining hair from one ear so the silver spray of earring showed.

"You think?" She patted her earring. He nodded yes, and her eyes, wild and intent, skittered avidly back to the stage, where Hank Snow was finishing his song. Deep in her throat, she began a quiet low humming.

Theo cupped his palms over the rounded curves of her shoulders. "How're you feeling?"

"Scared." she whispered, and leaned her head down, brushing her cheek against his fingers. "But I'll be okay. . . . Soon as I can get out there, I'll be fine." Bending, she ran both her hands from ankle to thigh, smoothing the length of black silk hose.

Applause rumbled towards the stage from the dark amphitheatre. A harmonizing family bowed and waved as they left the stage. The red digital seconds clicked forward on the clocks that directed each night's double show at the Opry with a ruthless precision cleverly disguised as easygoing, neighborly happenstance. A man read an ad for headache powders. Then there was more applause.

Then Hank Snow called Rhodora's name.

"Break a leg," Theo whispered; he'd been saying it all his life.

"I love you too," she said.

He kissed the back of her neck, and let her go.

Smiling, Rhodora stepped forward, taking the microphone smoothly from the man who held it out to her; with long quick strides she walked into the center of the heat of the lights, and opened her arms. And Theo thought—Amazing: She says she'll stop being scared as soon as she can get out there face-to-face with a colossal arena of strangers, where cameras flash and the arms of fans reach out of the darkness; where four thousand people she can't see sit waiting for her to make them feel something. Willing to love her if she can do it.

Rhodora threw back her head, shaking loose the long black hair, and then she leaned into the darkness and sang the first notes of the song that had won her her first record award. Back at her came a whistling roar of applause, and the fast sparkle of flashbulbs, like stars shooting across the southern sky outside.

Oh Lord, thought Theo Ryan, his chest lifting with the swell of his heart. Theatre people. . . .

Then smiling, he shook his head, shrugged, and told himself, I'll never be one of them, and I always knew it. Just give me my theatre on the page, just give me my books and my library. Give me, the professor grinned to himself, my scallop shell of quiet. Standing backstage while Rhodora sang her song, Theo began to chuckle. Be careful what you ask; the world may answer yes: The world had left him alone. Here he was, with (in a sense) two hit plays running tonight—*Principles of Aesthetic Distance* on Broadway, *Foolscap* in the West End—and if he'd wanted to see either one, he would have had to buy a ticket from a scalper.

All right, that was an exaggeration: Undoubtedly he could have pulled strings as Ford Rexford's literary executor (or as the author of the critically acclaimed *REXFORD, Volume I: Preacher's Boy*), and gotten in any night to see *Aesthetic Distance*. And he could have phoned London as curator of the Winifred Throckmorton Memorial Library of Theatre Arts, and arranged for at least a single house seat to that controversial drama, *Foolscap*. But still, as far as the world knew, neither one of these plays was *his* play; he was not named as author, or co-author, and certainly not as forger, on any marquee, program, poster, paperback, audio cassette, sweatshirt, review, or ad for either of them. He was as anonymous as an artisan who'd stained the glass or carved the stone of medieval cathedrals.

Theo thought back to how he'd waited in crowds at the previews of both those plays, handing his ticket to the usher, taking his place in the theatre and watching each show, with no one on the stage and no one in the audience knowing how large a role he had played in bringing them together. And each night's performance of *Foolscap* was just the next in the succession of collaborations that had begun with him and Ford Rexford, and had gone on to include Jonas Marsh and Mole Fontwell, Dame Winifred Throckmorton, and the actors, audience, producers, designers, and, yes, the director Scottie Smith, and—among many other co-authors— Sir Walter Raleigh himself. All of them authoring changes up to the curtain's rising on opening night, and at every performance after that, authoring more change.

It tickled Theo to think of Shakespeare scholars hunched over their critical microscopes for centuries, deciding which scenes, which lines, which words, belonged to the Bard, and which should be assigned to lower talents, to bad quartos or careless printers. But in fact who knew how many people had added their say as the plays made their way from page to stage, from stage to sacred text? Just think how many had already collaborated on *Foolscap* in its short history. Think how many would help before this new play of his, *From the Wings*, reached the audience it was made for.

The theatre professor looked around the wings. He smiled at a man with blacked-out teeth, in patched hat and baggy overalls, who was entertaining stagehands with his antics as he waited for his cue to go on. Theo smiled at a drummer in pink tuxedo, who slapped his wire whisk against his wrist as he waited to go on; at a cowboy in high-heeled boots, who sewed a tear in his alligator jacket as he waited to go on; at two women in strapless gold lamé (their hair, huge sprayed cascades of frosted curls), tapping their stiletto heels, and waiting their cue to go on.

Backstage at the Grand Ole Opry, Theo looked around at all these singers and dancers and clowns who stood here in the wings, all with gifts they wanted to offer strangers. And as he watched them, the troupe of performers grew into a crowd, filling the dark space between curtains and dressing rooms. Leaning against the walls and flats and props, perched on ladders and light boards, a great motley host of performers collected, whispering with one another, but all watching the stage, too, waiting their turn. In the shadows Theo could imagine seeing mingled together the unwanted Dead Indians and the medieval minstrels of Urswick Castle and Thayer Iddesleigh's chorus line of Hot Box girls with their ratty minks. Off in a corner he could see Uncle Wally doing card tricks, and Buster McBride practicing jokes with his dummy, the Latin lover Fernando-Teeno. Beside the shy ventriloquist, he could see Tara Bridges pressing her fingers against her throat where the notes of "Ah, Sweet Mystery of Life" waited to be sung. Like them, all over the world tonight, in theatres of every shape and size and style and measure of success, performers were waiting to go on, just as they had been for thousands of years.

In the crowd, he saw actors waiting to take on the roles of Antony and Cleopatra, of Sky Masterson and Sergeant Sarah Brown. There, whispering together, was the cast of *Principles of Aesthetic Distance*. And here was Sir Walter Raleigh, glittering silver and black, pearls and diamonds, with the cast of *Foolscap*. The wings of the Opry crowded with more and more players; masked actors in white Greek robes; dancers in Chinese brocades with fans in each hand; Richard Burbage, Maria Callas; curled courtiers in French pantaloons; a burlesque stripper, a beatnik poet, a vaudeville juggler, Edwin Booth and Ellen Terry and Ethel Merman, drawing-room lovers with slicked-back hair and villains with waxy mustaches. All here in the crowd.

And among all these players, Theo saw Ford. The playwright was leaning into his opened black army trunk, pulling person after person out of it, an endless procession of characters emerging from the small trunk, like a circus trick. Out of the trunk came Miss Rachel, came the preacher's boy, came the Mexican family in *Valley of the Shadow*, and the husband and wife in *Desert Slow Dance*. And all the hundreds of others. More and more people, lifted by

Ford from his small black trunk, and running to join the rest. Then Ford closed the trunk, leapt on top of it, and, smiling at Theo, bowed to him, a beautiful, grand, Elizabethan bow.

Out from the wings, Theo saw his father, Benny Ryan, slide tantalizingly onto a stage with his arms outflung, offering himself, a dream come true. And the young girls shrieked like Maenads the incantation of his name.

He saw his mother, Lorraine Page, beautiful, young, and safe in the light, talking to darkness from a summer-stock stage.

There in shadows of the wings, Theo saw his parents' friends, Sweets, the former child star, and Catherine, the former soaps star; all the former stars, now forgotten, and all the company of players who were never to be stars, all of them banded together waiting to go act out life so that people seeing their show could learn—or remember—how life feels.

The players bowed all together there in the shadows of the wings. Theo shouted and whistled as loudly as he could, and the heavy red swirls of curtain slowly closed between his wife, Rhodora, on stage, and the sharp echoing sound of strangers applauding out there in the dark.

NBC

MAL